PRAISE FOR
SHIRLEY ROUSSEAU MURPHY'S
PHENOMENAL EPIC FANTASY
THE CATSWOLD PORTAL

"A cult classic."
Virginian-Pilot

"Delightful fantasy . . . Murphy balances her rich,
detailed Netherworld with a vividly characterized
earthly realm. Her cat people, in particular, ring true."
Publishers Weekly

"Like Charles de Lint and Tanya Huff, Murphy
demonstrates a rare feel for crossworld fantasy,
bringing modern and mystical landscapes and people
into an illuminating juxtaposition. More than a 'feline
fantasy,' this engaging story should be considered a
priority purchase. Highly recommended."
Library Journal

"The fantasy buy for cat lovers."
Orlando Sentinel

"Rich, descriptive imagery is found on every page,
making this underground world come alive."
School Library Journal

"Lyrical . . . The interweaving between real and
fantasy worlds is well done . . . She is a writer to
watch."
Kirkus Reviews

Books by Shirley Rousseau Murphy

THE CATSWOLD PORTAL

SHIRLEY ROUSSEAU MURPHY

An Imprint of HarperCollinsPublishers

This is a work of fiction. Names, characters, places, and incidents are products of the author's imagination or are used fictitiously and are not to be construed as real. Any resemblance to actual events, locales, organizations, or persons, living or dead, is entirely coincidental.

EOS
An Imprint of HarperCollins*Publishers*
195 Broadway
New York, NY 10007

First Eos paperback printing: February 2005

HarperCollins® and Eos® are trademarks of HarperCollins Publishers Inc.

Printed in the U.S.A.

10 9 8 7 6 5 4

FOR MOUSSE

Cat's eyes in the face of a woman ... seem to promise the most unusual and selective delights as green and seductive they glitter ... The cat face is an ensemble of marvelously matched and balanced features and the total result is one to stir the heart. Where the human female is able to approach them, she becomes irresistible.

Paul Gallico, *Honorable Cat*

THE CATSWOLD PORTAL

Chapter 1

He ran pounding through the forest, his tennis shoes snapping dry branches as he stretched out in a long lope. Running eased the tightness, the tension. He was tall and lean, dark haired. Dodging between the broad trunks of redwood trees he headed uphill toward the mountain, swerving past deadfalls, trampling ferns that stroked his bare legs like animal paws. Strange thought, Alice's kind of thought, animal paws. He shivered, but not from the cold. It was dusk; Alice would be cleaning up, putting away her paints, washing her brushes, thinking about dinner, wondering whether to go out or open something. She wouldn't speak to him while he was still working, would go out to the kitchen and stand looking in the freezer.

She would have done those things. Had done them, once. The pain ran with him, he couldn't shake it, couldn't leave it alone.

Months after the funeral he had started to heal, to mend, the hurting began to dull, some feeling returning besides rage and grief. But now suddenly his pain was raw again, the last few days were as if her death had just happened, her body in the wrecked car . . . He swerved away from the ravine and ran steeply up between boulders, but at the foot of Mount Tamalpais he turned back. It was dark now within the forest, though the sky above the giant redwoods still held light. He ran downhill again for a long way before lights began to flicker between the trees from isolated houses braving the forest gloom. The chill air held the smoke of fireplaces and he could smell early suppers cooking. Alice would be saying, Let's just get a hamburger, I don't feel like cooking, don't feel like getting dressed. She'd fix herself a drink, go to shower off the smell of inks and fixative, slip on a clean pair of jeans. His breath caught, seeing her body wet from the shower, little droplets on her breasts, her long pale hair beaded with water.

He was in sight of the village now; it stretched away below him, the last light of evening clinging along the street and to the roofs of the shops. He could hear a radio somewhere ahead, and the swish of cars on the damp macadam, then suddenly the streetlights burst on all at once. His feet crushed fallen branches then he hit the sidewalk and an explosion of speed took him past the library, the building's tall windows reflecting car lights against the books. He could smell frying hamburgers from the Creek, and farther on something Italian from Anthea's. He swerved past villagers closing up shop, and each looked up at him. "Hey, Brade!" "Evening, Braden." He dodged the first Greyhound commuters returning from the city. "Hey there, West." "Nice night for running." He nodded, raised a hand, and pounded on past. His long body reflected running distortions in the shop windows. Crossing the dead-end lane to the garden where his studio stood among other houses, he glanced up the hill toward Sam's Bar that stood at the edge of the forest, thought of stopping for a beer, but then went on.

He cooled down on the veranda, poured himself a bourbon. Pulling off his tennis shoes, sitting sprawled in the campaign chair, he stared up at the tangled garden that began at his terrace and climbed the hill above him; a communal garden shared by the six houses that circled it. It was a pleasant, informal stretch of bushes and flowers and dwarf trees creating a small jungle. Two of the three houses above were dark. The lights in the center house went off as he watched, and his neighbor came out, her dark skin hardly visible against the falling night, her white dress a bright signal. She crossed the garden to the lane with long, easy strides, waving to him. "Evening, Brade," her voice rich as velvet. He lifted a hand, smiling, watched her slide into her convertible and turn at the dead end beside Sam's, drive slowly down the lane and into the traffic of the busier road, heading for the city. But when a cat cried on the terraces above, he shivered, unsteady again. He could see its eyes reflected for an instant, then it was gone.

As he rose to go in, he felt for a split second the warmth of anticipation. His eager mood burst suddenly: Alice wasn't there. Alice was dead. The loneliness hit him like a blow, and he turned back and poured another whiskey.

Evening was the worst. They had liked to sit on the terrace after a day's work, unwinding, watching the garden darken, watching the stars come spilling above the redwood forest that crowned the hill above the upper houses. In the evenings they had shared little things, random thoughts, coming together in a new way after working all day side by side in the studio, seldom talking, just being near each other. In the evenings Alice came alive in a different way from her deeply concentrating, working self, as if the night stirred a wild streak in her. Sometimes she would rise from the terrace and, carrying her drink, would walk up the garden to stand looking at the tool shed door.

And now suddenly Alice's death hit him as if it had just happened—his frenzy as he tore at the jammed car door, as he beat at the window. Alice lay twisted inside, her hair tangled in the steering wheel, blood running down her face. The rescue squad tried to cut the door away with gas torches, but he had fought them, crazy with fear that they'd burn her.

For forty-five minutes she was trapped, maybe dying, while the wrecking crew cut at the car slowly and methodically. The cops tried to pull him away; he kept fighting to get to her. When the door was wrenched open at last, he shoved the medics away, and her body spilled out into his arms, limp, sending a shock of sickness through him that had never, since, left him.

Her portfolio had been on the car seat beside her and she had a box in the back seat packed with ice, chilling two lobsters and a bottle of chablis. Later, when a police officer handed him the box, he'd thrown it hurtling down the cliff into the bay. He tried to kill the driver who had hit her. His plumbing truck lay on its side against a light post; it had crossed the meridian, plowing into her car. The driver was unhurt. He had grabbed the thin, pale-haired man and pounded him until the cops pulled him off.

Sometime before he left the scene a policeman had lifted her portfolio out of her car, wiped off the blood, and put it in his station wagon. Days later he brought it into the studio and shoved it out of sight in the map chest where she kept her work.

Three weeks after her death he had taken her lithographs and etchings off the walls of the studio, stripped her part of the work space, giving away everything—litho stones, etching plates, inks, handmade papers. He sent most of her work over to her gallery in the city. If he cleared away every reminder maybe he wouldn't keep seeing her there in the studio working on a drawing or a print, her long, pale hair bound back, her smock hanging crooked, her tongue tipping out as she concentrated. Maybe he wouldn't see her look up at him as she wiped charcoal off her hands, wanting a cup of tea, wanting to talk for a minute.

Fourteen months after she died he remembered the portfolio. He had taken it out of the map drawer and spread the drawings across his work table, searching for answers to the question that had begun to wake him at night.

The drawings were of the garden door.

The low oak door cut into the terraced hill like the door of an old-fashioned root cellar, though the small earthen room into which it opened had been built not for roots but to house gardening equipment: wheelbarrow, rake, ladder, pruning shears, sprinklers. The beautifully carved door was far too ornate to close a tool room, it belonged in medieval Europe closing away things exotic that rustled in the dark. It was made of thick, polished oak planks nearly black with age, rounded at the top beneath a thick, curved oak lintel, and carved in deep relief with cats' faces.

Nine rows of cats' heads protruded from the door, nine faces to a row. They were life-sized cats carved in such deep relief that two-thirds of each head thrust out of the wood. They were so real that one's first impression was of live cats looking out—dark furred, handsome. The cats in the top three rows seemed to be smiling with some inscrutable feline glee. Those in the center rows looked secretive. The cats in the bottom three rows screamed open mouthed with rage, their ears laid flat, their eyes slitted, their little oak teeth sharp as daggers. Each cat was so alive that no matter how many times one saw the door, the effect was always startling. As if the cats thrust their heads through some aperture in time or dimension from another place.

And after Alice's death, as he shuffled through her drawings looking at the individual cat faces, he felt his spine go cold for no reason. He had put the drawings away, filled with the unreasonable idea that the cats had caused her death. He had not, in succeeding months, been able to shake that thought.

He knew she had intended, on the day she died, to go to the Museum of History and try to trace the door's origin. That was why she had the drawings with her. Maybe she'd gone there, maybe she hadn't. Strangely, he hadn't wanted to find out.

When Alice was small and her aunt owned the house that was now their studio—that had been their studio—Alice had believed the door of the cats was magic. Though she'd outgrown that idea, she had never outgrown her fascination with its medieval aspects and with the cats themselves.

In her early childhood photographs Alice was a thin little girl, very blond, wiry and lively. She had studied at Art Institute where her father taught; she was the only child among classes of adults. She had spent hours of her childhood in the city's museums drawing skeletons, and at the zoo drawing the animals, while other children threw popcorn at the caged beasts. She had taught herself the intricacies of bone structure and of the movement of muscle over bone; she had learned how to bring alive the bright gleam of an eye, the sudden lifting of a paw. Some of her relatives, misunderstanding, had called her a prodigy. She had simply loved animals and wanted to paint them.

She was twenty when he met her; she was a student in the first classes he taught. He had found her dedication to animals too commercial, not painterly. He had told her that a true artist strove for the abstraction, for the heart of meaning, not just to reproduce an image. She told him she *was* striving for the heart of meaning, and that he was blindly misguided if he didn't see it. She told him he was too out of touch, too idealistic. That someone who had spent four years fighting in the Pacific should see more clearly than he did. He said being a Marine had nothing to do with what he saw as a painter. He had told her that if she wanted to be a commercial artist—and he had used the term like a four-letter word—she should go across the bay to the more commercial school, and not waste her time at Art Institute.

She had been the only student at Art Institute to be making good money long before she graduated. She had established a name for herself while most of the students were still trying to find out what they wanted to do. And as he worked with her in class, he began to see that her work was not simply realistic, that it had a deep, involving power.

He still got calls two years after her death from people in other states who didn't know Alice was dead, who wanted her to do a commission. Since the first of the year he'd talked with five thoroughbred breeders and more than a dozen hunting and show kennels. Her work had a richness and a quality of mystery that stole nothing from the strong aliveness of the animals she painted; as if she painted not only the animals, but aspects of their spirits as well.

He had given Alice's childhood diary to her parents, though he would have liked to keep it. It contained many of her small, early drawings, mostly of the pets she had as a child. One cat in particular she had drawn many times. There was a pastel of the same cat in their favorite restaurant in the city, a small French cafe. He hadn't been there since Alice died. The small, intimate cafe, whose walls were hung with the works of many Bay area artists, held too many painful memories of her.

In the map cabinet now were only the drawings of the garden door, and a few sketches of the child who had disappeared. He didn't know why he had kept the drawings of the child, likely the kidnapped child had been killed though Alice had refused to believe that.

The little girl had vanished from the garden when she and Alice were visiting Alice's aunt here, the child had been playing alone by the tool shed. Alice had searched frantically, gone to all the neighbors and into the village, and after several hours to the police, beginning the search that lasted long after Aunt Carrie died, that lasted until Alice was killed.

When he and Alice started dating, she had been so preoccupied over the child's disappearance that she seemed, often, hardly to see him. She would be white, shaken with the things she thought might have happened to the little girl.

The wind rose, soughing through the garden and through the tops of the redwoods that thrust black against the night sky. Above the trees against the stars, pale clouds blew. He rose and went into the dark studio and did not switch on the lights.

His new paintings covered the walls, in the darkness they were only black squares. They oppressed him, he did not want to look at them, he felt constricted by them and by his commitment to finish the series.

The date for his show at Chapman's was too close and he wasn't ready, the work wasn't ready. His lack of passion for the work, and his lack of professionalism in letting himself go like this, had no excuse. He told himself he'd lost the desire and thus the skill, that he wouldn't paint anything worthwhile again. He knew that was stupid. He wasn't some twenty-year-old who didn't know how to handle hard times. But he couldn't shake the depression, and the work reflected his barrenness—stilted and dry.

He turned away from the paintings restlessly and went back outside. Without conscious thought he crossed the brick veranda and headed up the dark garden toward the door of the cats.

The carved oak door was lit faintly by the scattered house lights at the outer boundaries of the garden. In the wind under the blowing trees the cats' faces seemed to move and change expression. They chilled him. As he stood looking, annoyed with himself for coming up here, he began to imagine space beyond the door. Unending hollowness. Deep spaces yawning down inside the hill. He imagined he could hear echoing sounds above the wind and voices whispering from deep beyond the door. And then he shook his head, and turned away, and went back to the terrace for a drink.

Chapter 2

Perhaps the universe tilted for an instant to allow Braden his perception of the dark, cavernous spaces. Surely some change in the natural forces permitted him to glimpse the tunnel plunging down, the teetering slabs of stone thrusting down into the hollow bowels of the earth. Though he didn't, for a moment, believe in such things. It was the next morning that, deep within the earth, an old woman stood saddling her horse.

Where the black caverns dropped at last to gentle meadows and cliffs and to wandering paths, dawn was coming, its green light seeping down from the stone sky—light laid down eons past by wizards long since turned to dust. The green light drifted like fog, turning the cliffs to emerald and embracing a stone cottage perched on the rim of the steep valley.

The old woman took her time saddling the horse and tying on her baskets full of woven cloth for trading. She was roundly built, with a face as wrinkled as an ancient apple.

The bay gelding she was saddling stood obediently tethered by her spell, his ears back in resentment. On the other side of the corral a pony snuffled at the hay manger. Behind them the valley dropped away, and across the ravine rose a line of cliffs jagged as dragons' teeth. As Mag tightened the girth and mounted, she glanced toward the cottage window and raised her hand to the girl.

From the open window Sarah waved back, and watched Mag force the gelding through the orchard and down along the ridge that lipped the valley.

She was seventeen, slim, and taller than Mag. There was a deceptive softness about her, like velvet over lean muscle. The corners of her wide mouth turned up as if with some secret pleasure. Her green eyes were wide, her lashes thick and black. She had long hands, clever at weaving. Her long brown dress was the typical valley coarsespun. As she watched the old woman and horse disappear down the cliff, intently she watched the pony, too, for he did not like being left behind. He was a big, sturdy pony of elven breed. When he raised his head and charged the fence suddenly, meaning to jump it, she lifted her hand in a sign that jerked him back. He turned away, his ears flat, his tail switching.

She could not see the village below, the land dropped too steeply. She would have gone with Mag but for the sow, due to farrow and as likely to eat her piglets as nurse them. The cottage felt larger without Mag, and she liked its emptiness. Mag's occasional absence was the only privacy she had. She loved Mag, but the cottage was small. She turned from the window, took up the mop, and began to scrub the wooden floor, mopping first without spells. When she tired of that she sent the mop alone over the boards, making it dodge around Mag's loom and around their two cots, around the table and their two chairs.

The one room served the two of them for cooking, for sleeping, for weaving and mending, and for canning and drying their garden produce. Its stone walls were smoke darkened, its rafters low, with herbs and onions hanging from them. She seldom went beyond the cottage and garden,

except when Mag took her trading to some small village.
There were no neighbors; she was used to the company of
the beasts. The cottage was the only home she remembered.
She thought she was no kin to Mag. Mag was as sturdy as a
turnip, always the same and always steady. Sarah was, Mag
said, as changeable as quicksilver. In this room Mag had
taught her the jeweler's arts and taught her to weave so she
could earn a living, and had taught her the spells for gardening and gentling the beasts.

She could remember nothing of her childhood. That part
of her life was without form, and Mag would tell her nothing
about her past. When they did travel to some small village
among other Netherworlders, the old woman sometimes put
the deaf spell on her so that, listening to the villagers' conversation, suddenly she would lose meaning and know that
she had for a few moments been deafened, made unaware.
Though Mag would never admit to such spells.

She took up a cloth and carefully dusted the clothes cupboard and the kitchen safe, then knelt to polish a carved
chest. She liked to dust by hand, rubbing oil into the ancient
wood. But now as she pulled out the drawers of the chest to
do the edges, the bottom drawer stuck. Kneeling, she tried to
straighten it by reaching underneath.

When she felt papers stuck there, up under the bottom of
the drawer, she drew back.

Then she reached again, fingering them. They crackled
dryly. When she started to pull them out, one tore. Dis-
mayed, she hissed a spell to free it. Three sheets came loose,
the old, yellowed papers dropping into her hand. She spread
them on the floor.

She thought Mag would not hide papers unless they had
to do with her. How furtive the old woman was. Sarah was
afraid to look at them. Maybe she wouldn't want to know
what they would tell her. She closed her eyes, trying to collect herself, torn between excitement and fear.

The earliest thing she could remember about her life was
her ninth birthday. She had become aware suddenly, as if
jerked from deep sleep, had been riding a horse double be-

hind an old woman who was a stranger to her, had sat
pressed against the woman's soft back as the horse worked
his way down a cliff. She didn't remember ever riding a
horse before; she didn't remember the landscape around her.
She had been bone tired, aching from a journey she could
not recall. Below them stood a thatch-roofed stone cottage,
a lonely, bare-looking hovel. The old woman had called her
Sarah, but the name had meant nothing to her.

At the cottage she had stood against the fence while the
woman unsaddled the horse and watered and fed him, then
the wrinkled old creature said, "I am Mag. Today is your
ninth birthday."

"It's not my birthday. I don't remember my birthday. Who
are you?"

Mag had led her into the cottage and sat her down in the
rocker before the cold wood stove, had knelt and built a fire,
lighting it with a flick of her hand. Then she took a clay
bowl from the shelf and began to mix gingerbread. Sarah
had watched, numb and angry. When the dough was rolled
out, Mag made a gesture with her hands that caused ginger
dolls to be cut from the dough without any cutter or tool.
"The dolls are tradition," Mag said. "Part of the birthday celebration."

"It's *not* my birthday."

"It is now. This is the first day of your new life. You are
nine years old."

Mag had set about decorating the dolls with magic runes
that appeared suddenly deep in the dough. She had baked
and cooled them, and made Sarah promise not to watch as
she hung them outdoors in the fruit trees.

But of course she had watched from the window, and
when, after her birthday supper, Mag sent her to search for
the ginger dolls she found the wishing doll at once. It was
the only one with emeralds baked in for eyes, in the fading
light its green eyes gleamed at her. Coming back with it, she
had stopped to look in the water trough at her reflection,
wanting to see her own face, and her image shone up at her
as unfamiliar as the face of the ginger doll. She was sur-

prised that her eyes were the same clear green as the doll's emerald eyes.

But from the cottage, Mag had seen her look into the trough and had been enraged. "You must not look at reflections. Not your own, not anyone's reflection. A reflection is an image, and it is powerful. In this kingdom the queen does not allow images."

After that, Sarah had avoided the water trough for a long time.

Now she touched the brittle papers, knowing they held a reflection too, a reflection of her own past. Her stomach felt hollow. The yellowed papers rattled in her shaking fingers.

Two sheets had been torn from books, their left-hand edges were ragged and they had page numbers. They were made of strange, foreign paper, very smooth, and the printing was not the usual handwritten script, but rigid and precise. The third paper had thin blue lines to guide a childish handwriting, and the child's words stirred her strangely.

May 9, 1938.

She is dead. My little Mari is dead. She was so small when I found her, just a little lost kitten alone and hungry in the garden. She had long white whiskers, she was so beautiful, her colors all swirled together like the silk tapestry that hangs in our hall. Her eyes were golden, with black lines around. She rolled over, flashing her eyes at me. She was starving, she wanted a home. Her throat was white, and her paws white, waving as she rolled. I picked her up and took her in the house and fed her leftover scrambled eggs and toast and milk. She ate until I thought she'd burst. I knew her name should be Mari, I don't know how I knew.

She slept with me every night of our lives together. Five years. She always met the school bus, racing across the neighbors' yards to the corner. She never went in the street after I scolded her. Sometimes when she looked at me I thought she wanted to tell me some-

thing. I thought she was trying to talk human language, but of course she couldn't. She could only talk with her beautiful golden eyes, or by touching me with her paw.

Now she is dead. The doctor couldn't mend her sickness.

I hate doctors.

I buried her under the fuchsia tree. I dug the hole, I wouldn't let Daddy help. I dug it deep, and I wrapped her in her blue blanket. I put in her favorite sofa pillow and her little dish. I made a clay headstone with her name and picture drawn into the wet clay, and baked it at an art school. I will miss her forever and I will love her forever.

There was no signature. Sarah knelt on the cottage floor holding the lined paper, shivering with pain for the child's agony.

Was this her own childhood grief, embossed into the page? Had she been that child? How could she forget such a thing as the death of a loved animal? And she didn't think she had ever seen a cat; cats were forbidden in the Netherworld. At least they were forbidden in Affandar—the queen's edict said cats belonged only in the upperworld among foreign evils. For an instant she felt on the brink of realization. Then the sensation of dawning knowledge vanished.

The other two papers only intensified her confusion.

I am Bast, I am beauty, I am all things sensuous. In Bubastis, in the temple of cats, my saffron fur was brushed by slaves, incense was burned to me and prayers raised to me, and kings fought for my favor. I strolled beside lotus ponds where virgins knelt at my silken paws or at my sandaled feet and served me delicacies in golden bowls.

I am Bast, child of moon's caress. I am Sekhmet, born of fiery suns. I have confronted the Serpent whose name is Deception and I have destroyed him.

Though the serpent will rise anew. My daughters
will confront him and their daughters will face him.
So I bequeath to my heirs the Amulet that holds the
power of truth. I tell my daughters this: only by truth
can the Serpent be defeated. Only by falsehood can
he survive.

She put down the paper, shivering.

To speak of Bast or Sekhmet in the Netherworld would be
to invite imprisonment. Cats and the gods of cats, by edict
of the queen, were forbidden—evil and unclean. Why had
Mag hidden this? What did it mean?

After a long time she took up the third page, and these
words were more comfortable, like the language of the
Netherworld tales; though strangely this page, too, spoke
of cats.

I tell you an old Irish saying that "There's crocks of
gold in all them forths, but there's cats and things
guarding them." And the Danaan people were driven
out of Irish lands into the burial mounds and secret re-
cesses. And they went down through crypts and graves
into the netherworld. And there were among them the
Cat Kings and the queens of the Catswold.

She did not know the meaning of Catswold. Yet the word
alarmed her. Fearing Mag would return, she put the papers
back beneath the drawer and sealed them with a spell. She
rose and stood at the window, searching the dropping cliff;
though if Mag had started up, she could not be seen. She
stood looking, then moved to the shelf and took down the
old woman's spell book.

Leafing through the yellowed pages, she found the spell
she wanted. She committed it to memory in one reading, and
returned the book to the shelf, casting a spell of dust across
it so Mag wouldn't know it had been moved. Then she
pulled on her cloak, snatched up a waterskin, and went to
saddle the pony. The Pit of Hell lay to the east, cutting

across a dry Netherworld valley where she had never been. She imagined the pit's flame-filled gorge bisecting the valley, its fires leaping high and searing the land on both sides. She imagined the Lamia she must call from the Hell Pit, the beast half-dragon, half-woman, a beast thirsty for human souls. She had no choice. These papers had to do with her past. The time had come to learn about her past, and only from a Hell Beast would she get answers.

Chapter 3

She pressed the pony fast along the high, grassy plateau, her heels dug hard to his sides; her long skirt whipped in the wind that sucked down from the granite sky. Fear of the Pit filled her. Her imagination toyed too vividly with the Hell Beasts and their hunger for human souls, and human flesh.

But with a powerful enough spell she would be safe. If she could call from the pit the Lamia and force it to answer three questions, she might learn who she was. She might learn why Mag had kept the past secret from her.

Soon they left the plateau and the pony made his way down a steep incline toward a dry, sandy valley. No blade grew here, no beast grazed. The brown expanse was surrounded by stone cliffs eaten with holes from the ancient seas. Above her the stone sky was eroded and scarred. She pushed the pony fast across the dry plain, and when at last they reached the far side, she pressed him up a new barrier of steep stone ledges.

At the top she paused to let him blow. Their shadow on the cliff shone thin as breath. Before her the land dropped again steeply, and the granite sky rose away like the top of a bubble. Her every instinct told her to turn back to the cottage and to Mag and safety. But she urged the pony on down the bank. He picked his way carefully, sure-footed, as were all elven-bred beasts. But at the bottom where they entered into a tunnel, he snorted uneasily. She had no doubt this was the way; already she could smell the reek of smoke from the fires of the Hell Pit. The tunnel, without the green wizard light, was totally black. When she brought a spell-light the pony moved on more easily, and when he saw far ahead the end of the tunnel he hurried; the gleam of green light cheered Sarah, too. They came out at the foot of high cliffs.

The air was hot, the land radiated heat. The smoke was so strong she sneezed. They climbed again, and by mid-morning, when they reached the highest ridge, the pony was sweating and balking. Now far, far below them stretched the Hell Pit. The scorched plain was dark with smoke, and was burned black in a wide swath along the edge of the pit. The pit belched smoke and seethed with flames leaping and sputtering. It was in some places wider than the broadest river, but portions of it were as narrow as a path. It was bottomless. Its magma burned and belched fire, bubbling up from the earth's molten core.

She forced the pony down the slick rock, the little beast skidding and sliding. The smoke smelled sulphurous. Soon sweat plastered her hair and ran into her eyes and glued her dress to her. The pony's neck and shoulders ran with sweat. Suddenly ahead something black flew toward her, separating into three winged shapes.

Three flying lizards skimmed along beneath the stone sky. When they were directly above her, they circled, watching her. She stared up at their little red eyes and shouted a spell at them. They flapped as if jolted, and flew away screaming. The winged lizards were the queen's spies. Why would they want to watch her?

As she drew near the bottom of the cliff, the stench of sulphur and smoke gagged her, and the pony put his ears back, wanting to bolt away. At the edge of the plain he balked completely, rearing and wheeling, fighting her. She slid off, let him run back up the cliff, then hobbled him halfway up with the strongest holding spell she knew. If he ran off, she'd walk home.

On foot she crossed the burnt plain and approached the Hell Pit, coughing from the fumes, dizzy with the heat. Near to the pit, flames licked out at her, and the heat warped her vision. She stepped nearer.

She could see deep down within the flames, dark shapes moving. Swallowing her terror, she choked out a summoning spell.

She waited, then repeated the spell. When after a long time she thought no Lamia would come, she felt weak with relief. But suddenly something dark shifted within the flames and began to rise.

A creature rose up within the licking flames, dragon-tailed and armored with scales, its woman's face and jutting breasts covered with bright scales that glinted and changed color in the hot, warping air. Its thick tail lashed at the edge of the pit, dislodging stones that fell away into the flames. The hot air warped and shifted, and the Lamia hung before her—half-dragon, half-woman—its woman's face fine featured but reptilian. Its mouth was red and wet, its black eyes hungry. Its hands darted out toward her: woman's hands ending in sharp dragon's claws. Its voice was a burning hiss. "What power have you, girl, to call me from the pit?"

Sarah had backed away, her mouth too dry to speak.

"Why do you call me, human girl? What do you want?"

"I—I call you to answer my questions."

The beast lunged at her. "If I answer your questions, what do you offer in return?"

She moved farther from the edge. "I offer nothing. You are bound by my spell to answer me." Her heart pounded too fast, she couldn't make her voice steady. "My spell allows three questions."

As the Lamia laughed, its colors changed, flickering into crimson spots and blue and silver bars that flashed across its breasts and thighs. It leaped at her suddenly, its claws pierced her shoulders and it jerked her into the smoke, swinging her out over the pit. She hung in space above the flames, the heat of molten earth and fire searing her, dizzying and sickening her. Below her, a dozen half-seen beasts writhed and reached, waiting for her to fall. She twisted, fighting the Lamia, sick with terror that she would fall, and she saw the hem of her dress burst afire. She grabbed the Lamia's arm and stared into its scale-lidded eyes, shouting a spell to save herself. The Lamia's eyes widened; it shifted, nearly dropped her. She screamed the spell again to ward away harm from herself, and suddenly the beast moved toward the bank and tossed her at the solid ground. She leaped from its claws sprawling, grasping at the earth, her heart thundering as she crawled away from the edge.

She crushed out her flaming hem against the earth and rose to face the Lamia, shaken, still so dizzy she dared not look down into the pit. "Do not touch me again. You are bound by the ancient powers to obey me."

"I am bound only by my own power or one stronger. Your powers cannot equal mine."

"I had the power to call you here. I had the power to free myself from your obscene hands."

Its black eyes blazed, then narrowed. "What is your question?"

"Who am I?"

"Melissa," it said obediently, its mouth widening in a bloody smile.

A surge of rightness filled her, a wave of excitement. The name seemed right, seemed almost familiar. *Melissa. I am Melissa.* But a name was not enough. She stared into the Lamia's hate-filled eyes. "I do not want to know only a name. I want to know *who.* What person? What family and history? What life did I have that I cannot remember?"

"You asked none of that. You are Melissa."

"But *who?* The question means more than a name."

"I have told what you required."

She swallowed back her rage. She did not dare to lose control of herself before this beast. "Tell me about my mother."

"That is not a question."

"What—what was the lineage of my mother?"

"Is that your second question?"

"It is." But even as she answered, she thought she had formed this question, too, unwisely. She had a sharp desire to attack the beast, some part of herself wanted to claw and kill the beast.

The Lamia said, "Your mother was wife to the brother of my sister."

"That is no answer, it's a riddle."

"I have told what you required."

"But she can't have been . . . Wife to the brother of your sister? But my mother wasn't . . . that is not possible."

When the Lamia began to fade, Melissa went rigid. "Child of Lillith! By the Ancient Wizards you are bound. You must answer my third question!"

"Then be quick. It's cold up here." It licked its red lips, eyeing her hungrily.

"What—what is the entire truth of my past?"

"Too broad a question. I need not answer that." It rubbed its dragon hands over its scaly breasts and began to grow indistinct, its body mingling with the smoke.

"By the old laws, you must answer me!" Melissa shouted. "From—from exactly where and whom, and by what power, can I learn the entire truth of my past?"

The Lamia stopped fading. Its colors were muddied now and sullen. Its voice was hollow, but its eyes glowed at her obscenely through the hot, warping air. "You can learn what you wish from the Toad."

"Give me the rest of the answer, child of Lillith. By the Ancient Wizards, you are bound to do so."

The Lamia's black eyes fixed on her throat. Its claws moved as if to tighten around her flesh. "The Toad sleeps in the dungeons of Affandar Palace. It will tell the past if you can wake it. And if it likes you."

"No toad could be kept in a dungeon, it would slip out through the bars."

The Lamia's colors flashed brighter. "I did not say how big a toad."

"Well? How big?"

"That is four questions." It shivered and began to vanish.

"You have not completed the third question," she shouted. "What power will I use to make the Toad tell me?"

The beast's voice was nearly bodiless. Flame and smoke warped her vision. "You need no special power," it hissed. "Use your wits." It appeared again faintly, its woman's shape more dragonlike, its face sharpened to a dragon's face. Then it disappeared in an explosion of licking flames.

When it was gone she turned from the pit quickly and fled up the cliff to the pony. She stood hugging the warm, sweet-scented pony, her arms around his neck, trying to calm herself.

At last she slid on and let him have his head. He leaped away up the cliff at a gallop, pounding upward as if pursued by the entire population of the Hell Pit. He didn't slow until they were well away from the valley, on the highest ridges.

Riding, clinging to him, she thought, *Melissa . . . I am Melissa . . .* Something of her true self had been given back to her, a tiny core of rightness. Perhaps now that she knew her real name—like knowing the key spell to potent magic—she could unravel her past.

The pony was climbing the last ridge when suddenly fire exploded in their path and a huge tree stood blocking their way where, a second before, there had been only bare stone. Its branches spread over them broad as a cottage. Its left side was consumed by flame, every branch burned, every leaf and limb was eaten by flame. But the right-hand side was green and alive, the leaves as fresh and tender as the first new shoots of spring.

She calmed the rearing pony and made him stand, though he shivered and trembled. This tree, that had burst suddenly into being before her, was the living symbol of the Netherworld: half of natural life, half of the shifting flame of enchantment. It held her powerfully. And it was the symbol of her own life, too: the half that lived with Mag in the cottage was natural and familiar. The other half was hidden within the flames of some inexplicable enchantment. And she knew that the tree, beneath its licking fires, was healthy and alive. Just as, beneath the secrecy of enchantment, her past was alive.

She did not leave the presence of the tree, the tree left her, vanishing as suddenly as it had appeared. She went on, filled with a strange anticipatory excitement. But then coming down the bank to the cottage she saw Mag's horse rolling in his pen, and she began desperately to invent a lie.

She dared not tell Mag she had been to the Hell Pit or that she knew her name. She led the pony into the corral and un-saddled him and rubbed him dry, delaying, unable to think of any reasonable lie.

In the cottage she found Mag kneeling before the wood stove bedding down newborn piglets in a basket, and she was filled with guilt. The sow had farrowed. Against Mag's instructions she had left the cannibalistic sow alone.

"I saved nine," Mag said, scowling up at her. "Who knows how many she ate."

"I—I was hunting mushrooms. I felt stifled in the cottage, I forgot the sow—I had to get out in the air."

"And where are the mushrooms?"

"I lost the basket down a ravine—the pony bolted, I dropped the basket. Flying lizards were everywhere."

Mag sat back on her heels. "Lizards don't come for nothing. What were you doing, that they would watch you?"

"I told you, hunting mushrooms. I'm sorry about the pig. Truly, I forgot her." Why had she mentioned the lizards?

Mag searched her face cannily. "Whatever you were doing, Sarah, it was to no good. And lizards promise no good. You'd best be wary, miss. You'd best stay in the cottage until the lizards tire of you." Mag looked deeply at her. "You could be asking for more trouble than you imagine."

She looked back at Mag innocently, but she was shaken. What did Mag know, or guess? Mag said nothing more until supper. She was, Melissa felt certain, angry about more than the sow. Could Mag know that she had gone to the Hell Pit? Or did the canny old woman know about the papers she had found beneath the linen chest?

Or was Mag's distress about something else, some village crisis perhaps, or something to do with the secret rebellion? The rebels' plans for war seemed so frail to Melissa. Yet the rebels were totally committed, and their ranks were growing. Selfishly she hoped Mag's anger was centered around their problems, and not on herself.

She waited until supper, than asked innocently, "Did you not trade well for your beautiful cloth? The blue one alone should—"

"Traded fine," Mag snapped, breaking the bread, her round, wrinkled face pulled into a scowl.

"Was—was there trouble for the rebels?"

"Yes, trouble!" Mag spread butter with an angry thrust. She had obviously been bursting to talk, and too upset to start the conversation herself. "Three leaders from Cressteane have been captured by the queen's soldiers."

"Oh, Mag. But how?" The rebels' movements and identity were so carefully hidden. It was only with well thought out plans that she and Mag ever approached a rebel cottage. Even where a whole village was against the queen, the rebels were painfully discreet.

"Betrayed by one of our own," Mag said. "And if those captured men are tortured into talking, our plans could be destroyed."

"Where are the captives?" she asked casually. "In—in the dungeons of Affandar Palace?" And the Lamia's voice filled her thoughts, *The Toad sleeps—in the dungeons of Affandar Palace.*

"Where else would they be but Siddonie's dungeons?"

She stared at her plate. "Who was captured? Are they men I know?"

Mag looked hard at her. "You have never asked rebel secrets."

"If they are captive, they are no longer secret."

"The queen will not learn their names easily. What you don't know, you can't be forced to tell."

They ate in silence until at last Melissa, too tightly wound to sit another minute, rose and picked up her plate. At the stove she heated water and did up the dishes while Mag took the piglets out to the sow, meaning to guard them while they nursed. Melissa worked idly at the spinning wheel while she made plans, her mind filled with the imprisoned rebels.

Rebellion had been building a long time against Queen Siddonie's increasing enslavement of other Netherworld nations. And Siddonie's rule within Affandar itself was crueler and more constricting each year. She had conscripted workers by enchantment, to go into the mines, and to serve in her growing army. She had torn families apart, and destroyed many of the traditional ways of making a living, destroyed people's will to work. As a result, villagers were starving.

When Mag came in and knelt before the cookstove, getting the piglets settled in their basket, Melissa climbed into her cot and pretended sleep. Not until hours later did she rise again and, in the near-dark, pull on her dress, pack some bread and ham, and take up a waterskin and lantern.

Chapter 4

Braden, barefoot and wearing cutoffs, set his coffee cup on the terrace table. The garden was barely light, the dawn air cool and smelling of wet leaves. He stood idly studying the tangle of flowers and small trees and bushes trying to get awake, trying to shake a faint but depressing hangover. The three houses up the hill were still dark. The studio behind him was dark, though if work had been going well it would be a blaze of light. He would already have set up a canvas, poured out turpentine and oil, and become lost in the painting.

When Alice was alive they used to walk at dawn on Sundays, Alice striding out fast but seeing every leaf and change of color, every bird, every animal in every yard. They'd end up at Anthea's in the village for breakfast, get the papers, read the reviews of the new exhibits. And when they were remodeling the house, they'd had breakfast out here on the terrace among the sawhorses and lumber, before the carpenters arrived. The front of the house had been torn out waiting for a new glass wall, gaping open to the garden like a bombed-out war casualty. They'd nailed canvas drop cloths over the forty-foot hole and Alice said that ought to be a big enough canvas for him to work on. Some of the inner walls had been torn away, too; they'd lived for ten weeks among bare studs and sheetrock dust. He could see Alice sitting here at the terrace table, her head bent, her long pale hair catching the light as she studied the blueprints. She'd been so happy to have the studio finished at last, to have her own place to work. The living room, dining room and entry hall had been turned into one forty-foot studio with rafters supporting the roof, and a skylight in Braden's work area. Alice liked the softer light of the windows. She had taken a week to get her half of the studio set up, installing shelves, arranging the printing plates and handmade papers and etching and litho inks. Thinking about her was still like digging into a fresh wound.

Above him up the terraces a sound jarred him—the snip, snip, snip of garden clippers. He stared up at the dark, thin gardener who was hunched over a bush methodically trimming away. Vrech was a greasy, unpleasant man. And what the hell was he doing here so early? Waking up everyone else in the garden houses. The snap of the clippers was like gnashing teeth.

The six houses that circled the garden shared Vrech's salary, but Olive Cleaver had hired him, years ago. The man did his job all right, kept the hillside tangle in just enough order to make the garden interesting, but he put Braden on edge; there was a cloying quality about him. Braden watched him, annoyed, pushing aside his sketch pad and pencils.

He had meant to plan a new painting this morning—as much as he ever planned, a rough start, some direction to give a model—but nothing stirred him. Nothing wanted to come to life, to make the light glow in his mind with the brilliance of a finished painting. Nothing he had considered lately had that brilliance. He felt as dull as if mind and spirit suffered from a toothache.

Sometimes he could jack up his lagging spirits by reading the reviews of his past shows or by recounting the frequent museum awards, a stupid ritual that meant nothing but would jolt his ego and get him started. He had less than two months to get the show together for Chapman, and he had only ten paintings and none of them meant a damn thing. Dull, uninspired. It would take twenty-five pieces to fill the gallery. He had thought of canceling the show—that would be the final admission of failure—but you just didn't cancel a show with Chapman, a show you'd had scheduled for over two years, not unless you were ready to admit total defeat.

He wasn't ready to do that. But it was nearly impossible to get himself to work. He'd done everything to avoid work—had gone sailing, climbed Mount Tam half a dozen times, even ridden a couple of times at the local stables as he used to ride with Alice, trying to make himself enjoy being out on the yellowed summer hills, maybe make some facet of the landscape come alive enough to want to paint it. But even going to the stables, glimpsing Alice's favorite mare, had thrown him into depression.

He'd made every excuse to avoid Chapman seeing the few dull paintings he had produced since his last show—he'd gone out of town, gone down the coast to Carmel. He had remained filled with defeat, feeling like he might as well be painting soup cans.

Maybe he should be, maybe someday they'd all paint soup cans—flat designs done with a mind as flat as that of a store mannequin, passionless, sexless.

But this was 1957 and the world of painters was filled with passion: the exploding passion of Still, of Kline, the inflamed vision fostered by Picasso, and echoes of the Bauhaus, and with his own kind of painting, with the work of the Bay area action painters, their colors the glowing hues of California, opulent as stained glass.

He dumped his coffee out, looking absently up the terraces. The gardener had moved to a hydrangea bush. Snip, snip, snip—an annoying, suggestive sound. Braden stared at his sketch pad thinking of excuses to do any number of unnecessary chores in the studio: stretch more canvases for more dull paintings, make a list of supplies, sweep the floor. The garden grew lighter, the hidden sun sending a blaze of gold along the top of the redwood forest. Halfway up the terraces a yellow cat came out from beneath a fuchsia bush and slipped warily away from Vrech; the cat's distrust of the gardener stirred sympathy in Braden even if it was only a cat.

There were five or six cats living in the garden. He ignored them and they ignored him; cats made him uneasy. Cats watched people too intently, and they weren't loving like dogs. He glanced up the hill to Olive's two-story house; its age-darkened siding blended into the dark forest behind it. There was a cat on Olive's front porch, crouched, watching the gardener. To the right in Morian's gray, two-story frame, a light had come on in Morian's bedroom behind her bamboo shades. He could see her moving around, caught a glimpse of her dark arm reaching just behind the shade. She would be getting ready for an early class. To the right of Morian's, nearest to the dead end lane, Anne Hollingsworth's one-story, white Cape Cod was still dark. Three neighbors, three single women—Anne divorced, Olive a dry old spinster, and dark-skinned Morian with plenty of men in her bed. The three were the most unlikely of friends, as different as three women could be, but they were close friends; and they had looked out for him tenderly since Alice died. In weak moments he admitted he needed them in the casual, secure context of neighbors. Though Morian was more than neighbor, gracing his bed occasionally with offhand pleasure and tenderness.

As he picked up his shoes and bent to put them on, the gardener came slouching down the terraces. Vrech looked straight through him, didn't acknowledge him, then turned and went into the tool shed, shutting the door. The action stirred a memory without any connection: he'd dreamed of Alice last night, the same nightmare he'd had a thousand times, Alice lying unconscious over the steering wheel. The flames of the cutting torches. His helpless rage. He had waked shouting and lashing out at the car in which she lay trapped.

Vrech came out of the tool room wearing a Levi jacket and carrying a brown paper bag. He shut the oak door, not turning to look at the carved cat faces that protruded from the old, darkened planks that formed the door. He headed across the garden to the lane, and quickly crossed the lane, heading toward the village.

The man usually drove a green Ford, but it wasn't there today. Strange that he'd come to work so early and stayed such a short time. Maybe his car was in the shop, maybe he'd left to pick it up. Braden stood looking after him idly, then on impulse he went up the garden to the tool shed and, despite his repugnance at touching the door, he opened it to look inside.

He didn't know what he'd expected to see. The dark little room contained only a wheelbarrow, the ladder, the work table, and some scattered garden tools. The table was littered with seed packets, and with clay pots to which dry earth clung. A hoe and shovel leaned against the dirt wall beside some bags of manure. He studied the stone wall that formed the back of the room, keeping the hill in check. Overhead, heavy timbers held the earth solidly. Someone had taken a lot of trouble building this hillside cellar. It had been in the garden longer than Alice's Aunt Carrie could remember. Carrie had played here when she was a child, as, later, Alice did, and then Alice's little foster sister. The cave seemed a depressing place for a child, though usually they had played on the brick pad in front of the door, making up games that included the carved cats, and talking to the cats. He breathed in the smell of raw earth, and backed out of the cave. A tendril of the cup of gold vine that framed the door slid across his neck, startling him. He grabbed the offending limb and broke it off. Why didn't the gardener keep the damn vine trimmed? The vine's ancient, twisted limbs were so old and thick they formed a heavy, rough frame for the carved door. Suddenly, watching the medieval cats' faces, he felt chilled. He turned away abruptly and headed down toward the studio; he could almost feel the damned cats watching him.

Chapter 5

Mag, I've gone to the Wizard in Marchell, please don't follow me. I must do this. I love you.

Melissa wrote the note in a thick layer of dust that she made appear on the supper table. Around it she wove a tangle of spells which would confuse Mag and make her laugh; the old woman was less likely to follow her if she showed some style. She didn't like hurting Mag, but it couldn't be helped. She dared not tell her where she was really going—Mag would come storming after her and with harsh words, maybe with spells, would force her home again. She pulled on her cloak, shoved her knife in its sheath, and fastened on her trinket bracelet for trading. With the pack, a lantern, and the full waterskin she quit the cottage, slipping out into the dark green night.

The way up the cliffs was precarious in the dark, with drop-offs and loose stones. But when at last she topped the cliff and started down the other side, the path was easier. Where the stone sky was lowest, white bats darted and squeaked overhead, skimming along after insects. She tied her hood to keep them out of her hair, though they stayed away usually, unless someone had laid a spell. Bat-spells were a prank children played, or feuding village women. When the sky rose again, black cliffs loomed against it, and on her right a precipice dropped. She didn't light the lantern but brought a spell-light; it could be doused faster in case of night-traveling horsemen who would surely be queen's soldiers. She thought it must be near to midnight when she turned onto a path between cliffs too narrow to be traveled by horsemen. She didn't want to happen on a band of rebels, either, going about some secret business. Too many of the rebels knew her and would tell Mag they had seen her. Soon she was skirting the ice caves, shivering with cold.

She had no notion how she would proceed when she reached Affandar Palace, except to ask for work in the scullery. She shivered with more than cold when she thought about descending into the palace dungeons to search for the Toad and for the captured rebels.

Soon she was in the labyrinth of the ancient, dry riverbed. She and Mag had sometimes come this way. The pot-holes and basins and thin arches were rimed with ice, and she laid a spell before her feet to keep from slipping. The Affandar River had flowed here until Queen Siddonie's powers changed its course so it brought water nearer the palace. That change had destroyed the economy of half a dozen villages which depended on the river's power for fulling cloth and for milling grain, but the queen cared nothing about that.

All night she followed the riverbed. As dawn began to seep down from the frozen arches above her, she scraped ice from a saucer of stone and curled up in its hollow, wrapping her cloak around her, and slept.

She woke at mid-morning filled with a fleeting dream, she could remember vast spaces reeling above her as if the stone sky had vanished, endless space filled with harsh white light. She lay puzzled, trying to understand what she had seen.

She rose finally and found a spring among the sculptured stone. Breaking the ice, she drank and washed. From the small pool her image shone back at her surprisingly clear. She looked away from it guiltily, but soon Mag's cautions faded and her curiosity overcame her fear of images. She looked at herself and laughed, forgetting caution.

All images were forbidden in Affandar and in most of the Netherworld. Everyone knew that an evil soul would cast destructive images and bring disaster.

But all souls were not evil. She didn't think she was evil; she didn't understand why all images should be avoided. And no one ever talked about what she had found in Mag's spell book, that images made with love were beneficial and that such images could heal. In Affandar there was no distinction between good images and evil; all images were forbidden by order of the queen.

There would be no mirrors in Affandar Palace. Or none that she would see. She had heard that the queen kept one small mirror for dressing, locked within her wardrobe where no eyes but her own would see it, and no spell could be cast upon her.

For a long time she knelt beside the spring looking down at her own reflection. Mag would have been furious, but Mag wasn't there. She liked her green eyes and dark lashes, and she felt happy to like what she saw.

Toward noon she came up out of the labyrinth onto rolling green pastures. The sky dropped close above her, radiating warmth. She could see ahead the village of Sesut. There was a rebel camp there. She had gone there with Mag, and she had learned to swim in the icy Sesut River with the daughters of a rebel leader. Now, she stayed behind a ridge, regretting the warm welcome she would miss and the good hot meal.

Soon she turned onto an animal trail through a woods, then followed a spring until it ended in a thin fall of water dropping into a ravine. Beyond the ravine she entered country she hadn't seen and knew only from hearing the rebels describe it. She knew she was passing caches of weapons and food hidden in scattered caves. Ahead the land was un-

stable, and she stepped lightly among shattered stone thinking of boulders imploding, of faulted, cracked caverns col-
lapsing in landslide. Families, whole villages had died,
buried in such implosions.

She came out of the faulted land at dusk to a place of fire-
stones. As she knelt to pick up the darkest, oiliest rocks with
which to cook her supper, pebbles fell from above her and a
small blue dragon slid out of a cleft. It was the size of a
pony, too small to be dangerous, but it snapped its forked
tongue at her. She was startled by her sudden desire to kill
it, an inexplicable need to leap on it and tear at it. A desire
so intense she caught herself moving stealthily, stalking it.
Only when she was very close did she freeze and draw back,
alarmed, not knowing what was wrong with her.

She had killed game, had hunted doves for Mag when
meat was scarce, bringing them down with a simple spell.
Even that killing had upset her unbearably. She had never
liked cleaning the birds; they hung too limply in her hands.
She didn't want to admit that she had been unpleasantly
stirred by the dead birds, that they awoke a horrifying desire
to eat raw meat. She was deeply ashamed of such bizarre
feelings.

And now, this night, sleeping beside her fire in a cleft of
stone, she dreamed of killing dragons and of shaking and
teasing dragons, and she woke sick with shock at herself.

Around her the first green of dawn was seeping from the
stone sky and cliffs. She drank some water, and set out walking fast, trying to escape her dream. She didn't feel like eating. When at mid-morning two winged lizards soared over
her, she started guiltily for no reason. The lizards' thin shadows slid along the roof of sky, but their ruby eyes looked
down directly into her eyes. Well, so she was journeying to
Affandar Palace. If they told the queen that, what difference?

Toward evening she crossed pastureland again, approaching a herder's cottage. She could see by the bales of reddish
wool in the shed that he kept long-coated russet sheep. She
thought he was likely on the high ridges where the russets

preferred to graze. Entering the cottage, she found cold mutton packed in peat and ice, and some bread and onions and dried peaches. She took a small amount of food as was the custom, leaving an opal from among the dangles on her bracelet. Some said it wasn't right to trade for food since the queen gave the common folk much of the food they needed. Mag said pay for what you get. Mag wanted nothing from the queen.

Queen Siddonie had gained her throne by marrying Affandar's child prince when he was twelve. She had come originally from Xendenton. She had been a little girl when Xendenton fell and her father and two brothers were killed. She and the one remaining brother had escaped the battle and were not seen again in the Netherworld for many years. When they returned, they quickly rallied an army to win back their kingdom. Siddonie herself killed its ruler, and she put her brother Ithilel on the throne.

Soon after, Siddonie married the boy king of Affandar. Once she was queen of Affandar, she set out to conquer other nations. At present she controlled five of the fourteen Netherworld nations, plus Xendenton and Affandar. She had taken the thrones not with war but with lies, with spells, with intrigue. It was said that Siddonie enjoyed toppling rule from within by forming alliances that turned against the true rulers.

Mag said that few Netherworlders would fight hard enough to preserve their own freedom; she said folk had grown too weak. She said the spirit of the Netherworld was dying. Surely the powers of protective magic had weakened. Spells failed, sometimes crops wouldn't grow. Too many babies were born dead, and many children sickened and died. Even the queen's own child was so ill no one expected him to live long. The rebels hoped Prince Wylles would die. Without an heir, Siddonie's rule would be weakened and she would more easily be dethroned.

Melissa came to the main road in late afternoon and crossed the Affandar River on a narrow bridge. Below her the wide water ran green and clear. She was startled to see, halfway across, three selkies swimming upriver, their dark horse heads poking up out of the fast water. She watched them with surprised pleasure, for seldom did the stocky, broad little horses show themselves. They turned in the water to look up at her with wide, dark eyes, friendly and shy. Then they swam to shore and came out of the river, galloping up the bank. And on the bank they shape shifted suddenly into stocky men—broad faced, dark eyed, their beards streaming water. She felt graced to witness such a sight.

The selkies were one of the few shape-shifting peoples left in the Netherworld. They were secretive; they clung to their own kind, their ways untouched by human concerns. When trouble boiled through the Netherworld, they disappeared into the rivers and buried seas, returning when peace was restored. She had no idea why these three would show themselves to her. They said no word, only looked at her, then the three stocky men dove back into the river and disappeared. Soon, far downriver she saw the three horses' heads pop up and move swiftly away.

At dusk she left the main road and settled in a shallow cleft between boulders, hoping she would not have nightmares again. She ate some ham and bread, and was nearly asleep when she heard hooves strike stone.

Saddle horses approached, moving at a controlled trot. She slid deeper down between the stones, thankful she had made no fire.

Five mounted soldiers passed close above her, their uniforms red against the darkening stone sky. Queen's soldiers. They were nearly past when suddenly the lead stallion snorted and stared behind him, sidestepping as if he had detected her scent. His uniformed soldier wheeled the horse and leaned down from the saddle, staring into the cleft straight at her.

"Come out of there! By the queen's order, come out!"

There was nowhere to run. She came out facing drawn swords.

The five men snickered when they saw it was a girl, and

glanced at one another. Her fingers itched for her knife, but it was in her pack. Three were older men. The captain was round faced and fat, his gray hair shaggy, his belly hanging over the saddle. One sergeant was dry and thin, the other a half-elven man, stocky and square faced. The two younger soldiers were Melissa's age, one a pasty boy, the other squat and freckled, full-blooded elven.

The captain's voice was thick and unpleasant. "Where do you travel? Why are you alone? What have you there? A pack? Where would a young girl travel alone in this wild country?"

"I come from Appian to seek work in the palace."

He looked her over with too much familiarity. "Why did you leave Appian? Why would you want work in the palace? What kind of work?" he said, snickering.

"We were too many in family," she said, keeping her voice calm. "My mother sent me to find work." She wanted to run, and she suspected she knew no spell strong enough to turn aside this crude man's attentions. Watching his eyes, she remembered every ugly story about the queen's guard.

He dismounted and jerked her to him. "How old are you?"

"Seventeen."

He stared at her stomach. "Are you with child? Is that why your mother turned you out?"

"I am not with child. I left home because there were too many to feed, nine sisters and brothers."

"There are never too many to feed. The queen gives food to all families."

"There are several big families in Appian. The queen's stores didn't stretch so far. And our cottage was crowded. Most of us slept on the floor. I am the oldest and they sent me to work." Why didn't he believe her? It was common practice to send a child to work at the palace or to apprentice in some wealthier village. Surely the two younger soldiers were apprentices.

The captain glanced up at the sergeant, licking the side of his mouth, then pulled her closer. He started to say something, then he looked at her more intently, grasping her chin, turning her head to left and right.

He lifted her hair, looking so closely she wondered if it needed dying again. Mag kept it dyed with spells and snake root, she was very particular about that. He looked intently from her hair to her eyes, then looked up again at the sergeant. Then, abruptly, he pulled his horse around, loosing her as the others drew close. He mounted heavily, off-balancing the horse. His look had changed, the lust had vanished. "Get on behind."

She thought of breaking away between the horses and running, but they would overtake her. The captain leaned from the saddle, snatched her arm, and pulled her up against the horse. "Get on. You want to go to the palace, you will come with us." He laughed. "You will go to the queen in style."

She had no choice. She got on, putting her foot over his in the stirrup, and sat behind the saddle clinging to it, not touching him.

Through the night they traveled, stopping only to water the horses. No one asked Melissa if she was thirsty. She fought sleep; she didn't want to doze and lean against the captain's fat back. She was tense with fear of what he might decide to do if they stopped to rest. It was nothing to rape a village girl—there was no law prohibiting it, not under Siddonie's rule. She didn't know why they hadn't tried already. Soon she heard a fox cry out in the dark woods, then they were skirting the Affandar River; in the darkness she could hear its waters gurgling over stones. They passed through a sleeping village, and another. She was relieved when morning began to gather misty green overhead.

They came out of the woods quite suddenly, and she sat up straighter. The meadow before them was very green, the road broad and smooth. Beyond the meadow lay rich orchards and vegetable gardens, and between these rose the pale towers of Affandar Palace. She stared at the huge, delicate structure, feeling uncertain again, and afraid.

Chapter 6

The soldiers kicked their horses to a trot, moving fast toward the palace. Five pale towers rose, the tallest reaching nearly to the stone sky. The curtain wall wandered in pleasing curves, and all around it lay the orchards and vineyards and vegetable gardens. Behind the palace were fenced meadows, then two small villages, then the ancient forest.

She had never before seen windows made of real glass. She could see the road clearly reflected, could see the large oak they were passing. But she could not see horses or riders beneath the broad branches, the road appeared empty. The windows were spell-cast; neither man nor beast would reflect in them.

The captain trotted his horse through the palace gates into a courtyard crowded with villagers working at the day's tasks. A smith pounded hot metal, vegetable carts drawn by small, stocky ponies stood at a side gate. A carpenter was mending a table, some scullery girls were husking corn. In a corner against the palace wall, six pages skirmished at sword practice.

She had thought to approach the palace at a servants' wing, unnoticed. Now the entire courtyard stopped work to watch the soldiers, and folk stared at her, too, and smirked as if they thought the captain had a new companion for his bed. Two scullery girls looked so knowing that Melissa wanted to smack them.

But then she was forgotten as heads turned toward another gate, and suddenly folk were kneeling and there was no sound but the soft thud of approaching hooves.

Through an archway beneath the palace a large group of mounted soldiers entered the courtyard. They were led by a dark-haired youth no older than she, dressed in a red and purple uniform pointed with ermine. "King Efil," she heard the captain mutter as, bowing, he reached back to nudge her. She bowed, looking up under her lashes.

The king was slim, dark haired, and very handsome. He rode directly past her, and he was looking at her. As his dark eyes seared hers, she felt her face go hot. He smiled intimately, and then with amusement, and then he was past. She glanced around to watch him move out the gate at the head of his uniformed troops.

"Get off," the captain said, shoving her. She slipped down and fell under the horse's legs, and breathed a quick spell to keep the stallion from kicking her. When she crawled out, red-faced, a soldier, the pasty one, pointed his sword to direct her ahead of him.

He guided her across the courtyard to a jutting stone wing of the palace, and flung open a door, shouting. She could hear the clang of pots and the cacophony of girls' voices. She stepped into a huge, cluttered scullery. A woman, uniformed in white, turned away from a stove of steaming saucepans, and the young soldier pushed Melissa toward her. "Village girl. Wants work." Quickly he was gone again, whether from embarrassment at herding women, or from boredom, she couldn't tell.

The big woman inspected her without expression. She had a fat, lined face. "I am Briccha. I am the Scullery Mistress. If you are allowed to stay, you will answer to me." Her braids were so tight they pulled her scalp. Her bodice clung tightly over ample breasts and belly. When Melissa didn't answer, Briccha grabbed her shoulder and jerked her through the scullery, shoving other girls aside.

They entered a small chamber with whitewashed stone walls. It held a chair, a table, a pitcher of water and a bowl, a towel and a crock of soap. "Wash yourself. Comb your hair. You *do* have a comb?"

"No."

The woman fished in her pocket and handed her a dirty comb. "And sponge your dress. Make yourself acceptable for the queen."

"I do not seek audience with the queen. I want only to work in the scullery."

"The queen sees all who seek scullery work. Don't dawdle." Briccha gave her a harsh stare, and left her.

Angrily Melissa spell-locked the door, then dropped her dress and scrubbed thoroughly and slowly, luxuriating in the soap and clean washcloth and clean towel.

Soon, refreshed, she washed the comb, scrubbing it with the washcloth then the towel, then she combed her hair.

She was left in the room for hours. She paced, then sat down and closed her eyes, trying to keep her temper in check. She loved idleness on her own terms. She detested idleness enforced by others. She was nearly asleep when the door rattled but didn't open. Hastily she removed the spell that locked it.

A thin serving girl entered bearing a plate of bread and a mug of milk—a bone-thin girl, maybe thirteen, with a bluish cast to her skin. She looked Melissa over shyly. "You are another," she said softly. "Do *you* know why you were brought here?"

"I wasn't brought. I came on my own. To work."

"But I saw you ride in behind the captain."

"I met the soldiers on the way. What do you mean, brought? Were you brought here by soldiers?"

The girl had gray smudges under her eyes. Her hair was lank, her eyes the color of mud. She was a valley elven child. "We all were brought here or summoned. Surely the soldiers brought you at the queen's orders."

"I told you, I met them by chance. Why would anyone want to bring me here?"

"The queen summons many girls. Some stay to work. Most are sent home again."

"Why would she summon them then send them home again?"

"I don't know why. But many of us are glad to be allowed

to stay. The palace food is good, and this life is better than herding sheep."

Melissa wondered if that was true. At least herding sheep, you were your own boss.

"What is your name?"

"Terlis."

"What if I refuse to talk to the queen?"

Terlis stared at her. "You wouldn't dare to do that. No one would dare."

A long time after Terlis left her, a woman soldier came for Melissa—a sturdy creature with a scar down her neck. She herded Melissa through passages and up two flights of stairs, then down a main passage to a black door. She knocked, pushed Melissa through, and shut the door behind her.

The huge chamber was nearly dark. She could see quantities of black furniture that crouched like waiting beasts. Splinters of green light pushed in through the far shutters. Across the room, five spell-lights began to glow, circling a black throne. Within the throne's dark embrace sat the queen of Affandar.

At first all that was visible was the white oval of the queen's face suspended in blackness, then slowly, as Melissa approached, she made out the queen's elaborately coiled black hair against the black throne, her black robe. When suddenly the queen moved, she revealed white hands flashing with jewels. "Kneel! You are to kneel!"

She knelt, feeling awe and fear. She thought that her own small powers of magic had likely been stripped away, that if she tried to use any spell to protect herself from this woman she would fail.

"Look up at me."

She looked up into the queen's black eyes, wary as a caged beast. The queen gave her a cold smile, but then her eyes widened, and her pale mouth twitched. She lifted her white hand and brought a spell-light bright across Melissa's face.

Queen Siddonie studied her for so long that Melissa, kneeling, felt her legs cramp. She could see no expression in the queen's black eyes. The power of the woman's stare made her weak and angry. Stories of Siddonie's cruelty filled her. She felt her heart pounding, and only with great effort did she keep her face blank.

At last the queen sat back and folded her hands. "You may rise. What is your name?"

"I am Sarah."

Rage flashed in Siddonie's eyes. "What village do you come from—Sarah? Tell me why you have come to Affandar."

"Appian is my village. My father could not keep us all. I came to find work in the palace."

"What work does your father do?"

"He mines a little," Melissa said, forcing quiet into her voice, counting on Appian to be so far away and so crowded that the queen would not bother to investigate. And why should she? What difference where she came from? "He makes some jewelry, and grows barley and pigs."

Another long silence as the queen watched her, a look that made her stomach twist with fear. But then suddenly in the queen's eyes something almost vulnerable shone: Siddonie's face softened, for an instant her smile was almost gentle. "You will start in the kitchens, Sarah. You will report to Briccha. If you are a good worker there may be other chores." Then suddenly her fists clenched and she half rose. "You are dismissed. Rise and get out. *Now!*"

Alarmed, Melissa backed quickly to the door. And her anger rose so fiercely she had to restrain herself from hissing curses or from striking out at the queen. She fled, enraged—and shocked at herself.

Outside the door she stood, regaining her breath, almost more frightened of her own fierce reactions than of Queen Siddonie.

Chapter 7

Braden was parking the station wagon after a pointless drive up the coast when he saw his neighbor, Olive Cleaver, come down the garden and go into the tool room carrying a camera and notebook. Olive was in her seventies, a skinny woman with parchment pale skin made more sallow by her garishly flowered house dresses: Woolworth designs of raw color so terrible they were wonderful. This one featured giant orange and yellow nasturtiums on a black ground. Its garishness shocked all color from Olive's bare legs and wrinkled arms and face. As she entered the tool room, she smiled and waved at him. He wondered what she was going to shoot in there with the Rolleiflex. Olive, strictly an amateur, did some passable work. He opened the back of the station wagon and retrieved his duffel bag and paint box. He'd packed extra shorts and socks and his razor, but he hadn't stayed anywhere, had turned around again and come home.

He had driven north toward the wine country and Russian River on a sudden whim, wanting to get away, but something—boredom, a sense of uselessness—had made him head back again. He had felt as confined in the car as he had felt in the studio; the same stifled sense of captive panic he'd had after the war when he marked time in England for three months without any action. Driving north, he had changed his mind about going to Russian River—the place stirred too many memories. He'd wondered why the hell he had thought he could go there, and he had cut off 101 suddenly onto the narrow road to Bodega Bay.

He and Alice had gone to Russian River before they were

married, in the middle of winter, and pitched a tent. They had had the place to themselves. They'd cooked on a campfire and had swum nude in the icy river. The first night, Alice spilled chocolate syrup in the sleeping bag, and for a week afterward they had made love and slept engulfed by the smell of chocolate.

Heading for Bodega Bay, passing green pastures where dairy cows grazed, he had let his mind stay numb and blank. At the shore he'd walked along the beach for several hours not thinking, watching the sea, trying to become a part of whatever it was out there—the rhythm of the waves pounding, the emptiness of sky and sea meeting unbroken, hinting at some kind of meaning he couldn't touch. Alice had loved the sea, she would have been running out in the cold water picking up shells, would have sat on a rock shivering, drawing the gulls and plovers.

Now as he carried his bag and unused sketching things across the terrace to the studio, he glanced up the hill again toward the open tool room, trying to focus on Olive Cleaver, get his mind off Alice. He was aware of flashes of light from inside the tool room as Olive worked with her flashbulbs, likely shooting still lifes of the garden tools, arranging earthy little studies.

He went into the studio, dropped his bag and paint box, and made himself a sandwich and opened a beer. When he came out of the house onto the terrace again, Olive was crouched before the oak door, taking pictures of the cats' faces. This should have amused him, but suddenly he wanted to tell Olive to stop it, stop taking pictures of the cats, stop fooling around with the door. He wanted to tell her to leave the cats alone, that they could be dangerous.

He didn't like that kind of thought in himself; he didn't like these crazy notions. Why the hell did he focus on cats? Everywhere he looked, his attention was drawn by cats; he'd gotten his mind fixated on cats. Even on the beach before he left Bodega Bay he'd seen a cat trotting along the sand, hunting among the seaweed, and he had to stop and stare at it. Black-and-white cat. It had stopped, too, and looked at him. Alice would have coaxed it to them, petted it, talked to it, given it part of their lunch. Watching the stray cat, he had imagined Alice there so clearly—her pale hair blowing in the sea wind, her fine-boned face concentrated as she talked to a stray cat. Alice had needed animals around her, had been more at home with animals than with people.

Annoyed with himself but unable to stop brooding, he got some stretcher bars and a roll of canvas and set to work stretching canvases, working on the terrace where it was cooler. Above him at the door of the cats, Olive was still at it. After a quarter hour of photographing the different cats' heads, Olive let her camera hang idle around her neck, and knelt by the door's lower hinge. She took a little knife from her pocket, and some envelopes, and began working the knife at the hinged edge of the door as if prying loose a splinter.

She dropped the splinter, or whatever it was, into an envelope, then pried out another from the next plank higher up, and put this in a second envelope. She stood up and took a third sample.

When she had five samples, one from each heavy oak plank that formed the door, she turned and saw him looking up at her. She smiled and waved to him again, went up the garden, and disappeared inside her dark-shingled house. He wanted to go up to the tool room and look at the door where she had cut into it; he wanted to figure out what the hell she had been doing.

But what difference? Anyway, it was her door. The way the lots were laid out in pie shapes joining in the center of the garden, the door was on Olive's land. If she wanted to pry off splinters, that was her business. Maybe she meant to send her splinters for a carbon-14 test. Maybe Olive suddenly burned to know how old the door was.

As Alice had longed to know.

Alice said if it was genuinely medieval, it shouldn't be in the garden but in a museum. She had thought it amazing that the door was in such good shape and not rotting. He thought the damn thing was a copy. Who would put a valuable antique in a garden? He had been singularly annoyed by her interest. She never had found out who built it into the hill, though she had gone over old land records and written to several families. Olive had been in on that little investigation—the two of them spending useless hours in the county tax office, complaining afterward because the office was not only cold but stunk of cigarette smoke. The whole thing was an exercise in wasting time, and after Alice died Olive had seemed to turn to other projects. A retired librarian, Olive had retained all her energy and interest in the world; she pursued with singleminded intensity the projects she undertook.

He finished the stretcher bars and began to cut canvas, anticipating four new canvases, pristine white and waiting.

For what? Waiting for what? Waiting for four new, dull, lifeless attempts which would be as unsatisfying as his drive up the coast.

Chapter 8

The scullery was steamy hot and noisy with the gossiping voices of two dozen scullery maids. Pots clanged, knives chopped against cutting boards, and Briccha's frequent commands cracked like rocks banged together. Smoke from the hearthfire mixed with the steam; the flames hissed and spat as fat dripped onto them from the deer turning on the spit. Beside the deer, braces of chickens roasted. Briccha took Melissa by the shoulders and pointed her toward a counter piled with dead doves and quail. "Pluck and dress them. Don't leave any feathers. Don't dawdle. Wash them in that bucket."

She set to work with distaste. Around her girls kneaded bread dough, mixed sauces, and cut and peeled piles of vegetables and fruits. She wasn't quick at cleaning birds, even with a simple-spell, and she didn't like doing it; their softly feathered bodies made her unbearably restless. She hated the blood and the smell of the birds' entrails because she was unsettled by them, feeling something stirring within herself that she didn't understand.

It was noon when she finished cleaning the last dove, but she hadn't earned a rest. Briccha directed her to a pile of greasy pots to scrub. She washed pots for the rest of the day, her hands and arms soon coated with grease, and she was sweating from the hot dishwater. The banter of the other girls distracted her, and a few remarks were directed her way, but she did not attempt to make friends. Late in the afternoon Briccha marched her up the back stairs four flights to the attic.

They entered a long, narrow room whose steep rafters rose to a high peak, and whose walls were lined with tiers of bunks. Briccha pointed to a top bunk at the end, up beneath the rafters. A ladder led up, skirting a small window.

"You'll sleep there. That'll do for a few days—you won't last longer. There's a blanket and towel on the bunk, a hook by the window for your dress."

Melissa looked at Briccha evenly. "Why won't I last longer? Did my work not suit you?"

"Your work was satisfactory." Briccha turned away. "I wake the early shift at four in the morning. You will go directly to the scullery. You will work until I release you in mid-afternoon." As she headed for the door, Melissa moved in front of her.

"Why won't I last?"

Briccha's narrow eyes widened. "You will not last at all if you cannot control your rudeness." She pushed past Melissa and strode out the attic door.

Melissa climbed into the high bunk, meaning to rest for only a little while. She didn't know what Briccha had meant, but she would find out. Pulling the thin blanket up, she lay thinking about the palace dungeons. She had glanced into the scullery storeroom when a girl was sent to get flour. She thought it likely the cellars were near the storeroom to give easy access to the larger food stores, and she wondered if they opened from within the storeroom. Soon she slept. She didn't wake until Briccha shouted up at her. "Four o'clock. Get down from there. Get dressed." A lantern burned at the far end of the room.

She climbed down, cramped and uncomfortable in her wrinkled dress. There was a crock of icy water beside the window. Two girls were dipping their towels into it, dabbing at their faces. She dropped her dress and washed herself all over, shivering, trying to wake up. Most of the girls still slept. Only five had been called. She dressed and followed the other four out, crowding sleepily down the dark stair. At home she would have built up the fire and gone back to bed until the cottage warmed, then risen to wake Mag.

As she pushed into the scullery behind the other girls, Briccha was already giving orders. Melissa tried to find humor in the woman's harsh manner, but it took her some days before she could let Briccha's scoldings roll off as the other girls did. Only Terlis seemed unduly upset by the scullery mistress's harshness. Melissa liked Terlis; the valley elven were shy, gentle people—though they hated to talk about unpleasant things, even to answer one's questions. The valley elven took the view that if you didn't talk about it, it would go away. When she asked Terlis why Briccha thought she would last for only a few days, Terlis didn't want to answer.

"What harm to tell me? It's too hard, not understanding."

"Look at yourself," Terlis said softly, "then look around you. You're the only pretty one. We're all either misshapen with the blood of cave dwarfs or just homely like me. You'll be sent home soon. The pretty ones are all sent home."

"But why are they brought here, then? And *why* are they sent home?"

Terlis smiled patiently. "Sent home to keep them out of the king's bed."

"Oh," Melissa said, her face reddening. She knew a dozen

tales of the king's adventures with various lovers. Of course the queen took lovers, too. She had a constant procession of bedmates as she tried to breed a healthy heir to strengthen her claim to the throne. Thus the kingdom was locked in a constant power struggle. Siddonie, if she could bear a healthy child, would surely throw King Efil out and make the new child's father king. She had married Efil to become queen; she didn't need him now. And if Efil could breed a healthy child first, he would dispossess Siddonie.

Terlis said, "Everyone knows a commoner is more likely to breed a strong baby."

"But," Melissa said, "if she's afraid of the king taking servant girls to bed, why does she bring them here at all?"

"No one knows." Terlis looked hard at Melissa. "The queen brought you here just as she brought us all, and no one knows why. Maybe her spells made you start out on your own, maybe she made you think you were coming on your own, but you can be sure that Queen Siddonie brought you to Affandar Palace."

She knew Terlis was wrong, but she didn't argue. What good to argue?

It was night when she found her chance to search further for the door to the cellars. She crept down from the attic after the other girls slept, and moved into the black shadows of the storeroom. Feeling her way along the shelves, her hand trailed over cloth bags of flour and jars of fruit, groping for the door that would lead down. She had tried for days to come in here, but there had always been people around. She knew that Briccha slept next to the storeroom, so she moved silently, but at last she brought a small spell-light—and froze.

Briccha stood in the shadows, broader than ever in a voluminous nightgown. "I thought so. What are you doing here? What are you looking for?"

"I was hungry. I came down for a slice of bread."

Briccha slapped her so hard she staggered against the shelves. "You don't need bread. The bread is in the scullery. I don't like nosiness. Nor does the queen. Get to bed."

For a week she didn't go near the storeroom. But in that moment she had seen, behind Briccha, two doors. One was open into a sleeping chamber—she could see inside a rumpled bed and a wrinkled white uniform hanging on the wall. The other door looked heavier, more stoutly made, and it was closed.

Convinced that was the door to the cellars, she waited until a morning when Briccha was in the vegetable gardens, then she approached it, slipping out of the scullery past the other girls, carrying an empty bowl as if she were going to fetch something. She hurried through the storeroom . . .

And she came face-to-face with Briccha. The Scullery Mistress had slipped in by a side door. Briccha held Melissa's arm with fingers like steel.

"I don't know what you're up to, young woman. The queen knows you have been snooping. I'm surprised she hasn't thrown you out or locked you up." Briccha's pinching fingers were bruising her, the broad woman stared into her face, but then, surprisingly, she released her. "You will not come here again. If you do, you will be eternally sorry. Now go fetch the prince's breakfast up to him. The regular girl is sick."

Melissa moved away thankfully, amused that Briccha thought such threats would stop her. Briccha said behind her, "Don't talk to Prince Wylles. And don't wake him. Put the tray by his bed. Don't wait for him to eat. He never eats."

Free of Briccha, she hurried up the two flights. The hot porridge and bacon steaming on the tray smelled so delicious it was hard not to sample the good food. She'd had only bread for breakfast. She felt no conscience about eating the prince's breakfast if he didn't, but she didn't want to get caught.

The upper hallway was lit by a jutting dormer window, with a pair of stone benches built into the recessed area, facing each other. She stepped into the deep bay, set the tray on a bench, and stood looking out through the glass.

She could see part of the kitchen gardens, and cages of doves and captive game birds awaiting slaughter for the palace table. The flutter of the birds behind the wire gave her a strange, excited urge. And there were cages of tiny birds, too, bright birds which were roasted with wine exclusively for the queen. She had heard Briccha call the birds Siddonie's morsels of spite, and she wondered what that meant.

Idly she watched a dozen horses and ponies grazing the fenced meadow behind the palace. Most of the palace mounts were kept in the stables that were entered by an archway in the courtyard. Beyond the meadows, the far forest looked dense and cold. In that ancient woods bears still roamed, and small dragons. It was the kind of forest where one might uncover the bones of still larger creatures no longer known in the Netherworld, bones that, when touched, moldered into powder. The wildness of the old forest excited her, she felt a hot desire to rove free there. And she felt lonely suddenly, too, and didn't know what she was lonely for.

She picked up the tray and went on. She knocked on the prince's door, then knocked again. When the child didn't answer, she slipped into the dim, curtained chamber.

The boy was asleep sprawled across wrinkled covers. She set the tray on the bedside table and brought a small spell-light to look at him.

His hair was dark, his face the same perfect oval as the queen's. But the child's face even in sleep was drawn with pain. Deep shadows stained his cheeks beneath his dark lashes. Everyone knew he was kept alive only by the queen's spells. No one thought Siddonie protected him because of love; she kept the dying prince alive because without an heir her claim to the throne would weaken. As Melissa turned away she saw an image on the wall, and started, shocked.

She had never before seen a picture, except those that children drew before their parents forced them to stop such practices. Why would there be an image in Affandar Palace, when every effort was made to avoid images? The windows were spell-cast, and it was said that even the horse trough was covered with a wooden lid before Siddonie came to the stables.

The picture was rich with smeared colors forming hills and trees. It showed a boy standing before a wood, and surely it was the prince, though in the picture he was not as thin.

Maybe this image was a charm meant to make the prince well. Such was not an accepted practice, and she knew of no one in the kingdom who would dare make such an image, or who would know how. Yet as she touched its rough surface, a sense of recognition filled her—a strange shadow of memory. But when she tried to bring the memory clear, it faded, was gone.

She straightened the tray on the bedside table and refolded the napkin. She had turned away from the sick boy's bed when suddenly the child spoke.

"What are you doing to my breakfast? What spell did you lay on my breakfast?"

She turned to look at him.

"Or were you eating it?"

"I'd thought of it," she said, amused. "It seems a waste, if you only send it back. How can you get well if you don't eat?"

He lifted an eyebrow. His pale face was regal in spite of the darkness under his eyes and his drawn look. A regal face, but emotionally empty, cold. His silk pajamas were rumpled and sweaty, and his dark hair was tangled. He said, "I don't want to get well. I don't like porridge and I detest pig meat. Throw it out."

She studied his black eyes, so like his mother's. He was pale to the point of grayness. "I can't imagine wanting to be sick." She looked at him for so long he began to fidget. She said, "You don't go out of this room at all? You don't ride? There are ponies in the pasture."

"Of course I don't ride anymore. I'm too sick. Horses are stupid beasts."

"You don't get tired of being in bed?" she said more softly. "You never want to be outside?"

"Why should I want to be outside? I'm too weak to go out. What business is it of yours?"

"It is none of my business." She looked him over severely. The little boy deeply angered her.

She had left him and was hurrying past the deep bay window when she realized a man stood there looking out. She paused. He had his back to her. He was dressed in hunting leathers, and not until he turned did she realize it was the king. She drew back, and because his look confused her, she knelt. It seemed strange to kneel to anyone, particularly someone no older than she.

He stared down at her and laughed, then grasped her hands and pulled her up. His hands were pleasantly cold, as if he had just come indoors. Unsettled by him, she drew her hands away. She had turned to hurry off when his voice stopped her. "The queen said your name is Sarah."

She faced him, waiting. He looked her over, then sat down on a bench, sprawling his legs comfortably in his fine soft boots, watching her. She looked back as calmly as she could.

"Come sit down, Sarah. Don't stand there like a frightened doe." His eyes were so dark she couldn't see the pupils—dark eyes that burned with life. His mouth curved in the hint of a smile, but it was a soft mouth. He took her hand and pulled her down beside him. "That's better—Sarah. That is the name you gave the queen." He smiled again. "What is your real name?"

"Sarah is my name."

"You can tell me your real name. I will keep your secret."

"Sarah is my real name. I must go. Briccha told me to hurry."

"I am king, not Briccha. You will go when I dismiss you." His features were soft, his chin rounded. But his eyes burned with stubbornness and the haughtiness of a young man used to getting his own way.

He said, "If you will not tell me your real name, then you will learn my name. Say, Efil, King of Affandar."

She said it hesitantly, not liking the feelings that he stirred in her. "Efil, King of Affandar."

"Say, *Efil*."

"Efil."

"Say it softly."

"Efil," she breathed, growing frightened.

"Say it as if it means something to you, as if it is the most wonderful name you know." His hands felt too warm on hers. His clothes were scented with vetiver, a magical herb that did nothing to calm her.

"Say it."

But she rose and pulled away from him. As she turned, a door creaked open down the passage. He thrust her away so suddenly she stumbled. "Go on, child. Don't stand in the passage dawdling. What will Briccha say?"

She went angrily, hearing men's voices behind her. She hurried down the stairs, fighting not only anger but a more complicated feeling that she didn't like.

All day she was irritable. When Briccha released her in mid-afternoon she slipped into the storeroom boldly, too tightly strung to wait longer. Snatching the moment, she fled for the cellar door and through it, and shut it soundlessly behind her.

She stood on the narrow, dark stairs, clutching the rail, listening. A damp, vegetable scent rose from below. But there was no sound. She started down through the blackness, feeling her way, daring not the smallest light.

Chapter 9

Feeling her way down the cellar stair clutching the rail, straining to see in the blackness, Melissa was afraid to bring a spell-light. Warily she listened for footsteps in the store-room above her.

At last, stumbling, she found the bottom step. On the stone floor her footsteps echoed softly, even her own breathing seemed to echo. From somewhere ahead came the faint drip, drip of water. She could smell onions and smoked meat, and a sour animal smell. After some moments, when she could hear no sound from the cellars or from above, she brought a spell-light.

Beside her, bins of vegetables flanked the narrow passage. She moved past hanging hams and barrels of pickled cabbage, past bags of nuts and grains. Shelf after shelf held jars of vegetables and fruits, and farther on stood barrels of flour and grains, and of ale, then rows of wine bottles. She lifted a bottle from its bin, brushing the dust away. Its foreign-looking label was beautifully wrought with pictures of grapes and fields, and with fancy gold lettering. This was no Netherworld label handwritten and applied with wax, this was upperworld wine, brought down through miles of tunnels from beyond doors that opened only by magic.

She didn't know whether the dungeons were on this level or a lower one, she only knew the palace cellars went deep, down into old caves and passages. Strangely, she felt a sense of repose here; the darkness seemed comforting, even the sense of being closed in seemed comforting. She felt almost as if she could see through the darkness.

Frowning, puzzled by her feelings, she searched for the dungeons, until at last, stumbling, she found a second flight of stairs. She had started down when a shriek from below made her douse her light.

She stood listening as the animal scream died. The smell of beasts rose so strongly she backed up a step. A second angry scream made her want to turn away. But she moved on, casting a strong spell-light down the steps. She found the lower corridor flanked with barred cells. Behind the bars, Hell Beasts stirred, their wings rustling in her light, their snaking coils unwinding, their eyes gleaming. Faces horned or scaled, all hostile, snarled and hissed at her. Paws and claws and deformed hands reached; she kept to the center of the aisle, moving on quickly.

She stopped, shocked, before a caged griffon.

She had never thought to see a griffon here. A griffon was not a Hell Beast; they roamed the oldest forests and were seldom seen. They were akin to the unicorns and the selkies and shape shifters. They were, like those beasts, generally creatures of goodness, though they could be unpredictable.

The Griffon slept pitifully cramped, his leonine body filling the cage, pressing against the bars, his golden wings crumpled in the tight space. His broad eagle's head, golden feathered, rested in sleep on his lion paws.

But as she drew close the Griffon came awake suddenly and raised his head, watching her with fierce, yellow eyes. She said, "You do not belong here. How did she bring you to this place?"

He didn't speak but lunged at her suddenly, roaring with uncharacterisic rage, crashing against the bars.

"What is it?" she said, coming close to him. "Oh, what has she done to you?"

He threw himself against the bars again, so hard she thought he would break through. But his yellow eyes were filled with pain. And when she reached through, stroking his face, all fierceness left him. He said, "Queen Siddonie killed my mate. And when I knelt before my dead love,

Siddonie's soldiers threw nets over me and pinioned my wings."

His eyes blazed. "I could have ripped an ordinary net, but I could not break her spells. Her evil is powerful."

"Maybe I can free you," she said, reaching to stroke his broad, soft paw.

She tried for a long time, but no spell she could remember would open the Griffon's cage. She left the Griffon at last, defeated.

Near the end of the long row of cells, she came to a caged harpy. The beast's long bird's legs made it ungainly. It stood taller than Melissa, and its feathers gleamed white in Melissa's spell-light. Its woman's torso and breasts were sleek with white feathers, but its white wings were so ragged she thought it must beat them against the bars. Its thin bird's face was stained brownish under its eyes and around its yellow beak. It stared between the bars at her pitifully. Its voice was soft and whining. "You have come to free me." It wrung its long white hands. "I am wasting in this cell, surely you are here to free me?" But in spite of its wheedling voice, its gaze was canny and appraising.

Melissa tried an opening spell, but she couldn't spring the lock. At last she said, "Can you tell me where to find the Toad?"

"In the next cell," it said, suddenly not pleading anymore but irritable. "Asleep. What could you want with the Toad?"

"I want to ask it a question, I want it to tell me about my past."

The Harpy laughed. "If you want a vision of the past, *he's* no use to you. All he does is sleep."

"Surely I can wake him."

"Do you no good. He has no powers left, the queen destroyed his vision-making powers. He can't tell so much as what you had for breakfast. He remembers only a few homilies, all useless."

"But . . ."

"Siddonie thought the Toad could tell the future. He never could do that. No one can tell the future. The queen is a fool.

Look at the beasts she has brought up from the Pit—for what? Not one of us can tell the future. Nor would we help her if we could."

"That's why she brought you all here? To tell the future?"

"That, and for her entertainment. She puts the fiercest among us in the courtyard to fight each other."

"I suppose the Griffon is the fiercest?"

"Oh, she doesn't do anything with the Griffon. She can't manage him."

"Then why does she keep him?"

"She likes to see him captive, of course. The more freedom a beast has known, the more she wants it behind bars."

"But you were all free."

"The Hell Beasts have been bound to the Pit of Hell. We are not totally free."

Melissa considered this as she moved to the next cell and looked in at the Toad. He lay sprawled on the stone floor, asleep. He was huge, nearly filling the cell. A lumpish beast, his green skin was covered with warts, his pale throat ballooning with each breath. Before she could try to wake him, the Harpy reached around with an icy hand and pulled her away. "If you wake him he'll blow himself into a stinking air ball. Phew. He won't speak to you."

Melissa's head was beginning to ache. "Are there human prisoners here?"

"Behind that wall." The Harpy pointed a white finger toward the featureless black interior of the cellar.

Melissa cast her spell-light, picking out barrels and shadowed pillars, and beyond these, a stone wall grown over with moss. "Do you know the spell to open it?"

The Harpy laughed, darting her pink tongue between sharp teeth. "Do you think I'd be in here if could command *any* of her spells? Do you think I haven't tried?" And quite suddenly the beast began to cry. Heaving sobs shook her, tears coursed down her white feathers, darkening the brown streaks. When at last the beast stopped crying, her eyes were red, and her voice was sharp with self-pity. "I thought you came to free me, but you didn't. You wanted the human prisoners. I'll never get out of this cell. I'll never see my little mirror again."

"What mirror?" Melissa asked, frowning.

"My mirror was my only companion, my only legacy from my dead mother, and that bitch queen has taken it from me. If you cannot free me I'll never see it again. Never." The Harpy combed distracted fingers through her feathers, and one white feather floated to the cell floor.

Melissa reached through the bars and took the Harpy's hand, trying to comfort her. "Why did the queen take your mirror?"

"I wouldn't bring images for her."

"I don't understand. The queen fears images."

"She fears images in the present," the Harpy said patiently. "My mirror could show the past. There is something in the past she wants to see."

"Then can you show me my past? I don't need the Toad. You can tell me who I am."

The Harpy stared at her cannily.

"I can remember nothing of my childhood," Melissa said. She considered the beast warily, searching its small cold eyes.

"I cannot bring any image," the Harpy said assessing Melissa with a keen avian stare. "Unless you steal my little mirror for me."

"Could you show me my childhood? Could you show me who my parents are? And where I come from?"

"If I had my mirror, I could show you those things."

"Where does she keep your mirror?"

"It *was* in her chambers, but not anymore. I can speak to my mirror from any distance. I made it give her images that drove her to nervous trembles." The Harpy laughed. "She couldn't rid herself of them. She kept taking my mirror out and looking, like digging your finger into a sore wound. At last she moved it to the king's chambers."

"How can you know where it is if you can't bring visions without it?"

"It calls to me. Every night my little mirror calls to me. Oh, I know where it lies hidden—in a wardrobe in the king's chambers. But that is not a vision, that is love calling."

"If I get it for you, will you show me my past?"

The Harpy reached through the bars to stroke Melissa's arm. "If you bring my mirror, I will give you whatever vision you choose."

"It would be terribly dangerous to go to the king's chambers."

"Two visions. And you will be safe enough; she never goes to his chambers anymore. Nor has the king slept in her bed since the weakling prince was born. The queen blames the king for the child's illness." The Harpy smiled. "The king blames her. He was a fool to marry her. Of course, he is still a fool. Go when the queen is at supper."

"If I were caught thieving in the king's chambers . . ."

"Everything in life is dangerous."

"I could be killed for such a thing. The laws would call it treason, to steal from the king's chambers."

"Three visions."

"As many visions as I choose."

"You already have the best of the bargain. The king will be no problem; any woman can twist him around one finger. All you need do is climb into his bed, and you can have anything."

"I do not intend to climb into his bed."

The Harpy smiled wickedly. "If you did not, that would be an opportunity lost, my dear. Think of it. The right woman has only to take herself to the king's bed to become the new queen of Affandar." She clasped her long white hands together. "Oh, I would like to see someone dispossess that bitch."

"If I steal the mirror, you will give me all the visions I choose."

"Five visions. That is my last offer." The Harpy fluffed her feathers, stirring ancient dust. "Someday the Netherworld kings and queens will fall and we will rule again. The Hell Beasts will rule again."

"Five visions," Melissa said. "But you must describe to me the queen's powers so I know them exactly."

"Everyone knows her powers."

"I don't. And I must know them if I am to steal the mirror."

The Harpy sighed with exasperation, as if Melissa were very dull. "A daughter of Lillith can open all that closes and close all that opens: locks and spell-doors, of course. And she can open a were-beast to his alter shape. And she can close his power to change. But her real strength lies in this:

"Siddonie can close away truth so only falsehood remains.

"Thus does she mean to twist the peasants so they follow her: she means to close their minds to truth. Thus," said the Harpy, "does she mean to enslave the Netherworld."

"And can nothing prevent her?"

"Many powers united might prevent her." The Harpy looked hard at Melissa. "The power of the Catswold might prevent her."

"Who are the Catswold?"

The Harpy stared at her, her eyes opening wide. "The Catswold are shape-shifting folk of the eastern nations." She searched Melissa's face. "You know nothing of the Catswold?"

"No, nothing." Uneasily she looked back at the woman-bird. "How can there be people in the Netherworld that I don't know about?" But she was reminded uncomfortably of the forgetting spells Mag wove over her when they visited the villages, those little deaf spells that had touched her in the middle of numerous conversations.

"The Catswold have many powers," the Harpy said. "But Catswold folk are independent and stubborn." She looked hard again at Melissa. "They will not easily unite, even to defeat Siddonie. Likely the Catswold will never organize into a formidable force against the queen, as the elven and the human rebels are organizing."

"How many rebels are imprisoned?" Melissa said impatiently. "When were the last ones brought down?"

"There are twenty-nine rebels here. The last three were brought five days ago. Siddonie tortured them. Their screaming kept me awake."

"You heard them through those thick stone walls?"

"My hearing, like my eyesight, is quite wonderful."

"When the queen tortured them, what information did she ask?"

"I couldn't hear *her*, just their screams. But she would want to know the rebels' plans, and she would want to know the names of their leaders."

"Couldn't you have shown her that, in your mirror?"

"Why should I? That is part of why she locked me here, because I wouldn't help her." The Harpy wiped her bill on her shoulder.

"You side with the rebels, then," Melissa said hopefully.

"I side with no one," the Harpy snapped. "Siddonie drew me out of the Pit with her cursed spells, and then she took my mirror. I want to see her dead. But I do not side with the rebels. Now go and fetch my mirror."

Melissa turned away, both amused by the Harpy and annoyed at the feathered beast. As she moved to the next cell, she saw that the Toad was awake. It had risen to sit on its haunches, its huge, warty belly distended. It fixed Melissa with a bulging stare that seemed empty of all intelligence. Melissa glanced back at the Harpy. "What are the homilies it remembers?"

"How to sour goat's milk. How to grow artichokes. How to please the Griffon."

Melissa stared in at the Toad. "Will you tell me how to please the Griffon?" She doubted that the Toad would answer, it looked so dull.

"Caress of gold warmed by sun," the Toad said in a slow, expressionless voice. "Kiss of emerald blessed by Bast, can please the steed of Nemesis." The beast looked at her without expression.

Melissa repeated its words, then, "Toad, can you tell me about my past? Can you help me remember who I am?"

The Toad stared at her then lay down again. In an instant it was asleep.

She shouted at it and reached through the bars, but her fingers could barely reach its warty hide. It slept on, deeply.

Well, at least it had told her how to please the Griffon, though likely she would never need to know that. The Harpy, looking out at her, seemed to divine her thoughts. "The Griffon would as soon eat you as look at you."

Melissa said nothing. She left the Harpy and approached the wall that hid the rebel prisoners, and pressed her ear to the mossy stone.

She could hear nothing. She tried all the opening spells she knew, but the wall remained solid. She drew her light over the mossy stones looking for seams, but found none. She turned away at last toward the stairs and climbed quickly.

Chapter 10

Uneasily Melissa approached the door of the queen's solar, wishing she knew why she had been summoned this time, and afraid she did know why. Yesterday when Briccha sent her up with the queen's new riding boots, she had paused in Siddonie's wardrobe to listen to the queen and two men talking in the chamber beyond. She had recognized the voice of the queen's seneschal. The dark, stooped man made her uneasy; Vrech came into the scullery sometimes to paw the girls, embarrassing most of them, and enraging Briccha. He was harsh, mean eyed, and not too clean.

Standing in the queen's wardrobe, she had listened to talk about imported wines and medicines from the upperworld, and Siddonie had said something about the portal in Xendenton and about a caravan carrying goods to Cressteane and Ferrathil. Vrech said they should not use the southern portal, that it opened on the upperworld in too crowded a location. Siddonie had snapped that she knew that, but it was less than an hour's ride away and he should be able to manage his affairs so no one suspected anything. The queen spoke with cool familiarity of the upperworld cities to which the tunnels led. When the conversation lagged and a chair scraped, Melissa had fled for the hall. She had reached the other end of the passage when Vrech came out, followed by a thick, stiffly moving man with grayish skin and mud-colored hair. The two men had started down the stair when Vrech glanced along the hall, looking her over.

"That's the girl," he said softly.

The men had paused, staring at her. She looked back boldly, but fear touched her. Finally they had moved on, laughing. She was terrified they knew she had been listening. And now, summoned by the queen, mounting the last steps and starting down the hall, she was certain she would be punished for spying.

She had been summoned not to the black door that led to the queen's dark chamber but to the adjoining solar which opened between the queen's rooms and the king's. She expected another dark room with black furniture and closed draperies.

But she entered a bright room, the draperies open to the green day, and four oil lamps burning. The walls were of a pale, smooth material she didn't recognize. The cream satin draperies, tied back, revealed a balcony then the far forest and a sweep of granite sky. The queen stood before a white marble mantel. She was dressed in pale riding pants, soft boots, and a white satin shirt clinging to her breasts and open at the collar. Her black hair was coiled elaborately, her black eyes were intense. A memory touched Melissa—she saw the queen dressed in strange clothes, a tight dress that ended at the knee. The vision filled her with fear and hatred. Even her dislike of the queen, and her knowledge of Siddonie's cruelties, seemed not enough to support the deep, total hatred that now swept her.

"I have decided to shorten your hours in the scullery, Sarah. Will that please you?"

"I . . . Of course it will please me." She was not to be punished, then? Did the queen not know she had eavesdropped?

"I plan to give you some tests. I believe you will find them interesting."

"What—what sort of tests?"

"Why, to discover your magic skills."

She shivered, puzzled and apprehensive. "I have no special skills."

"Did you not bring a light to guide your way up the passages to me, just now?"

"That is cottage magic—anyone can do that. There is no power to that—not like your powers." She didn't like treating this woman with deference, but she sensed that it was wise.

The queen smiled. "Do you remember the winged lizards which flew over you when you went to the Hell Pit? Ah, yes, I see that you do. My lizards saw clearly what you are capable of—Sarah. It takes a special talent to call the Lamia from the Hell Pit."

Melissa felt naked and defenseless, as if she were suddenly suspended again over the Pit, about to be dropped into the flames.

"It takes great talent to make the Lamia obey you." The queen's smile was so cold Melissa shivered. "I mean to train your talent in more complicated magic, Sarah." The queen looked at her deeply. "You are to be my disciple. You are to learn the powers of a queen."

Melissa gawked. She dare not speak. Why should the queen want to train her?

"And now, my dear, shall we begin to use your real name? I much prefer Melissa."

She swallowed. "If you wish."

"Why did you lie to me about your name?"

"I didn't mean to lie. I am used to Sarah; it is what I am called. Any other name seems uncomfortable." She was sweating, her throat was dry and constricted.

"I'm sure you will learn to respond to Melissa. It is your birth name. Come closer and kneel."

Melissa took three steps and knelt on the pale, richly patterned rug. Coldly she listened to the queen's spell binding her to a disciple's rules and submissions. She had not been asked if she wished to serve. Siddonie of Affandar did not ask, she commanded.

The spells were long and complicated. The queen's power pressed so strongly on Melissa she was hardly able to breathe. Silently, terrified, she wielded a counter-spell to block Siddonie's enchantment. But she began to feel deeply lazy as the malaise of enchantment took her. How rich was the queen's voice. And Siddonie was so beautiful, her pale skin creamy against the satin shirt, her black hair and black eyes gleaming like ebony.

Melissa jerked her thoughts back, alarmed. She fought Siddonie's charm harder with all the skill she knew. But blocking Siddonie's powers, keeping her face passive, again she imagined another room, where Siddonie sat at a desk, a very young Siddonie, no more than a child. The room glowed with a white, harsh light, and beyond the window loomed infinite space, as if the stone sky had vanished, leaving a void, a terrifying emptiness.

But then the memory faded, and she continued to fight Siddonie, keeping her eyes expressionless.

The queen watched her intently. "You may rise, Melissa." She nodded, smiling, as if she had seen in Melissa's face obedience to her spells. "You will return to the scullery when I dismiss you." She moved away from the mantel and drew her fingers along the back of a satin chair. "You will tell Briccha that from this day you are to work only in the mornings. Once you have spoken to her you will go to the dressmaker to be fitted for two plain, serviceable dresses. I have chosen the fabric. Then you will go to the bootmaker for sandals. You will come to me promptly each afternoon when you are summoned, not before.

"You will like my lessons, Melissa." She gave her a look of complicity, as if they were close now. "I mean to train you to skills you don't yet imagine, very special skills. If you learn as I expect you to do, you will know powers perhaps to equal my own power."

Melissa left the solar quickly, and stood in the wide passage shaking, sick with apprehension. She was exhausted from her resistance to Siddonie's spell, all strength seemed drained from her. She tried to recall the fleeting memories that had touched her but they were gone now and without meaning, leaving her puzzled and afraid.

In the scullery she delivered the queen's message to Briccha, then escaped quickly to find the sewing rooms. There she endured the slow ritual of being measured. She went to the bootmaker, and again was measured and prodded by strangers. And now, with Siddonie's unexplained interest in her, she might have little time to search for the Harpy's mirror. Once the queen's tests began, she would likely be watched more closely.

She must find the mirror quickly, she must look into the past and learn the spell Siddonie had used to lock away the rebel prisoners, she must free them and escape with them, escape the dark queen.

But that night when she went to search for the Harpy's mirror, slipping down from the attic toward the king's chambers, the queen's maid was on the landing. And the next afternoon when she tried again, two pages were waiting outside the king's door. The third time, very late as she approached the king's chamber, Vrech came out of the queen's door nearly on top of her. As she turned away, he caught her wrist.

"What are you doing down here? You belong in the attic at night."

"I'm hungry. I'm on my way to the scullery."

"This is not the way to the scullery, my dear." Smiling, Vrech began to stroke her cheek. She kicked him in the shin and jerked away, and went quickly up the back stairs, her nostrils filled with the smell of stale sweat.

She did not go down again that night. The queen's testing started the next day.

On foot she followed the queen's horse toward the woods south of the palace. She was flanked by four mounted soldiers. Walking between the horses she felt very small. And she felt stiff, sick, and cold with fear. She didn't know what would happen if she passed Siddonie's tests. But if she didn't pass she would be of no use to the queen and would likely be sent away.

When Siddonie drew her horse up, Melissa paused behind her at the edge of the woods.

The queen spun her horse suddenly to face Melissa and pointed toward a broad oak. "Do you see that dove?"

"I see it."

"Bring it down."

"I have no weapon."

"Don't sass me."

She stared up at the queen. The queen looked back impassively. "Bring it down or I will use a harsher spell on you."

Angered, Melissa made a simple killing spell. But she intentionally muffed it. The dove bleated and flapped away unharmed.

When it landed, the queen said, "Kill it now. Do not make another—error."

There was no help for it. She brought the dove down smoothly. The small bird screamed, fell struggling among the leaves, and lay dead.

"Fetch it," said the queen.

Obediently she picked up the limp, warm bird. As she gathered it in her hands, a sharp excitement filled her. Suddenly she longed to tease it, to play with it. Shocked, she stared at her grasping hands. Woodenly, not understanding herself, she carried the bird to Siddonie and dropped it at the feet of her horse.

The queen rode over the bird, crushing it, and began to describe the next test. "You will call a war horse to you—that bay gelding in the pasture. You will make it obey the commands I give you."

Melissa called the gelding. He jumped the fence and came galloping. He was tall and heavily made, and more willing than a stubborn pony.

"Make him run free to the forest then bring him back."

It was harder to control the gelding at a long distance,

but she brought him trotting back. Under Siddonie's direction, she worked with the gelding all afternoon. Only twice did he defy her; then the queen brought him back with her own spell, quickly, deftly. It was dusk when Siddonie released her.

There were no more tests for two days. The queen quit the palace before dawn the next morning, riding out with Vrech. Melissa watched from the window beside her bunk.

She had awakened feeling ill. For two days she dragged herself about wanly, making no effort to search for the Harpy's mirror. The illness was so sudden she thought perhaps the queen had laid a spell on her and when, the morning the queen returned, she felt completely fit, she was certain of it. An hour after her return, the queen summoned Melissa to a tiny courtyard at the back of the palace.

An armed soldier stood beside Siddonie. And there was, in the queen's eyes, an intensity that alarmed Melissa. Siddonie said, "You will turn his sword aside when he strikes at you."

Melissa stared at the queen, not understanding.

Siddonie repeated the order, as if to someone very stupid, "You will deflect his sword with your own powers. Only your own magic will save you from being struck through or beheaded."

"I cannot do such a thing. I never have done anything like that." And in truth she had not; this was beyond her powers. She watched the queen, terrified.

"He does not feign this," Siddonie said. "You will turn the sword or you will die."

But it was a test—surely it was only a test.

"If you cannot turn his sword, you are no use to me. He is instructed to kill you."

Fear and rage sickened her. She had no way to know the truth. If the soldier had been ordered to kill, he would kill. He moved suddenly, his blade flashed upward toward her face. Fear shocked through her. Her terrified spell wrenched the blade from his hand so sharply he went off balance.

She drew back, faint, not believing what she had done.

The queen smiled. "Very good. We shall try a few more."

"No. I will not do more. I don't like this. What are you training me for?"

In two strides the queen was before her, and slapped her against the wall. "You have no choice. You will do two more. Or you will die."

The soldier crouched, circling Melissa. When his sword thrust up at her she was so enraged, so hot with anger and fear, she shouted a spell that sent him sprawling across the tiles.

Again he came at her, crouching, dodging. Her blood pounded. She shouted a spell that turned his sword toward the queen's throat; only at the last instant did Siddonie's oath cast his blade aside.

"No more," Melissa said.

The queen smiled with triumph. "Very good, indeed. Soon, my dear, I will teach you some of my own skills."

Melissa's hands were sweating. She didn't like this; she was close to pure terror, close to losing control. She did not want to be Siddonie's disciple. She was frantic with the need to escape.

But she could not run away, not until the rebels were free. She watched Siddonie narrowly, waiting for the next test.

Chapter 11

The banquet hall was noisy—laughter and drunken shouts rose over the music. Melissa glanced in as she slipped past the serving door. There were three visiting kings with their queens and entourages. She had glimpsed King Ridgen of Mathe in the grand foyer, and Terlis had pointed out the king of Wexton and Siddonie's brother King Ithilel of Xendenton. Market Festival was the biggest celebration of the year. All day the scullery had seethed with strange servants added to the Affandar kitchen staff. And the courtyard had been in a turmoil of workers setting up the market booths and stringing colored banners. The visiting soldiers and the lesser servants were camped outside the castle, as were peasants from all over Affandar who had brought their wares for sale, their jewelry and weavings, their carvings and livestock.

Though the palace seemed bursting with people, surely at this moment with everyone at banquet, the upper halls would be empty. Melissa hurried up the back stairs and along the empty corridor toward the king's chambers, strung with nerves. She had vowed to herself that tonight she would find the Harpy's mirror, that she would learn her past, learn the spell to free the rebels, and get out of there. Leave the palace, get away from Siddonie's tests and training. Now as she reached for the knob to the king's chamber, from beyond the door she heard a woman laugh, a breathy giggle. She drew back against the wall, heard the king say, "It's only a little ruffle, come let me remove it," and the woman giggled again. Melissa fled for the back stairs and up to the safety of her attic chamber, both shocked and amused. The king had deliberately missed the banquet, flaunting his dalliance with some visiting serving girl, or perhaps with a visiting wife of royalty.

But not until the next morning in the scullery did she hear that the king had taken ill before the banquet, and of course she said nothing. The scullery was a turmoil of confusion as pastries and hams, sweets and sausages were prepared for the booths, as loaves were pulled from the ovens, and venison and game birds put to broil for royal breakfasts. As dawn touched the scullery shutters, Melissa stacked warm pastries onto a cart. She had been chosen to have a booth, and under the envious glances of the other girls, she wheeled her cart away to the courtyard. She was wearing one of the new dresses—a plain green wool that pleased her.

The courtyard was bright with draped booths and with colored banners blowing against the granite sky. When she had settled into her booth and laid out the pastries, she watched folk streaming in through the gates. The crowd was a mix of queen's peasants and visiting servants. Soon she was busy selling turnovers and meat pies as folk flocked to break their fasts. In the booth across from her, cider was sold, and in the next booth a jester juggled silver balls. Farther down the row, the puppeteers were warming up with smutty jokes. The music of lute and rota, horns and vielle echoed against the sky like a dozen bands.

How quickly her pastries vanished. Twice she sent a page for more. It was mid-morning when she saw King Efil descend the marble stairs, swinging a red cape over his purple jerkin and trousers. He began to tour the booths, stopping to throw darts, then to laugh at the puppets. He was so young, hardly older than she. She wondered where his partner was from last night, which of the visiting young women. Though it was common practice, she found the promiscuity of royalty unsettling. This was not the way of the peasant families; there could be nothing of loyalty or deep love in such a life. When the king turned suddenly toward her booth, she felt her face go hot.

A young page followed him, carrying two mugs of ale.

"Pastries, then!" the king said, laughing, his dark eyes fully on her. "A dozen pastries. The lamb, the currant—four of those peach—some scones." His gaze never left her. As she wrapped the pastries in a linen cloth, he leaned close across the counter. She backed off, handing him the package, but his hands lingered on hers and his voice was soft. "Come out from the booth, Melissa. My page will relieve you. You've been in there since daybreak."

"I—I can't do that."

His eyes hardened. "Come out now. You will join me for a picnic in the orchard." He took the mugs from the page and nodded, and the boy slipped under the counter into the booth beside her. The king balanced the mugs in one hand. The twitch at the corner of his mouth deepened, his eyes darkened with excitement. "Wander the fair for a moment, my dear, then come through the east gate to the vineyard. Don't be long. Come while the pastries are still hot and the ale has not gone flat." He gave her a last deep look that made her giddy, then he turned away and was gone into the crowd.

She looked after him, cold and still. She felt heated. Shamed. Uncertain.

One did not defy a king's orders.

Beside her the page was rearranging napkins over the pastries. He didn't look at her. She supposed he knew every lover the king took. Embarrassed, she slipped under the counter and moved away.

She watched the puppet antics of stag and dragon, hardly aware of them. She told herself she would share the king's picnic, that she need do nothing more. He couldn't force her; she didn't think he was strong enough to force her. Yet beyond her resolve her own heat built, and she saw again the dark, needing look in his eyes. She moved nearer the gate, but then paused beside the stall of a jeweler.

She need not go to meet the king. She need not if she was afraid.

Idly she examined the old dwarf's jewelry. It was plain, unremarkable work. But suddenly a different light shifted across his necklaces, suddenly she saw a brighter jewel shin-

ing above the common jewelry like a thin dream: she saw in
a vision a tear-shaped emerald, a magnificent stone. It was a
pendant: the oval emerald was circled by two gold cats
standing on hind legs, their paws joined as if they guarded
the gem. The pendant was so lovely she reached . . .

The vision vanished. The dwarf's jewelry lay dully across
the counter.

She stood clutching the edge of the booth, trying to understand what she had seen. The dwarf looked at her absently as he traded with a peasant family, taking their uncut
diamonds in exchange for a small pig he had tethered inside
the booth. Giddily she moved away, confused and light-
headed.

Had the jewel been a true vision? Some heightening of
perception she didn't understand?

Or had it been a memory from her past?

Still seeing the emerald pendant, she moved unaware
through the crowd until she realized she was approaching
the east wall. She stood uncertainly before the small gate.

If she didn't obey the king, he would make her wish she
had. She decided she would just go out and explain to him
that she didn't want to share his bed. Be direct was what
Mag always said. She would be nice to him, but firm. She
reached for the latch but then drew back.

To be nice to a man when he was primed for the bed,
could lead a girl straight into that bed.

She turned away. King or not, she wasn't going out there
to share his picnic.

She began to wonder how long he would wait in the vineyard. Suddenly, feeling giddy, she knew what she must do.

She fled for the scullery and the back stairs. At this one
moment she knew exactly where the king was, and if she
was fast, she could be in his chambers and out again with the
Harpy's mirror while he waited for her in the vineyard.

Chapter 12

"University of Chicago," Olive Cleaver said, dusting cake crumbs from her flowered dress. Under her brushing hand, orange birds of paradise jabbed across a purple field. She sat opposite Braden at his terrace table drinking coffee and eating the cake she had baked. Her frizzy gray hair and sallow face were not flattered by the bright afternoon light and the Woolworth dress, but her eyes were intelligent and lively. "The carbon fourteen test was developed there. It's a wonderful new test; it will entirely change historical research."

Braden watched Olive, amused not by her facts, which were perfectly correct, but by her enthusiasm. She had come down the garden bringing the carrot cake, wanting to talk. Such gifts embarrassed him, but he had made fresh coffee, brought some plates and forks out on the terrace, wiped off the table. Olive never bothered him when he was working, but seeing him on the terrace in the middle of the day was all the invitation she needed.

"I took only one splinter from each of the five planks," she said. "I wanted to know if they were all the same age. They were." She nodded when he lifted the coffeepot, accepting a refill. "All they do is burn the material. The gases from the burning are converted to carbon and put into a special Geiger counter—well, I'm sure you know more about it than I do. I know you do read something besides art magazines."

She blew delicately on her coffee. "Of course the test will tell only the age of the timbers, not of the carvings themselves. But still, it isn't so likely that new carvings would be made on very ancient timbers.

"I do wish, though, they wouldn't take so long. I suppose they have a backlog, and of course legitimate research comes first." She looked up the garden toward the oak door. Anne Hollingsworth's orange cat was sitting in the ferns staring intently at the door, almost as if drawn to it. Olive said, "If the door *is* very old, I feel as Alice did, that it should be in a museum. Yet I can't bear to think of removing it. That door is why I bought the house, it was the door that first led me into the garden." She cut her cake into small bites. "And after all, maybe it is a copy. Anne thinks it is."

And of course Anne would, Braden thought. Their neighbor, Anne Hollingsworth, had a mathematical mind that would never believe something so improbable as a valuable antique standing forgotten in their garden. He looked up the garden, fixing on Anne's staid Cape Cod house, traditional and unexciting. Anne wasn't given to Olive's fanciful flights and enthusiasms. Nor did she succumb, either, to Morian's brand of keen relish for living.

It amused him that he had three female neighbors who were his good friends. He toyed with his cake, wondering why, in his thoughts, he wanted to defend the antiquity of the door against Anne's unimaginative turn of mind.

Olive said, "If it *should* prove very old . . ." She didn't finish, but looked at Braden intently, her glasses catching the light. She was trying to say something she didn't know how to say. Above them the orange cat had risen and was coming down the garden toward the veranda.

She said, "The door makes me feel sometimes that it has more to it than . . . I don't know." She looked embarrassed. "Even if it should prove valuable, I would not like to move it from the garden." Some nebulous idea had taken hold of her. Olive got these hunches, went off on tangents. Braden really didn't want to hear it.

She watched him quietly. "You don't like the idea of it being an antique?"

"I didn't say that."

"You know my research is solid."

He nodded, trying to shake off the strangeness he felt. For all her quirks, Olive was a competent researcher; she didn't go off on wild chases in that respect, didn't use spurious sources. She was just so damned intense. Well, hell, maybe the door *was* ancient. He knew she had done weeks of careful work before she sent the splinters off to be analyzed. The orange cat came onto the veranda and lay down at Olive's feet, looking up at her expectantly. She cut a bite of cake and gave it to him.

Braden watched Olive, both amused and annoyed because he really didn't want to think about the damned door. But hell, she just wanted to talk. He said, "I know the test is supposed to be accurate, but did they say anything about possible misreading, a false result through some—oh, chemical change in the door itself, something unnatural?"

"Unnatural?" Olive said, her interest rising.

"Like garden chemicals," he said quickly, "something sprayed or spilled on it."

"Oh no, I didn't ask about that. Perhaps I should. Yes," she said, "I guess I'd better write and find out."

After she left, he wondered why he'd said that. He wondered why he felt so strongly that the door ought to be left alone.

Chapter 13

Melissa slipped quickly into the king's chamber. With any luck he would stay in the orchard for a while, waiting for her. The pastries would get cold, the ale would get warm, and he would be furious, but she would worry about that later. Maybe she would have found the mirror and escaped to the cellars before he left the orchard.

The king's chamber was dark, the purple draperies were drawn closed. The shadows were dominated by a huge canopied bed, its thick black bedposts were carved with four Hell Beasts: basilisk, hydras, lamia, and manticore. She had a quick, unwanted vision of making love with the king, observed by those beasts.

She tried to open the wardrobe but could not. She tried one spell then another, and had begun to think she would fail when, on the eighth spell, the door snapped open wide. Velvet and cashmere coats burgeoned out. Kneeling, she reached behind the rich garments and behind the soft leather boots, feeling for a hidden door.

But the wardrobe wall was smooth. She felt its floor. He must have twenty pairs of boots. She moved each pair, felt under it then put it back. She whispered all the opening spells she knew, but no part of the wardrobe stirred. She was standing on tiptoe, feeling beneath the upper shelf, when behind her the chamber door creaked open.

The king did not seem surprised to see her there. He shut and bolted the door, and with a flick of his hand he made the mantel lamp burn. "My dear, this is a much better place for a tryst. How clever of you." He took her hands and drew her close; she held herself very still.

He kissed her lightly. "I will do nothing you do not wish, my Melissa. But I can see in your eyes that you do wish it." He stroked her cheek. "Have you ever made love, sweet Melissa?"

She felt as nervous and spell-cast as a trapped beast. Her mind spun and fought, and still she stood frozen. He watched her knowingly, but then he released her and moved away.

He poured wine from the decanter on the mantel and handed her a goblet. "You did not come to join me in bed, sweet Melissa. What were you looking for?" Looking into his eyes was like swimming in black seas. As his look changed from heat to suspicion, she wanted to bolt out the door.

He said, "It takes a lot of nerve to search the chambers of royalty." He drew his hand down her cheek, letting it rest on her shoulder. "You are of value to the queen, Melissa. Surely you know that. Just as you are of value to me." He stroked the back of her neck. His touch was uncomfortably soft; she flinched with an almost animal repugnance.

"Why . . ." She choked. "Why should I be of value to the queen?"

He drew her close again, stirring her desire despite her repugnance. "How old are you, Melissa?"

"Seventeen."

"And where do you come from?"

"From Appian."

He smiled. "You do not need to tell me the lies you tell the queen. And, of course, she does not believe you. Melissa—do you remember your mother?"

"Of course I remember her. Why would you ask about my mother?"

"Perhaps we can make a bargain." He began to unbutton her dress.

She moved away. "You—could have any girl in the kingdom."

"Why should I have *any* girl, when I can have the loveliest? Melissa . . ." He drew her close and kissed her throat. "If you breed me a healthy heir, Melissa, by the laws of the Netherworld you will be the new queen of Affandar." Again he smiled, his look too intent. "If you were queen of Affandar, Melissa, what would you do?"

Excitement gripped her suddenly with the heady challenge. If she were queen of Affandar, she could free the peasants. She could free other nations, and dethrone Siddonie's puppet kings. She stared at him, mute.

He said, "Do you know that Siddonie fears you?"

She laughed.

"Do you call me a liar?"

"No."

He moved to the mantel to refill his glass, then turned, watching her. "Siddonie and I are locked in battle for Affandar. All the kingdom knows that. Siddonie would destroy me if she could. She wants no one to share her rule.

"You, Melissa—she sees in you the power to help her enslave Affandar and enslave the Netherworld."

"I don't understand. She mistakes me for something I am not."

"No, she sees truly. She would use you to enslave Affandar. But, Melissa, together you and I could defeat her."

She watched him intently, convinced that he wasn't lying and that this man could tell her all the secrets that had been locked away from her.

"Tell me, Melissa . . . Tell me what you remember of your childhood."

"The usual things. Working in the garden, caring for the sheep, collecting honey, learning to ride the pony—"

"Stop it. What do you really remember?" He held her shoulders hard, searching her face. "What do you remember? If you really remember nothing, why were you searching for the Harpy's mirror?"

"What is the Harpy's mirror?" she said dumbly.

He shook his head. "I can see it in your eyes. You do not lie very well. You have been to the Harpy in the cellars. She begged you to steal her mirror. What," Efil said softly, "would you trade for the Harpy's mirror, my Melissa?" He began again to caress her; he was so changeable, emotions danced and flickered across his face. She felt there was no real core to him, no one person. He stroked her throat, kissed her neck, until she pulled away. He turned from her, folding back the velvet bed cover, revealing dark satin sheets. He said, "Afterward, I will give you the Harpy's mirror."

"Give me the mirror first."

He only looked at her.

She looked back steadily. He might be selfish and quickly enraged, but underneath she sensed that he was weak. She said, "The mirror first."

"Your promise to come to my bed?"

"My promise."

He opened the wardrobe and pulled aside jackets and breeches, whispering a sharp, short spell—one she had never heard before. A panel slid away revealing a small cupboard. He took from within a mirror no bigger than her hand. It was oval, its platinum frame jeweled with opals and topaz and moonstones flashing in the lamplight. He placed it in her hands; it was surprisingly heavy. But it gave back no reflection. She could not see her face, or Efil's. Across its clear surface ran one fleeting shadow deep within, then its surface burned clear.

He said, "Did the Harpy promise to give you visions for this?"

"She—she did."

"You have the mirror. Now come to bed."

"Wait," she whispered.

His rage flared; he took her shoulders. "You will not take the mirror from this chamber until you have paid for it."

"That was my promise. But I cannot promise you a healthy child until the woman-spells are complete." She held the mirror tightly. "If you force me to bed too soon, there will be little chance of a healthy child."

Anger flashed in his eyes, and then uncertainty. "You can't think . . . ."

A noise from the solar stopped him. He froze, listening to movement in the next room. She panicked, not knowing where to run. He pushed her toward the draperies and behind them. "She's in the solar. Stay hidden." He straightened the heavy draperies, hiding her. She stood in darkness that smelled of dust from the thick velvet, her heart pounding, clutching the Harpy's mirror. She heard the chamber door open and close, then silence, and knew he had gone out to distract Siddonie. For the first time she was thankful for Siddonie's presence.

Chapter 14

From behind the draperies Melissa listened to the queen's muffled voice in the next chamber, heard the king reply to some question, then the queen snapped irritably at him. Slipping the mirror inside her bodice Melissa moved out from the draperies. Pressing against the door, she listened.

". . . be a fool," Siddonie was saying, "of course she is. You had a colossal nerve to approach *her*. And in public. Everyone saw you. Briccha has orders to confine her to the scullery. I have instructed the guards not to let her out of the palace. If you—"

"And I suppose you will put her in the dungeons," he interrupted.

"And what of it?"

"You'll never train her if you lock her up. She will be no use to you."

"And she will be no use to you," Siddonie said coldly. "Don't you understand that she would bring them all here, that they would destroy Affandar!" Another pause, then the queen's voice came closer. Melissa fled to the draperies. Behind them, she opened the glass door and slipped out onto the balcony. She had a leg over the rail, searching for a foothold in the vines, when she saw three guards below and drew back.

She stood against the wall listening to their idle conversation. She heard an inner door open, but when after a very long time she heard nothing more from the chamber, she slipped inside.

Efil's room was empty. She crossed to the door and listened, then drew it open, faint with fear.

The solar was empty. She hurried across the pale carpet between the satin chairs and cracked open the outer door. When she saw no one in the hall, she fled to the back stairs and down. She was halfway down the first flight when she saw a guard below, walking the corridor. She drew back into the shadows. When he moved away, she slipped down past him, silent and quick.

She reached the storeroom at last, her heart thundering. She slipped behind a row of shelves as two girls went out carrying a big bag of flour between them. When they had passed she fled for the cellar door. She didn't breathe until she was through and closing the door behind her.

She brought no light; she felt her way down through the blackness. She hadn't reached the bottom when she heard a man shout above, and a door slam. She raced down into the stench of the Hell Beasts and fled past them. When she reached the Harpy's cage she was shaking. Now she brought a light, so glad to see the white womanbird she almost hugged her. She slipped the mirror from her bodice and the Harpy cried out, flapping her wings and reaching for it. Melissa held it away from her. "First show me the spell to free the prisoners. Then show me the five visions you promised, then you will have your mirror."

"Don't be silly. I cannot make visions until I have my mirror."

"You can make visions at great distances. You made visions in the queen's chambers. I will hold the mirror."

"One vision."

"Five visions. First, the spell."

The Harpy sat down against the wall and turned her face away. But in Melissa's hands the mirror clouded, then reflected a stone wall.

The queen stood beside the wall in miniature that quickly enlarged until she seemed to stand beside Melissa. She was pressing her hands against the stone, speaking a spell of opening. Melissa had never heard these cadences. She memorized them at one hearing, but she made the Harpy show her again, to be sure. As the second vision faded she fled for the wall.

"Wait! My mirror! You can't . . ."

Pressing her hands against the stone, she cried out the spell. The stone under her hands vanished, and a ragged opening yawned. The stink of the cells made her gag. She stepped through, increasing her spell-light.

Inside the cages were crowded with men, ten and twelve to a cage, all watching her. They were thin, nearly naked, their beards straggling over bony chests. What clothes remained were shreds held together by matted filth. She saw hope in some eyes, fear and distrust in others. She repeated the spell and swung open the barred doors.

The prisoners surged out. As some brought spell-lights, she could see in their faces their despair etched deep. Three were not as thin as the others, and their beards were only stubble. She took the hands of stoop-shouldered Halek, and of thin little Methmen.

Methmen hugged her. He smelled terrible; they all did. She led them through the hole in the wall, then closed the barred doors and sealed the wall.

Halek said, "Did Mag send you?"

"She doesn't know I'm here. There is food above, on the next level."

Halek sent six men up the dark stairs. They returned with hams, a barrel of crackers, a bag of apples, canned fruit, and ale. Halek said, "Drink the juice of the fruit. Wash yourselves with the ale. We're too weak for spirits; we'd be drunk and couldn't fight." They wolfed the crackers and ham, slashing the meat into chunks with Melissa's knife. She watched them straighten the metal barrel rings into blunt weapons, and she helped them rip the apple bag apart and bind the barrel staves together as cudgels. They ate the fruit and broke the jars into weapons, tying the broken glass onto the ends of the cudgels. Then Halek took her hand. "Come, there must be passages deep within the cellars."

She drew back, pulling her hand away. "I can't come. There's something I must do. I will try to follow."

The men stared at her, then turned away. Halek, distressed, reached to touch her face. "You are certain?"

"Yes, certain." She watched them move away and begin to search along the walls for a hidden door, then she returned to the Harpy.

The womanbird said, "One vision, then I want my mirror."

"You promised five visions."

The Harpy combed her breast feathers with long fingers, looking sideways at Melissa, but at last she looked inward again, her gaze remote, and began to whisper in a soft, whistling bird language. The mirror's bright surface turned dark, then showed vast space unlike the Netherworld that faded into a dark forest with huge trees, not Netherworld trees. Images followed, quick and startling: a garden with flowers too bright to be real. A man, lean, bronze skinned, unlike a Netherworld man. Then a more familiar scene of the dark green Netherworld night. Flames reflected against the granite sky from torches set into a castle wall: not this castle but a dark, hulking structure. The vision was so real she felt that she stood beside the wall looking into the dark forest where armed shadows gathered, slipping toward her.

Chapter 15

The torchlight guttered and hissed, sending shadows running down the castle walls as a band of armed rebels moved out of the woods carrying ladders. They tilted them against the thick stone walls, but as they climbed suddenly mounted soldiers swept out of the castle gates. They picked men off with quick arrows, toppled the ladders and skewered men with their blades.

The king's soldiers were making quick work of the small band, when from the forest boiled a mass of dark, small beasts running. Cats! They were cats. Hundreds of cats stormed the attacking soldiers and leapt onto the backs of their horses, raking claws into soldiers' faces then leaping up the wall, swarming over. Cats dropped into the palace courtyard and onto the backs of mounted soldiers. And suddenly the cats changed to human warriors whose eyes reflected light.

Melissa stared into the mirror as, within the courtyard, a king tried to rally his troops against the attacking cat-folk. He was a broad, dark-haired man, and there was something familiar about him. She watched him kneel beside two fallen soldiers, touching their bloody wounds. She saw him pull a third man from battle, a young man so like the king, he must surely be the king's son. She watched the two of them snatch a child from the fighting, a little girl wielding a bloody lance though she could not have been more than nine. The king shoved her at the wounded prince, and pushed them toward a door. "Save yourself—save your sister." Melissa saw a woman join them, heard her whisper, "Ithilel." The prince grabbed her arm and dragged her with them as, behind them, the king turned to fight off their attackers. Then the king fell, with a sword in his chest. She saw the small daughter break free from her brother and run back to the king and try to lift him. She watched the three lift him and carry him through the battle, escaping down a dark passage.

In a cellar chamber son and daughter laid the dying king on the stone floor and knelt over him. The young woman moved apart from them, watching from the shadows. She had many-colored hair, all shades of gold. Beside the king, young Ithilel wept but the little girl's eyes held no tears, her dark eyes blazed. The dying king half rose, touching her face; then he stared toward the woman in the shadows. "How did the Catswold know my plan?"

"She is my wife," the prince said hotly.

The king coughed blood. "You are a fool, Ithilel. *She* has destroyed us, she has used you."

"No! She . . ."

Melissa caught her breath, realizing suddenly that if this was young Prince Ithilel, if she was seeing the fall of Xendenton, then the little girl was Queen Siddonie. But who was the young woman?

The king fixed his eyes on Ithilel. "If you were a man you would kill the Catswold traitor. Your wife has betrayed us. Do you not realize she has destroyed us?" He coughed, spitting blood, then looked evenly at Ithilel.

"There is no choice, you must go from the Netherworld. Take your cursed wife—do not leave her here to do more damage." He turned from Ithilel and reached to the child Siddonie, taking her hand.

"You are the strong one. You must keep yourself safe, my child, until you can win back Xendenton."

Siddonie's dark eyes were hard as glass. One thin hand remained clenched on her sword. "I will return." She stared at her father, brazen with a queen's challenge. "And when I return I will rule more than Xendenton." There were tears on her face, but she smiled coldly. "One day I will rule the Netherworld. And," she said, smiling, "I will build a formidable power in the upperworld as well—in memory of you, Father. And for my own amusement.

"And," she said, "I will take revenge on the Catswold beasts. Revenge such as they have never dreamed." She knelt before the king straight as a shaft, waiting without tears for his death. But the dying king clasped her to him, holding her rigid little body, his white face buried in her black hair.

The king of Xendenton breathed his last.

Melissa watched in the mirror as the prince crossed his father's hands over his chest to protect him from the creatures of the Hell Pit that could come for the souls of the dead. He closed the king's eyes with two gold *griffons* and then, rising, he took up a heavy bag of jewels from an iron chest by the door, and jerked his young wife out of the shadows.

Prince Ithilel sealed the wall behind them, making of the secret chamber the king's burial tomb. They hurried along dark passages, the prince holding the young wife's wrist. At last he opened the passage wall with words like spitting snakes and pulled his wife through the gaping hole and stepped aside for the child.

They lit three of the oil lamps stored within the tunnel, and then began to climb up the black twisting way. Their journey became a montage of the miles of tunnel. Melissa saw deep cracks in the ancient earth, dark trickles of water, falling space; time tilted and changed, and the earth around them changed as they rose within it. Melissa thought many hours had passed when suddenly thunder echoed above them and they entered a tunnel with smooth pale walls and a floor of glazed tiles marked with occasional shallow puddles. Then, where a black rune marked the pale wall, the prince said an opening spell.

A portion of the wall swung back. They passed into another smooth tunnel lit from above by yellow lights which were not oil lamps. This passage led to an echoing basement. They climbed iron steps strewn with paper and bottles. At the top of the long flight they pushed out through a metal door into white fog. Lights sped past them incredibly

fast, smeared within the fog. A hissing noise ran with the
lights, like wet snakes. The young woman drew back, afraid.
The prince took her hand, urging her on. But Siddonie
walked alone, small and erect, staring around her at this
world with a sharp, canny interest.

The three refugees crossed half the city, climbing hills
crowded with tall, pale buildings. High up, they left the fog
behind them. It lay below them like a white sea. Now above
them a black sky reeled away empty, pierced with lights that
Melissa knew were stars. The vast space in which those stars
swam terrified her.

Then came a scene of daylight painfully bright. Melissa
could see through a large window the city spread below,
the tall smooth buildings thrusting up through that vast
space that was bright now, pale blue and awash with the
yellow sun. She thought of elven tales of the sun. The yellow ball blinded her. The young wife stood at the window,
her hair more golden than the sun. Behind her Ithilel and
young Siddonie worked at a desk littered with papers. Another montage of scenes showed Siddonie and Ithilel writing in ledgers, entering figures, then the two out on the
street, going into buildings carrying a leather satchel. She
saw them enter a paneled room and empty Netherworld
trinkets from the satchel onto a desk: emeralds, opals, diamonds, sapphires. She watched them trade these for a slip
of paper. This happened many times. Their clothing became rich. Their dwelling changed to a huge house looking
down at a bay. She saw servants, rich food, and rich fab-
rics. She saw in a last sharp scene the face of the child Siddonie looking directly into the mirror. Her black eyes were
appraising and cold. Then Melissa was jerked back to the
dungeons.

She felt as weary and drained as if she herself had made
that terrible journey. Before her, the Harpy ruffled and
stroked her white feathers. Melissa saw that the rebels were
still in sight, searching the cellar as if no time had passed.
She faced the Harpy crossly. "That was a fine vision but it
told me nothing about who I am."

The Harpy snorted with disgust. "Yes, it told you. You will figure it out soon if you are using your mind." The beast looked hard at her then brought another vision. "After this I will have my mirror or I will yell so loud every guard in the palace will hear me."

Chapter 16

Now in the Harpy's mirror mist clung against the buildings of the upperworld city and shrouded the upperworld alleys where cats roamed lithe and restless. The sight of cats stirred a strange feeling in Melissa. She watched a yellow tom circle a doorway, watched a gray female shoulder out through the flimsy screen door in the back of a wineshop. She saw a thin tiger cat in the alley behind a grocery picking through trash, stopping often to stare up at the sky where, through fog, glowed the diffused light of the upperworld moon. She saw within a satin apartment a tan and brown cat waking her mistress with harsh cries then streaking past the woman's silk-gowned legs into the night. She watched a fat white female cat lead four starving cats through an open cellar door into a shabby room. There the female vanished; and a white-haired woman opened tins of cat food and fed the strays, then went out again, leaving the door ajar.

Inside apartments cats cried and paced, staring out through dirty back windows or through curtained front windows, or leaping over furniture and across desk-tops seeking a way out into the moonlit night. All over the city cats moved restlessly, caught by the moon's pull. Melissa knew more from the vision than simply what she saw. She knew that this night, not only the moon called to them.

In an alley between the Tracy Theater and a tall Victorian house, a big, heavy-boned tiger cat leaped from the fence to a rooftop. Pausing on the flat tar roof, he looked around, puzzled, restless and irritable, and a strange eagerness gripped him. Tail lashing, he jumped from that roof to the next, a four-foot span, and trotted to the next chasm and leaped again.

Covering the length of the block across the roofs of the store buildings, he dropped into the branches of a stunted tree that shouldered across an alley. There he settled himself in a crotch of branches as if he had done this many times. He listened, looking up at the sky, looking around him.

He was broad shouldered, with big paws and a broad, square head; he had the body of a fighter beneath his wide curving stripes of gray and silver. He lay limp along the branch, though beneath his indolence his spirit seemed coiled like a spring. His thick, striped tail swung idly. But then its tip began to twitch as, looking up through the mist, he watched the exact place where the moon would lift.

Suddenly he tensed. His tail stilled. He listened intently, tracking the faint hush of fur against brick, then the crackle of paper as an approaching cat disturbed a fallen poster.

Then he scented her and relaxed, letting his tail swing again; he knew her.

The old buff female climbed rheumatically into the tom's tree. He watched her, first lazily then intently, his yellow eyes suddenly widening. He saw that she was wild with news, her movements were jerky, he could smell her excitement.

He waited with growing impatience as she settled herself on a branch below him. When at last she spoke, her voice was harsh with agitation. "Three humans have come up."

He stared at her. "From below? Through a door?"

"Yes."

"Which door?"

"The warehouse on Telegraph. A man, a little girl, and a woman. The woman is like us."

The tom's body slid into a crouch. "Like us? Are you certain?"

"Quite certain. Her hair is piebald, her eyes are a cat's eyes."

"Who is she? Did you listen to them? Why have they come here?"

"I followed them last night. I have watched them all day." She looked to him for praise. He broadened his whiskers at her and raised his tail.

"There was war in the world below," she said. "These three have escaped a massacre. He is Prince Ithilel of Xendenton, the child is his sister. Xendenton has fallen, and these two seem all that is left of the royal family."

"And the Catswold woman? Why is she with them?"

"I don't know. But it was the Catswold who defeated Xendenton, fighting beside peasant rebels. The man and little girl discussed it last night after the Catswold woman slept; I listened from the roof next door through their open window. They think the woman is a traitor to them, that she is loyal only to the Catswold."

"Then is she their captive?"

"No, she is the wife of the prince."

The tom froze, his body going hard. He looked back at the female gently; she was old, and dear to him. "You did well, Loua." He didn't expect her to feel his distress. She had been born on the streets of the upperworld, her mother had no Catswold memories. Loua was as ignorant of her heritage as any common cat. "Why," he said softly, more to himself than to Loua, "why would a Catswold woman be married to a prince of Xendenton?"

Loua mewled her confusion. "The small princess hates her. She says the Catswold woman betrayed them. How could the woman turn against her husband? Why would they marry if they are enemies?" Loua was always miserable when life did not add up. She hunched down, staring at McCabe.

McCabe said, "Tell me, this Catswold woman . . . What does she look like?"

"She is beautiful," Loua said with envy. "Tall, sleek as silk. Her hair is gold striped with platinum and with red. Hair," Loua said jealously, "bright as hearthfire, and her eyes are like emeralds. She must be gorgeous as a cat. Her name is Timorell."

"Timorell . . ." McCabe tasted the name. "And where are they now?" His tail twitched with impatience.

"In an apartment on Russian Hill. From the roof next door you can see into the living room and into the couple's bedroom. It is the street of the Great Dane, third house north of him on the same side." She preened, expecting McCabe to praise her for bravery at circumventing the Dane. But McCabe was lost in speculation. Loua purred his name, moving closer; but then she turned away. She was too old to appeal to McCabe, too long past her prime. This Timorell would appeal. She hunched miserably, bereft of defense against beauty and youth.

As McCabe quit the tree he turned, his face filling the mirror. Melissa stared into his huge eyes, startled. He dug his claws into the branch, then leaped to the alley. In the shadows, before stepping into the street, he took another form.

McCabe stood tall under the fuzzy streetlight, adjusting his tie, then strode across Powell. His shoes made a soft echo in the fog. He was a tall man, powerfully made, broad shouldered, his dark gray hair streaked with pale gray. His hands were broad, capable, stained from work, the nails trimmed short and clean. His yellow eyes were light against his tanned skin. He was a man to whom most women were drawn, though some women avoided him with a strange fear.

He passed the house of the Great Dane without disturbing the beast. In the shadows he changed to cat again, his broad stripes sharply defined by the street light. He leaped, and flowed up the thick vine onto the apartment house roof.

He stared across six feet of space to the next apartment building, to the three dormers with their open windows. Inside, the rooms were dark. He leaped the six-foot span to the center dormer, and clung there on the ledge and pressed against a dusty-smelling screen, looking in.

The couple slept in an iron-footed, rumpled bed. The Catswold girl's pale hair spilled across the prince's shoulder. She was long, supple. The sheet clung to her, thrown back so McCabe could see that she slept raw. He admired the curves of her arm and shoulder and, beneath the sheet, the curve of her breast. He wanted to touch her, wanted to slash the screen and go in. She slept deeply, innocent of him. He wanted to wake her, touch her; he wanted to say the changing spell for her and slip away with her across the rooftops, to be with her in the secret night.

Melissa, watching McCabe in the mirror, knew his feelings as if they were her own. Gripped by the desire he felt, her own passions awoke in a way that shocked her.

McCabe watched Timorell a long time. He would have stayed near her all night, but suddenly in the silence he heard the brush of a hand across a window screen. He leaped from the dormer across the chasm onto the neighboring roof, then turned to look back.

The screen of the next window was pushed out. A child looked out. For one chilling moment McCabe saw her eyes. For one moment he stared into deep, complete evil.

The child drew back and closed the screen. McCabe sped across the roof and down the vine. He hit the sidewalk as the little girl came out the front door carrying a heavy lamp. Heart pounding, he pressed into the shadows. He changed to man as young Siddonie reached him, holding the lamp like a club.

He grabbed her arm, and threw the lamp to the street. It shattered. He held her wrists as she kicked and bit him, and he shook her until she became still.

"You were going to injure the cat—kill it."

"Catswold," she hissed. "Get away from me! Leave the girl alone!"

"What do you fear?" McCabe looked her over, laughing.

"That I will despoil your brother's wife?" He saw the child blanch. "Why have you come up from the Netherworld?"

"What business is it of yours?"

"Tell me." He twisted her arm, enjoying her pain, caring nothing that she was a child; she was evil, coldly evil. "Tell me what happened in Xendenton. Tell me, or I will kill you."

"You dare not kill me."

"The laws say only that I would endanger my immortal soul; that is my choice. Gladly would I do so to see you die, Princess!"

"If you know so much, why do you ask questions?"

He twisted her arm harder. "Who is the Catswold woman?"

"A traitor," she hissed. "A bitch—a traitor. And she will pay for her deeds—you all will."

"You are curiously indignant, for one whose kin has murdered thousands of Catswold." McCabe looked closely at her. "You are like a hard, sinewy little bat, Princess. Brittle and blood-hungry."

The child stared at McCabe, expressionless as glass, then touched her tongue to her lips with a dark, twisted laugh.

"Go back in the house, little girl. But know this: if you harm the Catswold woman in any way, you will know pain by my claws as you have never imagined pain." McCabe grasped her hair for a moment, hard. "Have you ever seen the guts torn out of a mouse so the creature, still alive, stares at its own offal, frozen with terror?"

She blanched, did not move. McCabe stared at her until she turned at last and went into the house, her back straight and ungiving.

The scene vanished, the mirror went smoky. Melissa stared, confused, into the blackness around her.

"You are in the cellars of Affandar Palace," the Harpy said softly.

Melissa brought a spell-light and reached to touch the bars, but she was still adrift between the two worlds. She was surprised to see the rebel prisoners crowded around her, silent, watching her. She was clutching the mirror so hard that when she dropped it in her pocket its mark was struck deep into her palm. When the Harpy reached through the bars toward the pocket, she backed away. She had started to speak when footsteps scuffed on the stair and she doused her spell-light.

A spell-light blazed above them, moving down the stair. The rebels fled. Halek grabbed Melissa and pulled her to a stack of barrels and down behind them.

Chapter 17

The spell-light came quickly down the stair striking across barrels and pillars and lighting King Efil's face. His voice struck sharp through the silence. "Melissa? Surely you are here. Melissa, guards are posted everywhere, but I can get you out. Come quickly."

She moved, wondering if she dare trust Efil. If she found a way out she could come back for the prisoners. But Halek jerked her back. "No! We are not to trust him." He clapped his hand over her mouth as Efil approached, passing within feet of them, heading straight for the Harpy's cage. His light picked out a shock of white feathers. "Where is the girl? She brought your mirror to you. Where is she?"

"What girl? Do I have my mirror? Do you see my mirror? Do you think if I had it I'd be behind these bars? The queen has my mirror, and if you were any kind of a king you would return it to me."

"I will search the cellars until I find her, so you might as well tell me, Harpy."

Melissa touched Halek's hand. "If he searches, he will find you. I can bargain with him. I—have something to bargain with."

He held her arm hard. "If he finds us, we will kill him. That's safer."

"But Halek, I can make him take you out of here. I can make him free you." She watched the king turn away from the Harpy. He approached and passed them again. Only this time he didn't pass them, he turned back and came toward the barrels that hid them. His light shot straight into her face.

She rose, but Halek was faster. He leaped and hit the king and pinned him against a pillar, forcing a shard of glass against Efil's throat.

Efil was very still, appraising Halek. "There's little time; the guards will come. Free me and I'll get you both out of here."

"You will get all the prisoners out," Melissa said. She nodded to Halek. "Call the men out."

Halek stood motionless a long time, pressing the broken glass against the king's throat. Melissa didn't know what she saw in Halek's face—fear, distrust—but at last he gave one soft whistle.

The men came out slowly, watching the king. When Efil saw the dozens of ragged, armed men, he blanched. "I can't take so many."

Halek pressed the glass harder.

"You dare not harm me," Efil said. "You would never get away without me, there are guards everywhere."

Melissa said, "Do you want my child?"

Halek stared at her. The men were watching her. She said, "If you get all the prisoners out, and the Harpy and Toad and the Griffon, if you see that all go free, I will bed with you."

"I have no way to trust you," Efil said.

"You have my promise," she said quietly.

They were a silent procession moving through the dark cellars. The prisoners followed Efil, then came the Harpy and the Toad. Efil could not, or would not, free the Griffon. Melissa was heartbroken for the poor Griffon. He was the most free of beasts, winging the Netherworld skies over mountains and valleys unknown by any land-bound creature. It was monstrous to leave him captive.

When they had pushed far back in the black cellars, Efil paused before a pillar and cast a complicated spell that drew the side of the pillar open. His spell-light picked out a thin stair leading down. The rebels crowded in and descended single file into blackness, the Harpy and Toad behind them. Efil waited, coming last with Melissa, forcing her along before him, and closing the pillar behind them.

They went down steeply for a long way, then pushed along a tunnel so low they walked doubled over, so narrow their shoulders scraped the damp walls. Thus they traveled until Melissa thought they must have crossed under all the palace farms and orchards. When at last they came to a flight leading up, the rebels clambered up eagerly. After a long climb they reached a trap door. It opened at Efil's voice, lifting up into a green-lit chamber. Halek's voice came back to her filled with awe. "The Grotto of Circe," he whispered. The others pressed behind him up into the jeweled chamber, into a mass of gem-wrought images so real they seemed alive.

The arched ceiling was mosaicked with jeweled branches tangling across it like the roof of a forest, and the branches were alive with birds made of emeralds and rubies and topaz, of lapis and garnet. The walls were filled with jeweled dragons and Hell Beasts and all Netherworld animals. A huge, carved bed stood against one jeweled wall. Melissa knew Efil must have kept this grotto hidden from Siddonie, for the dark queen would have destroyed it. She felt the power of the images, the power by which Circe, within a place of such magic, had first turned beasts into men, creating the shape shifters.

The ragged rebels trooped in followed by the Harpy and the Toad. Efil stroked a spell over the trap door so it swung closed and vanished into the mosaic floor. He stood looking the rebels over.

"The door I will open will take you into the woods south of the palace. You must go quickly; it is dusk but guards patrol the woods. You will be safe when you reach the eastern ridges."

He said, "I do this for Melissa, not for you. I may have differences with Siddonie, but I do not love rebels." He lifted his hand, made a sign, and opened a spell-door in the grotto wall. Dim green forest shone beyond. The Toad hopped through and away into the darkness between twisted trees. The rebels followed, glancing back at Melissa. She watched them go, torn between her promise to the king and fear of him that made her want to run after them.

The Harpy didn't offer to leave, but began to paw at Melissa, searching for her mirror. Melissa said, "One more vision."

"One vision," the womanbird said. "The last vision."

"I want to see my mother."

"You have already seen your mother."

"Queen Siddonie?" Ice touched her.

"No, not Siddonie."

Melissa stared at the Harpy. Her voice would hardly work. "The Catswold girl?"

"Yes. Timorell was your mother."

"But she was Catswold."

"You are Catswold."

"You are wrong, I am no shape shifter. Besides, the Lamia said my mother was wife of the Lamia's sister's brother, so I can't be . . ."

"Your mother's husband's half sister is a daughter of Lillith. All daughters of Lillith are sister to the Lamia."

"That is more confusing. Why can't you say, my father's half sister?"

"I am not speaking of your father. Your mother's husband was not your father." The Harpy glanced longingly toward the opening in the wall. From the forest, a cool breeze stirred her feathers.

"I want a vision to see my father."

"You have seen your father."

Melissa frowned.

The Harpy sighed. "I will show you your own conception. You will know your father, you will see yourself conceived. Then you will give me my mirror and free me."

Melissa nodded.

"Not many," said the Harpy, "are privileged to see their own beginnings." She lifted a wing, casting shadows across the mirror. There, the upperworld city gleamed suddenly with sunlight so bright Melissa squinted.

A man sat at a table in a sidewalk cafe. It was McCabe. She swallowed, watching him.

The cafe was beside long wharfs where huge ships were docked. White birds swooped over the smokestacks. Stevedores were off-loading wooden crates. At his table McCabe was drinking an amber brew, idly watching the street. When Timorell came swinging along he put down his ale, watching her intently, as if he had been waiting for her.

She was looking at everything, drinking in the colors and smells of the wharf. The wind blew her pale-streaked hair like a golden cloak around her shoulders. She was sleek as gold and ermine, her stride long and easy. She did not seem to be looking for anyone but simply walking. Her tongue tipped out, tasting the wind, and there was a little secret smile at the corners of her mouth. At the intersection where the street dead-ended before the cafe, she paused, looking around almost as if someone had spoken. Above her, McCabe had not moved. Timorell looked around her, puzzled, then suddenly she looked directly up at him.

She stood still as a hunting cat, her eyes widening. She was drawn to him, and McCabe rose, his gaze never leaving her.

She came up the four steps and stood looking at him. Then, drawn by his gaze, she slid into the chair he held for her. A power burned between them, filling Melissa with longing. This was their first meeting, this was Timorell's first awareness of another like herself in this foreign world. Then came a montage, she saw them walking the city streets, their hands touching, their looks slowly revealing and discovering. She saw them in shops, in cafes; talking, always talking. She saw Timorell at night slipping away from her apartment.

She saw McCabe and Timorell in a white room with jutting windows looking down on the city. The walls were covered with pictures of cats like benevolent talismans. She watched McCabe make love to Timorell on a pale rug before the open fire. They loved as man and woman, then as cat and cat, Timorell all gold and white to McCabe's dark gray beauty. Embarrassed at breaching their privacy, she was yet held by the prophecy their lovemaking wrought, sharp as Timorell's mewling cry.

And in the instant before the vision faded she saw, against Timorell's bare skin, an oval emerald pendant framed by two rearing cats.

When the vision fled, she felt she had fallen between the two worlds and was unable to cling to either. The strength of their love had taken her breath, and, too, the sight of the emerald left her stricken with a sense of power she could not unravel.

"What was that jewel . . . ?" she said weakly.

The Harpy flicked at her white feathers. "That was the Amulet of Bast. Your mother," the Harpy said softly, "was heir to the Catswold queens."

The Harpy fixed her with a beady stare. "You have forgotten all you ever heard about the Catswold. Only slowly is memory returning. Under Mag's spell you forgot there is a Catswold nation. Your mother, if she had lived, would be queen of that nation."

She showed Melissa a vision of white stone towers and caves, of little niches and high alcoves where cats slept on velvet and silk. "This is Zzadarray." Cats raced along the tops of the walls then leaped down to vanish, turning into silken-robed men and women. "They," said the Harpy, "are the Catswold of Zzadarray."

The vision hadn't faded when Efil shouldered the Harpy aside, facing Melissa scowling. "You don't need this. You don't need to see this." But then his looked softened and he began to stroke her and caress her. She shivered and tensed. He said, "Yes, my love, you are heir to the Catswold queens. You will be queen not only of Affandar but queen of the Catswold. Never has a Netherworld woman had such power." He kissed her and teased her, moving her toward the bed. But the Harpy pushed between them. She shoved Efil away and fixed Melissa with a hard gaze.

"Do you not understand? You are heir to the Catswold queens. This was why Siddonie wanted you. You could lead the Catswold people anywhere; they would follow you unquestioningly. If Siddonie rules *you* with her spells, she would rule the Catswold. She would force them to fight the rebels. Now, King Efil means to do that."

"No," Efil said. "I will not do such a thing. The woman-bird lies."

Melissa took the Harpy's thin hand, hardly attending to Efil. Slowly she was beginning to remember past remarks and conversations. The Amulet was a great power—it held the ancient power of Bast. She said, "The Catswold would not follow me if I do not wear the Amulet."

"Yes, they would follow you," said the Harpy. "Though your power would be stronger with the Amulet."

"The old tales say it is lost."

"Lost," said the Harpy, preening.

"Cannot the mirror show where it lies?"

The Harpy glanced longingly toward the spell-door then at her little mirror. "Spells were laid to protect the Amulet from visions."

Melissa looked back at her with all the command she could muster. "You will try," she said softly. "Afterward I will give you the mirror."

The Harpy tried. For a long time, muttering soft bird talk, she sought to bring a vision of the Amulet but the mirror remained blank. Suddenly the Harpy lost patience. She lunged at Melissa and snatched the mirror from her. The flurry of her white wings filled the grotto, then she was gone flapping into the night, hugging her little mirror. Melissa watched her disappear through the woods in awkward swoops. The woman-bird's voice echoed, "You have the power . . . if you will use it . . ." then her voice was only a bird cry, eerie in the darkness, and Melissa saw a last smear of white lift on the wind and vanish.

*   *   *

She watched Efil spell-close the wall so that no mark remained in the jewel mosaics and she thought, *I am Catswold*. She felt weak with wonder. And she was filled now with knowledge of the Catswold that had, moments before, not existed for her.

I bear the blood of queens, I bear the blood of Bast. That is why Mag hid the papers. That is why she made the deaf-spells. The stories were there in my mind, but I was deaf to them. This knowledge is part of my memory.

But this returned memory of the Catswold was not all that was lost. There was more. Still she did not remember her childhood.

Efil took her hands, drawing her close, stroking her hair, her throat. She turned her face away; she wanted to run from him, to lose herself in the woods. She wanted time to think. She was only beginning to see who she was. She wanted to understand and know herself; she did not want to be possessed now by another.

"Your promise will be honored now," he said softly.

He slid his hands down her back, his lips brushed her cheek and her throat. "You are frightened, queen of the Catswold. Do not be frightened, my love." His tongue touched her throat; his breath was hot against her.

She flinched away, holding herself tight and still. "I want time, I . . ."

But the fever he stirred was too strong, his caresses and his spells dizzied her. She fought the heat as he cupped her breasts, whispering love-spells. Stroking her, he moved her to the satin bed. He unbuttoned her dress, licking her breasts, weaving a spell that brought fire through her body. She clung to him, stroking him, begging him to caress her; all shame, all distaste vanished. All premonition of disaster vanished.

Chapter 18

The Harpy flew across the night, ducking through caverns and sweeping over valleys, drunk with her regained freedom. Her little mirror swung on its chain against her feathered breast. When she perched to rest high on a cliff, she gazed into the glass and brought a vision of Melissa bedding with the king. She watched with interest for some time, then grew bored and dropped the mirror so it nestled again among her feathers. She flew on, making straight for the Hell Pit, thinking of its warm blaze. She thought of her friend the Toad, and she supposed he had returned to the Hell Pit. She was surprised that she missed him. The Hell Beasts never cared for one another. Her wings stirred a solitary wind across the dark green night and when, banking around a cliff, she saw ahead firelight reflected across the sky, she paused.

The smell of roasting meat made her drool. She glided stealthily on, and soon she came in sight of a campfire with men crowded around. She circled.

The rebels were gathered eating their supper. The Toad was with them, eating ravenously. The roast rabbit smelled mouth-wateringly good. The Harpy dropped among them so abruptly the fire surged and spat.

Halek did not seem surprised. He looked the Harpy over. She, in turn, eyed the crisping rabbits. The rebel leader speared a rabbit from the fire and handed it to her. "Did you leave the girl with the king?"

"Can't say where she went." Intently the Harpy ate, picking the meat off with her beak.

"*Can't* say? Or won't say?"

She looked at Halek in silence, stuffing herself, smacking her beak. "Do you mean to sleep here tonight?"

Halek shifted his shoulders. "We mean to move on, make what miles we can. I did not like leaving Melissa."

"The girl is her own mentor. You cannot choose for her. The girl's venture, this night—if she were to become queen of Affandar—could win this war."

"I would not," Halek said, "like to depend on a trysting by King Efil to win a war."

"It could make more difference than you know."

"Speak plainly, Harpy. What more difference would there be, than that she should usurp the throne of the queen?"

"There is more to it."

Halek waited.

The Harpy studied Halek and studied his companions, then decided to keep her own counsel.

Annoyed with her, Halek rose. She turned away, sullen and mute. At once, the men stirred themselves, took up their crude weapons, and kicked out the fire.

The Harpy watched them depart. Soon she was alone, pecking at rabbit bones and dying coals. Sitting beside the dead fire, she looked forlornly into her mirror.

She watched Melissa and the king, observing their embraces with lusty interest. Then she brought a vision of a younger Melissa snug in Mag's cottage, carding wool beside the old woman. That homey scene soothed her.

She watched Mag and the girl over the years, saw Melissa as a child, stubborn minded and clever. She watched her grow up. She saw Melissa find the papers hidden in Mag's linen chest, and watched Melissa ride for the Hell Pit. She watched the Lamia rise from the flames at Melissa's bidding.

She watched Melissa leave home, and she watched Mag set out the next day to look for her. She saw Mag's useless searches, then watched Mag grieving by the cookstove. And suddenly, the Harpy did not want to go back to the Hell Pit.

She left the dead campfire and flew slowly over ridges and over a broad plain. She crossed above precipices and sheep pastures, her faint shadow cutting steadily along above her across the granite sky.

As dawn brightened she hovered above Mag's cottage, watching the old woman slopping nine squealing pigs. She swooped suddenly down onto the sty's rail.

Mag jumped, dropping her bucket. "Where did a harpy come from? What do you want? What's a harpy doing away from the Hell Pit?"

"She's in Circe's Grotto."

"Who is? What are you talking about?"

"The girl—Melissa."

Mag started. "You've seen her? Well, you know to call her Melissa, all right. But of course you would," she said, glancing at the dangling mirror. "What is she doing in Circe's Grotto? How did she find it? No one knows how to find that ancient cave." The old woman picked up her bucket, stepping around the guzzling pigs. "Why would you bother to bring such news to me?"

"The king knows where to find the grotto."

"So? What has King Efil to do with Melissa? And how did you get out of the Hell Pit?"

"She forced me out with spells."

"Melissa?"

"Of course not. The queen. Brought me up from the pit against my will. Locked me in her dungeon."

"How did you get out?"

"*She* freed me."

"The queen?"

"Melissa. Freed the rebels, too. They were half-starved. On their way home even now."

"Melissa freed the rebels?" Mag grinned. "All of them?"

The Harpy nodded.

"But what," Mag said, "has the king to do with that?"

The Harpy waited for Mag to figure it out.

Mag looked at the Harpy for a long time, her eyes slowly widening. At last, she said, "The king helped her? The king—oh, no."

"Oh yes," said the Harpy.

Mag stood quietly. Then she took the Harpy's hand and led her toward the cottage, speaking of hot tea and biscuits.

When the Harpy had finished her tale, while supping up four cups of tea and a dozen biscuits, Mag said, "I will go and bring her home. What a foolish thing to do—what a headstrong, exasperating girl."

"Leave her be," said the Harpy.

"Why would you say that?"

"What would you do if you went there? He has already bedded her—likely she is already with child."

Pained, Mag folded and unfolded her apron.

The Harpy said, "Why didn't you tell her the truth, old woman? Why didn't you tell her what she is?"

Mag looked at the Harpy intently. "She would have gone off among her own people. I'd have lost her. She needed to settle first. She is too headstrong; she would have done something foolish. I kept meaning to tell her."

The Harpy said nothing.

"I was working up to it when she went off. And now . . ." Mag shook her head. "Couldn't you have stopped her?"

"It was not my business to stop her." The Harpy smoothed her wing feathers. "Don't you see? What she has done could mean victory for the rebels—not that I care."

"I see clearly that it could mean victory. And I see that it could mean her death if Siddonie learns of this."

"Perhaps she will not learn of it."

"Siddonie's hatred goes back a long way." Mag looked at the Harpy. "If only your mirror could show the future."

"You would not want to see the future. This is Melissa's destiny, let her be with it."

"That is foolish talk—she is only a child."

"She is seventeen. Possibly she might bear a healthy baby and become, in truth, the next queen of Affandar."

"That, too, is foolish talk." Mag rose, angrily poking a stick in the fire.

"You have no right to be indignant," the Harpy said. "If she is successful, your rebels will have a bloodless victory."

Mag sighed, and returned to her chair. "She is only a child. She knows nothing."

The Harpy stroked her mirror, bringing a warming vision of Hell's fires. She had done all she could. Mortals were stupid and ungrateful. She wanted to be home among her own.

She waited until Mag dozed, then quit the cottage. Hours later when Mag woke, the Harpy was gone. Nothing remained of her but two white feathers clinging to the plank floor.

Chapter 19

Melissa woke hot and uncomfortable. The king slept sprawled across her, his leg pinning her. She slid out from under him so carefully he didn't stir.

Dawn light drifting across the mosaic ceiling made the jeweled branches seem to move. The ruby and amethyst and lapis birds stared down blindly, just as they had blindly watched the passion of lovemaking last night. She stretched languidly. In one night she had shaken off the last vestiges of Mag's little Sarah. In one night she had changed. Though the strongest change, that had nothing to do with Efil, was the knowledge of her heritage.

She pulled a satin pillow behind her and lay trying to remember a shape-shifting spell, but she could not. She could recall no such spell from Mag's book, though she remembered blank pages: pages surely enchanted so she had not seen what was there.

Slowly she brought back knowledge locked away from conscious thought. She dredged up casual remarks made by the rebels. She thought about the Catswold nation of Zzadarray, isolated far to the north, and about Catswold resistance to Siddonie's rule.

This was why Siddonie wanted her. To help enslave that rebellious nation.

And Efil wanted the same. He wanted her for the armies a Catswold queen could bring to support him. He had known what she was and had concealed that knowledge from her.

And she had yielded to his spells.

Remorse filled her. She had given herself freely to him. She, heir to the Catswold queens, had given herself not for love but to be used. She felt cheapened, shamed.

She told herself she had come to his bed to save the rebels, that she had kept a bargain.

Watching Efil, she understood sharply that she had lost last night more than her virginity. He had taken from her something more. An important part of her life had never occurred; she had been catapulted from child to someone already regretting the nature of that closest of alliances: wonder was missing. Joy was missing, and tenderness, and trust.

There was no honesty or trust between them. All was manipulation, playing the game.

That, she guessed, was the way Efil had lived all his life. His marriage to Siddonie had been political maneuvering as, surely, all their life together had been.

And now she was part of that manipulation. *My new queen of Affandar. My pretty Catswold queen.*

Yet in spite of her disgust, her pulse quickened as she watched him. In sleep he seemed younger, seemed almost innocent. Watching him, she vacillated between shame and desire.

How dark his lashes were, curled against his cheeks. His lips were soft, faintly pouting. He slept on a silk pillow embroidered with an ancient dragon, souvenir from the upperworld where he had traded a small jewel for it. Efil said that, eons past, Netherworld dragons had found their way up through the tunnels to the upperworld. Seen by men, tales had been created and images made of them in clay and paint and silk. He had amazed her, speaking so offhandedly of his trading journeys there. Such journeys were to Efil as ordinary as a ride to Xendenton.

He spoke just as casually of Siddonie's upperworld ventures. In the small hours as they lay talking, as he flipped open a crystal decanter causing its ruby wine to fill two goblets, he had looked deeply at her, with an expression she couldn't read. "You know nothing about Siddonie, my love. Well, but why should you?"

She had stroked his shoulder, tracing her finger down his cheek. "Tell me."

His face went sullen, filled with old angers. "She is obsessed with power. She lusts for power, and not only Netherworld power. She has built power in the upperworld, though perhaps it is small pickings by upperworld standards."

"I don't understand," she had said. "I thought there were no powers there."

"Not magic powers." He had lifted the crystal goblet, and winked at her. "Money. In the upperworld, money creates power. And upperworlders will pay ridiculously high sums for Netherworld trinkets—diamonds, emeralds, rubies. It was easy for Siddonie to buy power." He drained his goblet, and refilled it.

"She has established for herself a complicated investment structure, and she has recruited an army as well."

She had stared at him, perplexed.

"Oh, yes, my dear. Siddonie now has an army of upperworld rabble, derelicts, upperworld refuse. She has collected men no one wants or will miss. She has given them food and shelter, and trained them to our weapons."

"But why? To make war there, in the upperworld?"

He arched an eyebrow. "Of course not. She means to bring them here to fight beside our own soldiers against the rebels." Efil smiled. "Siddonie is more afraid of the rebels than one would guess."

"But upperworlders . . . Why would upperworlders fight for her?"

"When she befriended those men, few of them believed in anything. She has built allegiance among them. Now they believe in *her;* now she is their goddess. She has changed their need for liquor, through spells, to a need to serve her. She gives them security and material comforts. She furnishes Netherworld women to tease them and drive them nearly mad with lust." Efil smiled. "She has turned the upperworld rabble into her eager slaves."

He had seemed filled with talk. As if, Melissa thought, once he had laid claim on her, in bed, he must tell her all his secrets. Perhaps he needed someone to share his secrets.

"Have you not wondered, my dear, why her seneschals are so often gone from the palace? Three are concerned with Netherworld intrigues. Vrech is responsible for messages and instructions to her upperworld associate.

"Havermeyer comes down occasionally, but Vrech is the errand boy; he is back and forth often. Havermeyer is titular head of the corporation. Siddonie and her brother Ithilel hold title. The company operates barely on the edge of the law, but of course no one can touch Siddonie or Ithilel. They would simply disappear."

"But what use is power in that world, if there is no magic there? What does she gain?"

"Siddonie likes controlling others. She lusts for power, and more power."

"And does she plan to rule the upperworld as well as our world?"

He laughed, and traced his finger down her cheek. "You are an innocent one. The upperworld is immense. Even Siddonie has more sense than to challenge the giant corporations. Though she has amassed an interesting fortune. She does it for recreation. And she does it as well, of course, as a cover of respectability for the recruiting."

He drew her to him, stroking her hair. "Siddonie has established herself as a philanthropist. She has bought slum buildings and turned them into hostels for the poor. It is easy to recruit men without jobs or families from such a place. They welcome her offer of country air, warm clothes and beds, hot food in exchange for a few hours work each week. Once they are housed at the ranch, of course, the enchanting, skillful women from Xendenton and Mathe make sure they will not leave."

He cupped Melissa's face in his hands. "Do you see, my love, how vital our role will be? Do you see what we might prevent by wresting the throne from her? If she brings those hordes down, she will sweep across the Netherworld enslaving every land."

He looked deeply at her. "We can prevent that. Together we can free the Netherworld of Siddonie's tyranny."

Last night she had believed in him, she had believed all that Efil told her. Warm with lovemaking, feeling at one with him, she had burned to stop Siddonie. He had made her believe she would easily dethrone the dark queen, that Siddonie, without an heir, would fall and the Netherworld would be free.

He had driven away all her doubts, all her good sense. She had ignored his self-interest, had ignored the sure knowledge that within Efil there was no core of truth, no desire for good over evil. For right over wrong. She had pretended not to know that everything Efil did was for his own expediency and power. Now, for the first time in a long while she thought about the good, true things Mag had taught her, and she understood them. And she knew that Efil was not a part of that decency.

Efil stirred and woke, and lay watching her.

"I dreamed," he said, distraught. He reached for her hand. His palm was sweaty and cold.

His distress alarmed her. "What did you dream?" Dreams were too often prophetic.

"I dreamed of a changeling child. I dreamed that Vrech carried Wylles to the upperworld and brought a changeling down. That Vrech brought a healthy boy down to take Wylles' place."

"But it was only a dream," she said softly, seeing the pain in his eyes. She could not hate him when he felt such pain. "No one traffics in changelings anymore, Efil. That was all in ancient days—it was a dream."

"It was so real. I saw Vrech carry Wylles out through an

upperworld portal. I saw him bring the changeling child down into the tunnels, and the boy looked uncommonly like Wylles. But he was stronger, rosy and healthy."

"Maybe Wylles will get stronger. Maybe that was what the dream meant."

He sat up against the pillows, pale, shaken, trying to get hold of himself. After several minutes he said, "I suppose it was a dream. It would take Siddonie months, years to find a child who looked like Wylles." He drew her to him, kissing her nose and lips. "Before that our own son will be born and Siddonie will no longer be queen. Anyway, Vrech hasn't yet . . ." He faltered, then said too smoothly, "Vrech hasn't done anything to make me think . . ."

"Vrech hasn't yet what?" She pulled away, and sat staring at him, alarmed.

His face slid into a smile.

She caught her breath. "It wasn't just a dream! Siddonie *has* planned a changing! *You knew!* You knew before we—before you brought me here!"

"Of course I knew," he said easily. "And I have to stop her. Together, we can stop her."

She swung off the bed, snatching up her dress. "You bred a child with me. You—all the time you knew she could prevent that child from having claim on the throne. *You knew this! And you made a child in me!* I will—I will lay every spell I know to destroy it!"

He was out of bed, pulling her to him. "Our child will be stronger than any changeling. Trust me. You have the Catswold strength. And you will have the Catswold nation behind you. With our child, we will defeat Siddonie no matter if she does bring a changeling." He cupped her face in his hands. "There is a magic among the Catswold, a power for life that can defeat her." He backed her against the wall, stroking her, handling her too roughly, hurting her, whispering spells to dominate her.

She fought him, pushed him away. He threw her onto the bed, forcing her until in a tide of passion she clung to him.

Appalled at herself, she let him take her, driven by a wild, animal lust.

When they lay spent, she was ashamed. She hoped he would sleep. She made a sleep spell, silent and insistent. And when he did sleep, she slid off the bed and pulled on her rumpled dress. Angrily she cast the open-spell and watched the wall swing back. She was angry at herself, and angry at the powers that had lured her; angry because she could have resisted those powers. She was shamed because she had not.

Standing in the opening, she saw, away through the woods, the palace shining pale against the green-lit sky. She stood for some moments watching for guards, and when behind her Efil stirred from sleep, she spun around fiercely whispering another spell at him.

He slept deeply again.

She had stepped out into the woods when she saw riders leave the palace. She drew back, waiting until they had gone. Then a lone horseman came out the gate. It was the queen's seneschal, Vrech, hunch shouldered, booting his horse along in that ugly way he had. He was headed south, his yellow cape billowing.

She remembered that a tunnel lay to the south, and Efil's words exploded in her mind: *Vrech is responsible to her upperworld associate, he is back and forth often . . . I dreamed of a changeling child . . . I dreamed that Vrech carried Wylles to the upperworld . . . Vrech goes up more often . . .*

She closed the wall behind her and moved to follow Vrech. Soon she was running, keeping in sight his yellow cape. If there was a changeling she wanted to know it. She wanted to prevent the switch. She was determined not to let the tryst happen for nothing. She ran, her emotions and purposes all in a tangle, only knowing that she must follow Vrech.

Chapter 20

Melissa ran, ducking branches. She was just able to glimpse Vrech's yellow cape disappearing between the trees as his horse trotted away through the forest. Running, she felt twigs catch and pull her hair, and she jerked her skirt higher to avoid the grasping vines. Soon Vrech vanished beyond the palace among the forested hills. Her breath burned in her throat as she turned aside and ducked under the pasture fence.

With a quick spell she brought a pony to her. She grabbed his mane and slid on, opened the gate with a spell, and pushed the willing beast to a gallop. As, behind her, the gate slammed closed, she bent low over the pony, willing him to a run. Soon again she saw the yellow flash of Vrech's cape. He had slowed his horse. She slowed the pony and followed quietly in shadow. He was moving up along the river that wound through the forest. Her pony wanted to nicker but she quieted him with a spell.

Vrech followed the river for several miles. Among the trees flocks of birds fled away from him. Where a stream branched away from the river, he turned to follow it, but soon it flowed into a low cave and disappeared. As Vrech dismounted she turned the pony aside behind a tangle of mulberry bushes.

She watched him unsaddle his horse and tether it with a spell where it could graze and drink. He took from the saddle a lantern with a bundle. Carrying these, he disappeared into the cave, ducking low. She was cold with fear, wanted to go back. She spellbound the pony where it, too, could graze and drink, and followed Vrech. Ducking into the cave, she was terrified he had seen her, that he would be waiting for her on the other side.

But he had gone on. Beyond the opening the roof rose higher, and far ahead the earthen walls were lit by Vrech's receding light. Vrech's shadow humped and twisted as the lantern swung. Beyond him, the tunnel snaked away into blackness. She followed slowly, trying to made no sound. At her feet beside the narrow trail the stream ran deep and fast. But its faint churl did not hide the sound of Vrech's boots on the rough stone.

The echo of his steps grew fainter and his retreating light dimmer. She stayed close to the wall so the green daylight behind her would not silhouette her, but soon that light was lost as the tunnel curved. She could see nothing now in the blackness but the glow of Vrech's distant lantern. The air grew colder, soon the path became slippery. She knelt, feeling out across solid ice. Vrech had surely known it was here, and he had hardly paused. Carefully she crawled over the ice floe, then rose. This was the tunnel to the upperworld; she had no question but that that was where Vrech was headed. The thought of climbing out of her own world into the vast, unending emptiness of the world above filled her with hollow terror.

At last the air grew warm again, then the stream dropped away from her feet into a chasm, and here the trail narrowed, too. The spaces below her echoed back to her with the scuff of Vrech's boots. When his passage dislodged stones, each fell down and down clattering until its sound was lost. She did not hear the stones strike bottom. She clung close to the one solid wall, and soon she had lagged so far behind that Vrech's light had vanished. She wondered if he had heard or seen her and had doused his light and waited around the next bend. She dared not bring a spell-light.

Maybe the tunnel had split, maybe she was lost. She moved on faster, feeling ahead with each step to be sure there was solid earth under her reaching foot.

But then soon, frightened and wary in the darkness, she

began to sense the path ahead of her, began to know which way the path was turning, and to sense the spaces and densities around her. She was aware of the solid wall almost as if she could see it, aware of the thrusting slabs above her, acutely aware now of the hollow chasm beside the path, as if some other sense than sight picked out the contours.

She had never had this sense before; surely this was Catswold sense, and it excited her. Accurately perceiving the inky spaces around her, she hurried on until she could see Vrech's light again. Moving ever upward, curiosity filled her, about the world above.

Mag said the upperworld was awash with falling water, burnt by the spinning fire of the sun, and scoured by tearing wind. Mag said love was deeper there, babies healthier, and that there was in the upperworld a power that had been lost in the Netherworld. She said they did not have magic, but that other power was as strong as magic. The old woman grew morose sometimes, longing for that world. Melissa had no idea why she had left it, or why she never returned.

The dropping chasm disappeared, the stream ran again beside the path, sending spray across it. She knelt and drank, wishing she had a waterskin to fill. She was painfully hungry, and she was cold again. She imagined the queen making this journey wearing a fur cape and warm boots and gloves, her servants carrying food and wine; a safe, cosseting entourage within which the queen would travel warm and cared for. As I would, she thought, if I were queen.

Well, to Hell with that. She would rather be herself, and free, than be like Siddonie.

She waited impatiently while Vrech stopped to eat. She could smell onions, and could hear him chewing. Her stomach growled. They seemed to have been in the tunnel forever.

After many more hours walking, as the tunnel rose it narrowed so tightly and the ceiling dropped so low she panicked. Walking crouched, her head bent, then creeping, she held her fear in check, sweating, trembling. If she let her fear master her, there was no one to help. To beg help of Vrech would be to die in this tunnel.

But at last the constricted space eased, and the way rose more steeply. Twice more Vrech stopped to rest, and once to urinate. When she passed that place in the path she could smell his sour scent.

On and on up dark, winding ways. She sensed vast and dropping chasms, sensed jagged, tumbled boulders teetering across black space. Once she put her ear to the stone wall and heard beyond the stone the hushing roar of an under-earth sea. The tunnel grew so steep in places that steps were cut in the path. Hungry and afraid, she grew achingly tired. She went on heavily, wishing she were safe back in Mag's cottage. And then suddenly ahead Vrech stopped and spoke. The thunder of his voice, after the long silence, turned her cold.

But he wasn't speaking to her. He was reciting an opening spell. She heard stone scrape against stone and saw a stone wall swing in, then his light moved away beyond the wall, and the wall scraped closed, and she was alone in total darkness.

Tracing her hand along the rough wall, she felt adze marks where the earth and rock had been cut. She found the solid end of the tunnel and, to her right, a wall made of small stones set into mortar.

She repeated Vrech's spell.

The wall moved toward her, pressing in against her. She slipped around it ready to run back down the tunnel if Vrech was there. She stood looking into a storeroom, an earthen cave cluttered with a ladder, wheelbarrow, potting table, and garden tools. She was alone.

There was a door in the opposite wall. The streak of yellow-white light beneath it told her how bright this world must be. She moved to the door and pressed her ear to it. She could hear wind blowing; she could feel wind shake the door. And when she lifted the latch the door was pulled from her hands by the wind. Wind hit her, pummeling her. Sunlight exploded in her eyes. She stepped back, covering her eyes, pushing the door closed. Red spots swam across her vision.

When she opened the door again, she was ready for the light and the wind. Wind whipped her hair and dress against her. Light burned her. Squinting, she searched the brightness for Vrech.

She could make out nothing clearly. Masses of bright color swayed before her; tangled branches swung away to reveal blinding light, then swung back again. She was in a hillside garden. Down the hill stood three houses, their windows filled with the garden's bright, blowing reflections. When she turned she saw three more houses above, and above those rose the empty sky. She looked straight up at total emptiness and went dizzy, reeling. Clinging to the door she felt as if she would fall upward straight into that tilting and endless space.

And in the sky rode the sun. *Ra. Osiris.* Elven tales of the sun god filled her. She felt drawn by that powerful being. The sun made her feel weightless and giddy; she wanted to run through the garden leaping, wanted to bat crazily at blowing leaves. The wild abandon that filled her was beyond any human experience, made her long for claws to rake the trees, made her feel she must have a tail to lash.

And when, controlling her wildness, she turned to pull the door closed, she was facing cats, dozens of cats. She thought they were alive, then saw that they were carved from the wood of the door. They were familiar; she thought she had seen them before and she reached to touch their little oak faces.

Nine rows of cats, nine cats to a row. She didn't need to count, she remembered. She was a little girl again, wearing a short red dress, gazing up at the cats, waiting for them to speak, caught in an intense childhood game.

She stroked the dear cat faces and touched their little carved teeth, filled with raw longing for that lost time.

But the memory was connected to nothing. It hung in her mind suspended and alone.

She touched the heavy vine that framed the door, a vine

so old and thick that its cut branches, trimmed to clear the door, formed a deep, rough frame. How familiar the feel of the cut stubs, and of the young tendrils that had snaked out as if they would lash the door shut. How familiar the smell of crushed leaves where the vine had caught in the door's hinges.

Behind her the garden darkened suddenly, as if a huge beast had loomed over her. Alarmed, she spun around.

A gigantic shadow engulfed the flowers and small trees. When she looked above, she remembered Mag telling about clouds. The sun was hidden by clouds, like soft gray islands. And now, below the hill, the houses were absorbed by shadow. But as she looked she realized that the center house was familiar. Puzzled, intrigued, she started down the garden along a winding path. Ducking under small trees, skirting past tangles of flowers, she soon stood at the edge of the brick veranda that spanned the front of the house.

She remembered rolling a wheeled toy, bump bump, over that long expanse of brick. She remembered playing with dolls here.

She had been a child in this house. She had stood looking out at the garden. She could almost bring back the voices. In memory she could smell chocolate, and something lemony and sweet.

But again the memory was attached to nothing.

The front of the house was different. She did not remember all this glass, she had never seen so much glass; the whole front wall and door were glass. Its reflections of the blowing garden cast her own image back at her alarmingly.

She didn't want to look at her image, but she was drawn to look. She had never seen her full image. She put aside fear and studied her figure, and she liked what she saw. She was slim, long waisted. Her green dress looked darker in the glass. Her face was thin and pale against the blowing garden. She moved closer to look into her face and lost her image and could see into the room.

One big room ran the length of the house. Yet she remembered two rooms, with a little entry between them. In the entry had stood a red lacquer table. This ceiling was different, too. It was higher. There were rafters now where they had not been before, and there was a glass window in the roof between the heavy beams. The house in her memory was changed, as a dream changes.

These walls were white, not flowered. And on them hung images. Paintings—they were paintings. Their bright colors exploded in the light-filled room, forming bright hills and trees and sky and the images of people. Paintings like the small image in Prince Wylles' chamber, only these were huge.

To her right was a little seating area, a soft-looking chair and a couch covered with lengths of silk and velvet in all shades of reds and pinks and orange. Down at the other end of the room were more paintings, leaning several deep against the walls. A sound made her turn.

On a lane beside the garden, cars were parked. She remembered cars, remembered the feel of movement, the smell inside a new car. A car had pulled up now and was parking, but when its door opened she stared.

Vrech was getting out. She fled for the bushes at the end of the terrace, shocked to see him so suddenly, and amazed to see a Netherworlder using an upperworld machine.

As she huddled beneath the bushes, Vrech crossed diagonally up the garden carrying a bundle, and let himself into the tool room that led to the Netherworld.

She assumed he was going back, and despite her fear of him she was unnerved at being left alone in this world. But then as she watched, he came out again wearing different clothes, and got back in the car. He had hardly driven away when she saw a man running toward the lane. As he crossed it, she moved deeper into the bushes. He came directly through the garden toward her. She didn't breathe. But he didn't glance toward the bushes; he crossed the terrace and went into the house. He was tall, dark haired, bronze skinned: he was the man from the Harpy's montage of visions. His bare legs looked strong and muscled, not like Efil's pale legs.

Soon he came out carrying a tray with two glasses, a tall

bottle, and a bowl. He was pouring himself a drink as another car pulled into the lane and parked. The driver headed for the terrace.

This man was short, dressed in a suit and tie. This pleased her, that she could remember upperworld clothes. So many memories flashed at her, but none with meaning. The tall man poured a second glass and the two went in the house. She moved so she could see inside.

They were looking at the paintings, standing together talking, moving along from one painting to the next; but as they progressed from one end of the room to the other they began to argue.

They came out again arguing, their voices cold with anger. The shorter man said, "This is why you kept putting me off, telling me to wait until I got back from London, then until you got back from Carmel, from Sonoma, to wait until after Christmas. Why the hell didn't you say something, Braden? I hate to sound stuffy, but under contract, you don't have the right to cancel the show. *I* like the work—it's not as great as the Coloma series, but it's good. You can't back out of a show, not so late."

"Just put someone else in the date. Get Garcheff. Any painter in the Bay area would be pleased to have a show at the Chapman."

"If I'd known earlier I could have put the date up. Or I could have gotten someone. There's not enough time. And what about the New York show?" He set down his glass and picked up his keys. "The brochures are already at the printers. I won't cancel."

"Call the printer. I'll pay for the damn brochures."

"There isn't time to do new ones."

"The hell there isn't. Listen, Rye, you—"

"Christ, Braden. Be reasonable. If Alice were alive you wouldn't be doing this."

Braden went white. He drained his glass, staring at Rye. Rye looked at the glass pointedly. "Ever since Alice died, Brade, you've been letting yourself go to hell."

"That's a stupid damn remark."

Melissa hardly heard them. *Ever since Alice died—* *Alice . . . Ever since Alice died . . .* She hugged herself, shivering and hurt, so shocked she felt sick, but she didn't know why. She didn't remember anyone named Alice.

Rye said, "Where *is* Alice's work? That whole alcove used to be full of her prints."

"At her gallery. Where the hell else would it be?"

"The last etchings, too? The Thompson thoroughbreds? And those drawings of cats' faces from the garden door? The Blackeston retrievers? She was the only animal artist on the West Coast worth a damn, and you've hidden her work away."

Braden grabbed Rye, twisting him around. "I haven't hidden a damn thing! What the hell do you—?" Then he looked embarrassed and released the smaller man. "Sorry." He walked away toward the bushes where Melissa crouched, then turned to look at Rye.

"Alice hasn't anything to do with this. I'm painted out, run out of steam, that's all." He paused. "I have a dinner date, have to dress. Stay if you like. Maybe you can find something for the street fair."

Rye scowled at his retreating back. "You have ten weeks to get the show in shape." He left the terrace. As he crossed the garden, a woman's voice called from somewhere up the hill, "Tom? Tom?" Melissa watched Rye drive away, puzzled by the argument, and filled with emotions she didn't understand. Braden had gone inside.

When she looked up the hill again, a thin old woman in a brightly flowered dress was crossing from one house to another. The wind had stilled. Melissa could smell suppers cooking. As the sun vanished behind the woods she grew cold. She felt suddenly very alone.

When Braden came out and crossed the garden to a station wagon, she looked speculatively at the studio door. It would be warm in there, and there would be something to eat. She had a sense of delicious food within that childhood refuge. He gunned the engine, and squealed the tires as he turned around in the dead end lane and headed toward the highway. He had been dressed in a pale jacket and slacks, a white shirt and tie. He had left a light burning. She studied the niche between the brick terrace and the house where he had hidden his key. What good to lock a door, then put the key almost in plain sight? She was considering the wisdom of going in when a branch rustled behind her and a boy's voice said, "Where were you?"

She swallowed, frozen.

"There's chowder for supper; you'd better come on if you want any."

Every instinct told her to stay still. She tried to glance up without turning. Her heart was thundering.

The leaves rustled again. "There, that's better. Hey! Keep your claws in!" A boy strode past her close enough to touch, carrying an orange cat on his shoulder. As he moved away up the garden, silently she let out her breath.

The cat must have been standing just behind her. She wondered if it had been watching her. But it was the boy who had shocked her.

He was about twelve. He had the same dark brown hair as Prince Wylles, the same dark curling lashes and rounded chin—Efil's chin. The same straight nose as Wylles and Efil. He was fatter than Wylles, his color high and healthy, but still he looked like Prince Wylles. She watched him run up the steps of the white house carrying the cat and disappear inside, slamming the door. She could have been seeing Prince Wylles with only a few pounds added.

She had seen, close enough to touch, the boy who would be changed for Prince Wylles.

Surely Vrech had not simply discovered the boy here. He must have brought him here to this garden. She wondered how he had managed that. If Netherworld spells did not work here, what manipulations had Vrech used?

No matter. The changeling boy was here. Soon Vrech would take him down into the Netherworld. She wished powerfully she could undo her tryst with Efil last night. Thinking of bearing Efil's child, without clear promise to the throne, made her feel imprisoned, trapped and shamed.

When the garden was empty she came out from the bushes and approached the glass door. She wanted to see inside the house; she wanted to be in there, perhaps discover something to stir further memory. She felt torn between the two worlds, she did not know where she belonged.

Chapter 21

Night was drawing down over the garden, making the vast sky seem less daunting. Melissa approached the glass door and slipped into the shadows. Up the hill behind her, lights burst on suddenly in the center house: not the slow rising of lantern light, but all at once, bright and steady. She tried the knob, pushed the glass door open. Letting herself into the bright room, she moved away from the lighted lamp, hoping not to be seen through the windows.

The smell of the studio was of canvas and turpentine and linseed oil. Familiar smells that filled her with nostalgia. She touched a corner of the nearest painting, and finding the paint dry, she stroked the colors, caught by the comforting feel of the oils. But the memories that came glanced away too soon; she could make nothing more of them than pleasant, familiar sensations.

Tubes of paint were laid out neatly on the table in three rows. Clean brushes stood bristles up in a heavy mug. A can of turpentine and a bottle of oil stood behind the little cups which would hold them. Stretcher bars and rolls of canvas leaned against the wall. But these items used by a painter did not belong to the memory of this house; they belonged somewhere different. And no detail of that other place would reveal itself.

She entered the short hall knowing she would find, on her right, the kitchen, on her left, the bedroom, and the bath straight ahead.

In the kitchen she reacquainted herself with the taps for running water, with the refrigerator, and with the knobs that gave fire to the stove. She took two apples from a bowl, and a bottle of milk and some cheese from the refrigerator. She drank the milk and put the empty bottle back. She found the bread, ate two slices, and tied six more and the cheese and apples in a dish towel.

When she looked into the bathroom she remembered the floor of small, white tiles. She remembered bathing in the tub when she was a child, squeezing soap bubbles over the ornate fish spigots. Then in the bedroom she stood at the open window looking downhill to the highway, watching the lights of passing cars reflected in the marsh water, watching night fall across the bay, as she had done many times when she was small. She sniffed the familiar salty air, gripped by nostalgia, and distressed at her inability to remember more. She went slowly out again to the terrace, caught in the half-awake dream, and unable to put anything together.

The past that she could glimpse was not whole—feelings and places all were scattered. The people flashing vaguely in her memory could not be drawn forth—they were shadows, their voices were unidentifiable whispers.

Outside, looking up the darkening garden, she searched for Vrech, then went quickly up through the tangle of bushes and flowers and small trees, hurrying past the upper houses into the woods.

The scent of the trees was almost like a Netherworld forest, familiar and comforting. She found a nest of fallen boughs between three trees, and rearranged the dry, soft-needled limbs to make room for herself. Apparently this was the nest of some animal, but tonight it would be hers.

As she ate her supper of cheese and bread and apple, the night around her pushed the last long shadows together into chambers of darkness. Below her in the white house a light went out. The wind turned colder. In the dark-shingled house, a light went on upstairs. She could hear music, then strangely resonant voices that startled her until she remembered radios.

She remembered listening to the radio while lying snuggled in her bed with the lights out, listening to a radio story in the dark . . . whispering to someone in the bed across from her. They were shivering at the story and laughing together . . .

But who? Someone young and laughing. But nothing she could do would bring more than that fragment of memory.

Pressing deeper into the branches she became aware of the scent of cat on them, and without wondering how she could tell, she knew this was the scent of the yellow cat that she had seen from the bushes beside the terrace. As she considered her sudden sharp perception, she realized her vision had changed, too. Through the dark night, now she could see branches and deadfalls which, moments before, had been black smears. And she could see farther to the sides; as if she were seeing back past twitching, pointed ears. Excited, she sniffed the wind for new scents, waiting, wondering what it would feel like to change, to shape shift . . .

Waiting. Excited, afraid . . .

Waiting . . .

She didn't change. Her vision returned to normal human eyesight. Her sense of smell dulled again. Gone was the wild, skittery feeling that was so addicting.

She unclenched her fists, disappointed.

Perhaps she would not change until she knew a spell to help her. She must try to remember a changing spell.

Depressed, feeling flat and dull, she finished her supper, then curled down within the branches. How sad, to feel wonders dangled enticingly before her, then feel them jerked away. Nearing sleep, she felt again the sensation of being a child . . .

Only this time she had been terrified.

She was wearing a blue taffeta dress. She was perhaps four or five. She was huddled alone in an alley crying into the taffeta skirt when a stranger came and lifted her up and carried her into a strange house. She screamed and kicked . . .

She could not remember any more. She lay shivering, fully awake again, galvanized by a child's helpless fear.

She woke at dawn, alarmed at the heavy weight on her chest. When she opened her eyes she was staring into yellow eyes: the yellow cat sat atop her chest gazing down at her.

She didn't know whether to laugh or be afraid. When she stared back at him, he seemed suddenly to turn shy and retreated to the piled boughs and crouched there watching her. His golden tail twitched, his golden eyes remained intent. He was so alert, looked so intelligent, she felt her spine tingle.

She stayed still, knowing she was in his territory. She wasn't sure whether his intensity signaled interest or challenge. She did not want to battle a yellow tomcat for this space. The cat regarded her for some moments, self-possessed and bold. His coat looked so thick and silken she longed to touch it. She could still feel the warmth of his heavy body crouched on her chest. At last, deciding he was friendly, she started to reach to let him sniff her fingers, but the look in his eyes changed to active challenge and she drew her hand back.

But then his yellow eyes grew puzzled, as if he was as confused by this encounter as she. Then suddenly his ears twitched in the direction where the hill dropped, and he turned to stare down the garden. She heard a boy calling, "Pippin. Pippin." She raised herself up slightly above the branches, looking.

She saw the changeling boy, standing on the porch of the white house. When he spotted Pippin perched on the branches, he came directly up between the houses and into the woods. Not until he was very near did he see Melissa tucked down among the dry limbs. He stopped, startled; then he grinned.

"You're in his bed. Did you sleep there?" When she didn't answer, he flushed. "Sorry, didn't mean to pry. I'm Tom

Hollingsworth." He picked up the cat. The big tom flopped happily over the boy's shoulder, lying limp, looking down remotely at her.

She said, "I'm Sarah."

Tom studied her with a direct, comfortable gaze. She looked back boldly into the child's face, seeing a miraculously healed Prince Wylles.

He said, "You don't live in the village. I'd remember you."

"I live that way," she said, pointing off through the woods, wondering what lay in that direction.

"In the city?"

"Yes, in the city." She imagined tall buildings and steep hills as in the Harpy's vision. Or was she seeing something from her own memory?

She said, "Is there—someone who comes to the garden, someone named Vrech?"

Tom nodded, but his eyes hardened. "He's the gardener. He does all our yards, they're all mixed together." He looked at her deeply, with a child's honesty. "Do you know him? Do you like him?"

"I don't know him really, I just—I know his name. You don't like him?"

"He's always asking questions."

"I'm asking questions."

Tom grinned. "His questions are—pushy. He wants to know what I'm reading, what I'm learning in school, what my favorite foods are—he asked me a lot about that. What I'm doing this summer, even what foods my mother doesn't eat—really nervy."

"Do you answer his questions?"

"I guess I do," Tom said, surprised. "There's something about him—when he asks, I just—I suppose because he's a grown-up and—and because he frightens me a little," he confided. He bent his knee and scratched his leg without leaning over, so as not to disturb the cat. "He wanted to know what my father did before he died. One time, before we moved here, he asked me what my mother did in her work. He knew she was a broker's assistant, but he wanted to know exactly what she did, stuff that was none of his business."

"Has he always been gardener here?"

"Since before we came. He does gardening all over the village—for some of Mama's friends. That's how we found this house. He told Mama's friend Virginia about it right after our house burned. He said this house was empty, and the people might be willing to rent until we got settled. My mother thinks that was very nice. But I don't like him. I didn't like him helping us."

"Who—who lived in the house before it was empty?"

"Someone named—Santeth, I think. Did you know someone here?"

"No, I . . ."

But she did; there was a Santeth in Affandar Palace, a captain of the queen's guard.

Tom shifted his weight as if the cat was growing heavy. "Do you work in the city?" Then, seeing her expression, "Now I'm asking nosey questions. I'm sorry. I just thought . . ."

"It's all right. I—don't work—just now."

"You're out of a job? What do you do?"

"I clean," she said, trying it out. "I clean and cook."

"You're a maid? That's crazy. You ought to be a model, not a maid. You're too beautiful to clean someone's house. You can't like doing that."

"It's all right." She wasn't sure what a model was; she was pleased and touched that he thought her beautiful. Something about the word *model* struck her, but she couldn't make any memory come. When a car horn honked, Tom turned.

"It's my mother." He touched her hand by way of goodbye. "Come back," he said, spinning around so the cat flicked its tail to balance itself, and he was gone. She watched him set the cat down on the porch rail, where it jumped into a tree. Tom got into the car with his mother. They backed out and turned down the lane, going slowly past another cat trotting across the lane—a dark, tiger-

striped animal. Melissa wondered if everyone kept cats; she
wondered if they were all ordinary cats. The car was about
to turn onto the highway when another car swerved in
squealing, spun around at the end of the lane and out again,
just missing them. And something had happened. Tom and
his mother jumped out of their car. Tom started to kneel,
then his mother pushed him aside saying something, and he
ran shouting up the garden, leaving his mother crouched in
the lane over the small, still form.

   "Morian! Morian!" Tom shouted. "Tiger's hurt! Morian!"
   A door slammed and a black woman came quickly from
the gray house. She took the boy by the shoulders, staring
into his face. He said something, pointed, and she ran down
the terraces, her bare feet flying. Melissa forgot all need to
hide herself; she ran down the garden and stood watching
Tom and his mother and the black woman kneeling in the
middle of the road. The black woman's face was twisted
with pain as she rose cradling the little bundle in her arms,
and got into the car. Melissa was totally caught up in the
drama. A cat had been hurt, and they had rushed to it, were
surely taking it for help. In Affandar, a hurt animal would be
left to die, no one would attempt to save it. Perhaps no one
would love it deeply enough to save it.

   When the car had gone, she went quickly down to the portal and stood touching the carved cats' faces, letting their familiarity ease her confused feelings. She didn't belong in
this world; she was a foreigner here. Maybe she had lived
here once, but that time was gone; she had been only a small
child then. Now this world reached out too powerfully,
wanted too powerfully to draw her into it. Frightened, she
pulled open the portal and slipped through into the tool
room, and quickly she said the spell.

   The wall drew back. She pushed through into the darkness and closed the door behind her.

   Alone in the black tunnel she felt tears stinging. She
wasn't safe in the upperworld, yet something of that world
held her. Something of herself belonged there, something
raw and vulnerable. She felt she had torn herself physically

from that world. Confused, she hurried downward into the blackness, heading down fast toward the less complicated comfort of the Netherworld.

She traveled a long way, unable to bring a spell-light, running down through the blackness, trailing her hand along the rough stone, sensing the emptiness and the masses of stone with feline alacrity. She slowed when she reached the first drop.

And as she descended, the upperworld seemed not to diminish in size as a place does when one moves away. It seemed to grow larger behind her, the wind blowing wilder, the sun burning brighter.

Much later she managed to bring a spell-light dully gleaming against the tilting slabs, light swallowed by the dropping chasm beside which she fled. From far below came the churl of the stream hurrying down toward the Netherworld. And as she approached her own world she thought more kindly of Efil. Maybe she had been too hard on him. Efil had offered her a kingdom, offered her all that was his. In bedding her, he had only been trying to save the heritage he had so foolishly let Siddonie control.

She wondered if she and Efil together really could free the Netherworld. She wondered if they could stop the need for war, make every land free to govern itself, and if they might free the Catswold from their self-imposed exile. She remembered Halek saying once, when she and Mag had visited him in his village, that Siddonie longed to destroy the Catswold's stubborn independence, to break their spirit.

When she stopped to rest beside the stream, half of her wanted to join with Efil, while the other half wanted to avoid him. And there was within her, as well, a fierce, painful hunger to turn back again to the inexplicable world above.

But whatever she did, she must tell Efil that Vrech had found a changeling boy. No matter what she felt about Efil, no matter how he had deceived her, she must do this for him.

When long hours later she began to smell the deep green scent of pine she ran, bursting out from the tunnel into the familiar Netherworld night. She crossed the stream, and knelt, and snatched up Netherworld earth in her hands. Her cheeks were wet with tears.

She looked for Vrech's stallion, but it was gone. She wondered if Vrech, returning, had seen the pony behind the bushes. When she reached the pony she laughed at his impatient pawing. Quickly she swung onto his back, released him from the binding spell, and gave him his head. He flattened his ears and bolted for the palace.

Near the palace she slid down and loosed the pony in his pasture. Approaching the palace wall and slipping in through a side gate, she could see lamps burning in the scullery. And though it seemed to be very late, the big dining hall was brightly lit, and she could hear voices and laughter. She moved to the back of the palace, looking up at Efil's vine-choked balcony.

Chapter 22

She climbed the vine and swung onto Efil's balcony. She thought as she moved to the window to look in that maybe she would regret her return. Yet she must do this; she felt compelled to bring news of the changeling boy to Efil. She could see through the partially open draperies that the room was dark. She turned the latch and gently pushed the door open—it was jerked from her hand, and someone grabbed her arm, pulling her in. A spell-light shone in her face.

"Melissa!" Efil laughed drunkenly and pulled her into his arms. He stank of wine. "Where have you been? This is wonderful. Where did you go yesterday? I woke and you were gone." He began kissing her and fondling her.

She pulled away and moved to the mantel. "I have something to tell you, Efil. Something important. You weren't asleep?" She glanced toward the bed, then watched him light a lamp by snapping his fingers in a showy spell. He was really very drunk.

He said, "I just came in. Supper was endless. She's all worked up about the damned dwarfs in the north and their silver." He moved the lamp to a table; its light leaped up across his face to form unfamiliar contours. "She can't get the dwarf nation to settle on a king elect without turning it into a battle over silver taxes. What difference? She takes what she wants anyway." Again, eagerly, he reached for her.

She moved away and sat down on the bench before the cold hearth. "Please listen. This is important."

He sat down close beside her, smiling indulgently, and began kissing her neck. She pushed him away, prying his fingers loose. "You *must* listen, Efil. Vrech has found a changeling boy. He has found a boy to be changed for Wylles."

He stared at her, frowning. "There hasn't been time. She only—you're not serious? But of course, you're mistaken."

She shook her head. "There is a boy in the upperworld who looks exactly like Wylles. I have been there. I saw him."

He laughed, reaching for her. "You wouldn't go there . . . not alone, my love."

He was exasperating; she wanted to slap him. "That is where I went yesterday. I followed Vrech. He has brought the boy to live in the garden by the portal. Six houses," she said, trying to hold his attention. "Six houses surrounding a hillside garden. There is a door opening into the hill—a portal. Vrech has the boy living there, the child is the same age as Wylles. He looks exactly like Wylles only fatter, healthy, and strong." She wished Efil was sober. "Don't you understand? I followed Vrech up. I saw the boy. I talked with him myself."

Efil rose and moved irritably to the mantel. He stood looking at the row of dusty wine bottles, seeming not to see them. Absently he lifted one, wrapped a spell around the cork, and drew it forth.

"Oloroso," he said, seeming surprised that he held the

bottle. "Worth a fortune—brought down from Spain generations ago." He filled two goblets, holding the bottle carefully, not using a spell, as if with drunkenness his spells, too, were shaky. "In the upperworld they bid fortunes against fortunes for such wine." His eyes, when he turned to look at her, seemed caught between drunkenness and fear stirred by her words.

He handed her a glass. "Tonight you drink a fortune, my love. And tomorrow," he said, lifting his goblet unsteadily, "tomorrow we banish the queen."

"How can you banish her? You don't know yet if I'm with child."

"Tomorrow we will know." He smiled, regaining his composure. "This morning I sent a page to Ebenth to fetch an old woman who is a master at the spells of prediction. She will tell us if we have started a son." He watched her, laughing. "Oh yes, my love. She will tell us. She has a solid reputation among the peasants. Whether her prediction is true or not, the peasants will believe her."

She set her glass down. "No one can know so soon."

"This woman can. And if Siddonie *has* found a changeling as you say, then we must have proof at once. The old woman can give us that proof. A son, Melissa—a new prince of Affandar." He reached to pull her up from the chair, to hold her. She pushed him away.

He said, "Once the news is public, Siddonie wouldn't dare to harm you." He snatched up her glass, spilling wine. "Drink, Melissa—drink to our child—to a healthy new prince for Affandar."

She rose, took the glass, and set it on the mantel. "What about Wylles?" she said quietly. "*Wylles* is the true prince of Affandar."

"Everyone knows Wylles will die. Whether he dies here or in the upperworld makes little difference. It would be more convenient, though, if he died before any switch was attempted."

"You can't kill him." She watched Efil, shocked. "The Primal Law . . ."

"No one spoke of killing." He lifted her chin. "But poor Wylles knows pain. He could know more pain. Wylles knows fear, and that could turn to terror. Perhaps Wylles will find a way to ease his own hurts." He pulled her close, kissing her, open-mouthed and ardent, forcing her toward the bed. Fear and repugnance filled her.

"We daren't, Efil. Not here."

"There's no danger. Siddonie is occupied with a tinsmith from Cressteane, a hulking boar—as if size could assure her a breeding." Crudely he pulled at her dress, pinning her against the headboard, forcing her, seeming possessed. She fought him, stiff and clenched, hitting him. But even drunk he was stronger. His weight was on her, his hands invading her; this was not lovemaking, it was cruel. She was terrified she would cry out and be heard beyond this room. She bit him, twisting away, and heard the door crash open.

Light filled the room, blinding her, shattering across Siddonie's face twisted with rage. The queen lunged at her, grabbing her, wrenching her away, jerking her off the bed, shaking and slapping her, her nails biting into Melissa's shoulder. She hit back at Siddonie and broke free. She tried to run, but something unseen jerked her down; a power held her unmoving and helpless.

"On the taint of Catswold blood . . ." Siddonie hissed.

"No!" Efil shouted. "She bears my son! She bears the prince of Affandar!"

"To Catswold cleave . . ."

"The peasants already know," Efil yelled. "The news has been spread—they will rise against you . . ."

Melissa struggled, twisting at Siddonie's feet; above her Siddonie's voice echoed, "To cat do I command you . . ."

Her body constricted. She couldn't breathe.

"To cat I commit you. To cat you will cleave, to no other spirit yield." Siddonie had grown so tall, so huge. Melissa stared up at her, then stared at her own shaking hands. And her hands were changing into paws.

The queen glared down at her, her eyes filled with loathing. "To cat you are returning. Cat you will remain and never more than cat. You will *remember* no more than cat . . ."

Her body hurt, her legs were twisted with pain. She saw the disgust on Efil's face, saw him turn away. Siddonie's shouts deafened her. "Bring the guards!" Running feet pounded down the hall, and the queen's voice blurred, lost all meaning. The room was immense around her. She tried to rise, and fell panting. She stared in terror at her white paws scrabbling at the carpet as men pounded into the room, surrounding her. She spun around, facing one then another, torn with fear. "Get the creature out of here! Put it in a cage!"

The calico cat crouched, her eyes blazing, then leaped at the queen, clinging to Siddonie's thigh, slashing so brutally the queen screamed and knocked her away into a tangle of booted legs. The room seemed filled with boots, soldiers towered, spraddle-legged, blocking her, grabbing at her. She faced them spitting, raking their reaching hands, then dashed through between their legs and fled into blackness under the bed.

Two soldiers crawled in after her. When she lashed out at them they hit her. One grabbed her front legs, guarding his face, another jerked her up by the tail. They dragged her out, hurting her, and thrust a leather coat over her. She fought the coat. They held it closed like a bag, lifting her. For an instant something of Melissa surfaced, wild with terror, fighting so fiercely that the queen repeated the spell. Then she was simply cat again, raking at the leather. A blow made her sprawl, panting. The noise of loud voices pained her too. She was carried. Her captors' footsteps echoed down the corridors. A door banged open. She smelled fresh air. She heard leaves rustle under the marching feet.

Soon she smelled chicken coops. A latch clicked. The coat was tossed onto a hard surface and jerked open, and she was prodded out with sticks. She streaked out, ramming into the iron bars of a chicken cage.

Her back to the bars, she crouched facing the five soldiers.

They slammed the door and locked it, and began poking her with sticks, shouting and laughing. She fought their thrusting jabs for a long time, until she was so weak she began to shiver and salivate.

"It's going to have a fit."

"Let's get out of here. The queen said leave it alive."

They left, smirking.

The cat lay panting and shivering.

The cage was strong enough to keep small dragons and bears from the chickens. The floor was mucky with chicken droppings. Around her in other cages chickens flapped and squawked with fear of her. When she had revived somewhat, she watched the chickens with rising interest, her tail twitching. But soon she began to lick herself; she hurt in so many places that she worked frantically back and forth from one painful, tender area to another.

She was kept in the cage for five days. Darkness followed light. She had little to eat, and only a small bowl of dirty water that she avoided until she could bear her thirst no longer. On the fourth morning an apple-faced old woman came to look in at her, reaching her fingers through the close-set bars. The calico cat came to her mewling, rubbing her orange-and-black cheek against the old woman's hand.

Mag stood for a long time beside the cage, trying every spell she knew to open it. She was sick with despair for Melissa, wiping back tears. No spell she tried would work—Siddonie's powers were too strong. She could not slip the cat out between the bars; they were only inches apart. She could barely reach through to stroke the scrawny cat.

She found an iron stake in a pile of rubbish and tried to pry the bars apart, but the stake flew away, deflected by the queen's protective magic. And the cage was too small to turn the cat into Melissa, even if she could have breached the queen's power. Anyway, what would the girl do cramped in a chicken cage?

She thought that Siddonie wouldn't kill the little cat. She

thought that not even the queen would go against the Primal Law.

She rubbed the little cat's ears. Then, whispering, glancing around to be sure she was still alone, she repeated the most powerful strengthening spell she knew. If nothing else, she might give the child a measure of added endurance. The little cat pressed against the bars, staring up at her forlornly, but when the long, complicated spell was completed, something came into the calico cat's eyes that cheered Mag. She read it as heightened courage. She had barely finished when three guards came around the corner, saw her, and shouted and grabbed her.

She fought them; with hurting spells she made one back off, another double up with pain; but the three together were too strong. They forced her into the palace and through the scullery and storeroom, and down two flights. There, in the dungeons, they locked her in the cell vacated by the Toad.

For a long time after Mag disappeared the little cat watched for her, warmed by her caring. But Mag did not return. On the morning of the sixth day the calico was hauled out by a gloved hand and shoved into a leather bag. The man who held the bag smelled of sour sweat. She knew his smell; she hissed and spit through the leather at him, and clawed the bag until he hit her.

Panting, hurt again, she was hoisted and carried. She smelled horse. The pinprick of green light she could see through the tie hole of the bag changed as they moved, and the horse's movement jarred her. The light changed. The movement changed as the man got off the horse and began to walk.

Soon the green light disappeared, the hole in the bag went black. Then the tiny hole was pierced by a yellow light moving as the man moved. She could smell oil burning, and some part of her below the conscious level knew it was the smell of an oil lamp.

She could smell damp earth and stone, too, and could hear water rushing. She could feel the man climbing. The smell of water soon had her wild with thirst. But some sense told her it would be a long time before she drank.

Long after they entered the tunnel she had sensed a heightened awareness from deep inside herself. Frightened, she tried to back away from it. When she moved, shaking the bag, he hit her. And as they rose higher away from the Netherworld, the awareness seemed to diminish.

After many hours, the exhausted cat slept.

She woke when the smells changed again. The man had stopped climbing. He startled her by speaking; his voice made a guttural rhythm. Then came the soft, sucking sound of stone moving across stone, and something new stirred within the little cat. Some hidden part of her was trying desperately to wake. The sound of the moving wall brought a sense of promise. She crouched, tensed and listening. She could hear the wind. She could smell greenness. Weakly she lifted one paw, and her heartbeat quickened.

Chapter 23

Vrech left the portal and garden quickly, heading east along the busy two-lane road that led to Highway 101. The bag was heavy. When the cat tried to claw through the leather, he punched her. Each time after he hit her, he could hear her licking. He cursed having left the car with the damned mechanic in the city. He'd thought of going after it, then knew the delay would stir Siddonie's rage. She wanted everything done now.

When he reached 101 he headed north, walking along the concrete shoulder beside the fast traffic, jerking his thumb at every passing car. No one stopped for him. The day was growing hot. His upperworld pants bound his crotch, and his pants and shirt were sticky with sweat. Upperworld clothes were too tight. He dodged a reefer truck careening close to the shoulder, and when he stumbled, the cat yowled. He wished the beast was dead, but he daren't kill her. He didn't think much about the Primal Law, but he wouldn't go against Siddonie. The cat could die after he left her, but not while she was in his possession.

He had served Siddonie long before she married the twelve-year-old prince. He had been seneschal to the old king of Affandar and had adeptly managed the affairs that resulted in the king's death. For Siddonie, he would have killed the king with his own hands. Before she had any claim to the throne, when she was only visiting Affandar, she would meet him at night in the stables or in the woods beyond the palace. Her ways with him stirred passions no other woman was capable of; she knew his weaknesses; she knew how to touch him and when to cast a spell as she caressed and fondled and bit him, drawing from him the mind numbing, shuddering responses that no other woman could elicit. In turn, he had set the stage for the old king's illness and had helped her to reach the small prince, arranging her seemingly chance meetings with him. By the time the king died, Siddonie had enslaved young Efil with charms to drive a boy mad. Vrech had stoically endured the knowledge that Siddonie lay with him. Thus she had bound and corrupted the child. Within a month of the old king's death, Siddonie and Efil were wed, and she was crowned queen of Affandar. Once they were wed, he of course had returned to her bed, slipping into her chambers after young Efil slept.

The cat shifted position again, pawing at the bag. Along the highway the traffic was growing heavier, but the drivers looked at his lifted thumb and stepped on the gas. When at last a ride did stop, it was an ancient delivery truck, home-painted blue over the words, A-ACTION PLUMBING. He climbed into the hot, exhaust-smelling cab and dropped the bag on the floor next to the engine. "How far you going?"

"Portland." The boy was dirty, with pimples down his neck.

"I won't be going that far. Crescent City, maybe."

"What you got in the bag? It's moving."

"Trained monkey. It sleeps during the day." He nudged it with his toe. "Big dreamer—wiggles in its sleep." The bag jerked, and the cat gagged and heaved.

"Ate too many marshmallows. Makes him sick. Kids love to feed him marshmallows."

He parted with the van north of Crescent City. It was almost dark. Wind swept the tall grass in waves across the empty fields. He dropped the bag between the road and a clogged drainage ditch. If the cat was smart enough, it could get out. That should satisfy the Primal Law. He crossed the highway by running between cars, and in the diner he ordered a beer and a hamburger. Within half an hour he had eaten and caught a ride south again with a trucker.

As the eighteen-wheeler turned out of the diner's parking lot and passed the spot where Vrech had dumped the cat, he thought briefly of the girl Melissa with a pang almost of remorse. She was a toothsome thing, young and untried or nearly so. But then he put the little chit out of his thoughts; she was of no use to him. He belched comfortably and settled back, chewing on a toothpick.

Chapter 24

Speeding trucks made the roadbed tremble. Their hot diesel wind sloughed through the tall, dry grass, shaking the bag, bringing the cat up stumbling with fear, falling against her leather prison so it writhed and rolled. At the onslaught of each truck, she fought the bag, trying to run from the thun-

der and shaking; then she would stop fighting and lie panting until another eighteen-wheeler sped past nearly on top of
her, jerking her up again. At last, too exhausted to fight,
retching and dizzy, she curled into a little ball and escaped
into a trance-like sleep.

She was jerked up again when a semi careened off the
pavement nearly on top of her. She exploded, throwing herself stumbling and fighting the bag. Flecks of saliva flew
against the leather. Her tongue was thick from thirst and her
body was sore in a dozen places from Vrech's blows. She
was very thin from her days locked in the chicken cage, all
bones and fur, her calico coat cupping in ugly shadows
along her thin back and flanks. During her week-and-a-half
confinement in the cage, she had been fed only enough to
keep her from dying. And on the journey up the tunnel then
up the highway there had been no food or water. The shape
of her skull showed clearly beneath her matted orange-and-
black coat. Her left eye was swollen shut where Vrech had
struck her. Weak and sick, the stink of diesel fuel sucking in
through the hole where the bag was tied made her sicker.

But then through the hole came another smell, a healing
smell, making her more alert. The wind sucked in, carrying
the scent of earth and grass; and she could smell muddy
water. She pawed at the leather and licked at it, and tried to
push out through the tiny hole. She could get a paw out, but
no more. She had dug at the hole for some time when another smell reached her as the wind changed, a smell that
made her force her nose frantically into the tiny opening.

The shifting wind brought the smell of frying meat, from
the diner. She gulped at the greasy smell ravenously; it filled
her senses, tantalizing and rich.

Each thundering truck made her try to run, tripping and
fighting inside the bag. In between, when the highway was
silent, she dug and pushed toward the smell of food that
came to her from across the highway.

After more than two hours of fighting to get through the
hole, she had chewed through the cord. She did not realize
she was free. The puckered leather remained closed. She lay

heaving and weak, retching from the road fumes, wild with thirst. Her raw nerves made her muscles jump at every faint, distant approach of a truck. She could feel their approach in the shaking ground. She panted fast and shallowly. She had no more strength to fight. Yet when the next diesel roared by, the sudden blast of its horn jerked her violently to life. Inside the bag she tried to run, plunging away.

She hit the puckered hole, and was out, scrabbling at earth and grass, running blindly through the tall grass.

She might have run until she dropped, but in the darkness and confusion she didn't sense the ditch and she fell.

She landed six feet down in mud. She smelled the brackish water and crouched, licking frantically, swallowing mud.

When her thirst was slaked, she climbed out of the ditch sniffing the greasy, delicious smell from the diner. She approached the edge of the highway and crouched, watching the broad black expanse with her good eye. The macadam was warm under her paws. But the thunder began again, shaking the highway. She stared at the approaching lights growing larger, growing huge. The wind of the semi buffeted her; she leaped away into the grass and crouched and hissed.

When the highway was empty once more, the smell of food drew her back. Hunched and shivering, she crouched, tensed to dash across. There was thunder coming, but it was not very loud yet. She ran.

She was halfway across the first lane when the lights of a Greyhound bus exploded fast out of the distance; she froze; light bathed her small, still form and reflected from her eyes. Her white parts blazed bright. The driver didn't swerve. She leaped back from the speeding wheels barely in time.

When the bus had passed she sped forward again, confused, directly into the path of the next racing light. This time, an air horn drove her back as a pair of racing trucks bore down, their lights picking her out. The passenger of the nearer truck stared down at her laughing, as if he would like to see a cat mashed on the highway.

Then there was a lull in traffic. The four-lane was empty,

and silent. Only one set of lights was coming, very far away and with not so much noise. Eagerly she ran for the diner.

She misjudged. The car was quieter than trucks, but it was moving fast. The driver saw her and slammed on the brakes, skidding, screeching the tires. The cat was so terrified she didn't know which way to run, she crouched directly in the car's path, full in its light; then at the last second she leaped into blackness. She felt its wind behind her.

She crouched on the white line in the center of the highway, dazed by the lights now coming from both directions. Again tires squealed, another car skidded, and she ran wildly as it slid sideways. Through its open window a woman screamed at her. She could taste the smell of burning rubber as she fled toward the gravel ditch beside the diner.

She scrambled and slid down the side of the ditch to safety.

Above on the highway the car straightened and went on, the driver cursing.

There was water in the ditch. It tasted faintly of dog urine. She drank, gulping, then rested, panting and pawing at her sore eye.

At last her heaving heart slowed. She roused herself and began to stalk the smell of food. She climbed out of the ditch and crept across the parking lot, taking shelter under a car ten feet from the steps of the diner. She stared out at the door where the smell was strongest. The noise of the juke box, of boots moving inside on the wood floor, and of raised voices and occasional shouts made her tremble. Suddenly the door was flung open, noise blared out, and she fled as three men swung out loudly arguing, clumping down the steps toward her. Panicked, she streaked through the darkness toward the rear of the diner.

There she paused, drawn by the smells from the four garbage cans.

She could smell dog, too. Warily she stalked the garbage cans, then jumped onto one. She pawed at the lid and when she could not get inside, she moved to the next can.

All four were sealed tightly. At last she leaped down and slunk back to the front of the building.

As she crouched beside a truck, huddled against its rear tire, two women came out of the diner. They were quieter than the men, and she didn't run. They saw her white parts catching the light from the diner's window, and they began to croon over her. She backed away from them under the truck, tensed to run. But then the women went back inside.

She was still there when they returned, knelt down beside the porch, and pushed a paper plate under it. "Here, kitty. Here kitty, kitty, kitty."

She smelled the food, close enough to make her drool. She didn't come out until the women had left.

Then she fled underneath, and stalked the plate.

Convinced there was no danger, she attacked the food. She gulped fried hamburger, potato skins, and spaghetti. She ate until her stomach was distended. Then she curled down beside the plate and slept.

When she woke, the diner was silent. No noise, no lights. She stared out from under the porch at the expanse of black-top. The shelter of parked cars was gone. She crouched in the blackness beneath the porch, watching and listening. She saw no movement, and she heard no sound to threaten her. Far in the distance thrummed the soft hoot of an owl.

She finished the potato skins and spaghetti, then chewed the greasy paper plate to remove every last bit of goodness.

She came out from under the stair pawing at her sore left eye and staring warily around the parking lot.

When she was certain that nothing threatened, she sat down in the center of the blacktop and began to wash her front paws and her face. Then she sat staring toward the south. From that direction something drew her. Faint, incomprehensible images touched her. Dark spaces beckoned. In her puzzled feline thoughts, stone caverns waited, and safety.

She rose and left the parking lot, trotting due south along the shoulder of the highway.

When trucks passed she veered into the tall grass. She passed under an occasional oak tree, and glanced up into its branches, where instinct told her height meant safety. When she came across the fresh scent of another cat she ran. She kept moving steadily, obsessed with the sense of deep, sheltering caverns somewhere ahead.

She traveled all night. By morning her left eye was matted and oozing, and the pads of her feet were beginning to crack. At first light, as the sky began to redden, she climbed, exhausted, into an oak tree. She curled into a concave where three branches met, and slept.

She came down at mid-morning, hungry again. The sense of stone caverns drew her on, she kept moving and did not turn aside to hunt; she knew little about hunting; a kitten must be taught by its mother to hunt with skill.

Late in the afternoon she approached an abandoned shack. She was very hungry. She watched the shack and listened for a quarter of an hour, then she crawled underneath it to rest. Here she stumbled on the scent of mice. Investigating, she discovered a mouse nest. She ate the six baby mice, then stalked the cobwebby darkness where the mouse smell was strongest.

She caught a grown mouse not sufficiently wary. She killed it quickly and ate it, but she caught no more. It was that night, when she tried to catch a rat, that she learned how viciously a small beast could attack, and learned how to fight her prey.

She had crossed a cut field through heavy stubble. In the center was a small trash dump, and as she explored the rubble for food she smelled the rat in a half-buried wooden crate. The crate smelled of celery and of spoiled meat. The rat was a big male, old and rough coated. He had survived dogs, and had killed his share of kittens. Deep inside the barrel, he had heard her coming a long way off, but he hadn't bothered to hide himself. Now he crouched, listening to her approach, staring out at her.

The cat circled the crate, watching the gleam of his red eyes. She moved to the entry, to block him from running out. She crouched, tensed to spring, ready for him.

When after a moment he didn't run, she moved in.

She was close to the rat when he charged. She dodged and lashed at him. He swerved and clamped his teeth on her paw, biting clear through. He hung on as the cat thrashed and fought, and gnawed her paw brutally. Then before she could bite him he loosed her, dodged, and leaped at her throat, biting deep. She struck at him with her claws, then sank her teeth in his flank, trying to pull him off her throat.

The rat had miscalculated his distance; he had only the skin of her throat, not the jugular. She managed to jerk him free, tearing a piece of skin from her throat. She shook him, swinging him, and in her terror she hit him again and again against the sides of the barrel.

The rat went limp. She turned it loose, to lick at her wounded paw. The rat came to life, leaping straight into her face. She clawed at it and tore it away. Enraged, she grabbed it by the neck and bit and gnawed until it died.

After it was dead she thrashed it against the crate floor, heaving and shaking it.

She ate the rat, then licked her wounded paw. There was nothing of Melissa apparent in the little beast; she was all cat, learning to care for herself. Yet somewhere within the little calico, too deep to be sensed by animal instincts, breathed another presence. Within the little cat something waited poised, watching, learning.

Her hunger eased, the calico left the dump and headed south.

It took her ten days to cover the miles Vrech had covered in a few hours. The country remained open, with tall grass, occasional trees, and scattered farm houses and shacks. At first she hunted, but as her wounded paw grew painful and bloated with infection, she began to search out the easy pickings at garbage cans and dumps. Twice near dumps, half-wild farm cats attacked her. The first time, she ran. The second time, she fought the two females. She came away bitten and hurting, but she had taken her share of the garbage. Her hurting foot made it hard to run fast enough to avoid dogs, but the scattered trees gave her refuge beyond a dog's domain. She learned to stay near the trees if she scented or heard a pack of dogs. At one promising garbage dump she faced a family of raccoons, and when the big male charged her she fled. It was the next morning that she approached a salt water inlet on the outskirts of a town.

Houseboats and fishing boats were tied up along the banks. Somewhere a radio played music, but she had learned that this kind of sound didn't threaten her. She smelled human waste from the houseboats, and she smelled food cooking. Beside a dock, she smelled fish offal. Very hungry, she approached the fish cleanings, prepared for a feast.

She did not see at first the three big female cats who were already maneuvering for position over the fish, snatching at it, snarling and striking at one another. With the music playing, she didn't hear them. One cat was heavy with kittens, the other two were in nursing condition. Left alone they would have shared the food out in their usual desperate way. Now they froze, staring at the intruder, hissing at her and threatening with low growls. But the calico, as she traveled, had grown bolder: these were only cats, not dogs. She approached them, stalking stiff-legged.

A female's ear twitched. A tail dropped, and all three crouched.

The three attacked her together. They had her down, clawing and biting her when a little girl, fishing at the other end of the dock, threw a bait bucket at them.

The three cats fled. The calico fled, too, limping, her swollen right front paw sending shooting pains up her leg. Running, she stopped often to lick the lump that had formed as each day the abscess grew larger and more painful.

Five days after the rat bit her she came to the outskirts of a town. Her white parts were dirty now, her white chest matted with grit and road oil. And, cowed by the pain in her foot and by fear, she carried her ears and her tail low.

She crossed the fields of a small farm, walked under its last fence and stood surveying the city street and the houses lining the opposite sidewalk. She was less afraid of houses now. Houses sometimes meant food, and she was ravenous.

Her swollen paw throbbed with pain, hurting so badly that even though she kept her foot lifted and walked on three paws, every movement sent jarring pain through her body.

Now at the edge of the town she crossed the street behind two slow-moving cars. On the other side she trotted, limping, across yards until she came to an alley. Because it was narrower than the street and more sheltered, she turned into it, walking on three legs.

She traveled the alley quickly, crossing each residential street, never faltering from her destination south. She passed houses and scattered stores, then more houses. She was halfway through the town, in a small cluster of stores, when she smelled fish and paused.

Warily she turned into a side alley and approached the back door of a bait shop.

She stared up at the screen door. The smell of fish was strong. Boldly she picked her way through scattered trash and up three dilapidated wooden steps.

Crouching to run, she stared in through the screen. Inside, a man was cutting up fish. When he turned and saw her, he banged his cleaver on the table and shouted. She fled, leaping down on all fours: the pain jarred like fire through her.

But the jolt broke the abscess. As she fled it began to drain, the pus oozing out.

She ran for two blocks before she crouched under a car, licking and licking her hurting, oozing paw.

Soon the pain grew less. When she left the shelter of the car she was walking on all fours.

By nightfall she was out of the town and in an open field dotted with oaks, and she had forgotten her wound. She caught and ate three field mice, then sheltered high in an oak tree, resting, coming down once more to hunt. Her hurt eye had begun to heal, and the itching annoyed her. Several hours after dark the full moon rose. Its pull made her giddy, she lay out along a branch watching it, letting its power tease her.

At last, filled to brimming with the moon's madness, she leaped down out of the tree and raced the meadow, running up another tree and down, and up another. In each tree she paused to stare at the sky and out at the moon-whitened field. Then she raced on again. And if, as she ran madly, visions touched her, if she sensed underground spaces, and if mysterious voices whispered, these disembodied experiences seemed little different to her than the disembodied voices coming from radios and juke boxes.

She left the meadow that night, traveling south beside the highway. And now as she hurried on, feeling well again, she stopped sometimes to bathe thoroughly, sleeking and fluffing her fur. And she played more. She was drawing near the place coded in her feline spirit as home.

When on the tenth day she left Highway 101, a sense of rightness made her leap along through the marshy meadow that flanked the narrower road. With kittenish abandon she gamboled, jumping puddles. Her dodging play through the marsh grass made it dance and tremble. When she caught a mouse almost by accident, she ate it quickly then ran on swiftly toward home. Drawing near the portal, her green eyes shone. She smelled home. She stopped to stand on her hind legs, peering away over the grass toward the far hill. She smelled the garden. She galloped on, and soon she smelled a faint turpentine and oil scent caught on the breeze, speaking to her of a particular house. Wildly she fled along the edge of the highway, then crouched and sped across between cars, shaken by the cars' wind as they passed her. On the other side she slipped into the briar tangle at the base of the hill.

She climbed the hill beneath the briars, using a path worn by other cats and by rabbits. At the top, she came out behind the center house. Her whiskers twitched with interest at its scent, and she stood looking. But she did not approach the house. She went on past it, up through the garden, alert for the cats whose scent marked this territory as theirs. She could smell, ahead, the cup-of-gold vine and the ancient door, and she approached eagerly.

Olive Cleaver, standing at her window looking out at the garden, glimpsed a flash of calico and white move between

the bushes. Startled, she waited for the cat to emerge.
Strange that a neighborhood cat would have the nerve to
come into this garden, where the other cats were so possessive. Strange that it was a calico. She had never seen a calico cat near the garden or in the neighborhood. The cat soon
appeared nearer her, higher up the hill. She watched it slip
through a tangle of nasturtiums and disappear beneath the
jasmine bush before the tool shed door. Olive put down her
book, watching for it to come out.

When the calico cat did not appear after a long time, Olive
thought it must be hunting under the bushes. Maybe it was a
stray and really hungry. She thought of taking some food
down to it. But gooseflesh touched her because it was a calico, and she changed her mind.

Annoyed with herself, she went into the kitchen to brew
herself a cup of tea, thinking that she made too much of
things, let her imagination run away with her.

Strange, though, that a stray calico cat would appear in
the garden, going directly to the tool shed, as if it knew the
place.

Chapter 25

Riding fast, Siddonie and her two companions galloped
along the Mathe-Wexten border followed by the queen's
small entourage and by two dozen warriors belonging to
King Ridgen. The three monarchs had been in the saddle
since dawn, inspecting caches of arms and food laid ready in
spell-hidden caves. Siddonie watched King Ridgen propri-
etarily. She liked the way he rode, with an easy elegance. He
was dark haired, sleek, with a knowing body and knowing

hands, whether handling a horse or a woman. By contrast,
the older king, Moriethsten, was altogether sloppy. He rode
like a bag of oats. His excess weight shifted with the gelding's movement, and his pale hair, bound in gold filigree,
bounced unbecomingly in time to the horse's canter. His
face was too soft featured, matching his soft, undisciplined
thoughts.

Still, he kept the record books well enough. Since daybreak they had examined twenty caves, checking over and
counting barrels of crackers and dried meat and water, and
blankets and weapons and upperworld medical supplies.
Other caches waited farther on where Wexten spanned beneath upperworld waters. But now, though the stores must
be inspected, her mind was only half on the preparations
for war.

She was unable to dismiss her uneasiness about Melissa.
She knew Vrech had set the cat adrift in the upperworld, and
that should be the end of it. With luck, the cat was already
conveniently dead, rotting in some field. A natural death, for
which she could not by the Primal Law be blamed. Yet now
when she remembered Melissa as a small child, a certain remorse touched her.

She wondered if Melissa had already been pregnant with
Efil's child when she caught them in bed. Rage at Efil made
her boot the stallion and jerk his reins. Efil had been far too
bold to bed that girl. He had ruined a good many plans, and
he would pay for it.

Melissa's death was particularly bad timing. She must be
replaced now, quickly, and the chosen Catswold girl must be
trained to lead a Catswold army. They would have to quickly
find among the upperworld Catswold they had captured
some likely half-breed girl. A girl who had inherited some
latent talent for magic and could be trained to the task. The
result would not be as satisfying as having Melissa, but at
least an upperworld Catswold girl would be easier to handle
than Melissa.

The upperworld Catswold, strays from San Francisco's
streets, had not yet been allowed to take human form. They

must first be committed totally to the Catswold queen before they learned the changing spell and learned what they really were. They must be willing to fight for, and die for, that queen.

She moved her stallion up beside Ridgen as the trail widened. Soon, too, there would be the changeling boy to train, to teach how to behave like Prince Wylles. A boy to be turned into Prince Wylles, a healthy boy to insure her title to the throne.

The land around them was bare here, and craggy. It would grow nothing. There was no village, not one cottage. Even the most skilled growing spells would hardly bring a green spear. When she glanced at Ridgen, the dark king gave her a slow, promising smile. Beside him, Moriethsten noticed nothing; the man was as dull as a turnip. She was pleased that the pretty young queen of Chillings would not be joining them. She hadn't liked her, though she had thought her loyal until the girl was caught sending supplies to Zzadarray. Under the acts of war, the Primal Law against killing didn't hold. Likely the young queen's people were busy this day burying her. Siddonie considered the choices for a new ruler. Chillings should have a king—men were easier to handle.

Ahead, the stone sky rose abruptly, layered and ragged. Slivers of stone lay in their path where the sky had flaked and crumbled. She could see ahead, down the sloping, stony hills, the isolated inn: a dark, sprawling group of rock buildings forming the tri-border where Mathe, Wexten, and Saurthen joined. The horses began to fuss, sensing food and shelter ahead. As they came down the last expanse of stone, a dozen grooms ran out to take their reins.

Siddonie's soldiers dismounted and helped with the animals. They would join the grooms for ale in the inn's cellar, to glean whatever intelligence they could.

Soon Siddonie and the two kings were sipping spell-chilled ale in the small, intimate dining hall before the inn's fire. Ridgen and Moriethsten, discussing troop movements, quieted when the red-faced elven innkeeper returned with their meal of rare venison and roast quail. Siddonie watched the small, square innkeeper refill her stein, keeping the

pewter white-cold with a local elven charm. When the steins
were full Ridgen toasted her, dark-eyed and ardent, Moriethsten joining him innocently.

But Moriethsten was skillful in other ways, and reliable as
long as she kept close check on him. Their mutual cousins
staffed his palace in key positions. She had put Moriethsten
on the throne after the old king was unfortunately discovered selling Wexten children into Cathenn slavery and was
driven from the palace by a mob of enraged peasants. Very
nicely handled, in Vrech's usual style.

A metallic racket began. She watched, annoyed, as three
musicians strolled out from a curtained alcove with half a
dozen dancing girls around them—nearly naked girls dressed
in upperworld spangles. Ridgen and Moriethsten ogled them
until Siddonie caused Ridgen to choke, and caused both men
to find the girls dreary. Both kings turned away with bored
glances and returned to their discussion of war tactics.

When they had conquered Ferrathil and Cressteane, they
would move south. Once the south was won, they would destroy the eastern nations. "I want the Catswold finished," she
said softly.

Moriethsten pushed back a strand of pale hair. "When we
move east, our armies will be dangerously cut off from the
beltland."

"No," Siddonie corrected him. "We will not go through
the tunnel. We will draw the Catswold out to attack us."

The nations of Zzadarray, Ebenth, Cathenn, and Marchell,
Catswold dominated, were separated from the eleven belt
nations by the Hell Pit and by dense masses of stone passable only through a long, tedious tunnel. It would be suicide
to attack those nations on their own ground, the Catswold
had turned those peoples totally intractable. Siddonie traveled there seldom. She did not like the slow smiles of the
Catswold. She would not tolerate her horses being mysteri-
ously set loose, and her soldiers' weapons suddenly dulled
and broken.

It had taken her a long time to develop a suitable plan to
defeat the Catswold.

Several years ago she had purchased, with some manipulation, the hundred acres of cattle land in the upperworld, where there was an unused portal which led down through three miles of old gold mines and tunnels into Zzadarray. It was that portal through which, generations ago, many Catswold had emigrated to the upperworld. Now, very soon, Havermeyer would complete purchase of the old Victor mine, then the portal would be on her own land, a direct route into the Catswold nation of Zzadarray.

The Catswold didn't use the tunnel much now; their fascination with the upperworld seemed to have palled.

She regretted that upperworld weapons wouldn't operate in the Netherworld. If they would, she could wipe out Zzadarray in minutes, win the entire Netherworld in a matter of hours. She had, when she was quite young, sent pack animals down into the Netherworld laden with gunpowder and modern arms. But the old laws had held. Once in the Netherworld nothing would function; the gunpowder was as useless as sand. The Primal Spells, like the wizards who had laid them, were of incredible power.

The spell of light was needed, of course. But the spell that discouraged killing in the Netherworld except for official war was tedious, unwieldy, and outdated; the spell that would let no upperworld machine or mechanical device function was an abomination.

The dancing girls and musicians had gone. The fire had been built up and their mugs had been refilled. Siddonie raised a toast to their success, and saw Ridgen's color deepen. Under the table he stroked her hand as he lifted his glass in toast. But in spite of his touch, she was still thinking of Melissa.

If the cat accidentally survived, there was always the possibility that she could break the spell and free herself.

Though if she did, what matter? What damage could one Catswold do without training? Likely Melissa did not even know her powers. And likely she had no knowledge of the Amulet, or its considerable power.

And surely that gem was lost, inaccessible.

It was nineteen years ago that Siddonie had climbed the dark tunnel out of Xendenton beside Ithilel and his Catswold wife—Melissa's mother. She had thought then that Timorell had the Amulet, but later, searching Timorell's upperworld room and her possessions, she had found nothing.

After the earthquake she had searched the bodies of Timorell and McCabe, and had gone through the wreckage of McCabe's apartment. She had even searched the baby's clothes and its crib.

She had hated taking care of the baby; she didn't like babies. And what a difficult baby Melissa had been—mewling and spitting up. When she took her to the welfare people, she had meant to get her back when the child was old enough to be trained properly in magic. Even after Alice Kitchen's family took her, she had thought she could get the child any time.

She had tried, during those years, to establish some closeness with Melissa. Every trip she made to the city, she visited the child. She had done all she could to shape her thoughts and create some rapport with her. The child had been difficult even when she was small, so typically Catswold—stubborn, willful, and flighty, bursting into tears of terror for no reason. Then the problem had arisen with the Catswold Portal, and that was a situation that had seemed far more than coincidence.

That portal had been forgotten for generations. Havermeyer discovered it when he followed Alice Kitchen and the child. It had seemed a fortuitous find, entering down directly into Affandar as it did. She had, at that time, just begun to court eleven-year-old Efil of Affandar. She had been twenty-four.

Once Havermeyer found the Catswold Portal, they had used it regularly. But then Havermeyer, approaching it one afternoon, had stumbled upon Alice Kitchen making a drawing of it. He had pretended to admire her work, and Alice had told him, in the typically candid way of upperworlders, that she thought the door was ancient and that she meant to trace its history.

Siddonie sipped her ale, frowning. She had gone up through the tunnel herself the next day, to get Melissa out of there before Alice Kitchen learned too much about the portal, and perhaps began to suspect things about the child. It had been time to bring the girl down anyway. She was twelve years old and should begin training.

She remembered that day sharply. When she came out of the tunnel into the tool cave, the child was playing just outside the open door, in the garden. Siddonie had spell-bound her easily, had picked her up, and had carried her back through the wall when someone cast a spell over her. She went dizzy and felt the child pulled out of her arms.

She had remained trapped for hours in a spell as confining as stone, slumped at the end of the tunnel, unconscious, knowing nothing. When she regained her senses, she was certain the child had been taken down to the Netherworld. Then as she followed the tunnel down, she found behind a boulder some bread crusts where someone had eaten—smooth, commercially baked upperworld crusts. And beside these, a dark spot of earth had smelled sweet, as if some child's drink such as Grape Kool-Aid had been spilled.

Once in the Netherworld again, she had launched a thorough search for Melissa, but the child could not be found.

And in the upperworld Alice Kitchen began a search, too. It was later that she—Alice West by then—began to investigate the portal.

Vrech had taken care of Alice smoothly enough, crossing the Primal Laws only in a small way: a fear-spell that touched the truck driver, causing a swerve. That had been a long shot that had paid off.

Siddonie started as Ridgen squeezed her hand. She had been a long way off. Ridgen warmed her with a deep look. She winked back at him, and he smiled.

"The fire is dying. The chambers have been aired and warmed," he said.

As they watched Moriethsten, Ridgen's eyes narrowed, weaving a sleep-spell over the Wexten king—a simple enough charm when handling one person, though near impossible when dealing with a mob. Moriethsten yawned and began to nod.

Siddonie rose, taking Ridgen's arm. The two of them moved toward the stair, amused by Moriethsten asleep with his head on the table.

Chapter 26

In the Hell Pit the Harpy basked among flames, easing quickly again into her old habits. Her memories of the upperworld faded. She mingled with the hell-cast souls of the dead and whispered the grim songs of the dead, and nearly forgot the vibrant goodness of the living. Old lusts gripped her. Depression and anger drugged her; soon she was wallowing in all manner of depravity.

Only slowly did her preoccupation with the morose and sullen begin to pale, only slowly did the excesses of the damned begin to lose their charm, and the dead began to seem dull. At last the Harpy grew restless and began to think that warm, living people were more interesting. On a damp night when the Hell fires sulked and smoked, the Harpy looked deep into her mirror.

She saw Melissa climbing the vines at the back of Affandar Palace. She saw her fight the king's embrace, saw the queen storm in. She saw Siddonie change Melissa to cat, and she saw Mag agonizing beside the girl's cage, trying to free her. She saw Mag captured.

The Harpy watched Mag huddle shivering in the Toad's old cell, her round, wrinkled face pulled into despair. And when the Harpy tried to sleep, she could not.

What was it about this old woman that drew her sympathy? The Harpy was uncertain about leaving the Hell Pit. But she could leave. Siddonie's spell, that had originally freed her, was still strong.

She stood wakeful, pecking irritably at the flames and coals. Why shouldn't she go? Nothing bound her here. She would not admit even to herself how totally boring the Hell Pit seemed to her now.

When at last she rose, flapping, she headed straight for Affandar.

Three hours later in Siddonie's dungeons, a white wing swept against Mag's cage. A white arm reached through, and a thin hand shook Mag awake.

Mag stared muzzily into the white bird face as the Harpy whispered a spell that swung the door free. Waking fully, Mag quickly quit the cage, following the Harpy silently. The womanbird, excited over her increased strength over Siddonie's weakening spell, flapped and preened. She led Mag deep into the cellars, where she mumbled a charm that opened a pillar. Mag followed her down a thin flight of stairs and along a low tunnel. As they traveled, ducking, Mag sniffed the Harpy's smoky, sulphurous scent. "How was the Pit?"

"Warm. Lovely."

They walked a while in silence, then Mag said, "Why did you come away? Why did you rescue me?"

"The bitch queen took my mirror."

"That's no answer. You have your mirror."

"By freeing you, I am paying her back for my suffering."

"Am I that valuable to the queen?"

"She detests you."

Mag smiled. "And where is Melissa? What is happening to Melissa?"

The Harpy didn't answer. Walking ahead of Mag she looked down into her little mirror and saw the calico cat limping along beside the highway, thin and dirty. She saw the little cat in the garden staring up at the portal, her green eyes huge.

But the danger wasn't over. The cat remembered nothing; she was innocent and half-helpless.

"Well?" Mag said. "What of Melissa?"

"I can show you nothing."

"What do you mean, you can show me nothing?"

"If I gave you a vision you'd know where she was. You'd go barreling away to rescue her. She is best left alone."

"But what is happening to her?"

"She is resourceful," said the Harpy. "Trust me." She ran her fingers through her white feathers. "She is utterly content at the moment."

They had reached the stairs. They climbed and came out into Circe's Grotto. Mag caught her breath at its beauty, and she wanted to tarry and look, but the Harpy, pressing cold fingers into Mag's arm, shoved her on. The womanbird opened the wall and pushed Mag through, and they moved quickly away through the night-dark woods.

Chapter 27

Stiff-legged, the cat stalked the door, her eyes burning with green fire, her tail lashing against the bushes and vines. Warily she watched the cats' heads: they were not alive but there was life in them. She drew close then leaped away, then skidded toward them again, ignoring the clamor of the garden birds. Drawn to the oak cats, she reached a paw toward something invisible that seemed to move beyond the door, then, confused, turned quickly to lick her shoulder. But the vision amused her. She stared up at the door again, giddy, and rolled over, grabbing her tail, spinning and tumbling, her eyes flashing. Madly she played with the power she sensed. Leaping onto the vine that edged the door, she swarmed up it, drunk with the forces that pulled at her. She didn't see the garden cats on the hill above where they crouched watching her.

The five cats stared down, frozen with interest. They crept closer as the calico reached the top of the vine, watching her, stealthy as snipers. At the top of the vine she did a flip, then worked her way down again, slapping at the leaves. She leaped out of the vine at the base of the door and sat before it, ready for the door to open, willing it to open.

When it didn't open she rubbed against it. When it remained closed she pushed at it with her shoulder, then began to dig at the crack beneath, rolling down and thrusting her paw under.

When digging failed, she reared up on her hind legs and reached for the lowest row of snarling oak faces and raked her claws down them in long, satisfying scratches. When still the door didn't open, she turned away, pretending total boredom, and selected a shelter deep beneath the overgrown geraniums.

In the cool dark she stretched out full length, digging her claws into the earth, then lay washing herself. Drawing her barbed tongue across bright fur, she soon eased into a contented rhythm of purrs and tongue strokes. Soon she slept, exhausted from her long journey. The garden cats came down the hill and circled her. One by one they sniffed at her, then turned away puzzled. The big orange tom stayed a long time staring at her. The sun dropped behind the woods. The sky held a last smear of brilliance, then the garden darkened. The wind came up off the bay blowing branches and vines, but the calico slept on. She didn't hear the tool shed door push open. At first sign of the hunch-shouldered man, the orange cat bristled and fled. In sleep the calico smelled something unpleasant and her ears went flat and she curled up tighter, but she didn't wake.

Vrech stood in the low doorway staring around the garden, watching for activity in the six houses. The lights were on above in Morian's house. At Olive Cleaver's, only the porch light burned, suggesting that the old woman had gone out. In the low white Cape Cod, just the living room was lit. This was Anne Hollingsworth's night to work late. Likely Olive Cleaver was sitting with the boy. Tom would be asleep, suffering from the fever his mother thought was the flu.

Below, the yellow house on the left was dark. It was Wednesday, the Blakes' bridge night. He watched the center house as West left his easel and went down the short hall to the kitchen, likely to fix himself a drink. To the right of West's, the musician's house had lights on in the bedroom and bath. Wednesday was jazz night; soon those lights would go out and John the clarinetist would go up across the garden to Sam's Bar.

Vrech smiled. Olive Cleaver's hearing wasn't sharp, and the wind was making plenty of noise. With wind moving the foliage, he might never be noticed; he might seem just another blowing shadow.

He watched John cross the garden with his clarinet case, but decided to wait a few minutes more. Maybe the artist's model would go across to the tavern, and maybe West as well. They were both jazz freaks. Jazz made him nervous; he didn't call it music.

When neither Morian nor West came out, he grew impatient. Stepping back inside the door, he lifted his burden, bound in the burlap bag, easing its weight across his shoulder.

He left his lantern burning behind him on the tool table, pulled the door to, but not closed, and made his way up the terraces. The drugged prince was a heavy weight, and he was already tired from carrying Wylles up the tunnel.

He had neared the white house when the screams of trumpet and sax cut the night. The band was warming up; that would cover any sound he might make. As he moved in between the bushes beside Tom's window, something crashed past him, yowling. Damn cat.

He hid his bundle in the bushes, watching the house and thinking about the cat he had left on the highway. He saw it in his mind as the girl—a sexy creature. Suddenly another cat sped past his feet. They were all over the garden tonight—moonlight made them crazy.

He moved to the window and looked into the living room. Yes, skinny old Olive Cleaver was there reading a book. He returned to Tom's darkened window and felt with sensitive fingers for the hinges he had loosened earlier.

The blaring of loud, dissonant horns jerked the little calico awake and on her feet, cringing at the noise, staring with terror at the swaying, tossing garden. In the blowing moonlight the carved cats on the door seemed alive, and she reared up, looking at them with widening eyes. At that moment, the wind fingered open the door, exposing a crack of light. She stared at it and crept forward.

She sniffed the cat faces but was drawn, too, by the light space beyond the door; and by falling spaces on beyond the light. She hesitated, then she pushed through the door into the tool room, moving directly past the wheelbarrow and ladder to the stone wall, and stood looking up expectantly. She pressed her shoulder to the wall, then pawed at it. She was clawing hard at the stone when Vrech returned carrying his bundle. The cat tasted his scent and spun to face him. Her back pulled into an arch, her teeth bared in a spitting yowl.

Vrech set down his burden, swearing, wondering how the hell she had found her way back. He shoved the bundle against the wall, making sure Tom was too far gone to cry out, then closed in on the cat. When he lunged, she leaped clear.

He worked her into the corner behind the wheelbarrow. She darted past, upsetting two oil lamps and breaking a chimney.

He was sweating and furious by the time he caught her. She had clawed him in three long wounds; his hands and arms were bleeding. He grabbed a gunnysack and shoved her into it, but before he could close it she sank her teeth into his wrist. He knocked her loose, pushed her deeper in, then tied the bag and threw it against the door.

He barked a guttural opening spell that sent the wall swinging back, lifted Tom inside, laid the boy on the cold stone, and left him there.

Closing the wall, he picked up the sack with the cat inside and moved out into the blowing garden. He had to get rid of the beast; he dare not leave it so close to the portal for fear Siddonie would learn of it.

He'd leave it somewhere where it had a chance for life. That was all that was required. He wasn't carrying it back up the cursed highway.

He decided to buy a Greyhound ticket in the village, watch the bag loaded on as luggage, then disappear. Let the driver worry about what to do with it. One bus went clear to Coos Bay. He'd have a drink first, there was plenty of time. The Greyhound schedules were common knowledge in the village, and the Coos Bay bus didn't leave for two hours. He hoisted the cat to his shoulder, snuffed the lantern, and headed across the road. He didn't like the music at Sam's, but he liked to watch the women who came there.

Chapter 28

Basin Street jazz drowned the wind in the garden. The beat was solid, the music at once weeping and happy—primal music like a deep heartbeat. Braden, drowning in the good jazz, turned off the overhead studio lights and crossed the blowing moonlit garden, heading for Sam's.

He paused beside the tool room door, watching wind shake the door and whip the vine that grew around it. Feeling spooked, he wanted to move on, yet was held a moment watching the blowing shadows that raced across the garden, shadows running like live things. In the restless light the carved cats' faces seemed to move and change. Then from Sam's a blast of trumpet and trombone rose against the wind. And the wind leaping from tree to tree suddenly stilled.

The shadows stopped running. The garden was silent, deadly still.

Elder wind. It's an elder wind . . .

The term shocked him, surprised him. It was a term his Gram had used, a Welsh term from her girlhood. He hadn't thought of it since she died.

He could see her beside him standing on the rocks above the sea, the wind whipping her carroty hair, her arm around him because he was small and the wind was strong, wind that died, then suddenly blew again, throwing salt spray in their faces. "An elder wind," she said.

"What's that, Gram?"

"An elder wind can speak to you, if you know how to listen."

"How do you listen? I don't understand."

She had laughed, enjoying the wild evening. "You listen with something inside, the part of you that knows things."

"But what would an elder wind say?"

"Something of the future, something that's going to happen." Then, seeing his expression, she had said, "Something good. Something—beyond everyday things. Something—not everyone can hear."

He stood in the blowing garden, lost in that time that was forever gone. Lost to those he loved who were gone. Then, scowling at himself, he went on across the lane toward the warmth and the good, pure Dixieland. Above him the redwood forest loomed deep black, rattling and hushing as the wind once more tore at its branches.

Sam's Bar was an old converted house, dark shingled, nestled alone against the redwood forest. It had no neon and needed no advertising. Its patrons parked in the lane or on the skirt of blacktop by the front door, or left their cars at home. Inside, walls had been removed to allow for a sprawling openness with quiet corners, and to make space for the bandstand. You could get dark stout on draft, and hardboiled eggs pickled in pale, hot pepper juice. You could get bock beer in the spring, and during legal crabbing months you could get a sandwich made of green olives and crab fresh from the San Francisco fleets. Sam, ex-stevedore, jazz buff, was a good listener, and held within his graying head half the secrets of the village.

Braden threaded between the cars parked tightly around Sam's front door, and stood a moment awash in the plaintive, hypnotic rhythm of "Joe Avery's Blues." The porch was ten feet wide, with four steps leading up to it, and a dark wooden door with a small stained glass panel.

Inside, the room was warm, smoky, booze-smelling, and rocking with the gut-twisting music. He checked the bar, nodded to the band. Sam poured him a whisky, grinning through a short fringe of grizzled beard. The main room was to Braden's right. There was a good blaze in the fireplace. Long windows faced the windy, moonlit forest. Morian and Bob were at the corner table. Carrying his glass, he joined them. He took the chair in the corner, laying a hand companionably over Morian's. She was dressed in something white and low that showed off her beautiful umber skin. She was tall, not fat, but the sort of woman who, nude on the model stand, made fashionably skinny women look incomplete. After Morian, no model seemed worth drawing. No other model had the beautiful bones, the fine, long muscles and gorgeous breasts, the subtle turnings of shadows to study and capture and linger over. Her dark skin picked up reds, ambers: dark velvet skin clothing itself in deep lights and rich shadows, so any other clothing seemed out of place. She studied Braden.

"Work going badly, Brade?"

He looked at her; she always knew. She had been good friends with Alice, had always cared about their work, was a good critic. It was an experience to watch Morian rise from the model stand at break, slip on a wrap, walk around the classroom studying the work. A comment from Morian was always perceptive and valuable. She hugged a lot, companionably, as she admired and questioned. Low and velvet and fine, Morian was like a dark, rich sun rising in soft brilliance whenever she entered a classroom.

She watched him closely. "I suppose Rye's been over."

Braden nodded. "I told him to cancel the show."

Morian scowled.

Bob leaned back in his chair, watching them. He was smaller than Morian, a well-knit man. Sandy hair, a look in his hazel eyes that was sometimes too understanding—that was the trouble with shrinks. He was seldom without Leslie in the evenings—trim, tanned Leslie—except when she worked late doing the endless paperwork of the small village library. "That's pretty heavy, Brade. Rye's likely to take you up on it."

Braden gave him a questioning look.

Morian said, "Rye was over at school today. To see Garcheff's new work."

Braden put down his drink, instantly defensive. "He thinks I won't get the work together. He's planning to slip Garcheff in." And he knew that wasn't fair.

Morian said, "But you told him to cancel the show."

Now for the first time he didn't want to cancel. "Hell, I guess I had it coming." He reached for his drink, and spilled it.

They helped him mop up the whisky with paper napkins, stuffing them in the ashtray. Morian said, "You have almost two months. You aren't letting Garcheff take your date." She laid her hand over his, giving him a black velvet look, a soothsayer's look. Bob looked away, half embarassed, then left the table, muttering something about peanuts; Braden felt a quick, fleeting amusement because Bob was so straight. The band swung into "Just a Little While to Stay Here." The heat of the music drew them closer. Morian started to say something, then stared past him across the room, frowning. When she kept staring, he turned to look.

The gardener was sitting by the door. Vrech. The dark, hunched man was alone at a small table against the wall. Morian watched him intently.

"What the hell are you looking at?"

"That bag under his table," she said quietly.

"It's just an old gunnysack. What do you think he's got, Olive's jewelry?"

"It moved."

He hadn't seen it move.

She put her hand on his knee. "Keep looking—he's got something alive in there." Her eyes flashed. "You don't stuff a live creature into a gunnysack." She was getting worked up; it didn't take much.

"Listen, Mor—" He took her arm to keep her from getting up. "Wait a minute. At least be sure. What could he have?" He hadn't seen the bag so much as flinch.

Bob returned with pretzels, two beers, and a bourbon. "That's A'Plenty" ended in a high riff, the trumpet player mouthed inaudible words and they launched into "Salty Dog." Bob looked at Braden and at Morian's stormy face, and shifted his chair so he could glance across at the gardener.

Braden said, "She thinks the bag moved. Listen, Mor, just sit still a minute. What could he have?"

Morian picked up her purse. "There's something alive in there. What does he—he was in the tool room all afternoon with the door closed. Until after dark. He came out carrying a bundle—not that one, a big bundle. And now he has something alive. He's caught some poor animal . . ."

Bob looked mildly skeptical.

She scowled at him. "There's something in the bag. And he was in the shed for hours; I could see the door from where I was sewing. I saw him come out, but I never did see him go in."

Braden drained his glass and reached for the drink, amused at Morian. "You must have looked away once or twice."

"It takes more time than a glance away to go across the garden. I was watching the door." She looked faintly embarrassed. "The door seems to draw me. I see anything that moves around it. Vrech didn't go in while I was sewing. He came out well after dark, carrying a big, awkward bundle. The band was here, I could hear them warming up. Vrech came up across the garden carrying the bundle over his shoulder, then the moon went behind a cloud. When it cleared he was gone. I changed, made a phone call, and came on over. And there he was ordering a beer."

Bob shifted his chair again so he could prop his feet on the one next to him and see the gardener more easily.

Braden said, "Alice felt that way about the door."

Morian nodded. "I know."

When Bob left to meet Leslie, the bag had still not moved. Morian wouldn't leave. They sat quietly talking about the show at the de Young, obliquely watching the gardener. They avoided talking about Braden's paintings. Their hands touched as they worked up comfortably to a night at his place; it had been a long time. The band was into "Tailgate Ramble" when the bag moved again; they both saw it twitch then twist, as if something inside had flopped over. When Vrech prodded it with his toe, it lay still. But Morian was up, easing around the table. "I heard a cat cry. He has a cat in there." She stared at Braden, eyes flashing. "One of our cats?" He watched her, half amused, and followed her, hoping this wasn't going to turn into a brawl.

The gardener watched Morian coldly. When she knelt reaching for the bag, he snatched it from her and stood up swinging it away. The bag began to thrash and yowl. Vrech pushed Morian out of the way and spun past them out the door. Morian lunged after him. Braden could do nothing but go with her. He grabbed Vrech, swinging him around, and Morian jerked the bag from his hands. The rest was a tangle. Vrech punched Braden in the face, the cat screamed and raked Braden's cheek through the bag, then Vrech had the bag again, running. Morian ran after him; Braden, his jaw hurting, caught a glimpse of her face raging mad. He could only stay with her, knowing this was insane. As they crashed through the wood he gained on Vrech and tackled him running. He threw the bag clear, jabbing his knee in the man's belly.

Holding the gardener down, he watched Morian tear at
the bag, fighting the knots. Whatever was in there flopped
and fought. Every time Vrech tried to jerk free, Braden
twisted his arm tighter. He stared down at the man's angry
face, surprised that Vrech was so strong. He felt a powerful
distaste at touching the man; he wanted suddenly to flatten
that leering face.

"It's open. Oh Brade . . ."

A cat looked out, crouching and terrified. Its ears were
laid flat, its eyes immense with fear. Its face was part mottled dark, part white. As the wind hit it, it ducked down. But
when it saw Vrech it exploded out of the bag, clawing Morian's hand, leaped away, and ran. Like a streak it disappeared within the dark woods. Morian rose to chase after it,
then turned back.

"She was terrified, Brade. If I chase her she'll run forever."

He looked at her, exasperated. "What the hell am I going
to do with the gardener? What the hell are we doing out
here?" He was drained suddenly, and perplexed. Something
about the gardener sickened him. The man was tense as a
spring—he knew if he let up only a little, Vrech would be
all over him. He didn't feel like fighting anymore. His jaw
was already swelling and his fist felt like it was broken.
"Christ, Mor . . ." But she wasn't paying attention; she was
staring off into the woods looking for the damned cat. The
way the wind was tearing at the bushes, no one could see a
cat running.

"It was hardly more than a kitten, Brade. Little white
throat and paws. It was terrified." She turned on Vrech, her
black eyes blazing. "What did you want with it? What were
you going to do to it?"

The gardener glared and didn't answer. His dark eyes
were chilling, there was a strangeness about him that made
Braden force him harder against the earth.

Morian moved closer, touching Braden's shoulder. "Let
him up, Brade. The cat's gone—he won't catch her. Let
him go."

He didn't want to let him go, he wanted to pound him.

"Brade, let him go."

Unwillingly he loosed Vrech, ready to pulverize him if he so much as looked sideways.

Vrech moved away from him quickly, and headed back down through the blowing woods toward Sam's. He looked back at them once. In the darkness Braden couldn't see his face. The lights through the bar's windows illuminated his slouching walk, then he was gone around the building, heading toward the lane.

"Brade, go ask Sam for some hamburger. I'll go up in the woods, maybe she'll come to me. I think she's hurt. I couldn't tell, she fled so fast." She touched his face. "I can't just let her go, if she's hurt. Go on, Brade—cooked hamburger."

In the bar he got some hamburger scraps and two double whiskeys, and borrowed a flashlight from Sam.

It wasn't hard to find Morian in her blowing white dress, standing beside the spring. She took the hamburger, spread the wrapper out and weighted it with broken branches. She led him some distance away, into a shelter of wild azalea where the wind didn't reach them so strongly. "Talk softly, maybe the sound of our voices will soothe her. Maybe once she eats, she'll come to us."

He felt ridiculous sitting in the middle of the woods waiting for a cat. Alice would be very amused. He wondered what the gardener had been going to do with it. "Why do you think it's a female?"

"Most calico's are. And that little face—very female."

He didn't know how she could be sure—it was just a cat. Frightened, though, and young. Its eyes had been huge. "It won't come to you, Mor. It was too scared. Christ, what are we doing out here?"

"Just a little while, Brade."

They sat in silence, their hands touching, chilled by the wind, waiting for a stray cat. She said, "It hurts me to see them like that, so afraid, and maybe injured. They're so small; they weren't meant for our cruelty. Tiger—he was so terribly hurt. I couldn't help him. The vet says they go into shock, that they don't feel the pain. I don't know." Her hand was holding his too tightly. "I couldn't help him live, all I could do was help him die."

He looked at her and said nothing. She had the same empathy for animals that Alice had had, a deep, intimate fellowship that he had never really felt and found hard to understand. After a long time she said, "I guess she isn't going to come near the food while we're here. Poor little thing. I wonder where she came from, where she belongs."

"She's just a stray cat, Mor."

She gave him a hard look. "There's no such thing as just a stray cat." Then she grinned at him. "Are you just a stray person?" She rose and stood looking into the black woods. "The wind makes her all the more frightened. Maybe if I put out food tomorrow when it's calm, she'll come to me." She took his hand and they started down through the woods heading for his place.

The calico stalked the meat, but not until Braden and Morian had been gone for some time did she come near enough to gulp it. She ate all the hamburger, then drank from the spring, stopping several times to stare in the direction of the garden.

She was both drawn to the garden and afraid. She approached and shied away five times before she had worked her way down to the portal. Shivering, she smelled Vrech's scent in the door and leaped away again, but she did not head back to the woods. She bolted down the hill toward the brick veranda, sensing safety there.

She avoided the lighted portion of the veranda where yellow squares from the windows angled across the brick, and took cover in the bushes at the far end. Safe in the familiar shelter, she washed, circled deep in the dry leaves and curled down, tucking her nose under her tail. With her white parts hidden, even in the invading washes of moonlight she looked like part of the dry leaves, her mottled coat the same color as the leaves.

Her dreams were filled with fear. She mewled some-times, and her paws twitched and ran. But then as she slept more deeply the dreams became unclear to her cat nature. Meaningless dramas were played out, voices and scenes touched her which only the conscious Melissa would have understood.

Chapter 29

Braden was pulled out of a deep sleep, fighting to get his bearings. A sound had woken him—a scratching, clawing noise. Coming awake, he tried to figure out why he was sleeping on the model's couch. Then he remembered, and reached for Morian. The next moment he came fully awake and saw that she had gone—her clothes were gone. He could smell coffee; she had made coffee. The scratching sound was like fingernails on glass. He stared toward the window wall.

There was a cat out there, rearing up, scratching at the glass. It was the cat from last night; the cat they'd sat up half the night trying to catch. The one he'd bruised his fist for. What was it doing here? He didn't believe it was trying to get in through his door.

The cat had woken before daylight. The wind was gone. The garden was littered with broken branches, and birds flitted across them, searching for insects. She had started out from the bushes to hunt when a sound from the house made her draw back.

A figure had come out, her white dress rustling. She had crossed the veranda and headed up the hill, her scent on the still air familiar and comforting. The little cat rose to follow her, but then she glanced again toward the studio and settled down, yawning and stretching. She was dozing when a sparrow flew onto the veranda.

It took her some time to maneuver the sparrow into position. Skillfully she pounced, bit it behind the head, carried it into the bushes, and ate it. This morsel stirred her hunger, and she began to watch the studio. There was food there— she had gotten food there. Her green eyes blazed as she slipped out of the bushes onto the veranda and peered in through the glass door. She pressed against the door, and when no one came to let her in, she began to claw at it.

The door didn't open. Nothing moved inside. She clawed harder. Soon a figure moved on the couch.

The man stretched, and the cat backed away. But the next minute she pressed at the glass again, looking in sideways, her whiskers flattened in white lines across her cheek. She had received food in that room; she had known warmth and shelter in there, and love. Layers of her nature surfaced, layers of Melissa's childhood, but to the cat, she simply needed to be in there.

When the man didn't come to let her in, she raked again impatiently. She saw him swing his feet to the floor.

He couldn't believe this. The cat was staring in, raking its claws insolently down the glass. Why wasn't it still afraid? Why had it come down here? A chill touched him. What the hell did it want? As it reared up, its belly shone white against the glass. Its mottled and white face seemed curiously intent, its green eyes demanding. He snatched up a museum catalog and threw it hard at the glass. The cat stopped clawing. But it didn't run; it looked angry, almost looked incensed.

Maybe it smelled Morian, maybe had followed her because she fed it, maybe it thought she was in here. He pulled on his shorts, got a cup of coffee, sucking in the first sip, and went to shower and shave. The cat would be gone when he came out. He slammed the bathroom door on the sound of its claws.

When he came out the cat was still there. But it wasn't scratching now, it was mewling. He rushed at the door shouting, flung it open, and chased the cat into the bushes.

He put the canvas of *Natalie at Summer* on the easel, poured out turpentine and oil, got a fresh cup of coffee, and stood back to study the painting. Then, squeezing half a dozen tubes onto the palette, he got to work; softening Natalie's face and the purple shadow across her forehead, working in Indian Red, toning down the umbrella and its shadow across her shoulder. At some point the cat came back and began yowling stridently and clawing again. He wanted to throw the easel at it.

He worked steadily, ignoring the sound until his stomach began to growl either from frustration at the noise or from hunger. He refilled his coffee cop and stood in the hall looking at the painting. It was coming to life—there was warmth now. This was the one he'd wanted most to make right, the one Morian had looked at longest last night, though she had said nothing.

The cat was suddenly so quiet he looked up, hoping it was gone. It stared back at him, its green eyes huge and demanding. Christ, he and Morian had spent half the night waiting in the woods for the damned cat. It wouldn't come then, so why was it down here now, trying to get in? He went into the kitchen, started some bacon, and broke four eggs into a bowl. When he turned the skillet down he could hear the cat yowling.

Why the hell didn't it go to Morian's? She was the one who wanted to feed it and mother it. He went out to chase it off, but this time it didn't run. When he shouted it stood at the edge of the terrace looking so determined he almost laughed. For a little thing, it had a hell of a nerve.

Alice said cats went to the people who disliked them, that they found that amusing. He smelled the bacon burning, made a dash for the kitchen and flipped it onto a plate, swearing. He washed the skillet and started over, then turned the bacon low and went to phone Morian.

"That cat's down here."

"What cat?"

"The one last night."

"Don't be silly, Brade. It wouldn't come there, it was too frightened."

"The same cat. Clawing my door."

"It can't be. Are you sure? Calico with white paws and—"

"The same cat."

"I'll be down." She hung up, and in a minute she came down the garden dressed to go to work in a sleek *café au lait* suit. Before she reached the veranda the cat fled for the bushes. Morian stood looking after it as Braden opened the door.

"It's the same cat," she said, frowning. She approached the bushes and tried to coax it out, kneeling awkwardly in her high heels, talking softly. They could see the cat peering but it wouldn't come out.

Morian left at last, instructing Braden to feed it. "I'll come for her tonight—my class is in an hour. Please, Brade—she's just a young little thing, and frightened."

"She wasn't frightened while tearing up my door. And she looks old enough to hunt for her breakfast."

"Feed her, Brade." She cupped his chin in her hand, brushed his lips with hers, and left him.

He scrambled the eggs, put the burned bacon on a paper towel for the cat, and took his breakfast to the veranda. The sun rising at the back of the house left the terrace in shadow but washed golden light across the upper garden. The whole garden was torn and tangled from the wind, scattered with broken limbs. He put the burnt bacon by the bush, and his own plate on the table at the other end of the terrace.

He had eaten only a few bites when the cat came out. She sniffed the bacon but didn't eat it. She sat down, staring the length of the terrace directly at him. Directly into his eyes. He looked back at her for some time, strangely caught by her clear, green gaze. She blinked, and blinked again, then bent her head and began to eat the burnt bacon.

When she finished the bacon she looked up as if she

wanted more. He set his plate down at his feet, knowing she wouldn't have the nerve to come for it.

She approached the plate slowly, her body tensed to run. Her green stare didn't leave him. She was as dark as mink in the shadow of the terrace, her white markings sharply defined. She stalked the plate and watched him, seeming to hold both Braden and the plate in her wide gaze.

And, crouched at his feet, she licked up his scrambled eggs and bacon then got to work on the half piece of toast, holding it down with one white paw, tearing off small, neat bites, glancing up at him with a complacent warmth.

When she had cleaned his plate she gave him a slow shuttered look and flopped over at his feet to lie sprawled totally unprotected and trusting. Upside down, she began to wash her paws and face, glancing coyly up at him.

Amazed, he sat still, watching her. He guessed he didn't know much about cats. He would never have thought one so frightened would so quickly turn bold. Amused by her, he studied the painterly mixture of russet and black that patterned her thick coat with intricate swirls almost like batik.

Her four feet were white like small white gloves, and the bottoms of her paws were pink. Where the fur parted at her white throat, the skin was pink, making her look frail and vulnerable. Her mouth and triangular nose were pale pink, her ears so thin the light shone through.

When he moved to get up she fled to the bushes.

He scrambled four more eggs and ate them in the kitchen, put his plate in the sink, made more coffee, and got back to work. Working, he glanced occasionally through the glass at the cat, who lay trustingly asleep on the terrace.

Satisfied with *Natalie,* he tackled *Lady with a Yellow Buggy.* Garcheff wasn't having his gallery date. They were good friends; Garcheff would say he never dreamed of such a thing, unless of course Braden wanted to get off the hook. He was working steadily now, with a calm, sure sense. All he'd needed was Morian in his bed. He glazed gold into the shadows, worked life into the woman's face where before it had been stark, wove light into her figure and into the tree-tossed background until the painting began to glow. The old sure, elated feeling lifted him. When he looked up the door was ajar.

The cat was asleep on the model's couch, stretched across a piece of vermilion silk. He moved to grab her by the back of the neck and dump her out, but he thought she might scratch.

If she got behind the stacked canvases he'd never get her out. He bent and took her up carefully, sliding his hands under her warm, relaxed body. She hardly woke, she lay limp and trusting in his hands, raising her gaze full on him, her eyes languid.

He stood looking down at her, holding her. Her warmth radiated through his hands. At last he put her back down on the couch, on the warm indentation she had made in the silk.

This way, he'd know where to find her when Morian got home.

It was evening, almost six, when he finished *Lady with a Yellow Buggy.* Drained, he avoided looking at the work, had looked too long, the colors burned into his mind so he couldn't see anything clearly. But he knew the work had life now, resonance. Somewhere he had gone heavy-handed with this series, working as if with dead people. Still, maybe this was a false high, maybe he'd hate the stuff tomorrow. The cat was awake, staring up at him all languid ease and long emerald eyes, her mouth curved as if she were smiling. She jumped off the couch with a soft thud and came to him, wound around his bare ankles. The sensation was so strange he stepped away. Where the hell was Morian?

When the cat rolled onto her back, her white belly and throat exposed, he thought he could have crushed her throat with one kick. Before he knew it he was kneeling, stroking her.

She really was thin, all bones beneath the soft fur. Tiny little bones; he hadn't realized cats were so delicate. He must have known that once, because Alice was always petting cats on the street and he must have petted them to please her.

When he stopped stroking her, the cat touched his hand with a soft white paw, wanting him to keep on. Irritated, he turned from her to look up the garden, wondering if Morian was home. He saw Anne Hollingsworth pull in, leaving her car in the drive. When he rose to make himself a drink, the cat followed him to the kitchen.

"I'm not feeding you again—forget it. Morian can feed you. Cats stay where they're fed." The cat sat down in the middle of the kitchen and looked up at him demandingly. He turned away, relieved at the knock on the door. Morian could get the damned beast out of here.

It wasn't Morian, it was Anne—disheveled, red-faced from crying, her brown hair half damp and unknotted, her eyes swollen. Even her tailored suit looked limp.

"I'm sorry, Brade, but I can't—I wouldn't come barging in but . . ." She shivered and dug in her purse for a handkerchief. He put his arm around her and led her in, and handed her a clean paint rag. She blew her nose on it, then leaned bawling against him. He held her close, amazed; he'd never seen Anne cry. He'd never seen her messy and unkempt. She was the essence of the perfect professional woman.

Finally she got herself under control. Gulping back the last spasms, she stared up at him. Her face was blotched; she looked terrible. Damp hair clung to her forehead. She straightened her blouse, picked up his drink from the work table, and took a long, calming swallow.

"I'll make myself another, come on." He guided her toward the kitchen, like directing a small child. "Can you talk about it?"

"It's Tom." She leaned against the cupboard where he put her. "He's worse. Not—not sicker. Just . . . I don't know . . . His temperature's gone. Two weeks of flu has left him pale and he's lost a lot of weight. But it's not any of that, it's—the *way* he is." She looked up at him, her eyes filled with a fear that made him stare. "He looks at me like a stranger, Brade. As if he hates me. He . . ." She finished her drink and accepted the refill he had ready. He had made it weak—she wasn't a heavy drinker.

"He doesn't look at me the same. He doesn't speak to me the same. I could be the scrub woman. He's . . . totally unresponsive. I don't know how to describe it." She shook her head. "Braden, I'm afraid of him. I'm afraid of my own child."

He didn't understand what she was saying; she wasn't making sense. "Let me run it by you. Tom doesn't look at you the same way. He doesn't speak to you the same, and you're afraid of him."

She nodded.

"How long have you felt this way?"

"It's not the way I *feel!* It's the way he is!"

"I'm sorry, Anne. How long has he been this way?" She made him uneasy; he kept wanting to move around. He propelled her toward the studio.

She sat down, cradling her drink.

"How long?"

"This is going to sound insane. As if—as if I'm going on about nothing."

He waited.

"It started this morning. But he's so . . ."

Braden tried not to show his annoyance.

"Listen, Brade, I know how it sounds. But it's true. He's—it started this morning all at once. He is totally, completely different. He could be a different boy."

"But you can't . . ."

"He is so changed, Brade. As if—as if that boy up there is not my son." Anne looked up at him, her face puffy and desperate. He felt chills; he'd never known Anne to have flights of imagination. He wondered if she'd been working extra hard or if something had happened he didn't know about. Anne was the sensible one, always in charge of her life, perfectly groomed in her neat little business suits, able to juggle her work and care for Tom, planning things out, knowing exactly what to allow for in a given situation.

He said, "All the time Tom was sick he wasn't like this?"

She shook her head.

"But now, today, he's different."

"Yes."

"Did you call the doctor?"

"I called him and went to talk to him. I just got back. He said—he just said . . . to wait. To see how Tom is in a few days. See if he gets worse. Call him if he gets worse."

Braden took her glass and went to refill it. When he got back she was sitting just as he had left her, clutching her hands together in the same way, her knuckles white. She went on talking as if she hadn't stopped. "And the cat—he—Tom tried to kill Pippin."

She looked at Braden nakedly, her eyes like a hurt child. "You know how Tom loves Pippin. That cat hardly left Tom's room the whole time he was sick. Tom lay there with Pippin cuddled in his arms." She began to sob again, choking, then looked up at Braden with cold anger. "This morning Tom threw an iron bookend at Pippin—threw it hard enough to kill him, it made a terrible dent in the wall. It barely missed Pippin. Tom was white with rage. When Pippin leaped away, Tom grabbed up the lamp to throw that, jerking out the cord, standing up on the bed screaming. I snatched the lamp from him and got Pippin out of the house. The look on Tom's face, his eyes . . . The cold, horrible look in his eyes . . ."

Braden held her—he didn't know what else to do.

"Pippin won't even come to me now. He just runs; he won't come near the house. I don't blame him."

"Maybe it's Tom's medicine. Could the medicine have turned him strange?"

"He hasn't had that prescription for a week. He had Pippin on his bed last night while he ate dinner, loving and petting him. It was only this morning when I carried Pippin into his room that . . . Pippin tensed suddenly and stared at Tom and leaped away, clawing me and hissing. He has never done that. And the minute Tom saw him he went white and grabbed the bookend."

"But why did Pippin hiss when you brought him in? Tom hadn't hurt him yet."

"I'm trying to tell you. Tom . . ." She set her drink down, put her face in her hands.

He knelt beside the chair, holding her hand, puzzled and upset by her lack of control.

"When Tom got sick that first night, Brade, when his fever was so high, he kept saying strange things, crazy things. But he was never like this, not like today. He seems filled with hatred suddenly—with a cold, terrifying hatred."

"Drugs can cause mental change, Anne. Psychological change."

"When I reminded the doctor of that, he said, *Not with this drug.*"

"And a drug could cause him to smell different," Braden said reasonably. "Maybe to the cat he smells different. Maybe—Bob says . . ."

"I don't want to hear what Bob says." She glared at him, then lowered her glance. "I'm sorry. You touched a sore place. I don't want to think about—about Tom being . . ."

He held her close. "I know you don't. But if the drugs caused it, it isn't like his father was. It's—why don't you . . ."

"Talk to Bob?" She shook her head.

"Talk to the doctor. Ask him if—"

"I told you! I did talk to him! That's half of what's the matter. He doesn't believe me. He really doesn't give a damn!" She stared at him, enraged. "I just came from talking to him. He left me so—he said there was never a case of that happening with this drug. Never. But then when I pressed him he said maybe it could happen, he simply couldn't say. He didn't offer any help, he didn't offer to see Tom. He didn't want to run any tests, he just said to wait, see what happens. He just covered himself and left me hanging. That's what's so terrifying, that there's no one to understand or to help. No one to tell me what's wrong."

A crash cut them short. Braden remembered the cat and headed for the kitchen.

The cat was in the middle of the table ravaging a loaf of bread. Ravaging was the only word; she had shredded the wrapper and was hunched over the bread, gulping it down. She had, in the process, knocked a plate off, smashing it.

"When did you get a cat?" Anne said behind him. "Tom will—would have—would have laughed," she said faltering. "After all your remarks about cats. Braden, she's hungry. You can't feed her bread. Don't you have any cat food?"

"It's not my cat. I didn't feed it the bread—can't you see it just helped itself? I didn't ask it in here, it's Morian's cat. Go call her and tell her the damned cat's down here." Maybe that would distract Anne. And maybe Morian could do something to help her, make her feel better.

Anne knelt and took the cat in her arms, stroking it. It relaxed against her, staring into her face coquettishly, and purring. With the cat over her shoulder like a baby, she opened the cupboard door, found a can of chicken, as familiar with his kitchen as with her own. They often fixed meals together, platonic and comfortable, Anne and Tom, Morian and Olive Cleaver.

"For Christ sake, don't feed it my chicken. It'll never leave. Let Morian feed it."

"She's starving, Brade. Look how thin she is. She needs meat." She opened the can and dumped the boned chicken on a plate. The cat leaned out from Anne's shoulder, her paw reaching for the plate.

He said, "That cat ate two eggs this morning, five strips of bacon, and a piece of toast. It's had enough protein to run a polar bear. I eat that canned chicken for lunch."

"You eat hamburger and eggs for lunch. Go call Morian yourself." She sounded more like Anne again. She got the milk, poured some into a salad bowl, and watched tenderly as the cat slurped and gulped.

"That was the last can of chicken," he said, watching the cat with interest. He had always thought cats were neat, silent eaters.

"You can go to the store for more chicken. The cat can't."

"I wouldn't bank on that. It's got what it wanted so far."

"She really isn't yours? She's beautiful, Brade. Where did she come from? Her coat is lovely. And those eyes . . ." She

knelt, lifting the cat's chin, gazing into its eyes. "So green—
and a line of kohl around them, the way the Egyptian queens
did. Oh, you are beautiful, my dear." She seemed to need the
diversion. As she knelt there stroking the cat, the line of her
body softened, her face grew softer. "Did Morian bring her
to you? That would be like Morian." The cat had finished
eating. She picked it up again and rose, holding it against her
throat. "How can you hate her, Brade? She's so dear."

"I don't hate her. I just don't want a cat. She's a stray.
She's Morian's." The cat looked at him coolly and intently
from Anne's shoulder, her green eyes nearly on a level with
his. He stared back at her, annoyed, then headed for the
phone.

Morian picked up on the third ring. He tried to keep the
annoyance out of his voice.

"Mor, the cat's still here."

"I just got home. I'll be down in a while."

"Anne's here. She has a problem."

Morian came on down, took a look at Anne, and drew her
to the couch. As Anne talked Braden cleaned up the broken
plate, then began to clean his palette and brushes. The cat
lay curled in Anne's lap, asleep.

Morian didn't argue that Anne might be mistaken about
Tom or overtired, or that Tom needed mental help. She
didn't suggest seeing Bob, she just listened.

When at last Anne was eased, Morian took the cat from
her, cradling it in her arms. It hardly woke, relaxing against
her as it had against Anne. Nothing was changed about Tom,
Morian hadn't solved anything, but Anne felt better, had gotten it out of her system. The two left together, Morian giving Braden a pat on the cheek, carrying the cat away to make
it a bed and get it settled; there was no question of her wanting it.

Not until some hours later did Wylles wake from napping,
confused about where he was, feeling sick and cold then
hot. He rose and slumped to the window, sweaty and irritable in the unfamiliar, sticky pajamas. He was looking at a

garden he had never seen before. He tried to find some co-
herent memory, and could not. Everything was muddled,
unfamiliar, and confusing. He could remember nothing before this day.

He knew he did not belong here. Maybe he was caught in
some enchantment, though he could not remember much
about enchantments. He did not know where he belonged,
only that he did not belong here.

When he saw, in the window of the house next door, a cat
clawing at the glass trying to get out, he froze. He hated cats,
though in his crippled memory he didn't know why. But
watching the dark, white-marked beast, he was filled with
fear and disgust.

Chapter 30

The Harpy sat rocking beside Mag's wood stove, her expression content but remote, her thin hands cupping her little mirror, her wings lifting awkwardly to avoid the chair's
moving rockers. She regarded Mag stubbornly. "If I showed
you where Melissa is, you'd go charging off to find her. You
wouldn't leave her alone. This is her life; she must sort it out
for herself. I assure you she is all right."

"She's not all right. She's been changed into a cat, and she
has no idea how to change back. I never let her learn a
changing spell, never let her see one. Now," Mag said re-
morsefully, "she's in danger every minute. How can you say
she's all right? And if Siddonie learns she is still alive . . ."
Mag stopped speaking and glared at the Harpy.

The Harpy thought Mag would love to wring her feathered neck. She said, "I would not worry about Melissa. At

this moment she is content and happy." She wanted to spy on Melissa some more—she knew she was in Braden West's studio—but she would bring no vision until Mag had left the cottage. She closed her eyes, slowed her rocking, and pretended to doze.

Mag glared, flung on her cloak, grabbed up a bucket of slops from the corner by the door, and went to tend the pigs.

The Harpy sat petulantly, thinking. She didn't understand where her sudden streak of caring had come from; she had never cared about anyone, not since she was a fledgling pecking around her mother's feet among the flames of the Hell fires. Caring, feeling pain in her heart, wasn't a harpy's style.

But she did care. She found herself uncomfortably worried about Melissa, though she would not have told Mag that.

Maybe this burgeoning sentimentality was Mag's influence. Or maybe it stemmed from some genetic fault, some weakness left over from gentler times when harpies lived in the upperworld and consorted with humankind. Then, when harpies still lured sailors to their deaths, there had been tender moments, moments of passion and sometimes of real love and caring before they drowned their hapless victims.

Maybe she was a genetic throwback.

Now, alone in the cottage, she brought a scene which she hadn't shared with Mag, viewing again an encounter that had made her smile. As she watched Melissa and Braden West, the Harpy clacked her beak with pleasure.

In West's studio, the calico lay on the model's couch sprawled across a spill of vermilion silk. West was reaching for her angrily as if he would jerk her off the couch and throw her out the door. But then suddenly he drew back, his anger seemed to dampen, and he lifted the little cat gently, almost cuddling her.

The cat gazed up at him with languid ease and trust, her white paws limp, her small, pretty body limp in his comforting hands. The Harpy opened her beak with devilish interest as Braden carefully laid the cat down again on the silk, and stroked her. He was smitten, already infected with tenderness.

The Harpy liked West's tall, tanned leanness, his look of taut strength. But more than that, she liked his kindness. She was amazed at herself that she cared about kindness.

And there was something else she liked about West, something she couldn't sort out. Puzzling over the attraction, she thought maybe it was the fact that West didn't know he was kind; West thought of himself as hard-nosed and blunt. The Harpy watched him with interest, but at last she turned from Braden and Melissa to bring another vision: a conversation in the Netherworld that she had glimpsed earlier.

The queen and her seneschal stood in Prince Wylles' chamber observing the changeling boy they had stolen. Siddonie was dressed extravagantly for the royal ball in a swirling satin gown the color of the deepest Hell flames, and with rubies woven into her elaborately upswept hair.

On the bed, Tom Hollingsworth slept deeply. Drugged and spell-laden, the boy was now as pale as a Netherworlder. As the Harpy watched, Siddonie drew her hand across Tom's closed eyes, renewing and strengthening the spells she had laid on him earlier.

"You will remember nothing of the upperworld. You will learn willingly all I command you to learn. You will be healthy and strong in the Netherworld for as long as I require this of you."

The queen lowered her pale hands and turned to Vrech, her expression triumphant. "You did very well, my dear Vrech." She stroked Vrech's cheek, moving closer to him. "Now, of course, the boy must be properly trained."

Vrech nodded. "I have spoken with the horsemaster. In my absence, he will do quite well with the boy. He will put him on a horse, and teach him to handle weapons. The new Wylles should be ready soon to travel with you to the villages."

Siddonie brushed Vrech's lips with stroking fingers. "I plan to take the boy to every village in Affandar. I want him seen by every subject, every croft and herding family. Everyone in the Netherworld must know that Prince Wylles is again healthy."

Vrech's hands wandered over the queen's breasts. But his eyes, regarding the boy, were cold with another kind of promise.

Suddenly the boy stirred.

Vrech and Siddonie drew back, and quickly Siddonie cast a sign across Tom's face.

But still the child's eyelids moved. His hand slid across the cover, and his color rose. His eyes opened and he lay looking up at them, dazed, uncomprehending. Siddonie repeated a spell, and repeated it again.

The boy shivered, seemed to be trying to move. Then he dropped into sleep.

The Harpy, watching in her little mirror, saw in that instant when the boy had looked up something that perhaps the queen and Vrech did not. She saw deep in Tom's eyes a spark of sharp awareness. The boy was alert, intense; a look he quickly masked.

Siddonie watched the boy with cold anger. "He should not have awakened. What has caused this? What sort of boy did you bring me?"

Vrech had paled.

"I assume, Vrech, that you were more efficient in carrying out your other instructions. I assume you took more care in seeing to my wishes regarding Melissa."

"I told you that after I dropped the cat, I patrolled the highway. I am certain that pack of dogs tore her apart. There was orange-and-black fur everywhere."

"You might have waited and seen it happen."

"The Primal Law—if I saw it happen and didn't stop it . . ."

"A technicality, Vrech." The queen studied him with remote dislike, all her lust for him gone. "In the morning you will return to the upperworld. You will go directly to the ranch and set about replacing Melissa with a false queen. I want a girl who is sufficiently avaricious but who can be readily trained." She turned from him abruptly, her red satin gown swirling, her ruby encrusted hair catching the lamplight. She paced the room as if too filled with energy to be still; then she turned back suddenly, giving him an unexpected smile. "You may, of course, attend tonight's ball before you leave."

This ball, the Harpy knew, was another triumph for Siddonie. The wedding of Princess Natalia to King Allmond had brought into Siddonie's fold of politically subjugated nations the rich kingdom of Shenndeth, and King Allmond would be a loyal addition to Siddonie's cadre of obedient monarchs.

They left the chamber of the prince and moved into Siddonie's rooms, where Crandall Havermeyer waited.

Havermeyer's back was to them. He stood at the window looking out between the black draperies, his squarely built figure silhouetted by the fading green light. The upperworlder was so heavily built that he looked at first glance to be a strong, solid man. But at second look one perceived a frail construction, as if his body was made of hollow bones joined insubstantially by ill-fitting joints. The overall impression was of a body improperly designed, a rickety machine that could fall apart under physical strain.

The pant cuffs of Havermeyer's upperworld suit were wet, likely from the tunnel or the stream. His camel hair coat was wrinkled. His square jowls needed shaving. His skin always looked gray, dry as paper. His face was, as usual, without expression.

Siddonie looked him over with distaste. "Have you arranged to get Wylles and the Hollingsworth woman away from the garden?"

"I am arranging it. This is not something one does overnight."

She snorted. "You make a major project of everything, even something as simple as this. Have her fired, Havermeyer. See that she's offered a job in another state, one she can't refuse. I want this done immediately, not in your usual tedious fashion. I want Wylles away from the portal. If the spells on him don't hold, I don't want him trying to return here. You will arrange this quickly. Do you understand?"

He nodded, stone faced.

"Once this is done," she said, "I want you to go directly to the ranch." She moved to the window, looking out. Her view was of the courtyard, where the gates were wide open. In the dark green evening, carriages were already arriving from Cressteane and Ferrathil. Lanterns swung, sending arcs of light across the milling horses. Soon the courtyard would be full as a steady stream of richly dressed monarchs and their entourages made their way through the palace doors and into the ballroom. Siddonie turned, regarding Havermeyer impatiently. "You and Vrech will select, from among the captive Catswold, the girl to train in Melissa's place. She must be calico like all of their queens. She must be spirited, selfish, and tractable. I want a girl who is a fighter. I want a whelp of alleys, a slut who craves power."

Havermeyer's eyes hardened.

"Once the young woman is selected, Crandall, you will remain at the ranch for as long as Vrech needs you. You will help with her training in any way Vrech chooses. Do you understand me?"

Havermeyer nodded but still he didn't speak. Vrech said nothing.

"What is this silence? What's the matter with you two?"

Havermeyer shifted his weight. "You can't train one of them. No one can—no spell can make them tractable."

"Of course they can be trained," she barked. "The upperworld Catswold are nothing, not like these Netherworlders. I should think you would look forward to it—a young, fulsome Catswold girl to do with as you please."

She smiled. "You will train her to every power of magic you can force from her. I don't care how you train her. I don't care what methods you use. I want a Catswold woman who looks like a Catswold queen, who knows all possible Netherworld magic, who is totally ruthless. And who is totally obedient to me."

"But she won't have the power of a Catswold queen," Havermeyer said. "There is no way to train her to that."

"One can fake, with common magic, a formidable power. She must learn that magic. She must learn to manipulate. She must learn to feign sincerity just as convincingly as *you*, my dear Crandall, can fake honesty.

"And the girl must have charisma." She moved to Havermeyer, touching his cheek. "Charisma counts for much, Crandall. In both worlds."

The Harpy let the vision fade, preening her beak on her ragged feathers. To please herself, she brought a vision of the little calico being cuddled by the distraught Hollingsworth woman and then by the dark-skinned model. She smiled. Melissa would do all right.

When Mag came in from slopping the pigs, the Harpy's mirror hung idle and blank and the Harpy appeared to be sleeping.

Chapter 31

Morian carried the little cat up the garden, snuggling her, admiring her patterned coat of orange and black and white. The cat glanced up at her companionably, then flicked her tail at a winging bird and chattered a hunting cry. When Morian laughed at her, she looked back clear-eyed and snuggled closer, relaxed and trusting.

Reaching the porch, Morian shifted the calico to her shoulder, opened the door and, carrying her, emptied the laundry basket. She took it into the bedroom and found an old quilted robe to line it. Stroking the little calico and talking to her, she put her down near the basket, shutting her in the bedroom while she went to collect a litter box and cat food.

In the kitchen, as she filled a bowl with water, her thoughts were on Anne. She had been alarmed and puzzled by Anne's distress, and amazed at Anne's sudden helplessness. She couldn't believe Tom was as changed as Anne said. Yet Anne was not given to imaginative flights. She would have to see him for herself; maybe she could figure out what had made Anne react so alarmingly.

Anne's husband had died in a mental institution. Anne had had a hard time and was sensitive about mental problems. Morian shook her head; the thought that Anne herself might be having such a problem chilled her.

She had known Anne long before Anne and Tom had moved to the garden. Anne had kept her equilibrium remarkably well through the hard times with her husband. It seemed strange that now Anne would be losing her grip.

In the bedroom Morian arranged water and food dishes on a newspaper, knowing the little cat would be happier in one room until she got used to the house. She could let her deal with the black tom later. Morian smiled, speaking softly to the cat. "It'll take Skillet a while to get used to you." She stood watching as the calico peered with curiosity under the dressing table. Skillet had been lonely since Tiger died, but he wouldn't want another cat in the house.

She opened the window three inches from the top for fresh air, checking to be sure the screen was latched. The cat was sniffing the laundry basket. Morian watched her circle it then hop in and begin to knead the quilted satin as if she was pleased with the sleeping arrangements. This pleased Morian, too, and she knelt to stroke the little cat, admiring her brightly mixed colors against the cream robe. "You don't seem anxious to get out. Too bad Braden won't keep you— he needs something alive around him. He's getting morose."

The little cat's purr rumbled against Morian's stroking hand.

"You need a name, you know." Morian thought of several, but didn't offer any. The cat was beautiful and she'd like to keep her. But she didn't want this to get too permanent. Maybe Braden would change his mind.

In the kitchen again, she made a sandwich. She ate it looking out at the garden, thinking about Anne and Tom, then she left for an evening class.

In the bedroom the cat napped briefly. When she woke, she ate all the food. She used the litter box with interest, then prowled the room restlessly. Now that she was alone she felt shut in.

When the door wouldn't open under her demanding digging, she leaped to the windowsill. The breeze blew in above her. She leaped again and clung to the top. Under her weight the window dropped a few inches. Encouraged, she climbed atop the sash. It dropped farther. Balancing, she sniffed the night air, pushing at the screen, then she clawed the screen. It was an old screen and rusty, and when it ripped she stuck her nose through the small tear and pushed.

The hole expanded. She pushed through and, balancing awkwardly on the sash, she gauged her distance to the railing below. She quavered, rocking across the screen, found purchase with her hind legs, and leaped. Her rocketing jump ripped down the screen, sending her thudding onto the rail.

In a little while she was back at Braden's. Crouching on the bricks, she stared into the lighted room. When Braden didn't look up, she mewled. When he ignored her, she clawed the glass.

Braden heard her, and scowled. What the hell had Morian done—left the door open? After some moments of strained patience he picked up a folded newspaper and opened the door, meaning to scare the cat away. He smacked the wall loudly, but the cat only stared up at him and marched past him into the room.

Flicking her tail, she leaped onto the model's couch and circled, kneading the crimson velvet. He stood watching, amazed by her colossal nerve, and flattered by her determination. He watched her settle herself comfortably, her colors rich against the red. She gave him an unfathomable green look, lowered her eyes as if dismissing him, and began to wash herself.

He knew he ought to pitch her out.

But what harm could she do in the studio for a few hours? He felt like going out anyway, so let her stay. He stared out at the night, cold and perfect, pulled on his tennis shoes, and went running.

He ran through the hillside residential streets, breathing in the scent of the huge redwoods that stood guard among the houses. He stopped in the village after an hour's run, cooled down, and had a beer and a hamburger. Eating on the restaurant's deck overlooking the stream, he wondered if he should have left the cat in the studio. What if she made a mess? Yet he had a strange, unaccustomed feeling of pleasure at knowing she waited in the empty rooms to greet him.

When he got back, she seemed not to have moved. She looked up from the couch languidly yawning, her open mouth pale pink, her green eyes slitted sleepily, the pupils narrowing in the sudden light. Almost reluctantly he phoned Morian and explained that the cat had come back and that he didn't want a cat. Morian said her screen was torn. She said it looked to her as if the cat had made her own decision, so why didn't he relax and accept it.

She said, "If you don't want the cat, just put her out. She doesn't want to stay with me. You can't force a cat to live somewhere."

He knew he ought to put her out. He knew he shouldn't let her get the idea she belonged here. He glanced out to the garden, remembering the sharp chill as he walked home, and wondered where she would sleep. Well, where the hell had she slept before? Cats slept outside, that was where cats lived.

He didn't mean, passing the model's couch, to become interested in how the moonlight slanting down through the skylight stroked the cat's mottled coat. He stood studying the patterns of her orange and black markings against the shadow-crossed silk, seeing a rich painting. Then, annoyed at himself, he made a drink, got a book and went to bed.

* * *

The little cat woke in the small hours. The wind was up, rattling branches against the windows. Through the sky-light, clouds ran across the moon, hiding then revealing it. Moon shadows swam across the floor, and she leaped off the couch to chase them. The blackness under a campaign chair belled out then sucked back, and she leaped into it, her eyes huge, then charged out to chase the tracery of branches dancing along the walls. Twisting, spinning away she plunged into the black tunnel behind the stacked can-vases and raced along its length to burst out again, eyes blazing.

But suddenly different shadows were in the room with her. Four shadows fell through the glass where four cats stared in. She approached them stiffly, her lips drawn back in challenge.

They stood shoulder-to-shoulder: the black tom and the old white female, and her two half-grown kittens. The kit-tens, bolstered by their mother's presence, snarled and spat. And as the calico moved closer, all four cats screamed a challenge and forced against the glass. She held her ground, snarling, until the black leaped at the glass so hard it thrummed and vibrated. She backed fast, and took protec-tion behind the easel.

When he charged again, the glass shook as if he would come flying through. She fled for the kitchen, leaped to the counter then to the top of the refrigerator. There she crouched, listening.

When after some time no sound came from the studio, she began to prowl the kitchen counters.

She found nothing edible. She jumped to the floor, drank water from the bowl, then went to investigate the bathroom. Leaping to the counter she sniffed the tubes and bottles. They smelled like the man. When she grew bored with the bathroom she prowled the bedroom. He was asleep; the sound of his snoring interested her. Moonlight swam across the bed. She jumped up, patting at the streaks of light that shifted across the white sheets. She watched Braden. She

had never seen him lying down. She stood studying him,
sniffing his arm. In the chilly room she was drawn by his
warmth.

When he rolled over snoring she jumped clear. Then,
purring, she nosed down into the warm nest he had left. Settled against his warm back, she flexed her claws happily in
a wad of blanket.

She slept, her nose tucked under one paw. And within
Braden's sleeping consciousness something prevented him,
when next he turned over, from rolling on her; something
made him slide to the left before he turned, a sense of caring that rose without his volition.

He woke at dawn and lay looking out at the bay and marsh
stained red by sunrise. The blood red sky was reflected in
the wind-rippled water, cut through by sharp spears of marsh
grass. He had painted this marsh, an early series capturing
sunrise and storm and the clarity of summer light: a dozen
different moods of the salt marsh.

All night the wind had blown; he could remember waking
to wind. He frowned, remembering the cat jumping on the
bed, and he turned to look.

She slept soundly in a nest of tangled covers. He reached,
meaning to throw her off, but she looked too small and delicate to manhandle. Let her sleep.

He wished he had a cup of coffee. Alice used to bring the
pot into the bedroom at night, plug it in when she woke. He
got up finally, went into the kitchen, filled the coffee pot and
stood barefoot on the cold floor while it brewed, thinking
about the work, the show, and Rye Chapman. By the time he
carried the pot and a mug back to bed, his feet were freezing and the sunrise was past its peak. The cat hadn't moved.
He got back in bed and slid his feet under her, feeling her
warmth like an oven. She woke suddenly and turned her
green stare full on him, her expression chilling. Then she got
up, stalked across the bed, and resettled herself where his
feet couldn't reach her.

He grinned. Alice would be amused. A sense of Alice, a

sense of the empty spaces where she should be, lay behind all other thoughts.

He got up finally and got to work, not stopping until the cat rubbed against his leg, startling him because he'd forgotten her. He looked down, rigid with the shock of fur against his ankles. "What the hell do you want?"

She headed for the kitchen.

After nearly a week the cat was still there. Braden wouldn't admit she had moved in. She came and went at her pleasure, clawing at the door to get in, leaving deep scratches on the wood frame, waiting outside impatiently if he wasn't home or didn't come right away. He bought a few cans of cat food—he could always give them to Morian. The cat slept on his bed at night but was not allowed on the pillow; house rules began to grow up in spite of his insistence that she was temporary. She paid little heed to rules; though she did not get into the paint again after being cuffed lightly, probably because she didn't like the smell. And she had never offered to claw the canvases. He was completely caught up in the work again, the cat and everything else existing outside the real world of the paintings. He woke, painted, ate, slept, painted. He fed the cat and let her in and out to avoid her insistent yowling and scratching, or her insouciant rubbing against his legs. Twelve paintings were finished. Chapman came by and was pleased, and took some photographs for the papers. Braden wasn't on a real high, but he was working. Alice used to say the house could burn down around him when he was working.

Alice hadn't been so single-minded, shutting out everything else. She had been able to juggle several things at once—painting, print making, etching, housework, lectures. She had been such a careful draftsman, had always known what she was going to do before she did it, known what the work would look like. He could never manage that; his pleasure was in the exploration, in the discovery of forms unrevealed until he touched the right combination to free them. Alice had marveled at that. Well, Alice had been or-

ganized. She always said he lived by intuition—it was a
standing joke between them. Alice put things where she
could find them, then found them there. He put things where
he could find them, then forgot where that was. He missed
her. His occasional nights with Morian were warm and caring and completely casual. Morian was the earth mother—
giving, loving, but not involving herself. They were good
friends, as Morian had been with Alice. He couldn't stop
thinking of Alice; he was thinking of her more now than he
had done for months.

It had taken him a long time to learn to escape the raw
memories that tore at him. Now again they were like a fresh
wound—he was thinking of her again as he had just after she
died, lonely for her in the way he had been those first
months. As if she would walk into the room, as if when he
looked up she would be there working. Now again when he
woke at night he reached for her—and was startled and
angry when he touched the damn cat.

Bob maintained that patients in depression could be
helped by having a pet, a living creature that they would
hold and talk to, to let them know they were still among the
living. With that thought Braden almost chucked the cat out.
But she gave him the rolling over, green-eyed coquette treat-
ment, and he ended up stroking her. And he thought, as she
watched him so intelligently, that sometimes her eyes didn't
seem like a cat's eyes. Sometimes her green gaze seemed to
hold a greater knowledge. Braden studied her, puzzled and
intrigued.

Maybe Alice would know what that look was, maybe
Alice would be able to explain what he found so strange
about the small cat.

Chapter 32

Dawn. Melissa woke lying next to Braden deliciously warm curled on the blanket. Outside the bedroom window the sky was barely light. She stretched lazily, her toes touching the foot of the bed and her fingers tracking across the headboard. She jolted awake filled with panic: she wasn't a cat anymore.

She stared down at herself, at her rumpled dress. How close she lay to Braden, nearly touching him. His hand lay across her hair. She watched him, stricken, terrified he would wake. He slept sprawled naked, tangled in the blankets, blankets and sheet tumbled away from his bare back.

How long had she lain beside him as Melissa? She had felt no pain at the changing. Unless it was pain that woke her. Carefully, slowly, she slid off the bed.

He didn't stir. She tiptoed to the door, but then she turned back and stood watching him. Seeing him from the viewpoint of a woman was very different from seeing him through the eyes of a cat. The cat had seen height and strength and security, had been aware of his kindness and restraint, had seen a human she could be comfortable with, and one she could tease and manipulate when she chose. But now as a woman she saw him differently, and different emotions moved her.

He was strong and lean; she liked the clean line of his jaw and the little wrinkles at the corners of his eyes. She liked his deeply tanned face against the white pillow. He had a smear of green paint on his left ear; she wanted to wipe it off. She could still feel the heat of his body where she had slept against him. She knew his scent sharply, as the little cat had known it.

Beyond the windows, red streaks of dawn stained the bay. He would wake soon. He would look out at the sunrise then roll over and plug in the coffee. If she was still sleeping on the bed as the cat, he would stroke her and talk to her, and she would purr for him. If he found her gone he would call her, then pull on a pair of shorts and go into the studio looking for her, calling her.

He stirred suddenly and rolled over almost as if her thought had woken him. She fled down the hall and through the dark studio to the glass door. She was fumbling with the lock when he called, "Kitty? Kitty, kitty?" She wanted to giggle. He had never named her, just *kitty, kitty.* She heard his footsteps. Panicked, she got the door open at last and ran for the bushes.

She crouched down in the little space under the bushes at the end of the terrace, her back scraping against the branches. She wanted to change back to cat. But she didn't know how to change.

She didn't know why she had changed to a girl; she knew she had been a girl before, but she could remember nothing except being a cat. She remembered traveling through strange, hostile country, and before that a dark, smelly man shoving her into a leather bag. She remembered the smell of diesel fuel as she fought to get out of the bag. Then the diner. She remembered traveling, miserable and hungry, her swollen eye hurting her, and her swollen paw sending pain all through her body. She remembered the stray cats and the fights and the blazing eyes of the rat as it crouched to leap at her.

She looked up the garden to the door in the hill. The door had drawn her here, pulling her on, hungry and hurt and frightened. She heard a door slam somewhere up the hill and then in the lane a car started. She could smell bacon cooking, and could hear faint voices from the houses above. Soon Braden would come out searching for the little cat. She didn't want to be caught here hiding in the bushes. But she didn't know where to go. As a cat, she would simply have run up the garden and disappeared in the bushes. Now she didn't know where she could hide. In her distress, a memory touched her: a woman's face so pale it was nearly white, surrounded by blackness. Then she remembered animals; a huge toad as big as a person. A tall creature with a woman's breast and a bird's face and all covered in white feathers.

She pulled her skirt around her sandaled feet for warmth, listening to the din of birds in the garden. Their riot stirred her hunger; she wanted to slip out and grab one. She was appalled at herself, not at the thought of eating raw bird but of being seen catching and eating it.

The studio lights came on, and she could hear Braden inside calling the cat. Through the windows she could see him searching behind the stacked canvases. When he turned, she slid deeper under the bushes. He disappeared toward the kitchen, and she fled across the garden and across the lane.

Running toward the village brought new memories. She hurried past houses tucked among huge redwood trees. Scenes began to come to her: she was a child walking along this street holding a woman's hand, they were going to the village for ice cream. She couldn't remember the woman's face. Then she was inside a shop that sold bicycles, stroking a red bicycle. Then she and the woman were crouched together beside a stream looking for stones. These memories did not fit with the white feathered womanbird and the toad, or with the black room where a woman's white face seemed suspended.

Walking, she had soon passed all the houses. Now there were only shops. To her left the redwood trees rose up a hill above the stores, and there were houses tucked among the dark trunks.

She lingered before a hardware store, then stood looking into a dress shop. A sign reading "tool rental" meant nothing to her. But she remembered the art store.

Where the street dead-ended and a cross street cut through, she recognized the Greyhound station. She remembered riding the Greyhound to the city across a huge bridge. As she stood looking, a big black dog came around the corner and stopped, staring at her, his head lowered. She watched him warily. He sniffed her scent, and his lips drew back in a snarl. She backed away. He crouched to chase her and she fled through a shop door, slamming it in his face.

She was in a tea room. The tables had white cloths. It was half full of people eating small, leisurely meals. The smell of hot pastries stirred her hunger. She longed for a cup of tea and something delicious and sweet. She watched a man pay for his meal and she knew suddenly that she had no upper-world money.

She realized, shocked, that she was remembering not one world, but two.

Confused, light-headed, she left the tea room quickly, pushing out onto the street.

There was not one world, but two.

When she was able to look around her again, she saw that the dog was gone. Watching for him, she wandered the village—trying to jar her memory, trying to put pieces together. Certainly, whatever that other world was, it was far different from this world.

She looked at herself in a shop window, her figure an indistinct smear among shattered light and reflections. She touched the cloth of her dress and she remembered a loom. She fingered her jeweled bracelet and was aware of caves, and of a metal pick in her hand. Slowly she was able to reach back to that world, to glimpse stone ridges and stone sky and dark, cavernous wastes. Slowly, the Netherworld returned to her. Then suddenly and vividly she saw Mag's cottage, then Affandar Palace. She saw Efil's chambers; she saw the black bedposts carved into four leering Hell Beasts.

It was in that chamber that she had been changed into a cat.

She was Catswold. Half woman, half cat.

And she was still hungry.

She examined her bracelet again, and then turned back up the street, to the jewelry shop she had passed. She went in boldly, removing a small diamond bob from among the bangles.

The bland-faced, pudgy jeweler was reluctant to accept a jewel she had removed so casually. He looked at it in his glass, then asked to examine the whole bracelet. She gave it over, explaining patiently that she needed money. He looked for a long time at the individual jewels. When finally he made an offer, the amount had no meaning for her. She folded the paper bills into her pocket under his puzzled, uneasy gaze, and headed for the tea shop.

In the art store Braden bought half a dozen tubes of paint and some linseed oil, then he stopped at the Greyhound station for a paper to see the reviews of last night's opening at the de Young, then went across to Anthea's for breakfast. He ordered from Betty Jane, hiding a grin because her hair was the same too-red tangle that had always amused Alice. He asked how Betty Jane's mother was doing in the nursing home, then settled back to read the art page to see what Mettleson had said about his award in the annual. One thing about Rye, he got work around to the shows without Braden having to bother with it. This was one of the Coloma paintings, one of the semi-abstracts of ferns growing inside the roofless brick ruins of an old gold rush bank building. Rye had borrowed it from a collector for the show. Mettleson said it was ". . . reality blown apart and reassembled into lyric tapestry without seeming to have been rearranged, so discerning is West's eye for the essence of pure abstract poetry that exists in the everyday world."

Sure, Mettleson. Poetry. But the review pleased him. He was finishing his eggs and ham when his attention was caught by a girl just coming into the tea shop. She started in but suddenly she turned back, returning to the sidewalk and standing at the curb with her back to the window. The one glimpse he had of her was striking: a tangle of brown hair framing a cleanly sculptured face, gorgeous eyes fringed by thick, dark lashes. Now she stood looking up the street as if she were waiting for someone. Watching her, he began to see a painting—the girl's figure framed by the red awning, the white letters of the awning making abstract shapes against her hair, and these patterns blending into the blue building across the street. The whole scene was contorted by light warping across the glass. He made a sketch on his napkin, a quick memory-jogging study.

He had finished, memorizing the colors while eating the last of his biscuit, when the girl turned to look in, and he raised his hand in greeting—then wondered why he had done that. She looked startled and turned away, and he dropped his hand, feeling foolish. Why had he waved? He didn't know her. He had never seen her before. His aftervision was filled with her startled gaze before she spun around and headed up the street.

But, strangely, his shock of recognition remained.

He grabbed the check and dug in his pocket for change.

He searched the streets for her, wanting to talk to her, wanting to find out if he did know her. Wanting, suddenly and intensely, to paint this girl. Unable to shake the powerful, curious feeling that he knew her. Puzzled, and annoyed because he couldn't remember, he looked into shops and down side streets, and even walked up into the wooded residential area around the library and looked in through the long library windows, but she wasn't in there.

He went home at last, totally frustrated. He wanted to paint her beside the tea shop window. He could still see her dark-fringed green eyes. He dropped his sketch on the work table and unfolded it, but he didn't need it; the painting was surprisingly clear in his mind. Excited, he set up a fresh canvas, changed his shirt, and got to work.

Melissa had evaded Braden by ducking into the dress shop and browsing among the racks at the back. She wasn't sure why she was hiding. Braden couldn't know her. She wasn't sure, either, why she had turned to look back into the restaurant. She had just wanted to look at him; she hadn't thought he would be watching her, had thought she wouldn't be noticed. She had frozen, terrified, at his look of recognition.

But how could he recognize her?

She remained behind the dress racks until she saw him go past the window. She had avoided the sharp-faced saleswoman. Now the woman stood beyond the rack looking her over, taking in her long dress and unruly hair. "May I help you?"

"Help me?"

"May I show you something, my dear? Would you like to try on a dress?"

She felt confused, disoriented.

"Are you all right, my dear?"

"I—yes, I'm fine. A dress—the yellow dress in the window."

But then in the fitting room the saleswoman stared at her, shocked because she wore no undergarments. Cringing under the woman's disapproving gaze she dressed again quickly and left the shop.

She wouldn't go in there again. And she didn't want the suggested panties and bra and slip—she felt constricted thinking about them. Distraught and afraid Braden might still be searching, she headed for the edge of the village away from the shops. There on a deserted street the black dog found her again, and he had been joined by two big hounds. She turned to see them coming toward her fast, noses down, sniffing her trail. Before she could run, they circled her.

They lunged and drew back, baiting her. She was stricken not simply with her own fear, but with a child's total panic: this had happened when she was small. She had been chased and surrounded by dogs. She stood facing them, edging toward an oak tree in the yard of the nearest house.

When the black dog lunged, she kicked it. He snapped at her, and when she kicked again he jumped on her, knocking her against the tree. She twisted as she hit it, and climbed. The rough bark tore the skin inside her legs and scraped her arm, then she was up the tree clinging with all fours, holding tight with sharp claws.

The cat clung in the tree, spitting, her claws digging into the branch as below her the dogs leaped at the trunk, barking and snarling.

The little cat remained in the tree until late afternoon, backing along the branch each time the dogs leaped. She was only cat now, she remembered nothing else. Long after the dogs tired of the game and wandered off, she remained clinging in the branches. Only as darkness fell did hunger drive her down again, and instinct point her toward the garden. Hardly visible in the darkness except for her white markings, she fled between houses through the darkening woods, evading other cats, running in panic from dogs, streaking across streets in front of headlights. Twice she was nearly hit. When she crossed the lane to the garden, running, she almost collided with the black tom. He hissed and cuffed her and bit her. She dodged away and made for the veranda and safety.

Chapter 33

At dusk Braden made himself a drink and stood studying the painting of the girl in the tea shop window. He had captured her look, captured the intriguing sense of otherness he had glimpsed in that brief moment. The work filled him with excitement—this was right, this was what he wanted to do. He hadn't felt like this about a painting in a while. This was the beginning of a new series, one he had been waiting to do and not known it: a series of reflections all of this girl, her face caught in shattered light as if she had just stepped into this world from another dimension.

The reflections formed a montage: the shattered light striking across the tea shop window, shards of reflected color and light weaving around and through the girl's figure. She was turned away; he had caught her profile against the red awning and the blue building. The work was alive—it had the old, sure resonance. He was caught up totally, wildly eager, seeing other paintings . . .

He'd have to find her. He wanted the series to be of her. The planes of her face belonged to reflections, were uniquely made for reflections—in mirrors, in windows. He could see her in the shattered light of a dozen settings, the long sweep of her mouth, the hint of a secret smile, the look he couldn't define. He'd find her—he'd have to find her.

He had reached to turn off the bright studio lights, meaning to go into the village and look for her, when he realized the cat should have been winding around his feet demanding food. He remembered he hadn't seen her all day.

He opened the door and stood calling her, embarrassed to be shouting "kitty, kitty" across the garden. When she didn't come, he went up the hill carrying his drink, looking for her.

She didn't appear. She should be starving—he didn't think he'd fed her this morning, couldn't remember letting her out, then remembered looking for her when he got up. He began to worry about her, and to wonder if she was hurt. He got a flashlight out of the station wagon and looked for her along the lane, thinking how fast people drove in that lane, remembering that Morian's tiger cat had been run over there. Not finding her, he walked down the lane to the highway and up the highway, shining his light along the shoulder and into the bushes. He walked back on the other side, searching the marsh. The jagged grass caught his light, and once he saw the gleam of eyes, but it was a raccoon.

When he didn't find the calico, fear for her shook him. That annoyed him; he had never in his life worried about an animal. Abruptly, he turned back to the studio. She was probably in the woods hunting.

He made another drink and stood looking at the painting, too excited about it to leave it alone. He began to worry that the girl might not live in the village, that she had been passing through, maybe was already gone. If she lived here, why hadn't he seen her before? He grabbed a jacket and swung out the door to look for her, nearly stepping on the cat where she was pressed against the sill.

"Whoa. That's no damned place to sit in the dark!" Then he saw how frightened she was, crouching and shivering. She stared up at him wild eyed and sped past him into the room, huddling beside the easel, looking back, her pink mouth open in a silent cry. He knelt, afraid she would scratch in her panic, and he took her up against his shoulder, stroking her tense little body.

He petted her for a long time. Slowly she eased against him, relaxing. What the hell had frightened her? He looked out through the windows at the dark garden, wondering if Tom Hollingsworth really had tried to kill the yellow cat. If Tom was so violent with his own cat, how might he react to the pretty little calico?

When the calico had stopped shivering and lay warm against him, he carried her into the kitchen, opened a can of tuna, and watched her tie into it. Whoever said cats ate delicately hadn't seen this one; she acted as if she hadn't eaten in weeks, gulping and smacking. When she finished the tuna he gave her some milk. He watched her clean the bowl, then picked her up again. She belched, then lay limp against his shoulder purring. She was soon half asleep, drifting in some inscrutable feline dream. He stood in the hall holding her and looking at the painting. He had to find this girl. If the cat hadn't interrupted him he might already have found her somewhere in the village.

Two cats crouched in the garden watching the studio where the calico had disappeared. The black tom was filled with hate of her and wanted her gone from the garden. The white female felt no hatred as long as the calico stayed off her porch. She was a heavy, old cat, sway-backed from the weight of her pendulous, kitten-bearing belly. She sat with her belly protruding like a Buddha, bored by the black cat's anger. She grew more interested when the yellow tom appeared from the shadows. The black cat, conditioned by other confrontations, lowered his head and crept away.

The golden tom stood on the path staring after the retreating black, then went boldly down the garden to the terrace that ran the length of the studio. He took shelter under the bushes at the end, sniffing the calico's scent and watching the house for a glimpse of her. She interested him in a way he didn't understand: not as a female ready to go into heat, not in any ordinary way, but in a manner that both baffled and intrigued him.

Braden fried three hamburgers for dinner, two for himself and one for the cat, his mind on the girl and how the hell he was going to find her. He ate standing in the hall studying the painting, imagining the new series, ignited in the way a good series always stirred him. As if the series already existed somewhere, as if he had not to invent it but only to discover the individual paintings. Twice he put his hamburger down, once to let the cat out, and then to phone Bob for lunch the next day. Bob might know the girl. And he thought, if they had lunch, he could run Anne's problem by Bob and get that off his conscience.

He described the girl to Bob, but Bob didn't know her. He waited, holding the phone while Bob asked Leslie if she knew her, but Leslie didn't. Braden let the cat in, then made half a dozen more phone calls, but no one knew the girl. He went to bed late and tried to read, but couldn't keep his mind on the book.

He slept restlessly. He dreamed that he lay close to someone, he could feel her rough-textured dress against his skin; once he thought he touched her hair, tangled across his cheek.

He woke to a room gray with rain. The cat was sleeping soundly. It was raining hard when he left the house to meet Bob, sloshing out to his car under a battered corduroy cap, having no idea where to find an umbrella. He had left the cat inside; she seemed to have no intention of going out in the wet. The rain was a torrent when he pulled into the parking lot at the Dock. He made a run for the door and found Bob already at a table, perfectly dry, his umbrella dripping where he had leaned it against the window. Through the glass, sky and bay were joined in one dark curtain, the rain so heavy they could see only the first two boats tied to the quay.

"Working?" Bob said, nodding across the room to the waiter.

"Matter of fact, yes—the girl I mentioned." He explained about the sketch, and that he wanted to paint her again.

"She's no one I remember. Leslie will keep an eye out—nearly everyone passes through the library sooner or later." He looked at Braden intently. "This is important."

"Yes, a series—something very different. Something I want very much to do. Something . . . I haven't felt like this about the work in a long time." He could see Bob's look of relief in his returned enthusiasm and improved mental health, and was annoyed.

When they had ordered, he tried to describe Anne's situation, but now Anne's fear seemed silly. "You could drop by," he said. "I think she's gotten herself over the edge. She's called me twice since the night she came down, and she's talked to Morian, talked to Olive—she's talked herself into believing that Tom *isn't* Tom, that the boy isn't her child."

Bob shook his head. "If Anne doesn't want to see me, Brade, I can't intrude. Has Morian seen Tom? What does she think?"

"That's strange, too. When I asked her about it, she clammed up. I don't know what she thinks. She's talked with Tom, she just doesn't say anything."

"That's not like Morian, not to express an opinion." Bob paused, then, "Anne may be upset about some other things right now. Maybe that, plus Tom's illness, has gotten to her."

Braden waited.

"Two of my clients do business with Anne's company. A new brokerage firm is trying to elbow them out, giving them trouble, putting the screws to several small Bay area firms."

"Anne's not the kind to get upset over something like that."

"They have already taken over two small real estate firms

and fired the key personnel. This could mean her job. Have *you* seen Tom?"

"He's pale, irritable, lost a lot of weight."

The waiter came with their order. Braden on impulse asked for some fish or seafood scraps for the cat, receiving Bob's amazed stare. When the bag was brought, he realized he'd have to pick through other people's germs to remove shell and bone before the cat got it, and was sorry he'd asked.

Bob looked immensely amused. "When did you get a cat? I thought you hated cats."

"I don't hate cats. It's Morian's cat. I'm keeping it."

"The black one? The tiger cat was killed, I remember." Bob was big on cats—he and Leslie had several. "Where's Morian, some kind of vacation? I thought . . ."

"She's at home," Braden said patiently. "I'm just keeping the cat for a while. It's the stray, the one she—we—chased that night at Sam's, the one the gardener had in a bag."

Bob's expression was one of delighted superiority. Why were cat people so superior? Braden dropped the bag beside his chair and managed to ignore it, but as they rose to leave, Bob picked it up, handing it to him. "Have you named it yet?"

"What?"

"Have you named your cat?"

"It's Morian's cat. It's not my cat."

Bob buttoned his raincoat and picked up his umbrella. "I guess I can drop around, talk to Anne, see Tom. But I can't do anything, can't offer help unless she asks me." Then they were out the door, Braden running through the rain for his Chevy wagon, Bob sauntering beneath the black umbrella to his green MG. He waved as he spun out of the parking lot.

By the time Braden reached the house, the rain-damp paper bag was beginning to split. He wiped some juice off the seat, and carried the mess across the garden in both hands, cursing. He took it dripping through the studio to the kitchen and dropped it in the kitchen sink. The cat came yawning out of the bedroom sniffing the fish, winding around his ankles, her green eyes caressing him. He stood at the sink separating out bones and shells from potato skins—what the hell made the waiter think cats liked potato skins?

When he put the mess before her she set to with greed, holding a piece of lobster down with her paw and tearing at it. Finished, she gave him another loving look, followed him into the studio, and curled up by the easel so he had to step around her as he worked. When Chapman arrived around five, she jumped into Braden's lap and went to sleep.

He sat petting the cat, prepared for Chapman's long run-through of the mailing list, which was a lot of nonsense. But Rye always did this, as well as enumerate the kinds of liquor for the opening, champagne punch or whatever. He wanted to shout at Rye to do anything, just let him get back to work. But Christ, it made Rye happy. He had put *The Girl in the Window* in the bedroom before Rye got there to avoid making the rest of the work look dull.

That night the cat slept curled against his shoulder with her head on the pillow. And even though she smelled faintly of fish, he didn't push her away.

Melissa woke at dawn. Rain drenched the windows, cascading against the glass. She was unable to move her legs, her dress was tangled around her knees. She jerked awake, alarmed, and rolled away from Braden and swung off the bed.

This was too unnerving, to go to sleep as cat and wake as a girl lying next to him. Someday he was going to wake before she did. He was going to find her there. Her common sense told her to go away from here, to leave this garden and go away.

But she didn't want to go away. She had been a child here. If she remained in this house, she was certain she could recapture her lost memories. And, more powerfully, she didn't want to leave Braden.

But if she stayed here, she would have to learn how to change from girl to cat only at her own pleasure. And she would have to learn to retain her human thoughts when she was cat. It was terrifying to know that as cat she remembered nothing about Melissa, that she was totally ignorant and vulnerable.

Braden stirred, and she stiffened.

But he only turned over and slept again. She slipped out of the bedroom and into the studio.

Rain drummed on the skylight. The room was dim. The watery light made her think of shadowed caverns. And then another memory fell into place: she knew suddenly that the changing was done with a spell. There was a spell to make her change, a magic as natural to her as breathing.

She remembered Siddonie's voice, remembered the sharp pain of that first changing, felt herself jerked to the floor, could almost make out the cadences of Siddonie's shouted words. But then the spell faded. Absently she studied the painting before her, straining to bring back the spell. The girl in the painting was turned away, standing before a red awning.

Shock jolted her.

The painting was of her.

It was an image of her, standing before the red awning of the tea room, turned away looking up the street. Her dark hair, her green dress. She felt stricken with fear at seeing her own image. But yet she was deeply drawn to the painting. Soon fascination overcame fear. She stood looking, seeing herself in a way no mirror could show her.

The painting was beautiful, the colors warping together so rich they took her breath. She studied the line of her cheek against the red awning, her skin reflecting red. How could he have painted her from only one glimpse? She felt tremendously flattered and excited. She stood lost in his work until she heard the coffee pot start. Alarmed, she pushed quickly out onto the terrace.

Chapter 34

She fled through the rain to the tool shed, and in among the garden tools. Her dress was soaked. She stood in the little earthen room shivering, straining to remember the words for changing from cat to woman. Through the crack where the door was ajar, thin watery light seeped in. She thought about Mag's cottage: the cozy little room, the cookstove, the rocker and cots. And Mag's spell book lying on the shelf. Standing inside the tool cave, leaning against the ladder, she imagined taking the heavy book down, holding it in her lap, turning the pages, and imagined an empty page. She tried to let words come onto the page, tried to let her memory open. She could smell the onions hanging from Mag's rafters. She could feel the warmth of the cookstove, could feel the weight of the heavy book, could feel the thick, rough paper beneath her fingers. Slowly, as she stared at the blank paper, the words began to emblazon themselves, rising from the whiteness as if a licking flame drew them forth.

It was there. The spell was there.

"To cat do I cleave, to Catswold cleave, called forth leaping, careening joyous from spell-fettered caverns, to cat do I return . . ."

She changed to cat suddenly, without pain. The simple charm seemed part of her nature.

And she remembered. She was the little calico yet she knew she was Melissa. She was so pleased she wanted to race the garden madly. But suddenly she froze, rigid. The scent of Vrech clung in the tool room. Only now as cat could she smell it.

It was not a fresh scent, but it was not very old either. She left the tool shed quickly, pushing through the door into the rain, shaking her paws in the rain.

She sat under a tree near the portal, letting memories of the Netherworld come. Only when her fur was soaked and she was shivering with cold did she leave the shelter of the tree, heading straight for the terrace. She sped across the wet bricks and clawed at the door, crying pitifully.

He came at once, wiping paint off his hands. "How the hell did you get out this morning? You were on the bed last night when I went to sleep." He picked her up. "And this isn't the first time you've done that. Christ, you're soaked." He stood rubbing her wet ears, frowning. She snuggled deeper into his arms, getting him wet, purring so loudly her whole body shook. He carried her into the bathroom and began to towel her dry. Then in the kitchen he opened a can of cat food, and dumped the chopped liver in a dish. She watched him, wanting to laugh. This was perfect, to be cat but to have her own wits about her, her own awareness.

She finished the canned liver quickly. It was really quite good. Braden had returned to the easel. She strolled past him, leaped to the model's couch and gave her damp fur another cleaning, leaving dark stains on the velvet and silks. He was still working on the tea shop painting. She flipped onto her back, looking at the painting and the studio upside down. She felt so loose, so utterly comfortable both in spirit and in body. Upside down she watched Braden, then leaped to her feet and bolted the length of the studio and back, playing. She chased her tail in circles, sliding on the bare floor until, distracted, he left the easel. As he made himself a sandwich she sat down before the painting and studied the image of herself. She was still there when he came out of the kitchen. He stopped, watching her.

"What are you? Some kind of art critic?" He picked her up and stroked her absently. "I don't know why it's so important, cat, but I'm going to find this girl. I'm going to paint her again." His look was so intense, so deep, she shivered.

He said, "It's going to be the best work I've done. I've got two months to come up with, say, twenty new paintings." His excitement was infectious. She rubbed her face against him. He said, "Reflections. All reflections. Why the hell did she go off like that in such a damned hurry? And why did she stare at me like that? As if—as if she knew me." He frowned, puzzled. "Christ, cat. Think good thoughts for me. Think that I can find her."

He put her on the couch and turned away to clean his brushes, then went to wash. She could hear him splashing, then the creak of the closet door. When he crossed the hall to the kitchen she padded in behind him and jumped on the table to watch him. He was making a list of groceries. She wished she could add chicken and lobster, and cross off the cat food.

Well, why not make a list? What was to stop her?

Maybe not this time, but soon, she would make a list and see that he bought nothing but caviar. She wanted to shout with laughter, wanted to hug him. Now she could be anything she chose, for Braden. Cat or girl. Or both.

As he left the studio she bolted through the door ahead of him, switching her tail. From the terrace she watched him head across the lane toward the village. She would give him time to search for the girl before she introduced him to his phantom model.

She lingered in the garden, hunting. Her sharp cat's senses delighted her—her keener smell, hearing, and wider vision made every detail sharper. She could hear sounds she had never suspected as Melissa, could see the secrets within shadows that had been featureless darkness to Melissa.

She caught a bird, played with it, then killed and ate it. She caught a lizard, and turned it loose. And when she thought Braden had looked long enough for his model, she slipped into the tool room, changed to girl, and headed for the village.

She let Braden discover her outside the art store. He saw

her through the glass and came out shouting, flustered as a boy. He grabbed her hand as if she would vanish. He told her he had done a painting of her and asked her name. Sarah, she said. Sarah Affandar. He asked her to pose. He offered her union wages; he wanted her to pose for several weeks. She listened gravely. She loved his eagerness and his fear that she would refuse. It was hard to keep from howling with laughter. He told her he had a show scheduled soon at Chapman's. He said she could call Chapman's to check on him, call the Art Institute in the city where he sometimes taught. "I'm not making a pass, you're just—I simply want to paint you. I'd like the whole show of you—a series—your face caught in reflections, the planes of your face—you'll see. Before you say no, will you come back to the studio and take a look? I'm not making a pass, I promise."

"Your wife won't mind?" she asked, delighted with the game.

"I live alone. My wife died several years ago. But she wouldn't have minded; she brought models home, too." He grinned, making a joke. "Her models were dogs and cats."

She looked at him, questioning.

"She was a printmaker, etchings and drypoint, lithos. Alice Kitchen—the name she worked under, her maiden name."

She stared at him, sick, faint. The street seemed insubstantial, as if she would fall. *Alice . . . Alice is dead, Alice . . .* She saw Alice suddenly. Alice's face exploding back into consciousness so alive, her delicate features, her wry smile, her long, pale hair . . . . She saw Alice walking up Russian Hill, her peasant skirt blowing . . . *My wife died several years ago . . . Alice—Alice died . . . Alice . . .*

She was so faint, so sick, shaking with the pain of Alice's death.

She didn't remember clearly walking back to the studio. She didn't want to go in. She wanted to run away, curl up somewhere, and try to deal with Alice's death. He watched her, puzzled.

She moved on in woodenly, through the door he held

open, and stood uncertainly, looking around her. "You—you both painted here?"

He nodded, motioning to the left. "That part was Alice's studio, where the paintings are stacked. Would you like some coffee or tea?"

"I—tea would be nice." She wanted to sit down; she wanted to be alone; she wanted to cry and was too shocked to cry.

"Are you all right? You're so pale." He led her to the model's couch and got her settled, then stood looking down at her, concerned.

"I'm fine. Just—just—some tea will make me feel better."

When he had gone she touched the marks on the orange velvet where her wet cat feet had stained it. She ran her finger guiltily over the little holes she had made with her claws. One of her stiff white whiskers was caught in the velvet. She listened to Braden putting cups on a tray and tried to think about Alice, was afraid to think about her.

Her thin face, her warm, gentle eyes. Pale hair, long, pale hair. Long, full skirts. The smell of charcoal and fixative. Clear, beautiful skin.

And there had been another house. They had lived there, not here. She and Alice and Alice's parents. A tall house with jutting windows. She and Alice could see the bay from their bedroom. Her father was a painter, that's why the scent of paints and turpentine was so familiar.

Braden carried the tray out to the terrace and dried off the table and chairs with a towel. He had sliced some shortbread onto a blue ceramic plate. "Did you look at the painting?"

"I like it very much; it's beautiful. Rich." She saw that he was pleased. She said, "It's—it makes me feel like I'm swimming in color and light, like I'm made of color and light." But she could not, adequately, describe the way the painting made her feel.

He watched her, delighted with her. He thought maybe he had harbored a fear that she would turn out to be crude and unfeeling, because now he felt relieved. As the low sun threw amber light across her hair, he thought her brown hair wasn't the right color for her skin and light brows. Her lashes were dark, though, and so thick he had thought she used a black liner. But when she looked down, he decided she didn't use any makeup. He had a strange feeling of familiarity, watching her. As of someone he hadn't seen since he was a boy: a face he had known well, but which now was so changed he could put no place or time with it. He said, "Could you start posing today?"

She had been toying with her shortbread. When she looked up, he found it hard to look away. "I—yes, I could start today."

He left her to finish her tea while he got his sketching things together, stuffing charcoal, pastels, fixative and a sketch pad into a canvas bag.

In the village, they worked in front of the wine shop, the amber and red bottles reflected around her. He caught the quick reflection of a passing woman against her shoulder, and of a boy on a bike. Then in front of the little grocery she was mirrored against the yellows and reds and greens of the produce bins, distorted to jagged abstractions by the glass. He worked intently, feeling Melissa's response to him in her glances, in her languorous poses. They seemed caught together in a separate place, set apart from the pedestrians and occasional gawkers. Drawing the light along her cheek was like caressing her; drawing the line of her throat made him warm with desire.

As the afternoon dimmed they worked in front of the library, her image captured among reflections of the dark forest. But this sketch disturbed him. She looked, among the heavy shadows, not caught in reflections but caught in an atmosphere that wanted to swallow her, that reached out to make her vanish.

And he wondered suddenly what Alice would think of this girl. Then guilt touched him, and pain came powerfully. He closed the drawing pad and cleaned up his pastels.

As they walked back into the village she made no move to leave him. She didn't mention where she lived. At the corner by the Greyhound station, he asked her to have dinner with him. She said she would. They had walked for some minutes more beneath the street lights, heading back to the garden, when she asked him how his wife had died.

Chapter 35

The lights of the street lamps looked thin and insubstantial, as if they burned in another dimension. The evening air was chill. He told himself Melissa had asked the question casually, yet she seemed intense. She had turned pale when he had mentioned Alice. He watched her, frowning, not wanting to talk about Alice. He said shortly, "She was killed in a car accident. A truck went over the center line."

"Where?" she said softly. "Where did it happen?" Her look was naked, hurt, and unguarded. The next instant her eyes were veiled.

"On the approach to Golden Gate Bridge. The truck hit her sideways, her car went over the cliff." Her question had forced him to live it again: the phone call, then running to his car, barreling down Bayshore, running down the hill to her car, the fire truck hosing down the gas, men pulling at him to keep him from tearing at the rescue team.

He was sweating when they reached the garden. In the studio he left her looking at paintings while he made himself a drink and waited for the water to boil for her tea, stood in the kitchen trying to regain his composure. Why the hell had she asked about Alice? It wasn't any of her business. He heard her go into the bathroom to wash, going directly there, not searching for it. Well, it was a small house.

When he took the tray in she was curled up on the model's couch on the vermilion silk, her sandals off, looking comfortable and at home. She blushed under his intent stare, and looked down.

"I'm sorry," he said. "I was seeing a painting."

She looked up again and smiled, her eyes as green as sunlit sea. "Your wife was very young when she died."

"Twenty-nine." He fiddled with his drink, shaking the ice. Why did she keep asking? And yet now for some reason he wanted to tell her. "If she'd come home at a different time, hadn't been in that particular spot when the truck went over, hadn't stopped to get wine and lobster, hadn't stopped to take her cat drawings to the museum—a few seconds one way or the other, and the truck wouldn't have been there. All so useless, so damned useless." He got up and stood at the window with his back to her. "And so damned pointless to imagine what might have been if she'd just skipped one appointment."

"What—what were the cat drawings?"

He turned to look at her. "She'd done some drawings of a door with cat faces carved on it. It's up in the garden." He gestured toward the terraces. "The door in the side of the hill—the gardener keeps tools there. Alice wanted to see if anyone at the Museum of History might be interested in researching the door. It looks medieval, but of course it's probably a copy." He crossed the room abruptly and went to freshen his drink.

She sat looking after him, ashamed that she had upset him. But the pain was hers, too. Her memory of Alice was like pressing at a new, raw wound. Alice's deceptively delicate face, her cheek always smudged with charcoal, her funny twisted grin. The pain held Melissa in a grip like huge hands crushing out her breath.

She rose and went down the room. At the far end, above the stacked paintings, glassed-in bookcases faced the windows. Art books filled them now, but once there had been china animals. She and Alice used to play with them, making up stories. She reached beneath a glass door and slipped the hidden latch and felt the weight of the door as she drew it open. She imagined the set of white china horses they both had loved. But this was another unconnected memory; she couldn't bring it all together. She turned suddenly, sensing that Braden watched her.

"How did you know to do that? Open the latch?"

"I suppose I've seen one like it," she said quietly. "How long were you and Alice married?"

"Four years."

"And you lived here in the studio, and worked here together. But before that, who lived in this house?"

"Alice's aunt. We moved over from the city after she died; she left the house to Alice. We remodeled—tore out some walls to get the studio space."

"Aunt Carrie," she said softly, the pictures flooding back of a square, stocky Aunt Carrie, her short white hair always mussed, her thick ankles hidden in opaque stockings.

"When did she die, Braden?"

"A year before we were married," he said quietly. "Of heart failure. She was diabetic."

"Yes. Insulin shots." Pale white skin, the needle.

He looked at her evenly. "You gave me the impression you were a stranger."

"I suppose I did." The memories were fitting together now, the memory of her childhood far sharper now than any fragmented memory of the Netherworld.

He was very still, hadn't touched his drink. "Turn your head, Sarah."

She held the profile until he said, "All right," as he would if he were drawing her. He stood moments more looking at her, then turned away and knelt before an oversized chest with long, thin drawers. He pulled out the bottom drawer and began to shuffle through drawings. He removed one, studied it, and handed it to her.

She looked down into the face of a child, in profile against the door of the cats. The cats' faces surrounded hers. Braden got his sketch pad and held, next to Alice's drawing, his own drawing done an hour earlier as she had stood against the dark woods, her profile sharply defined in the library window.

They were the same. The child's wide mouth was turned up at the corners. She had the same nose, the same dark lashes and light brows. Only the hair was different. The child's hair was a patchwork of pale and dark streaks, several shades mixed together, tumbling down her shoulders.

He rose and went out to the veranda, and stood looking up the garden. She laid the drawings on the coffee table side by side, stared at them, then escaped to the bathroom.

She shut the door and stood looking into the mirror. She saw, superimposed over her present reflection, the face of the child who had, years ago, stood looking into this glass.

She and Alice used to come here to stay with Aunt Carrie for weekends. The door of the cats had been her special place. She remembered when Alice had drawn her there. "Just a few more minutes, Melissa—you can be still just a little while more . . ."

She remembered the last time she was alone by the door. Alice had gone into town to get something for Aunt Carrie. She had been playing and talking to the carved cats. She had been grabbed from behind and jerked into the tool room. The oak door slammed as she kicked and bit. Her screams were muffled by a hand over her mouth. A woman's voice hissed words she didn't know—rhythmic words.

The voice had been Siddonie's.

The next memory that would come was of riding double behind Mag, looking down the rocky cliff, seeing a thatched stone cottage, not knowing where she was or how she had gotten there.

When she came out of the bathroom, he was standing before the coffee table looking at the drawings. He looked up at her.

"Melissa."

"Yes."

"Alice thought you were dead."

"My memory was dead. For years I didn't know my true name—I thought it was Sarah. I didn't remember anything. I came here to try to remember. I saw you in the studio working, and I remembered this house."

"You met me on purpose today."

"Yes."

"And in front of the tea shop?"

"I had started to come in, then I saw you and I was afraid suddenly," she lied. "I knew you lived here but I didn't know who you were. I didn't remember Alice then—only the house."

She sat down on the edge of the couch. "Maybe I was afraid of finding out more." It was hard to tell him half the truth. She found it hard to lie to him. "I didn't even know what color my hair was. Someone kept it dyed. I . . ." She felt shaken because he was so angry—silent and pale and angry. "It—sounds silly but I—I would like to wash the dye out." She looked at him openly. "It would—maybe I would feel more like Melissa. Maybe *be* more like Melissa."

He nodded curtly. "The towels are in the bathroom cupboard, the shampoo on the shelf in the shower."

She fled for the bathroom, chagrined and hurt. If she'd had anywhere else to run to, she would have gone. In the bathroom she dropped her dress and turned on the shower, trying with panic to remember the spell Mag had used with the dye.

And, in the shower, whispering the reverse of the spell, scrubbing her mass of hair, she watched brown dye flow away mixing with the running water.

She toweled and knelt before the little electric wall heater, drying her hair just as she and Alice used to kneel side by side, warned by Aunt Carrie over and over never to touch the heater while their hair was wet.

When her hair was dry, she rose and stood looking at herself in the mirror.

Her hair was all in streaks: shades of rust, and streaks so pale they were almost white, and streaks nearly black, all in a patchwork of colors. This, with her green eyes, gave her such a resemblance to the calico she was afraid to go back into the studio, for fear that secret would be destroyed.

But that was silly. No upperworlder would think of shape shifting. To be Catswold would be beyond an upperworlder's ability to believe.

She dressed slowly, combed her hair with Braden's comb, and went out.

He was opening a bottle of wine. When he looked up at her, his dark eyes widened. She swallowed.

He said nothing for a long time, then, "It's beautiful. It suits you. It's the way she drew you." He paused, then, "She loved you, Melissa. She never stopped searching for you."

She took the wine he offered. She wanted to weep for Alice, not only with her own pain but with the pain in Braden's eyes.

She said, "When I was small, she would wake me in the mornings hugging me, her long, pale hair down around us like a tent, making me giggle." She took his hand. "You loved her very much. I am just beginning to remember how much I loved her."

They were quiet for a while, then she said, "There was another house, too. A tall house on a hill, with a view of the bay. I think that was where we lived."

"The Russian Hill house." He searched her face. "We can talk over dinner. I think we could both use something to eat. I'll wash, just be a minute."

Before he went to wash he put food on the veranda for the cat, and stood on the terrace calling her, looking up the garden as if he might see the white flash of her face threading along through the dark foliage. And Melissa sat alone in the studio trying to reconstruct the dark time before she knew Alice.

There had been a tangle of strangers, one after another. And Siddonie had come sometimes—a handsome, terrifying young woman with strange games she wanted Melissa to play. But then when she went to live with the Kitchens in the Russian Hill house, Siddonie had not come so often. There she was happy for the first time.

Braden returned wearing a sport coat and pale slacks. His glance slid across her long skirt, making her wish she had other clothes. She said, "I think your little cat was here. Is she orange and black and white? I tried to let her in but she ran. Cats don't like me much. I guess I should have let her eat in peace. How beautiful she is, really lovely." She hid her smile. "I expect she'll come back when I've gone."

Walking out to the car, she wanted to look at the door. But when they stood before it, a chill touched her. He would be thinking of the drawings and of Alice's death. And again she was ashamed and sorry that she had stirred his pain.

Chapter 36

The cars racing by them, the speeding lights and the speed of their own car dizzied and terrified her. Again she felt the little cat's panic as trucks roared past on the highway. She told herself that as a child she had ridden in cars. And she hid her fear from Braden. He was telling her about McCabe.

He had met McCabe only briefly, but he knew a lot about him from Alice and from McCabe's newspaper column. Her father had written regularly for the *Chronicle*. "An off-beat column," Braden said, "about art, politics, whatever came to mind. McCabe had an original, sharp way of looking at things. He was a building contractor but he also moved within the art community. He was a good friend of the Kitchens'. Before he met your mother, long before you were born, he encouraged Alice's interest in drawing animals. Later when Timorell moved in with him, Alice and she became friends. Timorell was about seventeen—she was eighteen when you were born. Alice was then about thirteen.

"McCabe knew that Timorell had a husband—she left him for McCabe, but he was in the city. He lived in a Russian Hill apartment with his small sister, a child about nine. Alice described her as totally evil; Alice was afraid of her."

He stopped for a signal, then moved on through traffic. She watched him, liking his lean good looks, his smile. He answered her questions honestly, she thought. He said, "Timorell was soon pregnant, and terrified her husband would find out. But the husband didn't contact her until after you were born." He turned onto the road to Tiburon, the car's lights slewing across the water.

"When you were three months old, Timorell's husband came to the apartment with his small sister. Alice was there visiting, and McCabe was at work on a house up in north Marin.

"The husband was in a rage about the baby. Timorell tried to get him to leave. As they argued, the earthquake hit. It rocked the building. The wall cracked, warping in at them. Alice described it quite graphically. Timorell was holding you, trying to protect you when the front windows collapsed inward and a huge bookcase toppled; it hit Timorell hard, she twisted and fell, and Alice grabbed you." Braden slowed for a cross street.

"Alice didn't remember clearly what happened next. She woke in the rubble, sprawled under the dining table clutching you. You were screaming. There were rafters down all around the table. Timorell was dead. Alice screamed at her and shook her, trying to wake her. The husband was alive, trapped by fallen timbers, watching Alice woodenly. But his small sister was standing over Alice staring down at the baby; she said something in a strange language, some kind of rhyme, then Alice fainted.

"When she came to, you were gone. And the sister was gone. Alice had no doubt she had taken you, and she was terrified for you. She felt things about that little girl . . ." He shook his head. "Alice was terrified of her.

"She got out of the building, got down the broken stairs, and searched for you. The street was all rubble, cars every which way, groceries scattered where they had exploded from shop windows. And there was looting, confusion everywhere. She searched until dark then made her way home hysterical and exhausted."

Melissa could see too clearly her mother lying dead. She could see young Siddonie snatching up the baby and running—stealing her, stealing the Catswold child. "And McCabe? What happened to my father?"

"He was working up here in Marin County, on a scaffolding four stories up. It fell with him. The police said that somehow he jumped free, but he was hit by falling bricks and killed."

Braden turned into a parking lot, under a row of muted lights. There were potted plants at the door of the restaurant. It was a weathered wood building set on rough pilings, extending out between the docks, over the bay.

Inside there was a small shop and then the bar. Braden led her into the shop to wait for their table. She didn't want to talk; she was filled with the past. But then in the shop, she saw on a top shelf a basket that intrigued her. When Braden lifted it down she knew she wanted it. She was fascinated by its smooth, octagonal sides and by its smell—it would be just right to nap in. She bought it, pulling the roll of bills out of her pocket, making Braden stare. "It's for your little cat." She handed the basket to him. "For her to sleep in."

He looked surprised, then faintly embarrassed. "She sleeps all over the silks I keep for models; she's clawed the hell out of them." He grinned. "Maybe, with a basket, she won't get on them."

When their table was called Braden watched the other women studying Melissa, her hair, her lithe beauty. It made no difference that she wore a long, rather strange dress, she would be smashing in anything. He was surprised she wasn't used to such stares, that the glances made her uneasy. Only when they were seated did she forget the other women watching her, as she became fascinated with the fishing boats crowding the dock outside their window. Her green eyes took in every detail of rigging, her mouth curving up in the little smile he liked. He wanted to touch her throat, her cheek. He wanted to make love to her. He wanted to know her better, to know what she thought, to show her new things, to take her sailing in the bay, or maybe riding. He felt a pang of guilt at being unfaithful to Alice, then realized how stupid that was.

When he asked her if she rode, she seemed surprised that he did. He told her he had learned to ride in England after the war. "Because of a girl whose name I've long since forgotten."

"The war," she said, watching him, seeming almost puzzled.

"I was in the Second Marines, in the Pacific. But after the armistice they sent me to England as an embassy guard. It was after I came home that I met Alice, when I was teaching." He picked up his menu. "What would you like? The lobster's usually good."

"Oh, yes, the lobster." She looked as if lobster was the most wonderful thing in the world. Everything seemed wonderful to her; she seemed to drink in every sight, every sound as if the whole world was spanking new, as if she had just been born.

But yet, watching her, he was sharply aware of another side. Despite her quiet enthusiasm, she gave him the impression she was holding something back, that there was far more to her life than she was letting him see.

"Wine?" he said. "The chablis?"

She nodded.

"Melissa, the Kitchens will be beside themselves when they learn you're alive." He watched her hands tighten on the menu. She had been reading the menu as eagerly as if it were deathless prose. "To the Kitchens, you were like their own child. Your disappearance caused a rift in that family that has never healed.

"They've gone to Europe for the summer. If I knew where, I'd call them. We could drive into the city tomorrow so you can see the house."

"Oh, yes. I'd like that."

*   *   *

When their dinner came she was starved, and the lobster smelled wonderful. She attacked it eagerly then realized he was staring. She felt her face redden. She slowed down, taking smaller bites. But it was the most wonderful food she had ever imagined—far richer than the rock lobsters which could sometimes be found in sea caves of the Netherworld.

He said, "The Kitchens have tenants in the house, but we can ask if they . . ."

She shook her head. "I don't want to disturb anyone. I don't—want to explain to strangers. It would be nice just to see it from the outside."

He nodded. "We could go to the Cat Museum, too—it's the best example I know of McCabe's work. He completely changed the old buildings. Alice must have taken you there."

She tried to remember and could not.

"We can get some nice poses in the museum gardens working against the windows—reflections of the oak trees and of the outdoor cat sculptures." And now she remembered. Bronze cats, brick paths beneath twisted branches, white walls and long windows.

She had loved the Cat Museum; how could it have faded from her memory? When she was small its galleries and gardens had been a haven for the part of herself that even Alice didn't see. She had always loved cats, had run to cats on the street to pet them, upsetting her foster parents and enraging some of the cats. And even though she and Alice had cats, some element had been missing, something she had come close to only in the Cat Museum.

He said, "The place has the feeling of a self-contained world. The reflections of the twisted trees and the sculpture are just what I want—you will fit perfectly. I think we can get some exciting work there."

She smiled at him, liking his intensity, his deep involvement in the work. She did not see such passion of purpose in the Netherworld. Except of course in Siddonie's dark passions.

"I'll pick you up in the morning if you'll tell me where, what part of the city."

"I'm staying in the village with someone, quite near to you. I'll walk over." She watched him set a morsel of lobster aside for the calico. She must have looked amused, because he grinned shyly.

"I spoil her. I never thought I'd have a cat, let alone spoil it."

"Doesn't she deserve to be spoiled?" she said softly. "She's so beautiful, a really lovely cat." She couldn't resist, the deception was delicious. And she could see his pleasure when she admired his cat. Their eyes met and held, and she shivered. But she thought, *I am Catswold. We are totally different. I should not let myself be so drawn to an upperworlder—I will be sorry. Already I can feel the pain this involvement would cause. I am Catswold, I am of the blood of Catswold queens, the blood of Bast.* She watched idly as the dessert cart was wheeled toward them, and let herself be distracted. Such desserts in the Netherworld were served only to royalty. She selected the most beautiful one, but it was too sweet and disappointed her. Sipping her tea, she said, "Did Timorell or McCabe leave anything personal? Something of—sentimental value? Jewelry, perhaps?" *An emerald pendant, perhaps?*

He watched her, frowning. "John Kitchen salvaged some of McCabe's paintings and prints. I think there was a safe deposit box. McCabe and Kitchen had the same attorney, one they both trusted. He might know. I'll give him a call, if you like."

She nodded. Things in this world were so complicated. She was yawning when they left the restaurant, was almost asleep when they turned into the lane. When he asked where she was staying, she said she would walk. He insisted he take her.

"But I really want to walk. The evening's lovely."

"Then I'll walk with you. It's late to be walking by yourself. I won't pry or question your living arrangements."

She looked at him, puzzled, then got out, handing him the basket. "I'll be fine. You have canvases to stretch. It's only a little way, and there are street lights."

"You can't *know* you'll be fine. The streets are empty, Melissa."

She touched his arm. "Please. I'll see you in the morning, early."

He stared at her then turned and left her, striking fast across the garden to the terrace. She watched him retrieve his key and push inside, not looking back. And she turned on her heel and hurried away, sorry she had angered him.

Deep in the woods she changed to cat. As cat she wandered the garden, thinking and enjoying her sharpened perceptions, her improved eyesight, the stronger smells. But then as she passed the white house she detected a scent that made her leap to cover, her tail lashing: Wylles. From the open bedroom window came the faint scent of Prince Wylles.

She crouched in the bushes, remembering the palace room where he had lain in bed when she took in his breakfast tray, remembering the boy's dark, cold eyes so like Siddonie's. She left the bushes and approached the house, rigid with fright. Crouching, she watched the open window.

She judged her distance and leaped, gaining the sill. Pressed against the screen, she watched Prince Wylles asleep in Tom Hollingsworth's bed. Seeing the prince here in this world gave her a strange, disoriented feeling, as if the two worlds were being forced unnaturally together.

And suddenly as she watched him, Wylles' breathing changed.

He didn't move, he still lay hunched around the pillow. But suddenly his eyes were open, staring straight at her. In the next instant he exploded to life, snatching a drinking glass from the table. He threw it as she leaped off the sill; crouched in the garden below she heard it smash against the wall. Then he was fumbling at the screen's latch. She backed into the bushes as Wylles shouted, "Stay away from me! I don't know what you are, but if you come near me I'll kill you!"

She waited until he left the window, then fled, streaking down the garden.

But as she leaped for the safety of the studio terrace, she realized that Wylles had driven away the last blocks to her memory. Her picture of the Netherworld was whole now—her life there with Mag, all the little details sharply fitted together. She saw clearly her days in Affandar Palace under Siddonie's domination. Frantically she clawed at the studio door, wanting Braden, wanting to be safe in the studio.

Yet when he came to let her in she sat down on the terrace switching her tail, suddenly feeling contrary and uncooperative. And highly amused. She might be, as girl, rather straightforward. But as cat she was a tease; and her own indomitable cat nature amused her.

He stood staring down at her, annoyed. "Come on in, for Christ sake! What the hell were you clawing the door for if you don't want in!"

She switched her tail.

"Christ, you're gone all day and half the night. You never come when I call you. But when *you* want in, you tear the hell out of the door. And then you just sit there." He glowered at her, enraged. "When you're gone the whole damned day, don't you think I worry about you? Get the hell in here if you want in!"

She got up and swaggered in, highly entertained, and headed for the couch.

"What's so funny? What's so goddamn funny?"

She stared at him, shocked. She hadn't thought he would see her amusement. She didn't know that a laugh showed on her cat face. She turned away quickly, jumped on the couch, and curled down on the satin.

Braden watched her. The damn cat had been laughing at him. And this wasn't the first time he'd had that feeling. And he wondered if he was getting a bit strange. Frowning, he took the piece of lobster to the kitchen and put it on a plate. "Your lobster's served, my lady."

She came running, and tied into the morsel as if she hadn't eaten in weeks.

When she finished he got her some cat food, then realized

he should have given her that first. Now she wouldn't touch it. She sauntered back to the studio, jumped on the couch, and began to wash, seeming as content as if she'd just gorged herself on the whole lobster. It was then that he remembered the basket.

He put it down on the couch for her.

She looked up at him, pleased. She seemed to like its smell. She got in, tail waving, circled, and curled down with a sensuous wiggle. Tucking her chin under, she smiled upside down at him, her green eyes slitted, her white throat exposed, her white paws drooping languidly over her belly. Her eyes, he thought, were as green as the sea—green as Melissa's eyes.

Chapter 37

Olive Cleaver didn't sleep well. She thought in the night that she heard Tom shout, *"Come near me—I'll kill you!"* She knew she had dreamed it, but she lay awake a long time thinking about Tom. She was puzzled by the change in the boy, distressed for him and for Anne.

She had gone over yesterday to ask Tom to help her with the research, thinking that might get him out of the house. But he had been so surly, so rude, that she had left after just a few minutes.

She had never seen Tom like that before. He said he had no use for books and why would he go anywhere with an old woman? She had left feeling very hurt. Now, lying awake, she tried to understand what she might have done to anger him and, worrying, she rose at last and went downstairs.

It was near dawn, beginning to grow light. She opened the

curtains to let in the sunrise, then made herself a pot of cocoa. She sat before the window sipping it, wrapped in her heavy robe and wearing her thick slippers, looking out at the garden.

She saw Braden let out the little calico cat. She was pleased that he had kept her. The cat trotted happily up the garden past her house, heading for the woods.

She was pouring a second cup of cocoa when a young woman passed her porch at the same spot, coming down from the woods, and went directly to Braden's. The same young woman she had seen around the garden the last few days. Maybe Braden had a new interest. Certainly she was a striking creature. Strange, Olive thought, she didn't remember her hair being so arresting. Maybe she had just had it done—she must have spent a fortune on it. Maybe she was an actress, made up for some part. Really, when you got used to her hair, it was stunning. Olive watched her knock, watched Braden let her in, then went to shower and dress, turning her thoughts to the research.

Chapter 38

"Get on the horse! Get on the horse *now!*"

"I won't! I'm afraid!" Tom backed away from the roan mare warily.

He wasn't afraid. He liked horses. But he stared at the queen stubbornly, defying her, determined she would not make him do anything. He hadn't asked to come here. He wanted to be home. The sooner she found she couldn't make him obey, the sooner . . .

The sooner, what? Tom thought, reining in his anger.

Did he think she would take him back to the upperworld? Why should she? As he turned away from the horse the pain hit him: a fire shot through his body so hard he was jerked to his knees. He couldn't move—the pain was so violent tears welled up involuntarily.

"Get on the horse." Siddonie grabbed his arm, jerking him up. "Get on."

"I won't."

The pain came, harder. He had never hated anyone, until this woman. He hated her. And was terrified of her.

"Get on now."

"Go fuck yourself."

Her rage was so great he thought she would kill him. He felt himself go dizzy then retchingly sick. His stomach heaved, and the sharp pain struck through him as if it ground his bones—he had never been so hurting and sick. He held himself straight, staring at her, filled with angry defiance until blackness tilted over him; he reeled, and fainted.

It was hours later that Efil, having watched the performance, was able to slip into the boy's room, breaking the locking spells on the chamber door. Siddonie had ridden off with Vrech toward the northern mines or maybe for a frolic in some deserted herder's cabin; he didn't care which. She didn't know he was in the palace, she thought he had ridden to Cressteane. He had doubled back, watching her ludicrous attempt to make the boy ride, an attempt she repeated every day.

The room was dim, the draperies pulled shut. He closed the door quickly and bound it with his own spells, then cast a light across the sleeping boy's face, not expecting him to stir. But when the light hit him, the boy woke.

Efil smiled. "You are strong, Tom Hollingsworth. Siddonie's spells are not as effective as she thinks. She means for you to sleep until she wants you in the stable yard again."

The boy watched him warily.

"Do you know where you are, Tom? Do you remember where you came from?"

The boy's eyes drooped as he fought the sleepiness stirred by such questions.

"No matter. You will know in time. I am Efil, king of Affandar."

"What is Affandar?" Tom sat up, punching a pillow behind him. "Where have you taken me? What is this all about? Who is this Queen Siddonie?" His brown eyes were very like Wylles'. Efil was fascinated by the resemblance. "Where is this place? Why did she bring me here? What does she want with me?"

"Vrech brought you here."

"The gardener, yes. He's a bastard." The boy swung off the bed; Efil caught him as he fell. With the spell Siddonie had put on him, he was surprised the boy could get up at all.

"The queen has plans for you, Tom. But perhaps we can change the outcome. If you will trust me."

The boy was silent, looking him over. At last he said, "I don't know whether I can trust you. But right now, I don't have any other choice." He leaned back against the pillows pulling for a full breath—that was the henbane. Efil made a quick healing spell, and the boy's breathing came easier and his color quickened. His eyes widened at the change within himself; he watched Efil with new interest.

"The queen's spells and the herbs make you ill. I have countered them, but that is not always possible. Nor will my spell last. I will lay what spells I can to help you, if you will do as I tell you."

"Can you get me away from here? Can you get me home? Is my mother all right?"

"I'm sure no one has bothered her. I will try to get you home, but it will take time. You must first help me."

Tom looked around the darkened room. "I don't want to stay here."

"You must, for the present. You must pretend obedience to the queen's powers. You must ride, as she tells you. Once she has trained you in horsemanship and to behave like the real Wylles of Affandar, she will take you out among the villages. You must do as she tells you—it is the only way I can help you."

"But what does she want? Why is she doing this?"

"She has brought you here to replace the sick prince. You look like him. Vrech searched a long time to find a boy who looks like him, then he—arranged for you to move to the house in the garden."

The boy's eyes widened. Efil put a hand on his arm. "There is no time for anger. You can only work at saving yourself. Siddonie will not harm you as long as you impersonate Wylles, as long as you are of value to her."

"But if I could get away . . ."

"It would do you no good to escape, Tom. You cannot leave the Netherworld alone. No portal will open for you; they will open only for a Netherworlder."

"But you can open this portal?"

"In time I can."

"I don't understand. And I don't understand about the Netherworld. A netherworld would be an imaginary place."

"This world lies below your world. You came here through the portal in the garden where you live—the door carved with cats."

"The tool shed door? But there's only a little room inside."

"That room opens to a tunnel. The wall behind it can be opened by a spell, but only by one of us."

The boy looked doubtful.

"Where do you think you are, then? What do you think has made you so ill and makes you sleep all the time?"

"Drugs, maybe."

"Drugs, yes. But magic, too," the king said. "I will try to get you home. But first you must follow the queen's lead—let her think you are spell-cast and obedient."

"And what do *you* want in return?"

"I want to get you out of here. Your presence will destroy my own plans." Efil smiled. "Don't fear, I cannot kill you. It is against the Primal Law. I can only get you home again—at my own time, in my own way."

He soon left the boy, satisfied with the conversation, certain that the boy would do as he ordered.

Already he had started rumors of the imminent birth of his child by another woman. Soon, he would let his subjects know the queen had brought a changeling into the Netherworld. Later, he would prove that was true. If that caused danger to the changeling boy, what difference?

He took the back stairs down to the stables, thinking about Melissa, hoping she was still alive. He would bring her down, surround her with divining ceremonies by the old soothsayer, let the peasants see her, create all the pomp he could to prove a child was on the way. A Catswold child, who could draw all the nations together—under his rule.

Chapter 39

The Harpy and Mag and the gathered rebels watched, in the Harpy's little mirror, as Efil talked with Tom. When the king promised to free Tom, the Harpy clacked her beak. "Certainly he will."

Halek laughed. "Might you show us the dispossessed Prince Wylles? Or does your mirror have the power to reach that far, Harpy?"

The Harpy jabbed her beak at Halek companionably, and brought a sharp reflection of Prince Wylles, alone in a bedroom of the Hollingsworth house.

Wylles had grown fatter, and he had some color now. His face was not pinched by sickness anymore, but only by his sour disposition. He was investigating the bedroom cupboards and closet, tossing the contents onto the floor. He seemed not to be stealing but simply destructive or inquisitive, perhaps fascinated with upperworld trinkets. As they watched he pulled out sweaters, a woman's shoes, an electric iron, examined each then tossed it aside. He stopped sometimes and looked around him as if he wondered where he was. "Likely," the Harpy said, "he has not fully regained his memory.

"But still," she said, watching him more closely, "there is a wariness about him. There is, don't you think, a look of fear in Wylles' eyes?" She glanced up at Mag, but held the vision steady as a dark-skinned woman entered the house.

This woman was there often overseeing the boy. She and the skinny, older, pale woman were neighbors in the little communal setting of the garden. The Harpy said, "She knows there's something strange about the boy. She half believes as his mother does that he is not Tom." They watched Morian look about her with disgust at the dirty kitchen. The boy, in the bedroom, hadn't bothered to answer her knock.

Morian considered the filthy kitchen table, where cracker crumbs had been smeared into chocolate syrup and peanut butter. Open jars of pickles, jam, and cocktail onions stood amid a clutter of dirty dishes. More dirty dishes were stacked in a tilting pile in the sink. She thought of cleaning up; it was only mid-morning, she had time before class. But she decided not to give the boy the satisfaction. She knew Anne hadn't left the kitchen in this mess.

She had grown to hate this chore of checking on Tom. Up until his illness, he had always been responsible when left alone.

She called to him, then went to look for him. She found him in Anne's bedroom.

He had everything out of the closet and the dresser drawers, dumped in a heap on the floor. Clothes were piled in corners and strewn tangled across the bed. The room looked like the Salvation Army sales room after a scatter bomb. She wanted to snatch the kid up and beat the tar out of him. She said, "I knocked. I guess you didn't hear me."

He glowered. "What do you want?"

She took a deep breath. "I promised Anne I'd look in. Anything you need?"

Silence. They stared at each other.

She moved nearer the boy. "I suggest you clean up this mess, and the mess in the kitchen, before Anne gets home."

"Why should I?"

"Because if Anne finally loses patience with you—and that could be very soon—she will do something about you. Tell me, have you ever been inside a mental hospital? Have you ever seen patients tied to the bedposts, or huddled into straitjackets with their arms wrapped around them so they can't even scratch their own noses? So they can't eat by themselves, or go to the bathroom by themselves? Have you ever seen patients with electric caps on their heads, with wires stuck into their brains giving them electric shock treatments?"

She had to suppress a smile. Whatever her description lacked in accuracy was made up for by the expression on the boy's face. And as she watched him, Morian was filled with the cold certainty she had had for days—that this boy wasn't Tom.

"If Anne thinks you are mentally ill, Tom, as your behavior suggests, she will certainly put you in a mental hospital. And they not only give the patients shock treatments, they put them on drugs that make vegetables of them.

"The windows have bars on them, Tom, and the steel doors are locked at night. And sometimes the medical students from the university come to—ah, study them."

Fear twisted deeper in the boy's eyes, and his lips were a tight line. But then hatred blazed from his eyes, raw and cold, stirring a dark fear in her.

She had no theory about what this boy was doing here or how he got here, or where Tom was; the idea of the boys being switched was too bizarre. Half her mind could not accept such a notion. But the other half—the deep, instinctual half—knew that Tom was gone.

She went away quietly, leaving the boy tearing up Anne's bedroom. Telling herself that her instinct was wrong, that no

sensible person would believe Tom had been kidnapped and
a stranger left in his place.

Going back across the garden she saw Braden and a girl
getting into his station wagon. She lifted a hand to him, admiring the girl's astonishing hair, wondering what kind of
fortune she spent on that wonderful mane. Maybe she was
an actress done up for a part. Braden looked pleased as hell
with her. Morian smiled and put Tom out of her thoughts.
She went on home feeling good.

That morning, Wylles changed his tactics. He began to co-
operate. Perhaps his increased wariness was engendered by
the cat he had seen watching him, or perhaps by Morian's
rage; likely even Wylles himself didn't know what ruled
him. He cleaned up Anne's bedroom, then he cleaned the
kitchen and did the dishes. Then he found an excuse to visit
Olive Cleaver, turning himself into a boy just as bright and
amiable as Tom had ever been.

Chapter 40

The tall Victorian house rose above the narrow street shadowed by the branches of twisted oaks laced across the slate
roof. The jutting bay windows stood open, their white curtains blowing just as they had blown when Melissa was a
child. The brick walk was mossy in patches just as it had
been, and the garden flowers looked the same. She wondered if the clay marker still stood in the garden where, long
before she was born, Alice had buried her little cat.

She realized Braden was watching her, and she took his
hand. When first he had turned onto the narrow street she

hadn't looked at the house, had sat looking down the hill at the familiar rooftops, afraid to look up at the windows of their old room. And then when she did look, the house was so familiar and warm that she might just have stepped off the school bus. And suddenly without warning she was crying.

Braden drew her to him and held her. She cried against him, unable to stop, stricken with the loss of those years and the loss of Alice, her memories jolting back with terrible power.

He held her a long time and didn't say anything. After a while she turned away and blew her nose, ashamed to have made a scene. She didn't want to get out of the car, she didn't want to look at the house anymore, it hurt too much. He touched her chin and turned her face back to him, wiped a tear away, and kissed her lightly on the cheeks and eyes. When he started the car he drove slowly on up the hill, in the direction she and Alice used to walk—up the winding street toward the Cat Museum, letting her look at the familiar neighborhood. After several blocks, at the top of the hill, he parked beside a sprawling cluster of white walls and twisted oaks. Memories of the Cat Museum came back to her all at once, so powerfully she might have really returned to the days of childhood.

The museum's grounds crowned the hill. The red tile roofs of its white stucco buildings were patterned by the trees' lacy shadows. Some of the buildings were low, some were two-storied. McCabe had tied existing houses and out-buildings together with garden walls and roofed walkways. On beyond the museum cluster rose the Victorian roofs of the neighborhood. She got out slowly, looking.

The iron gates stood open, and she slipped through as eagerly as she had hurried through as a child. She almost thought if she turned, Alice would be behind her, as if the two times had warped together. A cool breeze touched her, and she breathed in the sun-warmed scent of lilac.

Within the gardens, the galleries opened one to another, their white walls set at angles. She wandered, looking in through wide french doors. Sun and shadow swept across the sculptures, each on its individual white stand: a rearing stone cat, a black marble cat tumbling to catch its tail, a bronze cat hunting, a tangle of jade cats playing. Beyond the sculptures, paintings hung against the white walls, well placed, and of every school. She had a sharp memory of Alice walking away through an arch carrying her drawing pad, her long, straight hair swinging bright in the museum lights.

Where a series of sculpture shelves climbed to a niche beside a skylight, a gray cat slept. Other cats wandered the galleries and gardens. She wondered if McCabe had come here as a cat, leaping the wall at night to enjoy the vistas he had created.

When they got to work, Braden posed her in a walled garden where a window reflected two fighting bronze cats. He worked quickly, with charcoal. Then she posed beside a marble cat mirrored in the dark waters of a fish pond. As he worked, cats sauntered past her, rubbing against the sun-warmed sculpture stands. A white cat raced by, wild with play, and fled over the wall. Two striped cats chased along the top of the wall. Set into the garden walls were clay plaques inscribed with quotations. She remembered sounding out the words when first learning to read. Now, during her rest she wandered, reading them. Above a recessed bench were the words from one of the pages Mag had hidden under the dresser:

> *I am beauty, I am all things sensuous. In Bubastis in the time of Egypt's greatness within the temple of cats my saffron fur was brushed by slaves until it shone like Mandarin silk. Incense was burned to me and prayers raised, and temples built to please me. As I strolled beside lotus ponds the most beautiful virgins knelt before my silken paws, and served me delicacies in golden bowls, and lay silken cushions before me.*

But this version was different, and not complete; the human part was left out. She thought about Bast's Amulet and wondered if Timorell had had it when she came up through the tunnel into the streets of San Francisco. Surely, if Timorell had been wearing it the day of the earthquake, Siddonie would have taken it.

Or maybe Timorell and McCabe had secured it where Siddonie wouldn't find it.

She wondered if the Amulet *was* in McCabe's safe deposit box. All the powers of Bast locked away, here in the upperworld.

Braden finished four sketches quickly and put his pastels away. "That's enough—you're pale. Do you feel all right?" He took her hand. "Let's go get some lunch."

She nodded, walking close to him. She was comfortable with him, as if they had always known one another.

Well, at least they had known each other longer than Braden suspected.

As they passed through the gates she was startled to see Braden's neighbor of the flowered dresses stepping out of her car in a burst of red and orange poppies. On the other side, Wylles was getting out. Melissa drew back, but the boy had seen her.

When Braden introduced them, Wylles looked at her so blankly she couldn't tell what he might remember. Yet even if his memory had mended, he might not remember her. He had seen her only once, that day in his chamber. And he had been drugged and ill, and her hair had been brown, not calico. But what was he doing here? Why would Wylles come to the Cat Museum?

Braden said, "Are you here doing research, Olive? Or just for an outing?"

"You poke fun at me, Braden."

"I don't make fun at all. I think you've done some fine work. What did you find out about the radiocarbon tests?"

Olive smiled, her wrinkles deepening. "Tenth century, just as I suspected. The door is genuine, Braden. It is an ancient Celtic piece and quite valuable."

"Then you will remove it from the garden?"

"Not at all. No one has stolen it so far, and it's in amazingly good condition." The old woman shook her head. "No,

I like it where it is. I don't know who installed it in the garden, but for some reason I can't explain, I feel it would not be right to move it." She was watching Melissa, taking in her piebald hair and her long dress.

Braden said, "Melissa has been posing for me. We were working in the museum gardens."

Melissa saw Wylles' hand move faintly and his eyes narrow, but the next moment his face was dull, closed. She didn't know whether he had masked his sudden perception, or whether the awareness was fleeting and he had sunk again into the lethargy of drugs and spells.

When they were in the car heading down the hill, Braden said, "You really don't feel well. You've lost all color. Would you rather go straight home?"

"No, just some hot tea, and something to eat. I guess I was chilled. I'll be fine. Just hungry."

But she wasn't fine. She had seen, in Wylles' look, a quick hatred. Maybe because Braden was painting her, making images. Wylles' rage upset her, as had Olive's prying into the history of the portal. The old woman's interest could stir Siddonie's spite, or worse, could awaken some other power that would best be left alone.

She watched Braden maneuver between denser traffic, swerving around a cable car. "How would I look into McCabe's safe deposit box? Where would I find it?"

He braked for a light, glancing over at her. "I can call McCabe's attorney and find out." He slowed, looking intently at her. "This is important, isn't it? I'll call from the restaurant."

She ordered while he phoned. The attorney, Mathew Rhain, was out of town. He would not be back for a week. The safe deposit box was in his office. She said, "Is there no way we could see into the box before he gets back?"

"I asked. The secretary said no, Mathew is the executor. He's sailing—a call would have to be ship-to-shore, and that won't open the box. It would have to be a very unusual matter to bring him back before next week."

He looked at her deeply. "I left my phone number. Rhain will call as soon as he gets back." His dark eyes were so intent; she thought he saw her distress more clearly than she had meant and that alarmed her, though she was warmed and comforted by his caring.

He said, "Whatever it is, Melissa, I'll help if I can." Then their sandwiches came and he said nothing more; they ate companionably and he didn't pry. Driving back over the bridge, he took her hand, drawing her close, but he didn't question her. She said, "Your neighbor was doing research in the Cat Museum?"

"I doubt it. Probably just an outing for Tom, to help him get his strength back. He was pretty sick recently. Though he does help her with the research sometimes. He's very bright. But I don't think her project has anything to do with cats; it's about doors. She's been fooling around with this since before Alice died. They were both fascinated with the garden door."

"The door of the cats."

"Yes."

"She doesn't find the door of the cats—unpleasant, the way you do?"

He looked at her sharply. "Did I say that?"

"No, you didn't say it," she said softly.

He remained silent.

She said, "What does Olive do with her research? What's it for?"

"She's published half a dozen pamphlets on local history and artifacts. Small presses, no money in it, but it gives her something to do—makes her feel good. She's done some speaking to Bay area groups. Alice always encouraged her, but Olive can get carried away.

"Don't get me wrong," he said. "She's not a nut. The research she does is solid—she was a research librarian. I have a librarian friend who's worked with her, who says Olive is very demanding of herself, very careful. She's just—so intent about what she does. Well," he laughed, "I shouldn't criticize that."

She grinned at him. No one could be more intent: his

whole being, when he was working, seemed concentrated into one powerfully honed strength. As if Braden, in his own way, made strong magic.

They parted at the garden, Braden to rough in a painting, and Melissa heading for the village thinking, like all females since the time of the priestesses of Bast, about garments to adorn and entice.

Chapter 41

The beautifully dressed women on San Francisco's streets had filled her with envy, made her want to get rid of the heavy, long dress, to make herself new and modern. But when she reached the shop, the thought of buying upper-world clothes began to intimidate her. She hoped a different woman would wait on her; she didn't need any more shocked looks at her nakedness.

The same woman was there—thin faced, sour. Melissa moved through the racks away from her, choosing what she wanted quickly, a green-and-white leafy dress, and then orange silk pants and pink silk top as vivid as the silks on Braden's couch. She made a concession to panties, picking out several silk concoctions that looked like they would feel nice, went into the dressing room alone, and bolted the door.

The green-and-white dress felt light on her naked body. Its colors were as rich as the leafy tangles in the garden. In the mirror, she forgot about images and tried to see herself through Braden's eyes.

She bought the dress, the silk pants and top, and a pair of jeans and bright green sweat top. Wearing the jeans and sweatshirt, she let the saleswoman wrap her long dress with the new clothes. But when she reached across the counter to slip the roll of bills from her dress pocket, the woman gave her an amazed look.

"Do you want a purse for that, my dear? In the pocket of those jeans that roll will make a lump as big as your fist." The thin woman smiled at her for the first time, as if she liked Melissa better when she saw her money. Melissa hid a laugh, bought the little purse the woman offered, and dropped the money in it. She had picked up her package and turned to leave when she froze, staring out through the glass.

She had seen Efil. Already he was past, heading down the street. His face had been half-hidden by the hood of an upperworld jacket, but she had seen his profile—his rounded jaw, his thin cheek and pale skin. He had walked like Efil, a quick, light movement, faintly round shouldered. Clutching her package she hurried to the glass door to look out. Why would he be here? What was he doing here?

But of course he could be in the village. He came quite casually to the upperworld just as Vrech did, just as Siddonie came.

"May I clip the tags for you?" the saleswoman said, moving close behind her.

She stood still, feeling the woman's cold hand on her neck, wincing at the little snip of the scissors. Then she hurried out, scanning the street.

The street lights had come on, rushing the evening. The man had vanished; she had the uneasy feeling he was standing in some doorway watching for her. She thought of changing to cat and running into the woods where he wouldn't see her, but she was afraid to become small. She kept to the main street, hurrying.

She reached the garden without seeing Efil, and stood within a leafy maze looking for him. Dusk filled the garden with indistinct shadows. Above her, the forest was already dark. Down the hill, the studio lights were on; she could see the easel and Braden's legs below the painting, his occasional movement as he worked. She would be safe in the studio with Braden, protected and safe.

But she would not involve Braden in this.

Above on the hill, the three houses were dark. But there was a light on Olive's porch, and her car was gone from the drive. She went up the path quickly and around to Olive's back door where Olive kept the screen propped open for her cats. She had seen it from the woods, seen them going in and out—the white female dragging her tummy over the sill.

She hid her package on Olive's back porch behind some boxes, and in the shadows she changed to cat. She crouched, leaped to the sill, and from that high vantage she looked up into the forest.

The shadows were no longer solid black; she could see bushes between the trees. Crouching against the dark screen, she studied the forest for a long time.

She did not see Efil. She turned away at last, pushed under the open screen, and dropped onto Olive's kitchen counter.

The tile was cold under her paws. The tap was dripping, and she lapped water from it then jumped down to the linoleum and headed for the dining room. There she stood kneading her claws into the warm carpet, then reared up to see what was on the dining table. Yes, it was littered with books. She jumped on a chair then onto the table and prowled among the untidy stacks, but it was Olive's open notebook that drew her.

It was harder to read as cat. Her eyes didn't see the print so clearly, though everything else in the dim room was sharper. She dare not change to girl—if Olive came in suddenly she must find only a neighbor's cat innocently exploring. With her claws she managed to turn the notebook pages, but she had to back away to read Olive's writing.

The old woman had copied quotations, some from history books, some from collections of folklore and myth, all of them frightening. As the calico crouched reading the entries she felt her paws grow damp with sweat, felt her tail lashing as if it had a will of its own.

Some say that from within this hill they hear strange music. Closing the hill is a stone tall as a man, and it is carven with a cat. Myth says that if the right person knocks at this stone it will swing in, and he will enter into a world of ancient powers . . .

I asked them how they got under the hill, and they said that a door was hidden among the gorse. They said that door would open to an ancient world but they did not like to go there for the world was filled with cats who spoke like men.

These prehistoric burial mounds were built by an ancient Irish race, a folk whose power was broken when the ancestors of the modern Irish arrived in 3000 B.C. They fled underground and remained there among the were-beasts, and they are the Tuatha, the fairy folk.

There is a burial ground and a cave, both strong in magic, both belonging to the Cat-Kings. Both open into the antechambers of the underworld . . .

It was here in the British countries, where the Celtic witches dwelt, that the cats were taken down beneath the sod into the knowes and sithens and kept by the Tuatha, and they flourished.

Sudden footsteps made her start—someone was on the front porch. She leaped off the table and slid under the couch on her belly as the front door creaked open.

She heard Olive's voice, then the velvet voice of the black lady. She could smell her scent, musky and pleasing. Olive was saying, ". . . much more cheerful, he ate a huge plate of spaghetti at the Iron Pot. He's always loved spaghetti."

Morian said, "He's gaining weight, too. He seems—almost like the old Tom." As the two women crossed the dining room toward the kitchen, Olive paused by the table and laid her purse down among the books. "I know Anne's relieved. She's had a hard time, with things at work so chaotic, and Tom sick, too. Put the kettle on, Mor, while I cut the rum cake."

Melissa, from the dusty darkness under the couch, could see directly into the kitchen. She watched Morian move to the stove. The black woman was wearing a skimpy white sundress with plenty of honey-dark skin showing. Olive by contrast was so sallow she almost disappeared inside her red and orange flowers.

"The blue cups, or the white?" Morian said. "How's the research going?"

"The blue cups. It's going really well. I'm totally drawn in. Today we found reference to an Egyptian grave with a door inside that has a cat's head carved on it."

Melissa shivered. Braden had said the door in this garden was likely the only reference to cats Olive had come across.

Olive said, "That door led to a smaller tomb, and there were five mummified cats buried in it. I think that was the part Tom liked, the mummies. He copied the passage for me. I do think the research has helped him. He seems totally engrossed again, as he used to be."

Melissa heard the tea kettle sing. Morian said, "He seems—Tom seems all right to you?"

"He seems better. I know this has been hard for Anne, with this Lillith business. What *is* all this about the Lillith Corporation?"

"Anne thinks Lillith is trying to buy out her company. You know her firm isn't terribly big, but it's an old firm and it's always been solid. But since Lillith moved into the Bay area, through some kind of manipulation they've gained controlling interest of Meyer and Finley."

Morian carried a tray into the dining room. "Anne's boss quit last week, and that was a blow to her. And the sharpest financier they had was fired a month ago. Anne says the men who have taken their places are loud, hard to deal with, and really don't know what they're doing. Sloppy, she said. Or maybe worse. Files have disappeared, some records have been changed. Twice, Anne was blamed for important files being lost."

Olive began clearing books off the table. She didn't seem to notice that her notebook was open, though when Melissa came in it had been closed. "What a terrible thing to happen. Anne loves Meyer and Finley. That poor girl. I guess I was so interested in the research, and my sister Clara being sick—and my having to run down the Peninsula to be with her—I haven't really talked with Anne much."

"It's all happened pretty quickly. Anne's about ready to quit. She's so upset she imagines they *want* her to quit. She's applied to three other firms, one in Portland. The whole thing started just shortly before Tom got sick."

"But this Lillith firm—where has it come from?"

"Anne says they have holdings in several states, in diversified corporations and in land. The strange thing is, Anne says they put a large percent of their profits into charity."

"Here, come sit down, Mor. Why would they be so heavy into charity? Are they religiously backed?"

"No, Anne looked into that. They have no connection with any church, or with any other charity. They've set up soup kitchens and free hotels down on Mission and in several other areas of the city and down the Peninsula: one at Half Moon Bay, one at Stockton, several up around Mendocino. They have a big ranch in Mendocino, supposedly a training center for staff. But they send indigents up there, too. Men who need work. The men get bed and board for a few hours' work a day."

"That's very—altruistic."

"It's very strange," Morian said flatly.

Olive rose, startling Melissa. But she only went to refill the teapot. The rum cake smelled delicious.

Morian said, "I guess Anne's needed to talk to someone. I haven't been much help, except to listen. Lillith holds controlling stock in some Washington state businesses—a Puget Sound salmon fishing and canning operation, and some farming land."

Olive said, "Anne has checked them out pretty carefully."

"It's the charity thing that puzzles her. She's convinced Lillith is bent on destruction of the smaller Bay area firms. But why the charities?"

Olive poured more tea and passed the lemon. Melissa stretched out flat under the couch, trying not to sneeze from the dusty cloth mesh that covered its underside. Not until Olive rose to open the front screen door did she grow tense. When the yellow cat strolled in, she backed deeper under.

But the big cat didn't seem to see her; he headed straight for the table and stood sniffing as if drawn by the scent of rum cake. When he leaped onto a dining chair and stared across the table at Olive, the old woman laughed. "Pippin, the gourmet. He's been here almost constantly since Tom— since Tom grew so strange toward him." She put some rum cake on a plate and set it on the chair before the big golden cat. Melissa watched him tear into it, eating at Olive's dining table as if he were master of the house.

And Braden thought she was spoiled!

She had decided Pippin didn't know she was there when the golden cat, finished with the rum cake, jumped down and headed directly for her. She backed deeper under. He flopped down at the edge of the couch, staring in at her, his yellow eyes merry, his tail flipping. She looked back at him warily. And she realized for the first time that his eyes were not those of an ordinary cat. His gaze was far more aware and searching than a common cat, far more questioning.

Chapter 42

The golden tom stared under the couch at the calico, his eyes glowing with curiosity, his tail twitching in a semaphore of interest. She felt her own tail twitch in response. She was filled with a dangerous feeling of communion with this cat. She wanted to help him; she was certain he was more than an ordinary cat. And she dared not help him to shape shift. They gazed into each other's eyes unmoving until long after Morian had left and Olive had put her supper in the oven and gone upstairs. Pippin's expression was so filled with questions, she was certain he didn't know what he was. He seemed filled with distrust of her yet drawn to her as if longing to know what *she* was. When she stirred herself at last and came out from under the couch, he backed away from her.

She approached him and sniffed at him, then padded on past him. As she approached the door, she glanced back at him. He hadn't moved. He watched her with wide yellow eyes, but didn't attempt to follow her. She pushed quickly out through the screen, leaped off the lighted porch and underneath it, into deep shadows.

Crouching under the porch she stared out at the garden searching warily for Efil. The moon had risen, casting pale light across the garden. Below, Braden's studio lights beckoned. She could see him still at work, and she longed to be with him. She was filled with a desire so intense she was aware of his scent and could feel him stroking her.

Maybe it would be all right to go there. Efil wouldn't dare force himself into an upperworlder's house, nor would he dare challenge the tall, hard-muscled artist. She left the porch quickly and trotted down the path toward Braden's lights.

Efil was standing among the trees halfway down the garden, looking up at her. The fur along her spine and tail stiffened, she backed into shadow. She had begun the changing spell when he started up toward her. She couldn't see his face and didn't want to; he was a stranger to her now—they might never have lain together. She didn't know how she could have lain with him. The idea repelled her.

The change came quickly. She was girl now. He drew near and reached for her. She stepped aside.

"I came to take you home, Melissa. I came to take you back to the Netherworld, and to make you queen."

"No, Efil."

"But you must come back," he said, surprised. "We must formalize the child. There are ceremonies to be performed, the announcement to be made."

"I'm sorry, Efil."

He didn't seem to hear her. "Once the announcement is made I can begin the formal proceedings to dethrone Siddonie and crown you queen."

She said nothing.

"Melissa? Do you remember the Netherworld? Do you remember that you will be queen, that you are pregnant with my child? Siddonie can't have destroyed all your memory."

She stirred herself. "I am not pregnant, Efil. There is no child." She watched him narrowly. "I miscarried. The baby is dead."

He looked puzzled, then his face twisted in anger. He grabbed her shoulders hard. "You're lying. You're lying to me."

"It was very painful, there was a lot of blood. I still hurt, I still bleed some. I wept." She shuddered, turned her face away. "The child miscarried."

His fingers tightened on her shoulders. "You're lying— why would you lie?" His face had turned cruel. "You will have to come back to the Netherworld to prove that. The soothsayer will know." He bruised her, twisting her around, forcing her to stumble down the terraces toward the portal.

She fought him, kicking, nearly falling as he jerked her on. "There is no baby, Efil." She was terrified Braden would hear them from the studio, yet she longed to cry out to him. Efil jerked her arm behind her, shoving her on down the terraces. She quit fighting him and went limp so he had to drag her full weight. "I have nothing you want. I'm no use to you. Can't you understand? The baby was born dead."

"You're lying." Stubbornly he dragged her on. "I need you for the ceremonies whether or not the child is dead."

She willed herself to hang heavy, remained a dead weight until at last he turned her loose, holding her wrist. She stood facing him, so angry she trembled. "There is no child. I can't help you. Go find someone who can give you a child— someone who can carry a baby full term."

"Even if you were telling the truth," Efil said, "you are still my subject. You will do as I tell you." He forced her down the last terrace and against the portal, reaching for the handle. "It doesn't matter if you miscarried. The soothsayer will vouch there is a child—she will do whatever I tell her."

She stood with her back pressed against the faces of the carved cats, blocking the door. "I will not come with you. I don't want to be queen of Affandar. You must go back alone."

His touch was suddenly as soft as butter, making her wince. "We can make another child, Melissa. We can still defeat Siddonie. Why would you throw away wealth and power?"

"You're not listening, Efil. You're not hearing anything. I don't want to be queen of Affandar. Even if you dragged me back, forced me to bed—even if you could, I would make spells to lose the child. And," she said, "if you tried to force me to lead the Catswold, I would turn them against you, as well as against Siddonie."

"Listen, Melissa. I will tell you something you don't know." He watched her closely. She didn't like him to look at her so intently. He said, "If you do not return to lead the Catswold, Siddonie will kill them."

She looked back warily, trusting nothing he said.

"There is a false queen, Melissa. Siddonie is training a false queen to take your place—a Catswold woman from the alleys of the upperworld. Siddonie is teaching her all possible magic.

"If you do not come back, *that* young woman will lead the Catswold. And she will betray them. She will lead them into Siddonie's trap. Without you to show them the truth, she will lead them to defeat, and then kill them."

"I don't believe you. No Catswold would betray Catswold."

"This one will. She has no allegiance except to Siddonie." He smiled coldly. "This is the role Siddonie meant for you: to betray and destroy your own people." He looked deeply at her. "This is not just a war tactic, Melissa. This plan is Siddonie's final revenge for the fall of Xendenton. Ever since she was a child she has prepared for this."

He put his arm around her, drawing her close, his touch too soft. She shivered, drew away. He said, "Only you can stop her."

She felt cold, sick. She could not believe him, yet she felt the truth in his words.

"And," he said, "what about the old woman you lived with?"

"What about her?"

"Siddonie has imprisoned her in the palace dungeons."

"You're lying. That is a lie."

His look said it was not.

"Where is Mag now?"

"I told you. In the cellars."

But his eyes had changed. Now he was lying. She could sense his lie clearly, as if her inner vision, like her feline eyesight, had suddenly grown more intense. "Where is she, Efil?"

"They . . . someone freed her."

"Who freed her?"

"I don't know. She vanished from the cell."

"And this story about a false queen . . . That, too, is a lie?"

"No, that is not a lie."

She saw that it was not. Her increased perception was startling. She pressed her back against the protruding cats' faces, wondering if they were responsible for her sudden insight. Efil was watching her differently, almost fearfully. She pushed him aside, and swung the door open.

"Go back, Efil. Go back to the Netherworld. I am not part of your war."

He looked at her silently. He didn't touch her again. She saw his sudden distaste for her, as if, because he could no longer deceive her, she was of no use to him.

When he finally moved past her into the tool room he went quickly, his face impassive, turned away. Stepping in behind him, she listened to his spell and watched the wall swing away with a small suck of air.

He went through. She heard the little huff of air as the wall swung closed again. She stared around the homely tool room then went out, drew the Catswold Portal closed, and turned away.

Chapter 43

It was dawn. The dark green of night had hardly faded when three battalions of mounted Affandar soldiers rode out through the palace gates led by Siddonie on the tall, black stallion she favored. She had dreamed all night of slaughtering the Lettlehem peasants. She had dreamed for three nights running of the image doll some Lettlehem child had made of her, which had been hung at night in her own palace courtyard, and she lusted for revenge. Three battalions of foot soldiers followed her horse soldiers—the foot soldiers wearing heavy, curved swords and leading supply ponies.

They reached the mountains above Lettlehem near midnight. They struck the five villages one after another, routing out screaming peasants, burning their cottages and crops, driving off the sheep and pigs or slaughtering them. She had gone to war under justifiable duress, and she liked killing under that shield. Her soldiers herded together the best of the village horses for their own use, and destroyed the rest. Once the fields were blackened, they destroyed all tools so the Lettlehem peasants couldn't farm. Though Siddonie expected few of the peasants to survive their attack.

The slaughter lasted until dawn. The smell of blood and the cries of the maimed filled the burned out villages, and left Siddonie hungry for further war, lusting to attack every country in the Netherworld with full force. War was far

more satisfying than winning a country by intrigue; war
sharpened her senses and gave life meaning. Certainly Lettlehem had learned quickly this night, that no one made images of the queen of Affandar.

She watched the last of the peasants driven from hiding
and herded across the hills and into the last village square.
And there, in retribution for the incident of the image doll,
she watched twenty-five Lettlehem children hanged from a
gallows made of felled cedar trees.

The image doll had appeared in the courtyard of Affandar
Palace three nights before, hanging from a pole driven into
the earth. It was undeniably a Lettlehem doll, woven in the
same style as the Lettlehem rooftops and baskets, made of
the coarse flax grown only in Lettlehem. She did not know
who had brought the image to Affandar, but she would find
out. She did not admit to anyone the power the doll had had
to weaken her magic. For a full day after the thing was torn
down and burned, she had been unable even to cast a simple
spell-light. She could not influence the minds of her staff;
she could not manage her horse except with brute force; she
could not bring down game. The atrocity had left her sick
with certainty that the doll had indeed possessed a portion of
her soul.

Chapter 44

Braden was drinking his third cup of coffee and going
through some old sketches, waiting for Melissa, when he
saw her coming across the garden. He set down his coffee
cup, staring. No more long green dress hid her figure and
shortened her stride. She looked smashing—long and sleek,

with a lot more showing under the slim orange trousers and pink top of clinging silk. And the red silk scarf tied around her hair set off its multi-colored wildness. As she crossed the veranda and looked in at him, her green eyes nearly drowned him. When he remembered to breathe, he opened the door for her, moving the bowl of cat food out of her way. He had set it on the terrace after the cat marched out refusing to eat; he had thought that maybe later in the day she'd be hungry.

The cat had acted so strangely, glaring at him when he told her she was spoiled because she wouldn't eat her breakfast. "A little lobster and a few cans of chicken," he'd said, "and you're too good to eat anything else." And almost as if she understood, she had glowered up at him, then stuck her nose in the air and headed for the door, switching her tail impatiently until he let her out.

He watched Melissa now with more than an artist's appreciation, watched her with increasing desire. "You look great—you have an artist's eye for color. That orange and pink will be terrific. Have you had breakfast?"

"No, I . . ." She looked secretive, and blushed. "There was a problem about breakfast."

"Oh?"

"Nothing really. I just—didn't eat." She had a contrite, embarrassed look, and looked faintly amused, too. She didn't offer an explanation.

Maybe she was living with someone, maybe they'd had a fight and she had left without eating. But why the amusement? Or maybe lovemaking had gotten in the way of breakfast, he thought, annoyed. More than a little irritated, he picked up the canvas bag. "We'll run over to Tiburon for breakfast, then work in that Victorian house I mentioned. Are you ready?" He went on out ahead of her with his sketching things.

She picked up the picnic basket he had left and followed him. She didn't know what he was angry about. She didn't speak again until they were in the car headed for Tiburon. She leaned back in the seat watching the gleam of the bay,

searching for something to talk about. What had she done
to make him mad? The silence built, making her feel
trapped. What was the matter with him? Her feline reaction
was to turn away from him. Her human reaction was to try
to heal his anger. Was it her amusement about breakfast that
had annoyed him? But he couldn't know what had amused
her, so why was he angry? She watched him shyly under
lowered lashes, and when the silence grew too much she
grasped at the first thing she could think of to talk about.
"When you were a boy, when you went to live in Carmel,
how old were you?"

He rolled down the window and slowed for a turning car.
"Twelve," he said shortly. "It was when my father died."

"You and your mother must have had a hard time." She
tried to speak softly. When he glanced at her she said, "You
were very lucky to have your Gram."

She saw him slowly relax. She said, "I think she was a
very special person."

His expression softened reluctantly; he looked at her more
directly. "We were lucky to have her, and to have the home
she gave us. My mother wasn't trained to any skill, but she
liked working in the hotel. She was good at that—at manag-
ing the kitchen, and then at the bookkeeping. She learned
that quickly. It was just the right thing for her, and Carmel is
small. She liked being in a small place. She liked getting to
know people." He smiled for the first time. "We both liked
staying put, not moving around anymore."

He was quiet a few minutes, working through the heavy
morning traffic. She stretched, letting her muscles ease. He
said, "When my father was alive we moved from oil field to
oil field, my mother made few lasting friends. He was a
roustabout—Long Beach, Sunset Beach, Bakersfield. My
strongest memory is a succession of little shacky houses
with sandy front yards. Hot. There were always fleas in the
sand. I would wait all afternoon after school for my father to
come home and play ball with me—it was about all he liked
to do.

"Our move to Carmel was the first time I was in the same

school for more than six months. And Gram was my friend. She wore old faded jeans in a time when women didn't dress like that. She had worked in a boardinghouse when she was quite young—she was a wonderful cook.

"I used to sit on the dining terrace drawing the guests and waitresses. Gram was the only one who saw any value in my drawings."

"Your parents didn't?"

"My dad didn't think much of it. My mother thought I was clever and talented. She bragged and showed my pictures to the neighbors and to casual acquaintances, which enraged me. She meant well, but she didn't understand. Gram understood."

"Then she was special."

"We spent a lot of time together. We used to walk along the sea early in the morning after she had made the pies. She had a cook to do the breakfasts, but she always got up at four to make the pies.

"She loved the early morning sea. She loved fog pressing against the breakers, loved the wind. On Sundays we would go down to Point Lobos and walk there, watching the waves crashing on the rocks. She thought it good that I wanted to be a painter; she never thought it was sissy."

He slowed and turned the corner, and directly ahead of them was a theater marquee. She glanced at it and went cold. The legend on the marquee jolted her so hard she swallowed back a cry. Across the white face of the sign, in bold black letters, were three words that filled her with fear and confusion:

THE CAT PEOPLE
SIMONE SIMON

How could there be a movie about cat people? She didn't understand; she felt betrayed, exposed.

Braden was saying, "Pretty good old B movie. Ever see it?"

"I don't—I don't think so."

"About a girl turning into a cat. A silly story, but it's well cast. Simone Simon is good in it. She really looks like a cat—more like a pampered house cat, though, than a panther. The special effects are good—Jacques Tourneur directed it."

"A—a silly story?"

"Girls turning into cats. I like science fiction, but people turning into animals . . ." He grinned and shrugged. "Too silly." He turned into a parking area.

She said nothing. They got out and he held the restaurant door open for her. She felt cold. She shivered as she followed the waitress.

There were yellow flowers on the table. She touched them, sniffing their scent on her fingers. When the waitress had gone, she said, "What would you do if that story about cat people was real? If you were to see someone change into a cat?"

"Faint dead away," he said, laughing. "Or run like hell."

"I suppose it would be disgusting."

"I suppose it would—the arms and legs changing, fur sprouting all over, the shape of the head . . . Make an interesting series of anatomical drawings."

She toyed with her napkin, folding it into a small square, then smaller. She felt disappointed in him.

But what else would she have expected? She thought, *I am a cat person. I am that disgusting creature. I am your cat—the little calico who sleeps on your pillow.* She said, "Do you dismiss anything you don't understand?"

"Of course not. Would you like the waffles? They're really very good."

"Waffles would be fine."

When the waitress had gone he said, "Would you like to see the movie? It might be fun."

She didn't answer.

"Come on, Melissa—I'd *like* to see the damned movie!"

"You said you weren't much for that sort of thing, so why bother?"

"I only meant . . . I like Simone Simon. It would be fun with you, anything would."

"But you . . ."

"I only meant that things like that, things that can't really happen, people turning into cats—I just meant . . . Don't stare at me like that. What the hell's wrong? Oh, Christ. It seems silly to *make* such a movie, not silly to see it. Does that make any sense to you?"

"I—yes, I suppose it does." But it didn't. She watched the waitress set down his coffee and her tea, and she pushed her cup away.

"Are you all right? Are you not feeling well? Do you want me to take you home?"

"I'm fine." She looked at him steadily. "Your pictures aren't real. And reflections aren't real. They're not the real world any more than cat people are."

He started to speak, but she pressed on stubbornly. "For one thing, reflections make things go backward—your right hand is your left. They are illusions. So how can you say a movie about other illusions is silly?"

The waitress brought their waffles, letting her eyes slide down Melissa's bright tunic and pants.

Braden passed her the butter. "That's just the point. Light and reflections *are* real. The physics of light photons, electromagnetic radiation—all that is real."

The waitress came back with their orange juice, and apologized for having forgotten it. Melissa tasted it with curiosity. Cresteane Palace had orange trees. Five gardeners were kept to do nothing but maintain the spells for growing the delicate fruit, which was served only to the royal family.

Braden spread butter on his waffle and passed her the bacon. He gave her a deep, needing look, as if he wanted very much for her to understand. "Physics, the action of light, is a real science. But a woman turning into a cat is— that is just impossible. Physically, medically, scientifically impossible."

She ate in silence. There was no way to argue with him.

And why should she? What difference did it make? He was an upperworlder—they were different. Totally, irreconcilably different.

*   *   *

He signaled for more coffee, wondering why such a discussion should upset her. And why the hell he was so strung up.

But he knew why. He had thought she understood how he saw the world because she seemed to like his paintings. She had given him that impression, that she had a perception of color and light and meaning that was akin to his feelings. He had thought she understood what he was trying to do, what he wanted to say with his work.

Now he could see that she didn't understand at all. So all right, his stupid ego was hurt.

Why the hell did he want her to understand? He wanted her to model, not for some goddamned philosophical discussion.

They worked all morning around an abandoned, crumbling Victorian house set alone in the center of a grassy field. They didn't share half a dozen words. The empty rooms were filled with the sounds of the wind rattling the old doors and leaded windows. From beside a broken window she watched the wind running through the tall yellow grass that heaved like a sea. The chill, empty rooms made her feel forlorn and lost. She was very conscious of Braden's detachment, of his silent, intent concentration. His work overrode his anger. She knew she had hurt him, and she didn't like hurting him. She had said his paintings weren't real. In effect she had said that what he felt, what he wanted to bring alive for others, was not real. She had implied that his work was of no worth.

She hadn't meant that, and she hadn't meant to hurt him. She said, as he stood looking at a finished drawing, "I didn't mean that, about your work not being real."

He frowned, picking up the drawing. It was of the leaded glass window reflecting shattered images of grass and sky and of herself.

She said, "I meant, not physically real. But—there is something else in your work."

"You don't need to—"

"There is," she interrupted, "the spirit of what we see."

She looked at him deeply. "You bring alive the spirit of the physical world and make it real for others. That is your great strength, Braden West. In that way, what you do is very real."

He looked embarrassed, and looked at her deeply for a moment then turned away. She wanted to take his hand, wanted to touch him; but she dropped her hand and moved into the pose he wanted, turning casually, relaxed, until he told her to hold. And as he worked she watched him beneath lowered lashes, feeling the tension growing between them, a tension charged now not with anger and misunderstanding but with something intimate, a need drawing them together though he didn't touch her.

When they stopped to share the lunch he had packed, he wasn't angry, his glances still caressed her as they had when he drew her. In the last drawing she was standing before a stained glass door, her face streaked with its red and green light. She said, teasing him, "If physics makes things real, then this is the way I *was* at this minute. I was red and green."

He stared at her, scowling again, then started to laugh. He dropped the lid of the basket and reached for her, hugging her close, and when he kissed her it was a long, slow kiss. She leaned into him, kissing him back, forgetting what he thought about cat people.

Chapter 45

Melissa left Braden painting—already he had roughed in a canvas of the Victorian house. She went up the garden toward Olive Cleaver's, retying the scarf around her hair, watching Olive, above her, sweeping her front porch. She had decided to take the direct approach. Olive seemed gregarious, outgoing about her research, and Braden said the old woman liked to talk about what she was doing. What harm would it do to ask Olive, directly, what she was finding?

Within minutes Olive had hurried her inside, put the kettle on, and laid out her notebooks and a heavy, leatherbound volume. She cut some angel food cake, and as they waited for the tea to brew Olive opened the thick book. "This is on loan from the Cat Museum; it's quite valuable." The old woman sat with her back to the window, her face in shadow, her frizzed hair looking wild against the light. Carefully her wrinkled hands turned the frail pages, then she passed the book to Melissa. The open page showed the picture of a door carved with a running cat.

> This door of the galloping cat was discovered in a croft house in the south of England, in the village of Tiverton. It opens from the bottom of the cellar stair into the cellar itself, and had been boarded over, apparently for several centuries. The cottage, fallen past reclaim, had served as a feed storage shed. The myth of the galloping cat, which was believed locally, would allow no one to live in the house. Several families tried to move in but something, likely the stories

told by superstitious villagers, seems to have fright-
ened them off. In 1947 Dr. Alfred Stetsingwell ob-
tained permission from heirs to unboard the cellar
and examine the door. It far surpassed his expecta-
tions. Radiocarbon tests date the timbers at older than
the six centuries, probably from the first century B.C.
The carving is bold and primitive, and made with sim-
ple tools. All attempts to remove the door without
damage for exhibit in the British Museum have failed.
The frame wood splits, the hinges crack, and twice the
door itself has cracked. And these efforts give rise to
another chapter in the myth. Two of the workmen, re-
maining alone past quitting hours, swore that a figure
came down the cellar steps and told them to board up
the door again. The workers described the man as
having the face and paws of a cat. They boarded up
the door, but Dr. Stetsingwell later unboarded it. He
was never able to remove it, short of cutting apart the
wood, which he was not willing to do. The door re-
mains in the cellar in Tiverton, where this photograph
was made. The myths of the countryside center around
it, and around the strange disappearance and reap-
pearance of Tiverton's townsfolk. Tiverton is also
known in the area for its large, handsome cats, which
are said to be uncannily clever at mousing. In this
farming region, cats are valued for that purpose.

Olive said, "I've had a time searching out such examples.
I've used every resource in the city, and of course inter-
library loan."

Melissa was shaken. She watched the old woman warily.
"What the book says about the man being half-cat—that's
just made up, of course."

Olive smiled. "Of course that part is folktale. Oh, there
are wonderful tales. They've been all but lost." Her faded
brown eyes shone. "How lovely if they were true."

She opened a leather case and began shuffling through papers. "I've found mention of several such doors carved with

cats." She looked up at Melissa. "Are you sure you're interested in all this?"

"Oh, very interested."

"Well, you've seen the door in the garden, of course." She studied Melissa rather too intently. "There are curious stories surrounding each door—fears, superstitions. That's the aspect that interests me most. Are you a cat person?"

Melissa sat very still, fear swamping her. She daren't move, daren't speak.

"Do you like cats, my dear? Are you a person who likes cats?"

She let the fear drain away; she felt weak; her heart was pounding too fast. "Oh, yes, I like cats. But cats don't like me much. Tell me about the other doors."

"In a tomb in Egypt, a door was found hidden behind the sarcophagus. The cat carved on it is standing upright like a person. In her left hand she holds the crescent moon, in her right she holds the sun. She is wearing a tear-shaped pendant."

"A pendant?" Her heart thundered.

"An amulet. Surely it symbolized some power."

Melissa waited, afraid to speak.

"There are tales of an amulet," Olive said. "An emerald amulet with the powers of Bast."

"Do you mean magical powers? What—what kind of powers would such a thing have?"

"I have found several mentions of the pendant in works on ancient Egypt, but they do not describe the powers." Olive seemed to take the amulet very seriously. "The emerald is tear-shaped, and its setting is formed of two gold cats, their paws joined to protect it."

"I suppose it is in a museum?"

"Oh, no. It has never been found. And there seem to be no other really good pictures. I suppose if it really does exist, it lies buried in some undiscovered tomb."

Melissa studied Olive. "In the tomb where that pendant is shown in the carving—has anyone searched for it there?"

Olive smiled. "The archaeologist writes that behind that

door is a solid clay wall. I have wondered, if one dug there . . ." She shook her head. "I'm sure others have thought of that. I'm sure the archaeologist himself must have dug into that wall, though his published work doesn't mention it." She poured more tea, filling their cups. "There is a door in a Celtic grave which shows an amulet around the neck of a cat, though not such a clear image. All that remains of that door is a fragment, a piece of dark oak bearing the marks of a hinge, and the forequarters of the cat.

"And there is said to be such a door in Italy, where a cat wears a jewel around its neck, but I have found no good reference. But that's intriguing because—do you know about the cats of Italy, the Coliseum cats? Hundreds of cats living there in that magnificent ruin . . ."

There was no need to answer her, Melissa need only listen, Olive was completely engrossed.

"Hundreds of cats. And there's a strange myth in Italy that intrigues me, though I don't know how they could be connected. It is said that every now and then a stranger appears in Rome without money or identification—no passport, nothing. A stranger who is confused by the city and its traffic—innocent, like a child.

"He will be around the city for a few days then disappear. No one knows where such people go, or where they came from." Olive picked up the book, wrapping it in brown paper. Melissa's fists were clenched in her lap, her nails biting into her palms.

Chapter 46

Three hundred cats roamed within the fenced, wire-roofed compound in the center of the Lillith Ranch. Within the two-acre enclosure cats hunted through the high grass, played, slept, fought, and bred. Some had marked off territories and defended them. Beyond the cat compound and separated from it by low hills stood the barracks housing the human refugees from San Francisco's streets. The buildings crested the far side of the hill, and included besides the barracks a mess hall, recreation buildings, a gym, stables, tack rooms, and weapons rooms. There was a riding ring large enough to accommodate sword training and mock battles. The human trainees were encouraged to handle the horses under supervision, but they were not encouraged to visit the cat compound.

Some of the cats were strays. Some had been stolen from the yards and gardens of San Francisco's residential areas; some came from animal pounds. All were Catswold, carefully selected; one could tell by the eyes, by the unusually long ears, by something singularly unsettling in the expression. Vrech had not liked collecting them.

The toughest, most adaptable cats among the group did not bother to hunt, but sprawled arrogantly in the hot California sunshine, disdainful of hunting such easy game as the white mice freed daily into the enclosure for their pleasure. Instinctively they waited for normalcy to return to their lives, for times to fall again into the lean pattern of precarious survival they had learned in San Francisco's alleys. Here, the effort to hunt was wasted; here food was brought twice daily.

Some of the cats, feeling too crowded, skulked along the fence or climbed irritably up and down the oak trees that had been pruned to stubs to allow for the wire mesh roof; they clawed at the mesh, staring through to freedom. The more dependent cats simply gorged on the white mice, which hardly knew how to escape a cat's claws.

The area was relatively safe from idle discovery. It was protected by miles of fenced grassland owned by the Lillith Ranch, and the fences were spell-cast to discourage intruders. Small boys with twenty-two's would turn away from it white with fear, not knowing what they were afraid of. And of course the gates were spell-locked.

Within the compound Vrech and Havermeyer had for some days watched the cats and studied them, but it was Vrech who would do the training. Havermeyer had proven totally inept, and the night before last he had returned to the city offices of Lillith Corporation. Vrech knew he had been sent up to the ranch simply to oversee him. He preferred working alone, now that he had selected the female to be trained as the false Catswold queen.

She was darkly mottled, her coat a brindled, muddy mix of black and rust unrelieved by white. She was so mean she ran off males and females alike, and had lacerated the hands of two keepers who tried to pet her.

He caught her with raw meat, wearing heavy gloves. He put her into a cage, and carried her into a locked room with barred windows. When he said the spell, when she found herself turned into a woman, she leaped at Vrech, clawing at him. He grabbed her and turned her toward the full-length mirror he had provided. She stopped clawing him, and stood looking. A curiously childlike wonder transformed her face.

She was naked, of course, and she stared at her bare skin, at her breasts and her long legs and long slim arms, clasping and unclasping her hands as if her fingers had retractable claws.

Then she looked at her hands, examined them, and began to use them. She turned the doorknob, but couldn't open the door. She flipped the window latches and reached through to try to remove the bars. She pinched Vrech and stroked him, then tried to undo the buttons of his shirt.

She was thin, hard, angular, and well muscled. She had amber eyes, street-wise under her dark lashes, and dark, arching brows. Her black hair was red-streaked and lank, hanging to her shoulders. She watched Vrech with a shrewdness that kept him alert.

"Helsa," Vrech said. "Your name is Helsa, after a lesser entity of the Hell Pit."

"Helsa," she said, touching her breasts and cupping them. Vrech smiled.

Here in this room she was prisoner. She would remain so until she was sufficiently trained and trustworthy. He would be selective about the spells he taught her. She might be appealing and lusty, but he had no illusion that he could trust her. When he took her into the riding ring he would keep her spell-cast.

He clothed her in jeans and plain shirts. He spent three days teaching her horsemanship, then began to train her to the sword. He did not trust her sufficiently yet to take her to bed. In between riding lessons he taught her about the Catswold nation. When she understood its stubborn, defiant history and understood what Siddonie wanted of her, she saw at once the possibilities. Soon she lusted to lead the Catswold people, to hold absolute rule over them. She respected power and wanted power. She quickly understood that she would sell the Catswold nation for her own complete and absolute power. She understood that soon the queen herself would come to be with her and train her in further skills.

She could soon wield a spell to make the other cats storm the fence, make them leap and tear at the wire roof or fight one another. She could make the compound cats stop eating for days, or force them to gorge themselves. It was some weeks after Vrech began training her that Siddonie arrived at the ranch.

She was in the blue Rolls; Havermeyer had driven her up from the city. She had come up to San Francisco to sign business papers and check on him; he was good with the details but she didn't like to give him total freedom. The corporate takeover was so complicated that Havermeyer could too easily cross her.

She had used the tunnel that opened out of Xendenton. She kept a car in the parking garage into which the tunnel opened, deducting the monthly parking fee from her taxes. It was ludicrous to her that she must pay upperworld income taxes. She had brought only a dozen staff with her—they had gone directly to the hotel where she kept a suite.

She exited from the pale blue interior of the Rolls dressed in a black riding suit with diamond cuff links closing the sleeves of her white silk shirt, diamond earrings, and diamonds at her throat. Her black hair was piled into a complicated arrangement caught with diamond pins. Sleek and impeccably groomed, she ordered Vrech to bring Helsa to her in the compound office.

The office featured an orange-and-cream Khirman rug, and cream leather chairs against a wall covered entirely by a spell-cast antique mirror that did not reflect. Siddonie stood before the patterned gold mirror watching the Catswold girl enter, watching her eyes. Seeing Helsa's immediate envy.

Within an hour Siddonie, with skillful spells and with promises, had made Helsa her slave. The girl not only envied Siddonie's beauty and was determined to copy it, she lusted after the power Siddonie offered her. When she rode out with Siddonie in late afternoon, Helsa was totally committed to her.

Siddonie watched Helsa send her loose horse away and bring him back, watched her change shape in the saddle from woman to cat, balancing lightly; and when after an hour's ride they returned, she watched Helsa ride into the cat compound and lift her hand, drawing hundreds of cats running to her. She watched her make them swarm up the stunted trees, make them fight, stop fighting, watched her make them change to human then return at her command to cat. Siddonie meant, as soon as the girl was sufficiently trained, to bring all the upperworld Catswold and human troops down through the mining tunnel that led into Zzadar-ray, directly into the Catswold nation.

There the false queen would gather the Zzadarray Catswold, join them with her own armies, and move west until she joined Siddonie at the front lines. The Catswold would help defeat the rebels, and when the war was won Sid-donie's loyal soldiers would slaughter the Catswold soldiers, both those from the upperworld and those from Zzadarray.

And, when she had no more use for Helsa, she would kill the false Catswold queen herself.

Already in the south she had brought Shenndeth and Pearilleth into line without bloodshed, peacefully confiscat-ing most of the horses and all the food stores. And in the first skirmishes in the outlying lands, rebel soldiers had been driven mad with spells and had turned on their brothers and killed them. In Cressteane, spells of sickness had cut down dozens of rebels with illness of the bowels and stomach. And when the rebels' own healing spells failed, many among them had taken wine and, starving, quickly become too drunk to resist capture.

When Helsa turned and smiled at her, Siddonie smiled back with a cold, predatory satisfaction. This girl would pay, as would all the Catswold, for the fall of Xendenton.

Chapter 47

It was the evening the calico scratched Morian that Melissa saw the spirit of the cat hidden within Braden's paintings.

Morian had come down for a drink. Melissa watched her from the couch. The dark woman was beautiful in creamy satin and gold jewelry. Coming in, she kissed Braden on the cheek and Melissa felt a growl deep in her throat and felt her claws stiffen. And when Braden had gone to the kitchen and Morian came to the couch and reached to stroke her, she growled again.

Morian looked surprised and moved away. "All right, my dear. I know when I'm not wanted." She grinned. "Maybe a little jealous? You needn't be, you know."

Melissa turned her face away, but in a moment she looked back to watch Morian where she stood at the easel looking at the wet painting.

"You have a class?" Braden said from the kitchen.

"Mmm. I hate night classes—there's always some hobby painter who shouldn't be there and can't keep his mind on his drawing. I like this, Brade."

"New model. Starting a new series."

Morian looked at the three new paintings he had hung on the wall, then at the new sketches on the work table, handling them with care. When Braden returned with the drinks, she hugged him casually. "Nice. Very nice. This is going to be an exciting series. These—are these the Craydor house?"

He nodded. "We spent a morning there."

"Marvelous. Reflections . . . all reflections. Just right for you, Brade. And your model is perfect for it."

Melissa got into her basket and curled down, pretending to sleep, listening to the dry sounds of paper as Morian looked again through the sketches.

Morian said, "It's going to be the best series you've done. Even better than the Coloma series, and I didn't think any work could be better than that. Rye will go out of his mind. Has he seen them?"

"He's dropping by this evening on his way out to dinner."

Morian nodded and sat down on the couch near Melissa's basket, looking at the calico questioningly to see if she would growl again. "Nice basket—she just fits." She looked up at him, laughing. "For someone who didn't want a cat, you're doing right well by her." She reached to let the calico sniff her fingers, trying to make friends. But jealousy won, rage impelled the calico. She came up out of her basket striking fast, slashing across Morian's hand. Morian jerked away, her eyes wide. Blood beaded across her skin. Braden shouted and reached to grab the calico, but Morian caught his arm.

"Don't, Brade. Let her be. This is her house—she just doesn't want me so familiar." She moved away from the basket, pressing her fingers against the oozing blood, holding her hand away from her silk dress. "It's only a scratch." She stared into Melissa's eyes, not angry but curious, searching. Melissa hissed and spat.

Braden handed Morian a clean paint rag to stop the blood. "I'll get some iodine."

The medicine he brought smelled so strong it made Melissa's nose wrinkle. His look at her was cold, enraged.

Morian said, "She's only protecting her rights. She—Brade, look at her eyes."

"What about them?" He was furious. His voice made Melissa cringe. Why had she done that? Why had she embarrassed herself in front of him like that?

Morian said, "You've given the girl in the painting the cat's eyes. How droll—the same green eyes, black fringed. Lovely."

Braden looked puzzled. "No, they're Melissa's eyes. Melissa's eyes are green, she has dark lashes." He looked into the calico's eyes, frowning, staring so hard Melissa shivered. He said, softly, "They are alike." He was silent a moment, then he rose and took the empty glasses into the kitchen. Behind him Morian said softly, "It's about time." She reached a tentative hand to the calico to see what she would do. "You needn't be jealous of me, my dear. It's that gorgeous model you need to worry about."

Melissa relaxed, and pressed her head against Morian's fingers. Morian grinned at her. "That's better." She rubbed Melissa's ears, knowing just the right places. Braden returned and stood watching them. "That was a quick turnaround. Private conversation?"

"Just girl talk," Morian said as she glanced up through the windows. "Get a glass for Rye; here he comes. I'm on my way."

On the terrace Rye Chapman hugged Morian, then she headed for her car. He came into the studio and stood silently looking at the paintings. He spent a long time looking. He didn't say anything. He backed off, studying each painting, so obviously pleased that Melissa kneaded her claws with pleasure and purred extravagantly. It was much later, after Rye had gone, that she saw the shadow images.

Braden had started a new painting from the drawing with the stained glass window. Already the intricate pattern of reflections was rich and exciting, shifting across her figure, absorbing her, making her a part of the tangled colors.

As she sat in the hall behind him pretending to wash her paws, admiring the painting, she let a mewing sigh of pleasure escape her. Braden turned to look, and she froze. Then she rubbed innocently against his ankle.

He began painting again.

It was the next minute, watching the painting, that she grew disturbed. She padded farther down the hall to see it from a greater distance.

She moved again, looking.

She saw the phantom shape clearly: the faint shadow of a cat woven through her figure, a form so subtle she had to stand in just the right place to see it. Hardly more than a smoky stain, it was nearly as large as her figure: a cat lying up across her body within the folds of the orange and pink silk, its cheek forming her cheek, its muzzle barely discernible within her own face, its paws meshing into the folds of her shirt. A phantom cat, faint as a breath.

She sat behind him feeling sick. Why had he done this? Had he known about her all along? When they argued over the movie about cat people, was he making fun of her? Why else would he do this but to goad and tease her? She moved across the room to study the other paintings, and found a cat's shadow in each, woven through her figure.

Why would Braden do this?

Or did he not know he had done it?

Did he not know those faint, elusive spirits were there? Could it be that only his inner self knew? That something deep within him knew more than his conscious mind did? Upset and afraid, she felt her stomach churn. She was so upset that within a moment she had thrown up her supper in a little pile on the hardwood floor behind Braden.

He turned and stared at her, annoyed to be interrupted. Muttering, he got a rag and wiped up the mess.

But then after he had cleaned the spot on the floor he picked her up and held her, stroking her. "What's wrong with you? Why did you get sick? Is it the cat food?" He felt her nose; his hand smelled of paint. "How do I tell if you have a fever? *Are* you sick? Or did you eat a mole in the garden?" he asked hopefully. "Olive says moles make cats sick."

She snuggled down in his arms, basking in his gentle caring. How could she be angry that he had painted the shadow images, when he was so kind and loving? She couldn't believe he had done it deliberately. Maybe he didn't know the images were there. Maybe they came from some hidden inner perception.

Had Braden, in making images of her, touched some power centered around her? Centered around the Catswold?

The next morning she was certain that some power of the Catswold had been touched, for she had dreamed of Timorell. She saw her mother, tall and golden haired, wandering the darkened galleries of the Cat Museum. And Timorell wore the Amulet of Bast. In the dream Melissa looked into the emerald's green depths and saw the war in the Netherworld, and she heard someone call her name. She woke riveted with the thought that she must find the Amulet, that the outcome of the Netherworld wars could be changed if she could find the Amulet of Bast.

Chapter 48

Efil watched the compound from a nearby hill where he sat beneath a twisted oak behind an outcropping of granite, drinking a Budweiser.

He had not gone down the Catswold Portal when he left Melissa. He had waited until he felt certain she was gone, then come out again. He had gone into the city, then two days later had taken a Greyhound north. In San Andreas, he bought a used Cadillac and drove out to the compound. There he left the car on a side road and climbed under the fence, ignoring the fear that the spell-cast fence engendered. He had crossed the grassy fields staying near boulders and within the shadows of the oaks. He wanted to see what progress Vrech was making with the false queen, but he did not want to be gone too long from Affandar and the changeling boy.

He had been able to teach the boy a few tactics to protect him against Siddonie. The boy had no magic, of course, but there were ways of the mind that would help him, and Tom had a surprising ability to resist her. He had performed cleverly, letting Siddonie think she controlled him.

Efil had no intention of freeing the boy. He meant, at the right moment, to bring Wylles down to the Netherworld, to show the two together to Siddonie's armies and to the peasants, to prove there was a changeling.

Efil drained the Budweiser can, then popped open another beer and settled back. He watched the compound most of the day, watched the upperworld horse soldiers at drill and sword practice, and watched the false Catswold queen fight-

ing beside them in mock battle. The Affandar officers had
done well with San Francisco's drunks. They had dried them
out, and taught them to ride and to use a sword with modest
skill. He watched Helsa with far more interest, soon with
lust. She would be randy all right. And if he offered her
more power than Siddonie promised, he had no doubt she
would throw in with him. Once he convinced her that Siddonie planned to destroy her along with the rest of the
Catswold, she would be his.

In mid-afternoon an unsuspecting rattlesnake slid near
Efil. He killed it with a spell, then unwrapped the cheese
sandwich he had bought in San Andreas, and opened another
beer. He watched Helsa gather a dozen of the brawniest cats
in the enclosure and change them to human, watched her
lead them to the riding ring and drill them on horseback and
then, finished, turn them back into cats. He assumed that she
had not taught them the spell for changing. When he had
seen all he needed, he walked back over the hills to the dirt
lane, got in the Cadillac, drove into San Andreas and from
there to San Francisco. He meant to be back in Affandar by
the next night.

Chapter 49

The Greyhound bus smelled of cigarettes and stale food. A
large woman took up most of the seat, pressing Melissa
against the window. The bus was filled with morning commuters, with men in suits and ties, and women in tweed suits
flaunting bare, silky legs and high heels.

She had been half afraid to take the bus by herself, but she
had awoken excited by her dream. Curled up purring close

to Braden, her mind had been filled with Timorell and the Amulet.

As the bus moved through Sausalito, she watched the fishing boats rocking on the choppy water of the huge bay. Then soon, approaching the Golden Gate Bridge, she thought about Alice dying there and was blinded by sudden, sharp pain.

Once the bus had crossed the bridge she was afraid of missing her stop, worried about getting lost. But the driver let her off all right; nothing was so hard if she just asked questions. She left the morning commuters behind and swung up Telegraph in the sharp, bright wind. Above her the sky tilted in explosions of light; gulls screamed, banking over her, their wheeling flight exciting her. She turned up a familiar street that climbed Russian Hill but, passing the Kitchen house, she was filled with loss. The feeling nearly undid her; she was all opposites this morning, swinging from joy to pain.

When she reached the museum it was not yet open; the iron gates were locked. In the shadow of the wall she changed to cat and leaped up and over.

She wandered the gardens pawing into niches and behind sculpture stands. Her paws were more sensitive than hands, picking up every subtlety of the different surfaces and textures. She examined bronze and marble cats for possible openings, and explored along the tops of the garden walls, then climbed a vine to the roof and searched among vents and into an old chimney. When the museum doors opened at ten she slipped inside, into the open ladies room.

In a booth she changed to girl, and came out again to mingle with a busload of arriving tourists. Searching the galleries, looking into windowsills and shelves, she tried to think how Timorell would have marked the hiding place of the Amulet, with what sign to be recognized only by another Catswold.

She searched all morning and half the afternoon but found nothing. She left the museum late in the afternoon, tired and very hungry. Discouraged, she didn't catch the bus back across the bridge but took the Powell Mason cable car. Asking directions from the gray-haired driver, she got off at Union Square. She had a sandwich in a little cafe, then went shopping like any upperworld woman. She was back in the garden just after dark, feeling smug with her purchases, hiding her packages under Olive Cleaver's back porch.

Reflections of tall grasses tangled through Melissa's hair, shattered into angles by the rebounding light. Braden worked quickly, blocking in the canvas, excited by the emerging shadows, only absently aware that the cat was winding around his bare ankles.

She hadn't come in until after dark, then had prowled the studio restlessly. Several times he had noticed her looking up at the walls, and for a long time she sat behind him as if watching him work. She was doing that again now. She had left his ankles and sat down behind him again, looking. Soon her scrutiny began to annoy him. He laid down his brush and turned to face her. "What the hell are you looking at? Why would a cat stare at a painting?"

She looked so startled he laughed—the little cat looked truly shocked. And when he laughed, her eyes widened. She ducked her head and began to wash herself.

Grinning, he picked her up and scratched behind her ears. "You're a strange one. Pretty strange." But it was later when he stopped to fry a hamburger that he began to worry about her.

She came running into the kitchen at the smell of cooking meat. She hadn't touched her cat food. He realized she hadn't eaten since she threw up the night before.

Maybe this brand of cat food didn't agree with her. He cut up his hamburger to cool for her, and cooked himself another one. When hers was cool and he put it down, she wolfed it, ravenous.

But then in a little while she threw it up again. This was the second throw up, and she looked so miserable that he phoned Morian.

"Just on my way out, Brade. Let me run down." In a

minute she swished in, dressed to the teeth: sleek, honey-colored cocktail dress and strings of topaz and East Indian brass.

"Bring your date in, Mor."

"He's impatient—let him pace. He thinks it's stupid to be concerned about a cat." She knelt beside the couch stroking the calico, gently feeling down her sides, opening her mouth. She smelled the cat's breath with a familiarity that made Braden grin. She felt the calico's stomach, pressing carefully. Outside the glass her tall, dark-skinned date paced, glancing at his watch.

"Are you late for something?"

Morian shook her head. "He thinks we are." She stroked the little cat. "I can't see anything wrong. They'll throw up sometimes when they're pregnant."

"When they're what?"

"Pregnant, Brade. You know, it's when they—"

"Oh, Christ!"

"It happens, Brade

"What the hell am I going to do with a batch of kittens?"

"If she doesn't feel better by tomorrow, you'd better take her to the vet." She stood up and chucked him under the chin. "They'll be sweet, Brade. Sweet kittens."

He walked out with her and met her date, who stopped pacing long enough to shake hands. This was the boyfriend who worked for the *Chronicle,* in financial news or something; a promotion from the sports page, Morian had said. When they had gone Braden turned off the overhead studio lights and stood in the dark feeling suddenly, unreasonably encumbered. He didn't ask for a cat. He didn't ask for kittens. He didn't want to admit the concern he felt for the little calico. What the hell was he going to do with kittens?

Give a couple to Morian, he supposed, a couple to Olive. Give one to Melissa—maybe it could learn to like her.

She slept close to him that night, curled beside the pillow, her head tucked against his cheek. He kept his arm around her protectively, and she remained cat with difficulty. Lying wakeful, she wanted to change to woman, wanted to snuggle next to him as a woman.

In the morning she was still cat, sleeping beside him. She was proud of her control. He let her out and, on the veranda, arranged the table and chairs, preparing to paint Melissa there. She watched him from up the garden where she had climbed into a low acacia tree. When he seemed to be growing impatient she headed for Olive's back porch, and beneath it she changed to girl. With some difficulty she put on one of the new outfits from City of Paris, wishing she had a proper place to bathe and make herself look nice. She went down the garden dressed in the new gathered turquoise skirt and green blouse, and she felt a sharp excitement in the way he looked at her.

He posed her sitting at the veranda table, and drew her against the leafy reflections in the studio windows. She liked his absorbed excitement as he worked. In one sense he was very much with her, seemed so close to her it was as if he touched her. But in another sense he was totally removed. Strangely, the two feelings were compatible. She sat at the table thinking about her search in the Cat Museum and wondering if the Amulet could be in McCabe's safe deposit box. At mid-morning when he stopped to make tea for her, she asked if Alice might have had any keepsakes of Timorell's.

He seemed puzzled by her stubborn interest in possessions, and that embarrassed her. She rose, pretending to look for the cat, and went to stand at the edge of the veranda.

He said, "When we remodeled, Alice took some cartons and boxes up to Olive's to store in her attic. I think we got them all, but you could look."

She did look, late that afternoon. While Braden worked she went up the garden to Olive's.

The yellow cat watched her from the railing, then followed her into the house. She and Olive searched the attic but found nothing. Olive insisted on making tea, and when they sat down, Pippin jumped onto his chair and sat intently watching her. His golden eyes searched hers deeply, and when she let him sniff her fingers, he put his paw on her hand with innocent, almost pleading confidence.

"He likes you," Olive said. "He's nearly human, that cat. Much more intelligent than my own cats. He has been here constantly since Tom—since Tom turned so strange toward him. I feel sometimes as if Pippin could almost speak to me." She passed Melissa the thinly sliced pound cake. "Some cats seem so perceptive. As if they have a second side to them, secret and hidden from us."

Melissa sat sipping her tea, not daring to look at Olive.

Olive said, "Sometimes I wonder if that secret side could be—liberated." She reached to the sideboard for her leather-bound notebook.

Alarm spilled through Melissa. She rose hastily, tipping her chair and catching it before it fell. "I—Braden is waiting. I'm afraid I've kept him too long."

Olive paid no attention. "I copied this from Chaptainne's journal. He lived in the twelfth century, when people believed in magic. Or perhaps," the old woman said, as if Melissa had not risen to leave at all, "magic really existed then." And as Melissa backed toward the door, Olive began to read the slow, measured cadences of a spell.

Chapter 50

"*Call them forth leaping,*" Olive read, "*bring them ca-reening . . .*"

Melissa dared not run away and leave Pippin here alone to be changed. Sick and shivering, she felt her body want to change, and she blocked the spell. For while Olive could not make a spell, *she* was present, and the words echoed in her mind to bring the changing forces pummeling down.

"*. . . careening joyous from spell-fettered caverns . . .*"

The powers pulled at her. She stopped them, but when she looked at Pippin his tail was lashing, his eyes blazing. The expression on his face was so intense she reached out to him, stroking him, hoping to calm him, and for one instant she saw an aura around him, saw the faint, shadowed form of a man.

The sudden ringing of the doorbell made the yellow cat leap from the chair and streak for the back of the house.

Olive stared after him and rose to open the door, her expression unreadable. "He's heard that bell a million times. What gets into him?" she said innocently. "That will be my grandniece—I'm kitten-sitting for her."

A little blond girl came in carrying a tiny reddish kitten, and clutching a paper bag and a small quilt under her elbow as if her mother had tucked them there. From the window, Melissa could see a woman waiting in a green car parked in Olive's driveway. Olive took the bag and quilt, but the child didn't want to give over the kitten. The pale-haired little girl held the yawning cat baby against her cheek.

Olive knelt, hugging the child and stroking the kitten. "I'll take good care of her, Terry. A week isn't so very long, you'll see."

The child finally managed to hand the kitten over, reaching on tiptoe to kiss its nose as the little thing snuggled deep into Olive's hands. Melissa watched, very still. The kitten was so tiny. She wanted to hold it. She wanted to feel its soft fur, its delicate body. She wanted to lick it; she felt her tongue come out and had to bite it back. She could hardly keep from reaching out to gather the baby to her; she could smell its scent, infinitely personal and exciting. When she looked up, Olive was watching her.

As soon as the child had left, Olive brought the kitten to Melissa and settled it in her lap. Melissa cuddled it, hardly aware of Olive. It was so very small, so vulnerable. She lifted it to her cheek, felt its warmth against her, its baby-scent powerful. She stifled the urge to press her mouth into it, to lick it, to wash that lovely fur, to wash its little face and clean those tiny delicate ears.

She spent a long time stroking the kitten, playing with it, and holding it while it slept. Across the table, Olive seemed busy with her notebooks. The kitten purred so passionately that Melissa longed to feel a responding purr in her own throat. She longed to change to cat and snuggle it properly, let it chase her tail in the age-old hunting games. Meanwhile, Pippin stalked the room, watching her. She was sure his thoughts, as her own, still echoed with Olive's half-spoken spell. And then quite suddenly Olive looked up from her books and began to read the changing spell loudly and deliberately, shocking Melissa so she hardly breathed. In panic she said a silent counter-spell and felt the change in herself subside. But Pippin had leaped up, his yellow eyes agleam.

Olive's eyes were hard on Melissa. *"You who seek the form abandoned, you who seek the house deserted . . ."*

The change came quickly to Pippin. He yowled, was pulled straight, rearing and twisting, crying out, reaching with claws that became fingers as he was jerked tall.

The big golden cat was gone. A man stood before them, golden haired and naked.

He was a fine, muscular man, pale of skin, with short golden hair and the cat's golden eyes. He looked at his arms, at his naked body and long straight legs. He held one leg out and then the other, hopping like a marionette wild with pleasure; he seemed to have forgotten the two women.

But he stopped suddenly, regarding them with an expression of victory. "I am a—*man!*" The joy in his voice made Melissa laugh out loud.

"Why do you laugh at me?"

"A laugh of happiness. Like a purr." She could feel Olive's excitement. She thought, giddily, *Now the cat's out of the bag,* and felt herself falling into insane laughter. Olive left the room, returning with a blanket which she handed to Pippin.

"I am not—cold."

"To cover you," Olive said.

Obediently Pippin draped the blanket around his shoulders, covering nothing of importance. "What were those words? A—a spell. I want to know the spell."

Olive said it slowly. Pippin repeated it. In an instant he was cat again, his tail lashing.

But the next minute he returned to man, smiling wickedly.

Olive sat down at the table, regarding Melissa with composure. "I have read about this possibility. I have thought about it for a very long time." Pippin began to roam, looking at everything in the room, touching, sniffing. When Olive began to read the spell again, Melissa said hastily, "There is terrible danger in attempting things you don't understand."

"I did not attempt it, my dear. I did it. But why didn't you change? You are the same—your hair, your eyes. The way you hunger over the kitten." The kitten, innocent of the fuss, slept in Melissa's circling arm.

Melissa said, "Even with your research, it seems strange that you would believe."

"I believed because, when I was a young woman, I saw such a thing happen—or rather, I saw the results.

"I worked in the city, at the main library. I worked late two nights a week, and going home one night I saw a man step into an alley, and a cat come out.

"I thought little of that until it happened again. This time, the same cat went in and the same man came out.

"I grew curious, and began to wait near the alley on my late nights. I thought at first it was a man walking with his cat, though I never saw them together.

"I saw this happen three times more—the same man, the same cat, one emerging, the other disappearing into the alley.

"I began to investigate books on the occult, but they were so warped in their view that they told me nothing. I turned to folklore and then to archaeology. That was when I began to read about the doors with cats' faces."

She looked at Melissa coolly. "You are a part of whatever

is happening in this garden. The gardener, Vrech, is a part of it. And Tom—I don't know what to think about Tom. I'm not sure that boy *is* Tom Hollingsworth. Something has changed him greatly, something has come into this garden, something secret and pervasive and not—not of the normal world."

Olive poured cold tea from the pot and sipped it. They heard Pippin rummaging in the refrigerator, and he soon returned eating a fried chicken leg. He had forgotten his blanket.

He said, munching, "When I was cat, I didn't know . . ." He tried to bring up words from a language he had heard all his life but never used. "I didn't know . . ."

He gave up at last, finished the chicken leg, and laid the bone on the table. He said, slowly, "Now I am a man." He gave Melissa a deep golden stare. "Now I want to know where Tom is. I want to know what the gardener has done with Tom. I saw him take Tom away. He put the other boy in Tom's bed. That boy is not Tom. Where is Tom?"

Melissa sighed. Neither lies nor evasiveness would do. "Tom is in another place."

"Beyond the door?"

"Yes," she said, surprised. "Beyond the portal. How . . . ?"

"I saw the gardener come from there, smelling of deep, damp caverns. I saw him take Tom there. Tell me—all of it, please. If I am to help Tom I must know all of it."

Olive watched them intent and eager, absorbing every word, filled with a deep, excited wonder.

"There is a land," Melissa began, unable to do less than explain. "A land of caverns, deep down . . ."

"Beyond the door," Olive whispered.

"Beyond the door," Melissa said.

It took her a long time to explain sufficiently about the Netherworld, about the weakness of the Netherworld newborn and about the political importance of a changeling. Olive knew about changelings.

"Children stolen from our world, taken into the underworld through the cleft in a hill or through caves, another child put in their place."

Pippin said, "Will they hurt Tom?"

"I don't think so," Melissa said. "He's valuable to the queen. She will have put spells on him to make him forget his name, forget who he is, forget his life in the upperworld. She will do all she can to make him believe he is the prince of Affandar." She touched Pippin's hand. "Tom—a healthy child—is her assurance of her title to the throne. I don't think she'll hurt him."

"What will she do if he remembers who he is? If the spells do not—hold?"

"Likely they will hold. She has great power."

"Spells cannot be—broken? Go wrong?"

"They can," she said quietly.

"The door is the portal," Pippin said softly. "But is it not more than that? Is there not power within the door?" His eyes shone. "Power—that has increased since you came. I think it was the power of the portal that first made me know I was different. And then you came." His yellow eyes glowed in his strong human face. "You made me feel strange, uneasy." He began to pace. "You must teach me all spells. You must teach me everything about the Netherworld. You must do it at once."

She only looked at him.

"I must go quickly to find Tom."

"You can't go there. Siddonie would destroy you."

His feline gaze was searing, daunting. "I will go to find Tom."

"There are times for patience."

"I know that. I am cat, I know how to be patient. One is patient before a mouse hole. This," he said imperiously, "is not so simple. I will go into the Netherworld and I will return with Tom."

She sighed, stroking the sleeping kitten, filled with misgivings. Pippin was stubborn and hardheaded, truly Catswold. She said, "I will teach you all I can."

Chapter 51

Pippin sat naked in Olive's dining room reciting Netherworld spells. Already Melissa had taught him to bring a spell-light, to turn aside arrows, to open locks. He delighted her with his quick, thorough Catswold retention. She soon had taught him every spell he might need, and some just for his pleasure. He took her sandal from her foot and made it dance and hoot like an owl. He called forth a fear that made the kitten spit and left Melissa trembling, unable to pull herself free until he released her.

He said, "I am ready now. I am going now to find Tom."

"You aren't going naked."

"Why not?"

"You can't go around naked." She swallowed a laugh at his puzzled look. "You will be cold, Pippin. And you will have no pockets to put things in. You must wait until I buy you some clothes." She rose. "Just stay here until I come back." He nodded, perplexed, she was out the door before he could argue.

In the village she bought jeans and a sweatshirt, sandals that seemed the right size, and a backpack, a blanket, a rope, some candy bars and something called trail food, and a good knife. She was back at Olive's within an hour. Pippin dressed himself clumsily, complaining, and they went down through the garden. He had hugged Olive and rubbed his face against her by way of good-bye. The old woman had made him some sandwiches and put a thermos of milk in the pack. Melissa had drawn a map for him. She was nervous with worry, but there was no changing his mind.

In the tool room she brought a spell-light and spread out the map. She showed him how to travel from the tunnel to the palace, and from there to Mag's cottage. She showed him the three rebel camps he would pass, and described and named the rebel leaders she knew. She gave him enchantments to manage a horse. She was describing the inside of the palace, and how to get to Wylles' chambers, where Tom was likely to be, when something scraped against the oak door and it swung open.

Olive slipped in and shut the door quickly. She was dressed in heavy pants and a sweater, and carrying a faded backpack. "I took the kitten to Morian's. I got it settled in the bedroom and left her a note by the front door. I told her I was going to my sister's."

Pippin said, "You don't think—you don't plan to go with me? You . . ."

"I am going with you. I told Morian I was taking Pippin with me to my sister's in his carrier, that I thought it would do her good to have an animal around."

Pippin said, "It is not possible for you to go. I move too fast; you will be lost." He stood over Olive glowering down at her. "You are an upperworld person, you have no magic. What will you do when I turn to cat?"

Olive looked hard at Pippin. "I am an old woman. No one will miss me. I want more than anything to see that world. I will not hinder you. If I do, you can leave me behind. I want to see that world, and I want to help free Tom."

"But you don't—you aren't—"

"You can tell me what I need to know as we travel. And perhaps I can tell you a few useful things. I have gleaned many old spells from my research. Now open the wall, Pippin. I am older than you, and more stubborn."

He opened the wall.

Olive stared into the darkness and strode through beside Pippin. Just before the wall closed she glanced back at Melissa. Her look was filled with wonder, with the excitement of her final amazing discovery.

Melissa watched the wall seal itself and turned away

drained—and she was facing Wylles. He stood in the open doorway, white with rage.

He came in slowly and shut the door behind him. "They are upperworlders. You had no right to let them go through."

She said nothing.

"I saw you come down here, you and that Catswold—that nasty yellow cat. I saw the old woman come down. What are they up to? Why are they going down?" Wylles started for the wall, but she grabbed him and shoved him back.

"I am prince of Affandar. You dare not touch me, you are my subject." He swung to slap her, but she caught his arm. He was only twelve years old, and he had been near to death, but he was strong enough now—it was all she could do to hold him.

"Get out of here, Wylles. Go on back to Tom's house. What harm can two upperworlders do in the Netherworld?"

"What magic did you teach that Catswold?"

She only looked at him.

"You will pay for this. My mother knows what to do with meddlers—with a Catswold slut from my father's bed."

She clenched her fists to keep from hitting him. "I'm surprised at your loyalty to your mother, after she got rid of you."

"I admire my mother's power. She does what a queen must. My illness was a great hindrance to her." He moved away and picked up the hoe, watching her. "Siddonie lives for the grand plan. I admire that. I admire her skill for intrigue—both at home and in the upperworld. Anne Hollingsworth is beside herself because Lillith Corporation is disrupting her neat little life. She is like a beast caught in a trap; she has no notion what is happening to her, or why."

"And you would not help her."

"Why should I help her? I like seeing her squirm."

"And what would you do if you didn't have her to feed and shelter you?"

"I would manage." He smiled. "I won't be here long. When my mother has defeated the rebels, when she rules every kingdom in the Netherworld, I will return to take my rightful place."

"If you go back to the Netherworld you will sicken again."

"If I sicken I will return here to become well." The idea seemed to amuse him. "I will come here, just as upper-worlders take winter vacations in Hawaii. I can return as I please. What is to stop me?" He balanced the hoe, testing its weight. She laid a silent spell to deflect it, and realized that his own spells touched her; she felt suddenly weak and fearful. This was the real battle, the silent battle of enchantments. She wanted to run, and she knew that desire was born of Wylles' power warping her senses.

He said, "Siddonie will die in her time. And my father will die. Then I will rule the Netherworld that Siddonie is now winning for me." His weight shifted slightly as he tensed to swing the hoe.

She made the hoe so heavy he couldn't lift it. He dropped it and grabbed the shovel; their spells crashed between them, too evenly matched. *"Catswold,"* Wylles spat. "There will be no Catswold left when I am king."

"Why do you hate the Catswold? Why does Siddonie?"

His eyes darkened. "The Catswold stole Xendenton from us. They killed my grandfather and my uncles."

"It's more than that," she hissed, wanting to slap him. "You fear the Catswold powers. You fear the Catswold's stubborn independence because you can't defeat that independence. You fear their freedom. You can't admit the real reason you hate the Catswold—any more than you can admit why you fear images."

"You should know about images, Catswold girl. You stir them brazenly. You encourage West to do irreparable damage."

"Braden's paintings harm no one."

"West's images draw evil forces."

"Nonsense."

Wylles' face clouded. "Already evil has come to this place. I saw my father here with you, planning evil. I want to know what you are planning."

When she laughed at him, he turned white. "You are my subject. When I ask you a question you are obliged to answer."

"I am no one's subject. I am Catswold; I bow to no ruler."

He screamed a spell and swung the shovel; she drove heaviness into it so it dropped, and grabbed his hands. He struggled but soon they stood locked together by her grip, and by their powers. She burned to weaken him. He was only a boy, but he filled her with cold fear. Suddenly he jerked free and snatched up the hoe, and his spell, born of rage, overrode hers. They scuffled, she hit him. The hoe struck her in the head a blow that dizzied her, pain warped her vision. She faced him, dizzy, her back to the wall. She felt herself changing and was terrified to be small. Gasping, she shouted a forgetting spell as she felt herself change to cat.

She was cat, staring up at him. Wylles stared at her blankly, then looked at the hoe he held, puzzled, and he lowered it. She watched him, her ears back, then wiped her paw at the blood that ran down her cheek. She didn't know whether he had changed her or whether the pain had changed her.

He looked down at her, puzzled, made no effort to harm her though she was small. Silently she brought the changing spell, and brought it again—she became a woman again with effort. When she stood tall before him, he seemed startled. "Where did you come from? I don't . . ."

"We came in here together, don't you remember? I was just behind you. You were telling me your name. I had asked you where you live."

"I—Tom," he said, confused. "Tom Hollingsworth. I live up—up the garden. In the white house. You're hurt—you've hurt your head."

"I hit my head. I must go and tend to it. Maybe you'd better go home, Tom."

Wylles nodded obediently and went out. She stood outside the portal watching him meander up the garden. Then she headed for the studio, dizzy and weak.

When Braden opened the door and saw the blood he put his arm around her and helped her to the couch. "Better lie down. I'll get some ice." She lay down gratefully on the vermilion silk. He left her, and soon she could hear the rattle of the ice tray. He returned to hold an icy towel to her forehead and cheek, his dark eyes intense. "Are you dizzy? Can you see clearly? Are you sick to your stomach? Melissa? My God, what happened to you?"

Gratefully she let him doctor her. Even under the cold pack she could feel her cheek and forehead swelling, and then, terrified, she felt the falling sensation that came with change. Pain made the change, she was sure of it now. She blocked the metamorphosis stubbornly, willing herself to hold human shape, sick with terror that she would become the little cat as he watched.

"Are you dizzy, Melissa? Do you feel nauseated?"

"Not dizzy, not sick. It just hurts. The ice makes it better."

Kneeling beside the couch he drew her to him, holding her close, his lips against her hurt forehead. "Will you tell me what happened?"

"I fell, up in the woods—I tripped on something, a branch. So stupid." She was steadying now. The sense of turning to cat was fading. "I fell against a tree and hit my head."

"But you're trembling."

"It frightened me. It hurt."

He tilted her chin up, kissing her. "You're completely white. Is that all that happened? Or was it someone—did someone hurt you?"

"No, there was no one. The pain made me dizzy, the fall frightened me. I—I'm all right now."

"Rest a while. I'll get a blanket."

She watched him tuck the blanket around her, already she was drifting.

He said, "Don't go to sleep. If it's a concussion you mustn't sleep. Talk to me."

She didn't want to sleep; she was terrified of going to sleep and changing. But she was very sleepy. Fighting to stay awake she rose at last, went into the bathroom, and washed her face. When she came out of the bathroom she stood behind him looking at the new painting, one from the Victorian house.

This painting had a dark quality. She saw herself standing beside the bevelled mirror in a bedroom of the Victorian house, wrapped in reflected shadows. She stared into her own face, startled.

She had, in this painting, a quality the other paintings did not show. Her face reflected power. Her eyes, within the shadows, reflected magic.

He was working away, oblivious to her. She stared at his back, frightened. Braden was seeing too much. First the secret cat shadows through her figure, and now this revealing glint of magic, far too explicit to be comfortable.

But he didn't know anything consciously, she was convinced of it. Whatever Braden perceived was seen not with his conscious mind.

When she had stood behind him for some minutes held by the painting, and upset by it, he turned. He was frowning, annoyed that she was standing there. But she supposed this was natural—no one wanted someone looking over his shoulder. He said, "Do you feel any better?"

She nodded.

"I have some steaks," he said. "Will you stay for dinner?"

"I—I'd like that," she said softly.

He glanced toward the darkening garden and began to clean up his paints. At his direction she washed two potatoes and put them to bake, feeling smug that she was cooking in an upperworld kitchen. He went to wash, then put some records on and fixed her a whiskey. He made a salad, and while the steaks broiled he called the little cat. He looked disappointed when she didn't appear. "I guess it's silly to be concerned, but she's gotten sick a couple of times."

"It isn't silly at all, just very caring. But I don't think she'll come while I'm here. Cats always avoid me."

They ate on the terrace by candlelight, watching the garden for the cat and listening to records. The music was strange to her, exciting. There were trumpets, clarinets; he called it swing. Then one number struck her memory, making her unbearably nostalgic, and Braden said Alice had liked it.

They washed the dishes together and played another stack of records and talked about nothing and about everything—about McCabe, about Alice and the Kitchens, about the city, its galleries and museums. Isolated memories touched her, of pollarded trees in Golden Gate Park, and then of wind on the ocean. Of a room with a skylight and a fountain. Ugly memories touched her, too—pictures of a dozen different schools where she was always the new child, picked on, hazed. He had the same kind of memories, from moving so often as his father followed the oil fields. She remembered being thought a strange child because she liked cats, but she kept that memory to herself. As they discovered mutual childhood fears and pains she found her need for him rising in a way she had never felt before.

She got him to talk about his work, though she had to read between his remarks. Slowly she began to understand the search he embarked on with each new painting. She began to see how he groped, each time, for some entity almost beyond the painter's grasp. He laughed at himself. "Late night talk." But she liked very much the way he explained his feelings.

He was not self-conscious. His words seemed to be a way of exploring, as if he seldom put his intentions into conscious thought. She understood that his vision of the work came from deep inside; she thought that his deep response to the world was almost like an inner enchantment.

Late in the evening he called the cat again, then brought Melissa a cup of tea. She said, "The moon's full—it makes cats crazy. She's probably playing up in the garden, climbing trees." She smiled at him. "She'll be home in the morning, don't worry."

Leaning to set the cup down he touched her hair, then tilted her chin up, looking deeply at her. She swallowed, ducking her head to press her face into his hand. Rubbing her cheek against him, she rose and led him to the bedroom.

In the dim moonlight, touched by the cool salt wind, she

let him undress her. She was already used to his nakedness, and was amused because she couldn't tell him that. She rose to his stroking, to his lips on her, as if she had never before been loved, as if this was the first time.

Chapter 52

Wylles reached the top of the garden filled with rage at Melissa for the spell she had tried to lay on him. There was too much power in the Catswold woman. Though her spell hadn't destroyed his memory, he had felt his face go slack, had felt himself starting to drop into the dull state of forgetfulness, had used all his power to counter her enchantment. He was pleased that he had hurt her, saw the blood as she turned away. Saw with disgust Braden West open the studio door for her and put his arm around her. And then at the top of the garden, when he spied Olive's two kittens sunning on her porch, all his fury focused on them. He thought about cat blood spurting and thin bones broken, thought how the kittens resembled Melissa, if not in color, at least in their soft, furry weakness.

He approached the kittens casually, as if he didn't really see them. Ignoring them, he sat down on the top step.

They looked at him with curiosity and soon the bolder kitten approached him. It was gangly despite its thick, soft fur. The thought of wounding it made him hard; he cupped his hand over his crotch. With a sudden hot, shivering bliss he pictured not the gray-and-white kitten rent in his hands, but Melissa: he saw the calico rent and torn.

The kitten approached innocently and stood looking up into his face. The second kitten skittered close behind it. He waited until they were both winding around his knees, then he grabbed them suddenly, one in each hand, meaning to bash them together, seeing Melissa crushed.

Pain hit him: hot pain shot through his neck and throat. Then someone knocked him up off the porch, hitting him from behind.

The blow was so sharp his arms jerked and his hands released the kittens. His vision faltered, blackness washed over the garden. He felt himself being shaken, hard. The porch and garden warped and swam before him. He was jerked around, hands biting into his arms.

He was facing the black woman; she held him in a grip like steel.

Morian slapped him. Her eyes blazed. His fear of her was so complete and debilitating he wet himself.

Morian tried to control her rage; she didn't want to injure him, just terrify. Whoever this boy was, he needed to experience the terror of quick retribution. She shook him until she was afraid she would do him damage, then she held him away, staring into his white, frightened face.

She knew this could not be Tom. Tom would never harm an animal, he was too strong inwardly. The real Tom had a deep, sure core of lightness that would not allow him to do something so weak.

She tried to see physical differences between this boy and Tom, in the set of the boy's eyes, in the shape of his brows or mouth, his round chin. As she watched him, a shiver of vertigo touched her, a swarming dizziness that puzzled and alarmed her. She held the boy tighter, digging her fingers into his shoulders.

"If I ever see you near any cat, if I see you *touch* a cat again, I will break your bones, boy. I will smash your face."

"I wasn't going to hurt them. What makes—makes you think I would hurt them, Mor? I was petting them, picking the kittens up to pet them."

She jerked him up off the steps, bringing him close to her face. "If any cat, in this garden or near it, is harmed in any way—even if you are not responsible—I will make pudding of that white, pasty little face."

His stare told her that he would like to crush her, just as he had meant to crush the helpless kittens.

She shook him and twisted his ear until tears spurted from his glaring eyes. "Do you understand me!" she shouted. "I will twist your face like I am twisting that ear. I will twist your body like that, and break it." She dropped him and held up her hands. "These black hands could kill you, boy. If you touch any cat again, these hands will break you in little pieces."

He backed away from her. And she saw as he turned away from her something distant and cold crawling out of his eyes.

Then he was gone, into the Hollingsworth house. She stood looking after him, wondering who, or what, this boy was.

Chapter 53

The Harpy cupped her little mirror in her hands and watched with interest as Morian shook and slapped Wylles. She was perched alone on a ridge of black rock far north of Chillings, catching her breath. She opened her beak wide as, in the flashing light of her mirror, Morian dealt with Wylles. She liked the black woman's style. The prince deserved whatever he got.

She felt that the fates were working now in a fascinating way. The events in the two worlds were linking, meshing together. Even Wylles' role was notable. She had begun to think that, after all, the powers of good would triumph.

She surprised herself that she cared.

She was a Hell Beast. She should be rooting for Siddonie and the dark forces. She had tried, but she could not. She felt drawn to Melissa and to Mag and the rebels. Her fondness embraced, as well, the inhabitants of the upperworld garden—Braden, Olive, certainly Morian. All of them had a passion for life that warmed and excited her.

She realized that she was, for all practical purposes, no longer a true Hell Beast. She had, in becoming drawn toward the most spirited living souls, abandoned the flames of Hell. Win the war, that was the first order. After that— maybe she would move in with Mag and raise pigs.

She shook her tired wings, and let them droop and rest. Every muscle ached. She had been flying for days, moving endlessly beneath the Netherworld's skies and sometimes running through tunnels too narrow for flight. She was the only flying beast willing to help the rebels, willing to gather together the ancient folk. How many miles she had flown she didn't count. She had routed dwarfs from deep cave communities, and had summoned small dark men from clefts so remote they had no green sky of wizard light, only spell-lights. At her call, shy bands of white-skinned elven folk had scaled down sheer cliffs to gather in valleys their races hadn't seen in generations. Goat-hooved urisks small as rabbits had come carrying immense spears, and a tribe of dorricks with twisted backs had joined the rebels.

Under her recruiting, the small, disciplined rebel army was swelling into a formidable band, taking on so many troops it was becoming cumbersome and unruly. She had even routed out the last few dragons, though they were puny beasts. She had brought into the rebel camps folk so long forgotten that no one knew what to call them. But all were warriors, or soon would be, though they might be armed only with picks and axes and sharpened shovels and with fighting spells not used in generations.

And now, not only were the tribes joining together, but the fates of key individuals were joining: the fate of the real Tom Hollingsworth, who had already escaped from Siddonie.

The fate of Melissa. Of Wylles. The fate of Siddonie herself. And the fate of Braden West.

When, rested, the Harpy exploded suddenly into flight again, she took off with such vigor that her wings scraped the granite cliff and she bumped up against the granite sky. When she recovered from the jolt she set off in a long, powerful flight, heading north straight for Mag and the rebel camp, her shadow winging above her thin and fast. She arrived at the camp in mid-afternoon.

At once, Mag set about preparing a pot of cricket soup for her. "What of the false queen, Harpy? What does your mirror show?"

The Harpy smiled. "Just as we hoped, the street cat has embraced the advances of King Efil. Or," she said, "she seems to have embraced his proposition. Though in my opinion, the king is a fool to trust her." She reached, took the ladle from Mag impatiently, and began supping up crickets from it.

"The king was always a fool," Mag said.

The Harpy nodded, her mouth full. "He thinks the false queen idolizes him. Ah," she said, smacking a cricket, "lovely soup."

Mag said, "It's hardly cooked yet. I do not like this business of the false queen."

"Siddonie has trained her well," the Harpy said glumly.

"And?" said Mag.

"The Catswold have long been without a queen. They may be eager, indeed, to follow this woman."

"Then tell them she is an imposter—tell them before she comes down the tunnel and into the Catswold nation."

"No."

"Well, why not? If you don't, I will send a messenger to tell them. And I myself will go to fetch Melissa home. The Catswold need their true queen."

"No," said the Harpy. "Not yet."

"I do not understand you. Why are you so stubborn? You will have to tell me where she is. Do you want me to waste time searching for her? She is needed now."

The Harpy turned away to ladle out more soup, then grew impatient and dipped her bill into the pot, spearing crickets.

"No matter how much you have helped us so far," Mag said, "if you impede us in this you will destroy us."

"No, I will not. Do not go after Melissa. Let the fates have their way."

Mag stared at her. "Then you know what will happen? I thought you couldn't see the future."

The Harpy raised her dripping beak, a cricket caught in the side, squirming. She gulped it before she spoke. Her words were far too poetic for her nature. "I do not see the future. But I sense the whisper of fate like a rising wind against the granite sky."

Mag snorted.

"I sense fate powerfully," the Harpy said, her little black eyes widening. "If I did not, I would go myself to fetch Melissa."

She resumed eating.

It was much later, after she had left Mag and was flying alone beneath the dark sky, that the Harpy saw in her little mirror a scene that made her pause in flight, dropping and shivering.

She saw a blackness stirring deep down within the flames of the Hell Pit: a dark, primal evil that, she thought, not even Siddonie's powers could have roused. She watched it for a long time, shaken. She might sense fate, but she had not sensed this. She did not know how to deal with this cold black essence of the Hell Pit.

Chapter 54

T hrough the open bedroom window the bay was dark under low clouds. Wind rattled the reeds in the marsh, bringing to Melissa as she woke a memory of running among the reeds. She frowned, thinking some noise had awakened her. She heard nothing now but the wind. She woke fully and stretched, watching Braden sleeping beside her, deliriously aware that she need not sneak away now, that she belonged here, that he would wake soon and hold her and love her. She slid closer to him, fitting herself against him, her desire rising. In sleep his arms went around her and his embrace tightened but he didn't wake. Hungrily she touched her lips to his face, breathing his scent, wanting him. The noise came again, the noise that had awakened her. She came fully alert, listening to the sliding, metallic scraping.

It came from the studio, the scraping then a click. Puzzled, she slipped out from Braden's arms, slid off the bed, and pulled on his robe. She went out barefoot, silently padding toward the studio.

The room was unnaturally dark with the draperies closed. The only light was a faint gray pool beneath the skylight, and a dull pallor spilling in through the open front door.

Wind from the open door fingered coldly against her ankles. She looked for whoever had come in. Where she stood in the hall, in Braden's dark robe, perhaps she had not been seen.

She could see little in the dark room. She breathed a silent spell and changed to cat. The shadows thinned, the room was lighter.

She saw a black figure barely visible in front of the closed draperies. She could hear him breathing now, and she knew his scent. Frightened, she slipped into the blackness behind the stacked canvases.

From the dense shadows between canvases she watched Wylles move toward the easel. He made no sign that he had seen her. Suddenly his face was lit, not by a spell-light but by a flashlight. Its yellow circle moved toward the paintings hanging on the wall above her.

The light paused at each painting as Wylles moved slowly down the room, looking. Then he moved to the easel; she saw too late the glint of a knife.

She heard the canvas rip as she leaped. She landed on his back raking her claws into his flesh. He threw himself against the wall to crush her.

She jumped from his shoulders and changed to girl. She hit him and grabbed his arms. The studio lights flared on.

Braden stood half awake, half asleep, wearing a pair of cutoffs, looking at the slashed painting, at her, and at the paint-smeared blade in Wylles' hand. Looking at the painting where her face was slashed, with a hole in it where a flap of canvas hung down. It began to rain, pattering against the glass.

Braden took the paint-smeared knife from Wylles' hand. He examined the paint on Wylles' fingers.

Then, not speaking, he clamped a hand on Wylles' shoulder and propelled him out the door. Melissa watched him guide Wylles up the dim garden, watched them mount the stairs to the white house, watched Braden push Wylles against the wall like a limp doll. She could see that Braden was talking to Wylles. Wylles didn't move. At last Braden opened the door and shoved Wylles inside the house.

He came back down the garden and pushed past her, not speaking. Was he angry with her? She heard the coffeepot start. She stood looking at the ruined canvas. If she had not come in, Wylles would have destroyed all Braden's paintings of her.

Images—he stirs violent powers with his images . . .

She went into the bedroom and slipped back into bed to wait for Braden to cool down.

At last he brought his coffee and her tea to bed. She touched his face. "Did you wake Tom's mother? Did you tell her?"

"No. My business was with Tom." His dark eyes burned with anger, but not at her.

"What did you say to him?"

"I explained how I would feel if anything else of mine was touched. I told him I had killed men in the war. I told him killing meant nothing to me." For the first time, he grinned. "I demonstrated with his butcher knife a diversity of things I could think of to do to him."

"Would you?"

He smiled.

She buried her face against his bare shoulder. "I loved that painting."

"I'll do it over."

"He'll come back, Braden. No matter what you told him. Is—is there somewhere we could take the paintings?"

"He won't come back."

"Yes."

He looked at her, frowning. "How could you know that? Is there something you're not telling me?"

"No, but—did you see his face? I just feel that he could come back."

"Was it Tom who hit you yesterday? The blow on your head . . . ?"

"I fell. Why would Tom hit me?"

"Why would he slash my painting?"

"Could you take the paintings to the gallery now? The show is only three weeks away. We—we could go down to Carmel. You said last night it would be nice to paint in Carmel."

He looked at her silently, trying to see more than she was telling him. "He's only a child, Melissa. Why would I run away from a little boy?"

She touched his face, tracing the line of his jaw, turning

her own face so the wound on her forehead and the bruise on her cheek caught the light.

He stared at her then drew her close, kissing her, holding her. At last he said, "So why not? We could get some good work in Carmel, the light is wonderful, the sea . . . But I don't think I want to dump the whole show on Rye so early, fill up his storage space."

She busied herself with her tea.

He touched under her chin, tipping her face up. "There's more to this than you're telling me."

"He slashed one painting. He will destroy the rest." She looked back at him steadily.

He sighed, took her cup from her, and kissed her. "I suppose I could take them to the gallery. But some aren't dry. They're a bother to handle."

She watched him.

"All right. Rye can order frames. And he can have frames ready for the paintings we do in Carmel." Then he laughed. "This kind of last minute thing drives him crazy."

He touched the tip of her nose with his finger. "You don't need to say much to get your own way, do you? With that green-eyed stare, you're as hardheaded as the damn cat." He gathered her close, burying his face against her, kissing her, making slow, easy love to her.

When they lay spent, his mouth resting against her throat, he said, muffled against her, "Just before I woke this morning I was dreaming of a green world. Green cliffs, green sky, green caves." He raised up, looking at her, his eyes filled with pleasure from the dream. "I could see in the rock formations how water had cut through, and how the earth had twisted and warped. The green light seemed to seep out of every stone."

She stared at him, her heart pounding, trying to look enchanted by his tale, wondering what power they had made together, to allow him to see her world so clearly.

He fixed breakfast while she showered. The rain had stopped, the sky was clearing and the morning turning hot.

He took their tray to the terrace and stood calling the little cat; he hadn't seen her since the day before. "Tom can't have hurt her? He tried to kill his own cat. I swear I'll kill him if he touches her."

"She would scratch him, Braden. She would run from him."

"Go ahead and eat. I'm going to look for her. Maybe while we're gone she would be safer in a kennel."

Dismay made her choke. "Wouldn't she be terrified? Has she ever been in such a place?" But he had already started up the garden. She saw him glance up at the white house, his hands tightening into fists.

She ate as he searched; she put his plate in the oven. She watched him tramp through the woods then go down toward the highway. She loved him for caring so much. When he returned she said, "I'd look for her, but she won't come to me."

"You'll need to pack a few things."

"Yes. I'll go do that."

"You won't need much: a bathing suit, some shorts, and that smashing green-and-white dress for dinner. I'll call Mathew Rhain about the safe deposit box. If he's back, we'll stop there on our way, after we drop off the paintings."

She headed across the lane toward the village then doubled back through the wood where Braden wouldn't see her. Within five minutes the calico came running down the garden. He scooped her up, hugging and rubbing her, unashamed of his pleasure. "Where the hell have you been? Dammit, you scared the hell out of me." He held her away, looking into her eyes. "I hope to hell you're sufficiently afraid of that—of Tom. Where do you go when you disappear?" He carried her to the kitchen. "You don't give a damn that people worry about you." He put her down and opened a can of chicken. She wolfed down the chicken, then wound around his legs as he assembled the painting rack, put it in the station wagon, and began to load paintings. Before he went up to talk with Morian about taking care of her, he shut her securely in the house.

* * *

Morian put her arm around him, scowling. She was enraged by the slashed painting, but, Braden thought, she
didn't seem surprised. She said, "Of course I'll keep the
calico. I'll shut her in my bedroom when I'm gone, and
fix the windows so no cat could open them. Olive should
be back soon; she'll watch the house when I'm not
home."

"What about the key? Doesn't Anne have a key?"

"Not anymore. I got it back from her."

He waited for her to explain but she didn't. She said, "The
calico will be fine, Brade. Sleep on my bed, eat caviar."

He hugged her companionably. "She's shut in the studio,
I'll bring her up before we leave."

But when he returned to the house, the calico had disappeared. He had left the door locked. Melissa wasn't back, no
one had come in. The windows were closed. He searched the
house, puzzled, then worried, then angry. And why was he
so damned upset, worrying over a damned cat?

But he kept searching, behind the stacked canvases,
under the bed, even in the cupboards. There was no way she
could get out. He had given up at last and was taking out the
last two paintings when she appeared from the bedroom
and shot past him out the front door. He watched her race
away up the garden to disappear behind Olive's house, and
he leaned the paintings against the station wagon and went
after her.

He didn't find her. He went back to the studio and called
Morian. Hell, if the cat could evade him like that, she could
sure as hell evade Tom.

In the village Melissa shopped for a small suitcase, a bathing
suit, and tennis shoes. She returned to the garden to find
Braden irritated because the cat had disappeared again, and
Morian trying to soothe him, promising him she would
search for the cat and care for her. Morian said there was
nothing for Braden to worry about, she'd call him if there
was a problem; and she gave Melissa a look that startled and

alarmed her—as if Morian knew very well where the little calico would be.

But of course she was imagining that; there was no way Morian could know.

Chapter 55

She was afraid of taking the elevator by herself. She got out of the station wagon nervously as Braden paused in traffic. She entered the brick office building, pushed the elevator button, and steeled her nerve to slip inside. She was glad she was alone and not among strangers. She rode up feeling skittery, wanting to climb the wall. She tripped as she left the moving box and thought the door would close on her. Unnerved, she fled to find Mathew Rhain's office.

A blond, tight-lipped secretary took her name. Melissa turned her back on the woman and stood looking at the watercolors of sailing ships that decorated the waiting room. When Mathew Rhain came out of the inner office she froze, so startled she found it hard to speak.

Rhain was a short, stocky man with hair the color of red clay. He had a broad, freckled face and broad, short-fingered hands. He was taller than an elven man, and he greeted her with the smooth manners of an upperworlder; but Mathew Rhain had elven blood.

Why would a Netherworlder be living and working in the upperworld?

But why shouldn't he? McCabe had. Mag had, once. No one knew how many Netherworlders had escaped the tyrannies of enslaved nations to live in the free world above.

Rhain studied her with intense interest, as curious about her as she was about him. He took her hand, searching her face. "You are McCabe's daughter. Even if West hadn't told me, I would see it." He drew her into his private office and closed the door. The room was furnished with colored leather chairs, an oriental rug, and more sailing ships, in paintings, and as models arranged along the tops of the bookshelves. On a table at one end of the room lay three black leather binders.

Rhain seated her at the table. "McCabe was my good friend. I wish he could know that you are well—that you are here."

She squeezed his stubby, square hand. "Braden said you would want some proof of who I am, but I'm afraid I don't have any proof."

"I think I can arrange some proof. These are McCabe's journals. I have kept them safe since he died."

"Was there—anything besides the journals?"

He settled a quiet look on her. His eyes were rust colored, with little lights that softened them. "There was nothing else. John Kitchen has McCabe's paintings, those that were left, and what few books survived the earthquake. Perhaps he has other things. Do the Kitchens know you've—returned?"

She supposed Braden had explained to him about her memory. She said, "Not yet. Braden says they are in Europe."

"They're expected back in a few weeks."

She said, "Have you lived in the city long? Did you know my father long?"

"My grandfather and McCabe's grandfather were friends, in the gold fields. I—have lived in many places." He reached for the leatherbound books. "You may find the journals difficult to open." He sat down opposite her, watching her. Reaching to open the first journal, she understood why she would need no identification. The journals were sealed. She glanced up at Rhain. If she wanted to open her father's journals she must use Netherworld powers. She must put all her trust in this sandy-haired elven man if she were to find any clue to the Amulet.

She was afraid—of being discovered, of Braden learning about her.

But she must do this.

The books had dates on the front, written on a white label in a bold script. She chose the volume that would cover the year Timorell came up into the upperworld. Not looking at Rhain, she made a silent spell for opening.

The cover freed itself. She opened McCabe's journal then looked up to meet Rhain's eyes. Their secrets were shared, and she knew he must trust her now, as she was forced to trust him. He rose, and left her, shutting the door behind him.

She touched the velum page, admiring McCabe's neat, square script. She meant to flip through until she found Mc-Cabe's description of Timorell, but the journal fell open to that page as if McCabe had gone back often to this passage where he first saw Timorell.

Thursday, May 6:
Through her window I could see her asleep, the cover thrown back. She and her husband and the child have taken a rented apartment; it smelled of stale cooking and dust. I thought she should not be in such a place. She is like the sun, her hair is all shades of gold and red. She is tall, sleek, a silken woman. I wanted to wake her, to touch her, to whisper a spell and see her leap to the sill as golden cat. She stirred and sighed as if she sensed me there. I waited for her to wake, never patient, until I realized that someone watched me. Her husband's sister watched me: an evil child. Darkly evil.

Saturday, May 8:
I returned to her this morning before dawn: She stood at the window letting the sharp wind bathe her bare skin. I stayed out of sight. She seemed excited by the wind, by the smell of the bay and the city smells; the wind carried its scents to her like a feast, she kept

*scenting out, and perhaps she was aware of me, too.
She seemed fascinated with the rooftops that spread
below her. I could imagine the golden cat chasing
across them. But when she looked up at the sky she
seemed to go dizzy; as morning came brighter she
could not avoid looking. She gripped the window
frame, she looked up slowly, staring directly up. The
distances seemed to make her faint; she leaned her
head against the window frame as if to regain her balance. I think it unnatural to live all your life with a
solid granite roof above you.*

Tuesday, May 11:
*I spent the morning inspecting the job up on Glasgow
Street, then drove down the Peninsula to pick up the
kitchen tile and the cabinets. I returned, unloaded
them, and knocked off at noon thankful I have a good
foreman, good men. I think of Grandfather mining
gold in Coloma—and in deeper mines. This was the
only thing we didn't agree on: where best to work,
above ground or below. I am restless and unable to
settle. I have seen her twice more, walking the neighborhood near their apartment; I must confess I cruise
near her apartment. When she goes walking she tries
to look at everything at once, tries to take in every
new detail, every scent and sound; but she is nervy,
skittish.*

*I have talked with others who have come up, it took
them weeks to get used to so much space and to the
open sky and the sun. I cannot conceive of living all
my life beneath that weight of earth. I think I would
tear the stone apart to get out. I remember too well
Grandfather's tales of earth shifting and chasms col-
lapsing—though folk seemed to take that as much for
granted as we take earthquakes and/or hurricanes.*

Friday, May 14:
The sharp wind sweeping in through the Golden Gate

makes me wild. I can't settle. I drove by the piers, stopped to watch a Norwegian ship offloading rubber, a Chilean ship discharging leather; but the ships didn't hold me as they usually do. I can think only of her. She is seeing this world for the first time and I long to be with her. But she must make her discoveries on her own; and perhaps she is happy with her husband. I can't bear to think that; he is not Catswold; how can he appreciate her?

Monday, May 17:
I have followed her. She is a delight to watch, everything is new and wonderful. I think this is a time of growing for her, and I feel that it is a time of pain. Her husband seems to share nothing with her. He seldom goes out with her. I am glad. I couldn't bear it if she loved him. We will meet soon. My patience will not hold much longer.

Wednesday, May 19:
I have not written anything for a long time. We have met, we are together. I need not write of this.

Friday, May 21:
Her husband deals in stocks, bonds, land, small corporate trades. His young sister absorbs adult business affairs with a shocking hunger and rapidity, with the same commitment and trained memory that she absorbed spells and enchantments. A voracious child, singleminded as a young vulture. Tim fears her.

Saturday, May 22:
My love has moved in with me; she is all my happiness. She relishes everything about the city: the wind, the shops, the little restaurants, the wharves. We walk, we laugh, we eat and listen to music, and make love.
She is fascinated by the sleek cats of the city basking under stairs or on balconies. She will kneel to

stroke them; she is aware of every cat—and they, of her. Cats wait for her behind curtained windows and in alleys, though she talks to them in a language that none of them understands.

Wednesday, May 26:
Tim doesn't know what to make of my collection of paintings of cats—they fascinate her in an uneasy way. She has grown up to feel that images are evil. I try to tell her that these were made with love. There is one sketch she keeps returning to, of the young calico, a charcoal sketch Alice did. I told her it was done by the daughter of a friend, and I took her to meet the family. She and Alice were drawn to one another. Tim took the child's hand in a strange, tender gesture, delighting Alice. They are already fast friends.

Saturday, May 29:
I have taken Tim to the Cat Museum. She was charmed; she wanted to know how I happened to do the designing. I told her Alice's father suggested me, that the old doctor who commissioned it didn't know half how interested I was. That amused her. And Tim has done a strange thing, she has commissioned a piece of sculpture for the museum. She wanted me to help her choose an artist. I have suggested Smith, a metal piece. He is already at work on it.

Melissa paused, feeling her pulse pound. Why would Timorell commission a sculpture in a museum strange to her, in a world strange to her?

Unless she had a special use for that sculpture. She tried to remember an iron or bronze cat with the artist's name Smith.

In the succeeding pages, she found no further mention of the sculpture. Braden had come in; the two men sat at the other end of the office deep in conversation. She felt unnerved to see him talking comfortably with a Netherworlder:

how strange that the two worlds kept pushing together, flowing together. She had thought of Braden as totally removed from the realms of the Netherworld, but now that separation seemed less severe.

Wednesday, January 12:
Tim's husband saw her on the street yesterday. He could see that she was pregnant and he thought the child was his. She told him it is not, that she is not his wife anymore, not in her eyes. She was in a rage when she got back to the apartment; she did not like having such anger while she carried the child. She made spells to drive the anger away.

Thursday, February 16:
Our baby was born at one o'clock this morning in a small hospital in Marin County. We were concerned about Tim going into a hospital, but Rhain knew some people, a doctor we could trust. And I was in the room, whispering spells to keep her and the baby from changing. Tim's labor was relatively easy. Our child is the most beautiful little girl, with lovely calico hair. A nurse said her hair would turn the right color soon, not to worry. We laughed about that. We named her Melissa. Melissa McCabe. Tim made a quick recovery; we were out of the hospital and back in the apartment the next afternoon. When Alice came to visit she was ecstatic with the baby. Melissa took to her, reaching for her with a little mewling cry that startled Tim, but it was only a human baby cry. Of course Alice doesn't suspect.

Melissa turned forward to the last two entries.

Wednesday, August 9:
Something is happening—the common street cats sense it. All morning they have been out on the streets, acting strangely, searching restlessly for places to

*hide, then moving on. Dogs run the streets nervously.
The earth is trembling, though so far only we and the
animals can feel it. I am afraid for Tim and Melissa. I
will not leave them.*

*Saturday, August 12:
The trembling was three days ago. My nerves are like
hot wires, and not only with fear of the physical damage. I cannot help but equate the earth's trembling
with forces of evil, as my grandfather believed.*

   *But this is not the Netherworld, and the trembling
has settled now; I will work on the Marin house today
only because Tim insists.*

The empty pages that followed should have been filled
with their lives together, with their love, with their baby
growing up, learning to walk and talk, learning to live as
McCabe and Timorell did, both as cat and as human.

She imagined too vividly her father falling from a rooftop,
twisting, fighting himself, then hit by falling bricks. She
tried not to see Timorell sprawled under the fallen bookcase
in the wrecked apartment. She was trembling with pain for
them, wanted to weep for them.

When Rhain rose, she said, "I must give the journals
back."

"It is only a formality. They have been safe here for a long
time."

She laid her hand over the volumes, closing them with a
silent spell. She rose, handing them to him. Their eyes met,
sharing their secret.

Chapter 56

The coast was ragged and wild. Waves crashed against the dark, wet cliffs. Occasional cypress trees thrust out of the stone, trees as gnarled and bent as if giant hands had twisted them. Seaspray leaped on the wind, beading Melissa's blowing hair, dampening Braden's shirt. They stood together looking straight down the rocks at the sea where the water heaved and fell. Dark kelp beds soughed up and down, and surface breakers crashed thundering against the pitted stone. The smell of salt and iodine made Melissa tip her tongue out to taste the sharp scent. Braden watched her, powerfully immersed in her animal pleasure at the wildness of sea and wind. She seemed as totally engrossed as if she had never seen the sea. Each time gulls wheeled over them her hands moved involuntarily, as if she wanted to fly with them—or snatch them from the wind and hold them.

Driving down from San Francisco they had stopped at Half Moon Bay for lunch, had sat at a window table facing the beach, eating clam chowder and French bread. Outside the glass, the deserted white sand stretched to an empty sea, and even that flat expanse had held her. She had seemed fascinated with the wheeling gulls; her mouth had curved up with pleasure when gulls screamed by their window. Now he watched her, charmed by her eagerness, wanting to show her everything, to share with her the village where he had grown up, its red-roofed cottages, its hilly, winding streets, its little restaurants and galleries. Wanting her to love the inn that had been his home, wanting her to be a part of it.

Within an hour he was showing her Carmel, the narrow,

shop-lined alleys, the Monterey pines marching down the divided main street. The inn stood a block from the shore; he
could see that she liked its white stucco walls and red tile
roof, and its balconies bright with potted red geraniums.
Mrs. Trask kept it just as neat and welcoming as it was the
day she bought it from Gram. He parked and reached behind
the seat for their bags and his painting things. Melissa
swung out, took her bag and his and went ahead up the brick
walk, looking.

The lobby pleased her; she entered slowly. Sunlight through
tall windows played over the white walls and potted ferns.
The large cool room was high ceilinged, its brown tile floors
bare, its white wicker chairs cushioned in pale blue. Only
the proprietress looked out of place, black as a raven in her
long black dress and thick black stockings and flat black
shoes. Mrs. Trask was a hard-looking old woman with gray,
grizzled hair knotted behind her head. But when she saw
Braden and cried out a greeting and hugged him, her face
changed; she was all smiles and warmth. "I save your usual
room. Is enough space for easel. Do you bring a cloth to
cover my floor?"

Braden nodded and grinned, hugging her.

The woman looked at Melissa shyly, perhaps comparing
her to Alice, but then she smiled and took Melissa's hand in
a warm, engulfing grip.

Their room was on the third floor. Its wide corner windows looked down over the village to the sand and sea. Its
tile floors showed off white embroidered rugs, and the thick
white spread was embroidered with flowers; crewel work,
Braden said. He unfolded his drop cloth in a corner and set
up his easel, then grabbed her in a hug. "I don't know
whether to take you to bed, or swimming. Either way, take
your clothes off."

It was much later that they swam. The sea frightened her
and was ice cold. Behind them the beach was nearly deserted except for a few walkers; no one else was swim-

ming. The waves hit her so hard she could hardly stand.
Beyond the waves, Braden swam strongly, and she
wouldn't be outdone. She followed, thankful Mag had
made her learn in the swift Sesut River. But they came out
soon, freezing, and lay warming on the sand, holding
hands, feeling the heat build, thinking of lovemaking until
they rose and returned to the inn.

They entered the inn through the rear patio where they
could hose off their feet. The bricks had just been washed.
The round tables were pushed together and the chairs piled
on top, and a man in coveralls was setting mouse traps behind the potted geraniums. Mrs. Trask sat at a table cutting
up raw bacon for mouse-bait. Her face looked angry and
sullen, as if she trusted no one, but again when she smiled
the sun came out. Melissa wondered if she had had a very
hard life.

The old woman looked them over. "You have goose
bumps. No one swims in that water—water like ice. Foolish,
Braden. People drown in that water." She saw Melissa staring at the traps, and smiled.

"Mouse somewhere. It overruns us. I tell Arnol, either we
must catch him or we have to have a cat. I never see mouse
so bad."

And there were mice; that night in the small hours when
Braden slept, she heard scratching in the wall and lay trying to decide exactly where. The sound drew her, teased
her; she was afraid of the way it made her feel. She rose at
last and stood looking out toward the sea where the breakers rolled white in the moonlight, trying to hear only the
pounding waves, trying to ignore the scratching in the walls
behind her.

But soon she could smell the mouse, too, and her muscles
tensed, and she felt the dropping feeling that heralded
change. She resisted change, but all her senses were honed
on the mouse. Its smell was too strong to bear. Its scratching
teased and tormented.

Maybe she could change to the calico for just a moment.

Braden slept so soundly. As she watched the wall where it was scratching, it suddenly darted out into the room and reared up in the moonlight, scenting out with a twitching nose.

She moved silently, stalking it.

Halfway across the room she stopped, clenched her fists, and turned away. She got back in bed and curled down close to Braden. He half woke and pulled her close, then slept again. She lay awake for the rest of the night, knowing that she must control this. Knowing that being with Braden constantly, never apart to turn into the calico and hunt, was going to cause problems. She had no way to work off her killing instincts. Quite suddenly, her love for him had pulled her into a gentle, passionate prison.

In the morning when she kept yawning, she said the moon had kept her awake. They had breakfast on the inn's patio, then got to work. He drew her on the beach beside a wrecked boat with shattered glass in the windows, then before a shop with leaded windows that mirrored a red, flowering tree. That evening after dinner he chose his favorite from the day's four drawings, stretched a canvas, and blocked in a painting. He had brought books for her—she read California history and some poetry, but the poetry made her uncomfortable. It was too much like reading spells.

They had the windows open because the smell of turpentine bothered her. When he came to bed they made love in the cool breeze; their passion echoed the pounding pulse of the sea, as if they partook of the spirit of the earth itself, elemental and primal. That night she more easily ignored the mouse, snuggling close to Braden, though again the nervy little beast came into the room with them as if irresistibly drawn to the contemplation of its own death.

And the next day, giddy with the excitement of wind and waves, as they walked on the rocks above the churning sea, she did something so stupid and foolish that she wallowed afterward in remorse.

Mrs. Trask had packed a lunch for them, and they drove down to Point Lobos, where gigantic stone slabs jutted into the sea. Among the wet, reflecting slabs of water-sculptured stone Braden posed her. The sea light, running and changing across the rocks, excited her, made her giddy. The sea made her wild—she wanted to run beside it, she wanted to chase the waves. She felt fidgety and impatient as they carried their lunch up a rock escarpment. Braden climbed slow and sure-footed, but Melissa, on the rocks above him, could not resist the razor-thin crest. She didn't mean to run, but suddenly she was running and leaping along the crest, laughing, giddy.

His shout stopped her. "For Christ sake! Get the hell down from there! What the hell are you doing!"

She stared down at him, deflated, ashamed, enraged at herself.

"What the hell were you doing? You could have fallen, killed yourself." He held her too tight. "You scared the hell out of me."

She was quiet while they ate. She knew she was being sullen, and she didn't like sullenness in herself.

But she didn't like being so constricted. She had been perfectly safe on the rocks; she hadn't been in danger. She felt contrary, willful. She wanted to run; she was crazy to be free a moment, just to run in the wind. Being cooped up within herself, having no chance to work off her pent-up wildness made her irritable.

It was mid-afternoon when Braden left her to walk around a point looking for the next place to work. She snatched the moment of freedom and ran crazily along the top of the cliff; and suddenly a rock broke under her feet. She fell headlong, clutching.

She righted herself in mid-air and landed lightly at the bottom of the cliff, on the rocks where the waves were crashing. Her tennis shoes slipped on the wet surface and she almost went in. As she turned, starting back up the cliff, she saw Braden on the rocks above her staring down at her, his face twisted with disbelief.

She came on up the cliff, sick and afraid. Why had she done that? So stupid. So tragic and stupid. He said nothing.

She couldn't look at his face. She wanted to run away from him, but she couldn't.

He shoved the sketch pad into the canvas bag, dropped the charcoal and pastels in without even putting them in the little wooden sketch box. "Let's go." She went silently ahead of him to the car, and got in without speaking.

He started the car then turned toward her. He grabbed her suddenly, pulling her across the seat, holding her so tightly she gasped.

"Do you want to tell me what you were doing back there? You could have killed yourself." He held her away, and looked and looked at her. "Do you want to tell me how you did that? Like . . . Christ, like an acrobat—twisting like that—landing on your feet . . ."

"I don't know how I did it. I—I was afraid. You were right, the rocks are dangerous. I was afraid. I just—tried to right myself. I don't know how I did it." She looked at him helplessly.

He held her closer, kissed her fiercely. "Christ, Melissa. I love you, for Christ sake. You can't—you might have been killed. Why . . . ?"

But he didn't finish, he only looked at her, holding her. She clung to him, remorseful and lost.

Chapter 57

The Harpy's mirror was red with flame. In the little glass, the fires of the Hell Pit writhed, and deep among the licking blaze a blackness stirred. Half-hidden by fire the black beast thrust up, shoving aside the manticore like a toy, flicking the lamia away. The creature was so huge its head was an island rising up from the fires. Its eyes were pools of fire that could drown a war horse and rider, its jaws dripped with the flesh of men who suffered eternal damnation in the Hell Pit. As it rose, above it on the edge of the precipice stood Siddonie of Affandar.

Siddonie smiled and called the black dragon to her, summoning its ancient power, summoning the one power that reached beyond all worlds. This beast, part of the primal dark, of the eternal malevolence, was carnal, depraved, absolute in its viciousness, and it was indestructible. If it were destroyed in one place, it would return in another; it was birthed in the black emptiness beyond all worlds.

When the worlds were formed and the common beasts appeared, it had torn apart generations of creatures and eaten them. When men came into the many worlds, it took the weakest to itself and filled those men with evil, and it lived in each of them. In the upperworld it was known as Grendel, as Hecate, as the Mara and Black Annis, and it took the name of modern slavemasters. In the Netherworld it made its nest in the Hell Pit. On every world it nested, yet never did it diminish. It was everywhere, its get were the lamia and the basilisk, the manticore, the daughters of Lillith. Often it ate them then bore them anew. And now, from above, the queen of Affandar spoke.

"I am daughter to Lillith. Lillith's power is my power, and so I hold power over you."

The beast smiled, its cavernous mouth filled with viscous flame.

Siddonie said, "I direct you and you must obey. I bid you lead all Netherworld men to me and make them my slaves. I bid you battle beside me and make me victorious in this war."

The Harpy held her mirror in shaking white hands. When she looked up at Mag, her voice was subdued. "She has called the powers of the black dragon. She has called the embodiment of the primal dark. She is a fool. The beast will destroy her. And it will destroy us all."

Mag's hands were still, hovering over the scraps she was cutting up for the pigs. "You didn't tell me this before."

"I did not know before. The vision has come only now. Siddonie has called it. She is a fool if she thinks she can control that darkness." The Harpy's little yellow bird eyes were hot with anger and grief. "No one can say now what will happen. If the primal dark is loosed unchallenged across the Netherworld, it could destroy everything. Just as," the Harpy said, "worlds have exploded in the heavens. Just so, this land could know destruction. We could lose all magic, and all wizard light, and be steeped in blackness again for all eternity—a chasm without life."

Mag scraped the pig food into a bowl. "And will nothing stop the power she has summoned?"

"The power of vigorous life can stop it," the Harpy said. "But that power is dying in the Netherworld. It is that vital strength that has, in every world, driven the beast back."

Chapter 58

The restaurant rambled along the cliff high above the sea. It was a weathered gray building, old and casual. They had a window table facing an explosion of sunset. As they sipped their drinks they watched the colors change, watched the red sweep of sky slowly invaded by storm clouds. But Melissa could hardly keep her eyes on the sunset and away from the caged birds that flitted and chirped beside their table.

The cage was rectangular, some ten feet long with an arrangement of tree branches inside. The two dozen jewel-colored birds were as lovely as real jewels. They were vibrant, swift, enticing. They were every combination of colors: red and purple, orange and green, peach and turquoise, each as rich and spectacular as the jeweled birds of Circe's Grotto. Their chirping voices were hypnotic, and she was drawn irresistibly by their constant darting flight. The fast hush of feathers made her stomach constrict and her hands clench. She could smell bird, almost taste bird. She tried to study her menu, but could not keep her eyes from them.

For nearly a week she had been docile, had stayed away from the cliff, had not darted her hands into the shallow sea to catch the little crabs that scurried there. And at night when she heard the mouse scratching she had pulled the pillow over her head and clenched her teeth and ignored the little morsel. But the mouse was bold; she found its droppings in front of the dresser and around her suitcase. And with the pressure of restraining herself she had grown irritable, and their lovemaking had suffered. And now Braden had, innocently, seated her next to the birds and she wanted to snatch at them, to rip the wire and grab them.

"What will you have? What looks good?"

Bird! I'll have bird—raw please, with the feathers on! She pressed her knuckles to her lips.

"Melissa?"

"I—the lobster would be nice."

"But you've been eating lobster all week. Well, I don't care . . ."

"The—the crab, maybe?"

"That would be a nice change," he said caustically, watching her, his eyes faintly narrowed. She lowered her gaze to the white tablecloth and laced her fingers together in her lap, hard, to keep them still, fighting the passions of the little cat.

But soon her gaze wandered to the birds again. The cat was nervy, demanding, like a bonfire inside her threatening to take over, take charge. When she could stand it no longer she excused herself and rushed to the ladies' room.

She stood looking into the mirror at her haunted face; she could see the cat's passion and hunger looking out. She tried to calm herself, tried to drive the little cat away and ended up crying, her thoughts out of control. And why did she keep wanting to curl down into dark places? Everywhere they went, she was drawn to the shadows behind chairs, to the dark caves under tables or beneath bushes. On the beach among the rocks she would stare into little crevices, wanting to crawl into them. In the lobby, it was the secluded darknesses behind the tall ceramic planters. The little cat had never been so drawn to darkness. What was happening to her?

She returned to the table feeling wrung out, weak, and still the birds flitted and darted. She got through dinner taut and uncomfortable, and it was that night, nervy and upset, that she began to save scraps for the mouse, tucking a bit of bread into her purse beside the roll of bills.

From then on, at each meal she tucked away a crumb, tiny morsels that she put down late at night after Braden slept. Each night she told herself she wouldn't do this anymore, and each night she placed her bait closer to the bed.

Each night the guilt, the furtive slipping out of bed then back again to lie listening. She was being very stupid; he was going to find out. And the mouse became bold—it would run out, snatch her offering, then sit up holding the bread in its paws, eating right in front of her. And at last the night came when she could no longer lie still.

She could see the mouse across the room in the faint hint of moonlight. She rose, her fingers curling and straightening with the need to make claws, and she knew she dare not change. Half-naked in her panties, she slipped toward the mouse, light and quick. It was just behind Braden's shoe. She could see it and smell it, could see its whiskers twitching. She crept close and crouched and snatched it in her cupped hands.

She drew her hands up, ecstatic with the feel of the mouse squirming against her palm. She stood up, gripping it tightly; she shook it and felt it wriggle with terror and she smiled and turned . . .

Braden was awake, watching her.

She backed away from him. "I—I heard it scratching. It was—it was so loud. Scratching at something. It woke me. I—I don't know how I did this. What—what shall I do with it? Oh, it's moving in my hand, it's horrible." Its movement excited her unbearably. She wanted to loose it and chase it, wanted to bat at it and play with it. She looked at Braden pleadingly. "What—what shall I do with it?"

He looked back at her, expressionless.

She went into the bathroom and dropped the mouse into the toilet. She pulled the handle. It fought as it was swept away from the sides in the churning water. It thrashed wildly as it was sucked out of sight. She stared after it regretfully. What a waste of a perfectly good mouse. She longed to have kept it, to have played with it then killed it. She washed her hands because Braden would expect it, and returned to the bedroom. "It's gone. Horrible."

He was still staring. She stood looking at him, her expression as surprised as she could manage. And she was filled with terror. He knew. He knew what she was. It was over. It was all over between them.

She picked up the heavy bedspread they had kicked to the floor, wrapped it around herself, and curled up in the upholstered chair, her face turned away from him. As soon as it was dawn she would leave. She should have gone before. She should never have come here with him. She closed her eyes, keeping her face hidden.

She heard him rise. She felt the chair give as he sat down on its upholstered arm. He drew her to him, held her against him. "Come to bed, Melissa."

"You don't want me there."

"Why wouldn't I?"

"You were horrified by—by the mouse. You were looking at me as if . . ."

"As if what?"

"I don't know what. As if you thought me disgusting because I happened to catch a mouse in the closet."

"You have to admit, it isn't something every girl does, catching mice in the middle of the night with her bare hands. Most girls won't go into a room with a mouse, let alone catch it with—that way."

"But I had a mouse when I was a child. I used to catch it like that when—when it got out of its cage. Tonight—it was so loud. And how else would I have caught it? I just—I didn't think . . ."

He picked her up and carried her to the bed and put her down, pushing a pillow behind her. "Any other girl would have told me, let me deal with the mouse."

"You were asleep. Are you disappointed? Did you want to catch it yourself?"

He looked startled, then scowled. He didn't see anything funny.

"I just didn't think," she repeated contritely. "I used to catch my mouse that way, so I just . . ." She looked at him innocently.

He stared at her then began to laugh, a choke at first, then he doubled over laughing, fell across the bed laughing. "You caught a mouse—a mouse . . . flushed it down the john . . ." He shook with laughter until she was laughing too. "You slipped up on a mouse in the middle of the night . . ." He rolled over, consumed with helpless laughter.

When their laughter had died they lay limp, gasping. A giggle escaped her, then she sighed against him and curled down in his arms.

But the catharsis of laughter didn't last. The next day they began to argue about nothing, tense and irritable with each other. She would catch him looking at her, puzzled, and she would lash out at him with something rude. The hot sun in her face made her feel sick and dizzy. Once she had to leave him, hurrying back to the hotel, barely reaching the bathroom before she threw up her breakfast.

She returned to Braden weak and cross.

"You're awfully pale. I'm nearly finished with this drawing. Can you hang on a little while?"

"Yes," she said. But all he wanted was the paintings, he didn't care anything about her. And then she wondered what was wrong with her. It didn't make sense to be so angry. She loved him—they were together, in this lovely village. She should be so happy; she should be warmed and replenished by their love, by Braden's knowing lovemaking and by his caring. And the paintings were part of his lovemaking, his painting her brought them together in a way few lovers could know.

Yet the little cat was driving him away.

The stupid cat couldn't be still, and her wildness and hungers were ruining everything. She did not feel at one with the calico at this moment; she felt led by her, used and intimidated by her.

That afternoon when Braden started another painting, he said it would be the last. That when this one was finished they would do nothing but play. He was working on the painting when Morian called. Melissa picked up the phone thinking it was the boy who brought room service because she had ordered some sandwiches.

Morian said a registered package had come from the History Museum, that it looked like drawings. Braden said, "Ask her to open it. And ask her about the cat."

"Open it, Morian. And he—he wants to know if his little cat is all right," Melissa said weakly.

Morian said, "She hasn't come home, Melissa. Not since you left. I didn't want to tell him but . . . Maybe I don't need to tell him?" There was a long silence, then, "Maybe I needn't worry about—the cat—just now?"

Melissa's heart had nearly stopped.

"Melissa? I'm opening the package now."

"Yes."

"Do you remember that Olive left me a note when she brought the kitten here?"

"Yes."

Braden glanced up, wondering what they were talking about.

Morian said, "It was pretty cryptic. I couldn't figure it out." Again a pause. Then, "Now I think I know what Olive was saying. Now I think I don't have to worry about Braden's cat. Now," Morian said, "I see that you can take care of her."

Melissa couldn't speak.

"Shall we tell Braden that his little cat is here, and safe?"

"That—that's right, Morian." She felt so weak she had to sit down.

Braden scowled at the silence, put down his brush, came across the room, and took the phone from her. "What's wrong, Mor? What's happened?" He sat down on the bed beside Melissa, putting his arm around her. She pressed her face to his, listening to the low voice at the other end of the phone.

Morian said, "Nothing's wrong, Brade. Everything's fine. The calico's doing just fine."

Melissa's heart thundered. Her hands were shaking, her mouth was dry. Morian said, "She's safe and happy and cared for, Brade. Loved. Your calico cat is very loved."

She felt sick. She couldn't stop shaking.

"I have the package open, Brade. It's two of Alice's draw-ings of the garden door. There's a letter."

"Read it," he said tensely, watching Melissa.

"Let's see, they—they found the drawings while going through the archives. It's from the director Alice saw that day. He says . . . he thought they had all been returned—tried to phone you, guess your phone is unlisted—sorry for the inconvenience. That's all, nothing urgent, just returning the drawings."

Melissa went into the bathroom, washed her face in cold water, and stayed there until she was calmer. When she came out he was painting again, eating a sandwich with a painty hand. The tray sat beside the bed; she poured herself some tea. He hardly looked up at her. She ate and drank her tea but couldn't settle down. She went out at last to shop, and paced the village until dusk thinking about Morian, about what she knew, what Olive knew. Knowing that Braden would find out eventually, and when he found out, her life would be over. There would be nothing more for her.

She lay awake that night long after Braden slept. Near mid-night she rose and stood restlessly at the window, then pulled on shorts and a shirt, and went out.

The village was dark, the moon veiled behind clouds. She walked to the beach but didn't go out on the sand. She followed beside it through tangled bushes and tall grass, compulsively moving toward the darkest shadows. Soon she knelt, crawled on hands and knees in among the bushes and she changed to cat. She had no choice but to change.

The calico paced and wound among the bushes feeling sick. Her coat felt matted, and she didn't want to groom herself. She came out from the bushes once to stare away toward the sea, and when a sharp pain gripped her, she crouched. The pounding sea sounded like a giant heartbeat. When the pain was gone she moved back under the bushes and crept along through the tangle. She was all instinct now, searching for the darkest shelter, searching for the driest, softest bed. Another pain caught her, and she crouched, panting.

When the pain was gone she moved on again, seeking urgently. She pushed through the tall grass and wild holly, and another pain brought her down.

When the pain passed she remained hunched on her forelegs, breathing hard. Another pain pressed, and another. She rose, searching. She found no place better than the last. All the ground was damp. Pains forced her into another crouch, her claws dug into the earth; her thoughts sank into mindless pain and the need to lick, to push out; frightened and alone, she felt water break. Her pain and her cry tangled together. She felt the first kitten come. Turning her head she saw it, gauze covered, dropping down in the wetness.

She tore the damp, spider-web gauze away. She licked the tiny kitten frantically, wanting to clean it before the next one came. She licked its tiny closed eyes, its little face, its minute ears. Why was it so still? She licked harder, pushing at it, waiting for it to move, waiting for the next pain.

The gauze was gone from the kitten. She severed the cord. But still the kitten didn't move.

She pushed at it, rasping along its skin with her rough tongue to wake it and make it breathe.

The kitten didn't wake. It lay mute and still.

There were no more pains.

She lay quiet at last, her one dead kitten cuddled against her throat, her paws curved around its little, still body.

It was much later, as dawn touched the sea, that she licked herself clean and rose wearily to her four paws, looking down at her dead kitten.

She was unwilling to leave it alone.

Yet she knew she must leave it.

She dug a grave for it, first as cat, her claws tearing at the earth, then as Melissa, her hands scrabbling into the torn soil. She buried her kitten deep, and covered its grave with holly thorns and stones.

She backed out of the bushes and stood up. Her hands were caked with dirt, her nails filled with grit, her clothes dirty. Her legs were scratched from the bushes. Mourning deeply, she made her way back through the early dawn to the inn, to Braden. Wanting him to hold her, wanting to be held, to be safe and held.

Chapter 59

She returned slowly to the inn. The dawn sky was dark gray streaked with silver, pierced by the dark Monterey pines marching down the center of the empty, divided street. Her thoughts, all her being, were centered on her kitten. She could still see its tiny claws, its blind eyes. Too sharply she could see her little kit lying still and lifeless.

She had said spells over him, knowing that was useless but needing to say them, needing their comfort. She was terrified that when she told Efil she had miscarried, she had cursed her unborn Catswold kit. She passed Braden's station wagon parked at the curb, then turned back because she had felt along her bare arm a wave of heat from it. When she touched the hood, it was hot. He had been out; he had been looking for her.

She met him on the stairs. He was wearing cutoffs and a sweat shirt. He followed her back to the room, stood waiting for an explanation.

"I went for a walk."

"In the middle of the night? I woke at three o'clock and you were gone, Melissa. I've been driving around this damn town looking for you. I came back to see if you were here. I was about to go to the police."

"I couldn't sleep."

"Why the hell didn't you wake me? I thought—Christ, I didn't know what to think." He grabbed her hands, then saw the caked dirt, the grime in her nails. "Where did you walk?"

"On the beach. I—collected some shells and rocks, but then I left them. And I picked some grasses and holly."

"For a bouquet?"

"The grass wilted, the holly stuck me. I threw it all away." Must he press her? Couldn't he just gather her in and hold her? She went into the bathroom and shut the door. She washed her hands, and scrubbed her nails. Her face was dirty, her eyes red. She filled the basin with cold water and ducked her face in, letting the coolness pull away the grainy, hot feeling, scrubbing her face hard with the washcloth.

When she came out his anger had abated. "I'm sorry. I was so damned scared. I didn't know where you went, I didn't know what happened to you. I remembered how you came to the studio that evening with the wound on your head as if someone had beaten you. I thought . . ." He sat down on the bed, just looking at her.

She sat down beside him and leaned into his warmth. "I'm sorry. I didn't mean to frighten you." She was so tired. She could still see her tiny lifeless kit, could still feel his delicate little body, his tiny paws and tiny, perfectly formed claws. Braden stroked her hair and rubbed the back of her neck. But she couldn't bear to make love. She shook her head weakly; mourning her kit, and already mourning her inevitable parting from Braden. He held her, letting her doze.

It was much later that he held her away from him with a deeply searching, uneasy look. "When we go back, Melissa, will you move in with me? Will you live with me? I have this irrational feeling you're going to disappear." His dark eyes searched hers, loving her. "I don't mean to press, to smother you. But I don't want to lose you." She snuggled closer, touching his cheek. He said, "Will you live with me? Will you think about getting married? We could think about that."

"I . . ." She looked at him helplessly.

He waited.

"We—we could think about it." But they could never

marry. She must go back to the Netherworld; she did not belong in this world; she did not belong with him. And soon he would begin to put the strange occurrences together. He would figure out what she was—an impossible creature, half woman, half cat, and he would be sickened.

"Melissa? Will you marry me?"

"We—we need time to—think about it."

The line at the corner of his mouth deepened. She hugged and kissed him, making herself go soft and relax against him, teasing him until at last he made love to her; his loving should have been healing, but their tender, passionate loving made her mourn him, drove her into deep depression for what she had already lost, so all she wanted to do was weep.

They showered together, and he washed her back. Turned away from him, she let her tears mingle with the hot water.

As he toweled her off, he said, "Shall I send down for some breakfast? You look so tired. Climb into bed. I'll call the kitchen." He tucked the towel around his middle and went in to straighten the bed for her. She climbed in gratefully, but then she saw his suitcase sitting by the door, his closed paint box, the folded easel, and remembered that this was the day to go back; they had no choice, the opening was tonight. She swallowed tears that threatened to swamp her, and turned her face into the pillow.

Braden watched her as he phoned in their breakfast order. She was crying silently, trying to hide her long, quivering shudders into the pillow. What the hell happened last night? It was almost impossible not to ask questions, not to demand answers, yet common sense said to leave her alone. He wondered if someone had followed her here. A husband or lover? He lay down beside her, gathering her close, holding her close in the circle of his arms. And after a while he said softly, "Were you with someone else?"

She turned over, looking at him blankly. Her face was red and sad, and her wet lashes beaded together. "Someone else?" Then her eyes widened. "A man? Oh, no." She touched his face. "No! It wasn't that!" She seemed truly

shocked. "It wasn't that. Just—sick. I feel better, truly I do."
She held his face, looking deep into his eyes. "There is no
one else. I could love no one else but you."

He got up and tucked the covers around her, wondering
why he couldn't believe her. It wasn't even that he didn't believe her; but he couldn't escape the things left unexplained.

When the breakfast cart came she drank and ate dutifully,
then curled up again, spent, and was soon asleep. He stood
looking down at her, his breakfast untouched. Then he
picked up his suitcase and painting box, the folded tarp and
easel, and headed for the car.

They would have to leave when she woke, go directly to
the gallery, frame these six paintings and hang them. Rye
would be pacing, having anxiety attacks waiting for them.
They had planned to change clothes at the gallery, have a
leisurely dinner. The opening wasn't until nine, and Rye
liked his artists to arrive late, liked them to come in when
there was already a good crowd.

He loaded five paintings into the station wagon, and
Melissa was still asleep when he went back to the room for
the last one. He had started to pick it up, making sure it was
dry, when something about the painting made him stop. He
set the canvas down and backed off to look at it.

The pale sand made a shocking contrast to the dark, cloud-
riven sky, and to the reds in Melissa's clothes, and the faded
red of the derelict boat, where her face reflected in the broken window. She was looking down, the reflections of her
cheek and hair woven through the reflections of five winging
gulls. This was a strong painting; why should it bother him?
He kept looking, felt he was missing something, an eerie and
disruptive sense, like a strange premonition; a feeling as
wildly unsettling as Melissa's fall from the rocks, or as seeing her catch the mouse in the middle of the night, or as her
nervousness in the restaurant beside the caged finches.

Fairy tales chittered at him like bats in a black windstorm,
as if insanity had reached to wriggle probing fingers deep inside his drowning brain. And the message that was trying to
get through to his conscious mind could not be tolerated. He

shoved it back deep into the dark places where he couldn't see it—a sick nightmare message, an aberration. He turned to watch her sleeping, and in sleep she was as pure and innocent as a wild creature. He loved the way she slept curled around the pillow, totally limp. He wanted to gather her in and love her and keep on loving her. He rejected the nagging fear that made him see shadows across her face.

He felt certain there was no one else. She wasn't a tramp or a flirt; she hadn't glanced at another man, though nearly every man stared at her. He didn't think any deeper than that, didn't dare to think deeper. He gave it up at last, looked at the painting again, saw nothing strange in it. He picked it up and carried it down to the station wagon.

She was still asleep when he got back, her lashes moving in a dream. Even watching her dream made him edgy. He kept wondering what she was dreaming about. And why the hell did every damned thing set him off into wild, impossible speculations? He went back downstairs, and in Mrs. Trask's office he called Morian.

"We'll be late getting back. We'll go directly to the gallery—see you there. How's the calico?"

"Happy, Brade. Loved and spoiled and luxuriously cared for. What's wrong? There's something."

"Nothing. We're just loading up to come home." How did she always know? How did she sense that he had called her for comforting, for reassurance? "Everything's great."

"You two haven't fought?"

"Of course not. Why would we fight?"

"I see. Well, whatever it is, Brade," she said softly, "I think you're very lucky to have Melissa. Don't—don't hurt her, Brade."

She didn't wake until nearly noon; the depression didn't hit her until she was fully awake. Quite suddenly she remembered her dead kit, and the hurting hit her.

The room was hot, the sun slanting in; she was sweaty, tangled in the sheet. Braden was gone. She rolled over clutching the pillow, heavy with depression.

She wished they could stay here in this little village and never go back, that she could forget the Netherworld, that they could forget everything but each other and she could forget the feline part of herself.

Deliberately she made herself think about the gallery opening. She was terrified of the evening to come, terrified someone would see the cat images in Braden's paintings. *How very clever of you, Mr. West. Phantom cats. What a droll idea, so subtle. What, exactly, is their significance?*

And at the opening she would have to face Morian: a woman who knew everything about her, who had told her clearly that she knew. She wanted to run away now, but he wanted her at the opening. She would hurt him if she went away now. He said the paintings were hers, that without her they would not have happened, that without her there would be no opening and he would still be sunk in gloom.

She knew she must go, and that she must smile and meet strangers and be nice to them. She would disappear afterward. She would go back to the portal alone, and down, and would never see him again.

She rose and dressed and packed her few things. Braden returned and they went downstairs to Mrs. Trask's office to say good-bye. The office was as bright and cheerful as the rest of the inn, white wicker furniture and potted plants, and a collection of prints that covered three walls. Some were Alice's: an etching of winging gulls, a lithograph of swimming seals, and one of horses wheeling at the edge of the sea. Behind the desk hung an etching of a cat sculpture, the cat leaping after a bird. Her pulse quickened. She recognized it from the Cat Museum. And Braden said, "Timorell commissioned the sculpture shortly before she was killed in the earthquake. Alice thought it had some special meaning for her, that was why she did the etching, several years after Timorell's death."

Now her heart was thundering.

In the museum, she had examined that cat sculpture. She had found no clue that it might contain the Amulet. Now, she burned to go back and look at it again. She moved behind the desk, to study it.

The bronze cat's fur was roughly done. One could see the globs of clay from which the casting had been made. And within the rough clay patterns, across the cat's flank, was an oval shape unlike the other texture. A little teardrop shape so subtly different one could easily overlook it, but a shape a bit too perfect. A teardrop the same shape as the Amulet. Excited, she turned away when Braden took her hand. She said good-bye to Mrs. Trask and hugged her. The old woman felt like a rock, draped in her black mourning, but her smile was full of joy.

Chapter 60

Twenty paintings hung on the white gallery walls, each with space around it, each well lighted from spotlights recessed into the ceiling. Hung all together, the rich, abstracted studies had such power they jolted Melissa.

She stood alone in the center of the gallery turning in a slow circle, drinking in the colors and shadows, the reflections, so overwhelmed she felt tears come. Glowing with Braden's passionate vision, each painting seemed to her beyond what any human could bring forth. She had no experience, from the Netherworld, of the passion or skill that could create such beauty. Braden had brought this power out of himself, out of what he was; she stood alone in the gallery wiping away tears stirred by beauty, by his power; and tears of pain because they would soon be parted.

And she tried not to see the cat images shadowed within the canvases. She prayed no one would see them. Yet each painting whispered with the faint spirit of the cat, lithe and dreamlike, nearly hidden.

She had left Braden and Rye in the gallery office unloading and framing the six paintings from Carmel. The two office desks had been laid with white cloths and stacked with ice containers and liquor bottles, silver trays and boxes of canapes. A long table in the gallery itself held cocktail napkins, stacks of glasses, little plates, a cut glass punch bowl, enough for a huge crowd. And the thought of a crowd terrified her.

Through the fog-softened San Francisco night, they walked two blocks to an East Indian restaurant, leaving Rye to mix champagne punch and hang the last of the show. They sat in wicker chairs with deep cushions dining on lamb curry and a lovely rum drink. It was late when they returned to the gallery. Its street was lined with cars. She felt her heart thudding as they pushed in through the crowd. Braden greeted friends and introduced her. She didn't like being pressed among so many people, nor did she like the noise of dozens of conversations all at once. Everyone wanted to meet Braden's model, everyone wanted to compare her face with the work. She wondered why they couldn't just look at the paintings, just *see* the paintings. She wanted only to drift unnoticed, hearing their comments about the work, not about her. She smiled and answered questions, trying to be what Braden expected, and it was not until late in the evening that she began to notice something was wrong.

Braden had drifted away. A dark, intense man was suddenly beside her. When she turned to look at him, ice crawled down her spine.

He wasn't tall. He was well knit, with short, dark hair. His yellow eyes were vivid in his thin, tanned face. His voice was soft and purring; brazenly intimate. "I like the work tremendously. So subtle."

She wanted to run from him. He did not belong in this room. He did not belong in this world. He said, "You're a marvelous model."

She looked at him coolly. "The model is unimportant; only the painter is important."

He smiled. "A painter must have—inspiration."

She glanced around the room for Braden but couldn't see him. The man moved closer to her. "I'm enchanted by the shadows in West's work."

"All paintings have shadows," she said shortly, edging away from him. Distraught, she backed into the woman behind her, almost spilling the woman's drink.

He said, "These are unique shadows." He took her elbow, easing her away to a little space in the crowd. "Unusual shadows. Shadows that speak to me."

She didn't want this, she'd been so afraid of this. And suddenly other people were crowding around them: a portly man in a black suit, two women in cocktail dresses. They circled her, blocking her retreat, muttering compliments. They watched her through eyes not ordinary. Her discomfort turned to panic as four sets of feline eyes studied her. Then suddenly Morian was there, moving toward her.

Morian slipped between the two women. She was dressed in a short silver shift, and had silver clips in her hair. She took Melissa's hand. "There's a phone call for you in the office." She patted the dark-haired man on the shoulder. "You can talk with her later, Terrel. She's a popular lady tonight." She turned away, guiding Melissa before her.

They went through the office, where two waiters were replenishing trays, into the deserted framing room. Melissa leaned against the work table, weak. She could not look at Morian, she could not look up into Morian's knowing eyes.

Morian cleared a stack of papers from the couch and sat Melissa down as if she were arranging a small child. She brought her a glass of water from the sink at one end of the work bench. "That was Terrel Black. He's harmless, but he's pretty intense. He paints and teaches up at the school. You're awfully pale. Can I get you something to eat, or an aspirin?"

"No, nothing. Not an aspirin, they don't—I can't take them." Too late she saw the knowing look in Morian's eyes. "Thank you for getting me away. I just felt sick suddenly. Maybe the crowd, too many people." She was trying not to prattle, and afraid to stop talking. She didn't want Morian to say anything. She felt ice cold. She didn't know what Morian would do.

Morian watched her, then rose. She found a man's sweater and dropped it around her shoulders. "Stay here, rest a while. I'll tell Braden where you are."

"I . . ."

Morian turned back, her dark eyes questioning.

"Nothing," Melissa said. "Thank you."

Morian nodded, her face expressionless, hiding her own thoughts, then turned away and left her.

She sat shivering, sipping the water. There was a door at the far end of the framing room beyond the painting racks. It led to the alley—they had brought the paintings in that way. She could leave now, slip away down the alley, take a taxi to the Cat Museum, retrieve the Amulet . . .

Before she could decide Braden came in, preoccupied, frowning. "Mettleson is here. Are you too sick just to meet him? He saw the show this afternoon but he wanted to see the Carmel paintings even in this crowd. He wants to meet you. Could you just say hello, then come back and lie down?"

She followed him out. If she stayed with Braden she could avoid Terrel Black.

Braden introduced her to Mettleson. He was a short, balding man with thick gray hair at the sides of his head running down into a beard. They exchanged polite, meaningless talk. He told her she was beautiful. He praised the paintings. But then Braden turned away to speak to someone, and the next minute there was a shift in the crowd, and she had been separated from Mettleson. Terrel Black took her arm. His friends crowded close, locking her in a circle. She did not see Braden, did not see Mettleson. And the pale blond girl looked deeply at her, her blue, feline eyes intent. "Do you think Mr. West would paint me? Do you think Braden West would paint my spirit as he has painted yours?"

Melissa wanted to claw her. Terrel moved casually between them. "It's the finest work Braden's done. I'm awed at his—perception. I didn't know he—I'm amazed at how much he sees."

She held her temper. "Braden sees only the color and form, and the reflections of light. He sees only the things he knows."

Terrel smiled. "He has to see in order to paint. Are you telling us that he doesn't know what he sees?"

"Surely you see something he does not?" she said coldly, and tried to shoulder past him out of the tight circle, but they closed more tightly around her. Their voices were low, caressing.

"Beautiful paintings . . ." the red-haired girl said.

"The lovely shadow of the spirit . . ." said the pale one.

"You know things we don't," the portly man said softly.

"Show us," Terrel said. "Show us, Melissa . . . Show us how to change . . ."

She forced between them and ran. She dodged through the crowd knocking people aside, spilling drinks, shouldering and pushing through. She was out the door, running across the dark street between the moving lights of cars. Brakes squealed, a car swerved, lights blazed in her face.

She gained the curb ahead of a squealing car, but nearly fell when she caught her heel. She was panting. She righted herself and ran, trying to lose herself in the blackness between street lights.

But feet pounded behind her and Terrel shouted her name. When she glanced back, four sets of eyes reflected headlights. She ran as she had never run, but she heard them gaining, their feet pounding . . .

Terrel was too fast; he grabbed her, spinning her around. She scratched at him and kicked.

"We won't hurt you, we only want . . ." He held her in a steel grip. "Tell us, Melissa. Tell us how to change."

"I don't know what you're talking about." She faced him shivering. And then in spite of herself, his pleading touched her.

They stood frozen staring at each other. "Please, will you tell us? That is all we want, only to know how to change."

It was no good to pretend. It was too late to pretend. She said, "You don't know. None of you know."

"None of us. We . . ." Light flashed suddenly across Terrel's eyes as Braden's station wagon skidded to the curb. Braden jumped out reaching for her, but Terrel jerked her away. "Tell us, Melissa!" But Braden was on him, knocking him aside, pulling Melissa close. She pressed against him, hid her face against him.

"What do they want?" Braden said.

"I don't know. Please, will you take me home?"

He tilted her chin so she had to look at him. "I think you do know." The others stood poised. Braden looked from Terrel to the blond girl to Melissa. "I think you know, Melissa. I think you must do what they ask. I think you must help them."

"I don't know what you're talking about."

"I think you must free them, Melissa. As you are free."

She couldn't take her eyes from his. The two worlds tilted and fell together and she was falling, destroyed.

"Free them, Melissa."

He held her away, his hands tight on her shoulders. "Do you think I didn't wonder? You caught a mouse in your bare hands. You were shaking it and smiling until you saw me watching you. You fell from the ledge, turned over in midair and landed on your feet. Do you think I didn't wonder?"

His lips were a thin line. "Don't you think I saw how the birds in the restaurant upset you—excited you? And the day you got so angry when we talked about people changing into . . ." He shook his head, his eyes pleading. "Don't you think I wondered why the cat was never there when you were? Not once did I see you both at the same time."

"But Morian said she was there."

"Morian lied."

"But . . ."

He drew a breath, silencing her. "Tonight for the first time I saw the shadow-cats in my paintings." His face was like stone. "Images I did not consciously put there." His hands were hot on her shoulders.

"And just now, Melissa, when you turned and saw my car, your eyes . . ." He swallowed. She could see the muscles working in his jaw. "Your eyes reflected the headlights—like mirrors. Like jewels. Like a cat's eyes."

She tried to pull out of his grasp.

"Tell them what they want to know. Tell them now."

She looked at him a long time. It didn't matter anymore, nothing mattered, she had lost him. She turned within his grip and faced the waiting Catswold. There were more now, ten—twelve—more coming out of the shadows.

And within the shadows someone said, "There is a world—other than this. There is a passage, my family told of it. Tell us about that land. Tell us where the passage opens."

"There is war there," she said. "The passage leads to war, to death for the Catswold. Please . . ." She didn't believe this was happening. This couldn't be happening. "I—I can only free you. I can only give you the spell. I won't tell you how to go there. There is danger there." She felt displaced, sick. But she must help them, give them the spell. It no longer mattered what Braden saw and heard, she had already destroyed his love.

She said the spell quickly and turned away, pulling Braden toward the car. She didn't want him to see the changing. As she got in the car she heard the words repeated behind her, and repeated again. She got in. "Go quickly, please." But he had turned and was watching them. He saw in the darkness the tall shadows vanish into small swift beasts, saw the cats running away into the night.

Chapter 61

Outdoor lights brightened the fluted borders of the museum's tile roofs, and the brick paths. Light slanted down through the gnarled limbs of the oak trees to cast their twisting shadows along the garden walls. Braden parked on the empty street and Melissa left him quickly.

She had remained silent as he drove up Telegraph and then up Russian Hill. She didn't know what to say to him and she didn't want to know what he thought; she couldn't bear to know. She didn't want to hear his accusations. She had lost him. She was filled with the pain of that loss and if he spoke to her she would weep.

She moved quickly away from the car through light then shadow, and in the darkness beyond a garden wall where Braden couldn't see her, she changed to cat. She crouched uncertainly, then leaped up the wall and over.

She searched the gardens one by one for the sculpture of the rearing bronze cat which Timorell had commissioned. She was not alone within the gardens; other cats prowled, hunting mice and crickets or eating the cat food the museum put out for them. Some challenged her, but none attacked. They seemed more possessive at night, when the museum was exclusively theirs. She found the sculpture at last in a small circular garden planted with lavender. She changed to girl and stood against the sculpture stand touching the cool bronze. The cat was rearing up, the texture of its coat rough with the clay that had originally formed it, from which the cast had been made. She ran her hands along its rough flank, tracing the texture of the metal until her seeking fingers found one perfect oval.

She pressed it, fingered it, but it did nothing. Maybe this was simply the tear-shaped symbol of the Amulet. She could feel no cracks along the cat's body where the sculpture might open. She tried to tilt the cat but it was bolted down. Discouraged, she whispered an opening spell.

The bronze cat fell apart in two halves.

Within lay the Amulet of Bast, gleaming green in the faint garden lights. When she lifted it, it was heavy and cold to her fingers. She touched the setting that circled it, could feel the two rearing bronze cats. She tried a spell-light, not believing one would come, but her bright light struck across the emerald and deep into it, glowing green.

She saw that the two golden cats circling it were not mirror images. One looked gentle, that was Bast. The other, Sekhmet, was fierce. And deep within the emerald, cut by some magic she didn't know, shone the sun. Here was the trinity of the cat goddess: Bast the gentle; Sekhmet the warrior; and Ra the sun.

How many Catswold women had looked into this emerald and considered their dual natures? How many women, over how many centuries? She slipped the chain over her head and let the Amulet drop against her, heavy, powerful.

Now the commitment was made. Soon she must face Siddonie and try to destroy the dark queen—the Lillith woman. The power of the Amulet held and terrified her. She felt as if generations of Catswold women had come alive within her, as if their spirits had joined, waiting to see what she would do.

And when at last she faced Siddonie she would be facing not only the queen of Affandar, but the eternal evil. As Bast had killed the Serpent, so she again must kill it.

She returned to Braden, needing desperately to be with him for the few moments more they had left. In the car he sat looking at her, and reached for her, drawing her close. "Can you tell me what you did in there? Can you tell me any of this?"

She looked at him in the darkness, then brought a small spell-light so the emerald shone, hanging at her breast. His eyes widened. She let the light dim and she went into his arms again. He touched her face, stroked her hair, but he didn't speak. She moved close within his arms, desolate.

With the finding of the Amulet, the Netherworld and the upperworld had warped together. But their own two worlds had shattered totally apart.

He touched her face, holding

Chapter 62

Braden turned the station wagon into the lane, his headlights slewing across the flowered hill. Melissa kissed him and slid out of the car and ran. He jammed on the brakes and was out, too, running, grabbing her. "You're not going down alone." She had told him everything, had described the Netherworld for him, had built a picture of Siddonie's evil, and of the rising war. "I'm going with you." He held her wrists, so insistent she couldn't break free.

"You can't go, you have no protection, no magic. They—"

"I have other skills. I'm coming with you."

His eyes burned her, his grip bruised. There was no use to argue with him. She said, "Then you must do as I say. There are things you must have—things I wouldn't need alone."

"Like what?"

"A lantern or oil lamp—not a flashlight. A knife strong enough for a good weapon. Some food."

"Why do *you* not need a weapon?"

"I can turn a weapon away. I told you, magic is a weapon there."

He didn't move, just held her prisoner.

"Please, Braden, there is little time."

"I'm not leaving you alone." Gripping her hand, he headed for the studio.

"I'll wait for you, I promise. I must make slow, careful preparations. Please—hurry, get some food for us. And bring a blanket."

He searched her face, holding her tightly.

"You're wasting time, Braden! I promise I will wait! You must trust me!"

He released her at last and turned away, running for the studio. She saw the studio lights go on as she pushed in through the portal. She said the spell, she was through the wall when Braden burst into the tool room. She shouted the closing spell; the wall swung closed in his face.

"Christ! Melissa!" His voice was muffled.

"Are you hurt?" she screamed.

"No, for Christ sake. Open the damn wall!"

"I love you, Braden. I will love you forever. I will come back to you." *If I can,* she thought, turning away and choking back her tears. She ran down into the blackness.

She was soon cold in the thin dress. And the upperworld sandals were not meant for rocky paths. She kept repeating over and over, *Please, Braden, know that I love you. I must do this. There is no way I can avoid facing Siddonie.*

But she had no plan. It was madness to think she could destroy Siddonie alone, even with the Amulet.

Never had a journey seemed so long. She was very cold, and grew despondent. On and on down the rocky path, longing to turn back and be in Braden's arms. Longing to forget Siddonie and the war, and knowing she could not.

Even if she turned back, she would not be safe. Nothing would ever be safe.

When at last after long hours she saw the green light beyond the tunnel mouth she ran. She splashed through the stream into the full green glow of morning—and came face to face with a saddled gray gelding. He shied at her and snorted, backing away within his spell-tether. She stood in the mouth of the tunnel looking for his master.

This was not a horse she had seen in the stables or pastures of Affandar. And his saddle had not come from the palace—it was an elven saddle, square and plain. Seeing no one, she broke the spell, snatched up his reins, mounted, and headed for the palace. She didn't care where he had come from. If Affandar was already at war there wouldn't be a horse left anywhere.

In sight of the pale wall she pulled up the gelding to a walk. The pasture was empty. There was no sound from the palace, and no person visible. No smoke rose from the chimneys. She could see no movement at the windows, no one in the gardens. She tethered the gelding by the wall, not wanting him trapped in the courtyard, and she slipped through the side door into the scullery.

She found the scullery deserted, the cookstove cold. No food had been left on the counters. She searched the main floor chambers; the corridors echoed with her footsteps. Every room was empty. She went into the courtyard; and there, from a side door she saw Terlis and Briccha gathering vegetables in the garden. When Terlis looked up and saw her, the pale girl moved behind a row of bean vines and slipped away from Briccha. Soon a side gate flew open into the courtyard and Terlis was hugging Melissa. Melissa was surprised at how glad she was to see the child. She clung to Terlis almost desperately. How thin Terlis was, and how dark the shadows under her eyes.

"It's been so long, Melissa. I knew you would come today, the Harpy said you would. I've watched all day for you."

"Was it she who left the gray gelding?"

"Yes, he was the last decent horse and he wouldn't have been here, except a deserter came home. The Harpy was here last night. She terrified me—I've never before seen a harpy."

"Are we at war? Has the whole palace gone to war?"

"Yes. It's strange for the palace to be so empty; most everyone rode out with the army." Terlis shivered, and Melissa saw in her eyes the same fear of war she had seen in the faces of the rebel families: a fear of the loss of home and sustenance, loss of a way of life.

"The queen was so cruel and nervous before she rode out, worse than ever, pacing, shouting orders. She was still here when the dying prince recovered. When he ran away she had the whole palace upside down."

"He recovered? Tell me."

"He began to eat. I took his food up sometimes; he was actually hungry. His color came back almost overnight. Though he didn't talk much. But then soon he was out of bed riding beside the queen. He was weak of course, clumsy in the saddle, but far from dying. Siddonie took him everywhere; soon all Affandar knew he'd recovered.

"But two weeks ago he disappeared. The queen was in a rage. She called the seneschals into her chambers, questioned everyone in the palace. She sent every seneschal and half the guard to search for him."

"He just disappeared? What happened?"

Terlis' eyes widened with delight. "A cat, Melissa. I saw a cat hiding in the gardens. The queen would have caged it if she knew. A fine big cat, all golden, and I know it was more than cat, too." Terlis grinned. "After the prince vanished I didn't see the cat anymore." She looked at Melissa strangely, and touched her cheek.

"Then soon afterward the Harpy came. She'd been a long time gathering folk to join the rebels. There are none that can fly except her. Except the lizards, but they belong to the queen."

"The Griffon can fly."

"The Harpy was afraid to release him; she is afraid of him. She said he might do anything. You can hear him roaring in his cage. All the Hell Beasts are nervous and screaming."

"The Griffon is not a Hell Beast."

Terlis only looked at her. "Rumor is that the selkies have all disappeared from the rivers, that an elven man saw dozens of selkies fleeing toward the eastern mountains."

Melissa gripped Terlis' shoulders. "Tell me exactly where the fighting is. Tell me everything you know."

"The Harpy left a long message. I helped her strip the beds, and she talked all the while. She made me repeat it to be sure I remembered."

"She stripped the beds? In the palace? Why would she do that?"

"I don't know. She took all the bed sheets, every sheet in the palace, clean or soiled.

"The queen has told her armies the rebels mean to en-slave the Netherworld. She tells them the rebels plan to take all the land. She has made her troops afraid of being enslaved by the rebels so they will fight more fiercely. The Harpy says that at the front lines the rebel troops are caught by the queen's spells, that they sicken with fever and are torn by thirst. Even where the streams run cold, they often cannot touch water. Her magic drives them back as if by a wall."

Terlis shook her head. "Canteens containing water go dry, and the Harpy says Siddonie has laid rotting-spells to tear the rebels' clothes from them. Naked, they are the more vul-nerable to every blade, and they are cold and demoralized."

"Has Siddonie spell-cast all our forces?"

"She puts her spells only on the ones that draw near the front lines of battle. The Harpy thinks she hasn't enough power to hold spells upon all the attacking troops."

"Is there anyone left in the villages?"

"Only a few old men and women, and the smallest chil-dren. The villages have little to eat—Siddonie has destroyed everything."

"Where is the fighting?"

"In Ferrathil now, but moving toward Cressteane. Sid-donie means to cause the Catswold troops from Zzadarray to fight beside her. The Harpy said to tell you that."

"How did the Harpy know I would come? Of course, her mirror. But—"

"The Harpy said to tell you this: You are Timorell's daughter. You have found what you needed to find. Now use it." Terlis looked at her, shivering.

Melissa said, "You must go back to the gardens and keep

Briccha occupied. The horse will still be here when I'm gone. You can put him in the pasture."

At Terlis' puzzled look she turned and headed for the dungeons.

Chapter 63

Braden tore at the wall with his hands, smashed his shoulder against it, threw all his weight against it. It refused to move. She had opened it; her words had opened it. He had seen the wall swing inward, had seen her go through. The solid stone wall had slammed in his face, had hit him in the face, scraping his jaw and arm, bruising his hands. For an instant he had seen into the tunnel, had smelled the damp, raw earth. In the light that Melissa had made he had seen the walls of the tunnel leading down deeper into the earth. Then the wall had shut her away.

He fought the wall, battering at it and swearing, then he grabbed the ladder and ran at it, rammed the ladder's end against the stone with such force that he broke the heavy side bar and the first two rungs. He flung it down, knowing coldly that only by magic could the wall be moved though he did not believe in magic.

Hadn't believed in it.

He shoved the ladder aside, grabbed the metal wheelbarrow and swung it, hitting the stone with all his weight and force. Chips of stone flew in his face, pale gouges bloomed in the dark stone. The wall didn't move. She was gone, where he could no longer reach her. He found the shovel and dug into the mortar, trying to pry the stones apart. Then he dug into the earth beside the stone. He would dig into the damned tunnel that way.

But then digging, jamming his foot hard on the shovel to ram it into the earth, he felt a draft behind him, and a beam of light hit the dirt in front of him. He swung around.

Morian stood looking, taking in the toppled wheelbarrow, the broken ladder, the shovel in his hand, the broken earth where he had begun to dig.

"She's gone," she said softly.

"Yes, she's gone! Through the damned wall! You knew!" He stared at her, totally enraged. "She went through the goddamn wall. She went into the goddamn hill—and you knew it. *How did you know?* Christ, you knew what she would do."

"You saw her go through the wall?" She was so damned calm he wanted to hit her.

"Yes, I saw her. The damned wall *opened*. She slammed the stone wall in my face."

Morian laid her flashlight on the work table, leaving it burning. It cast a pool of viscous yellow onto the wall and left the rest of the room dark. She took the shovel from his hand. She pulled his hand into hers, holding it tightly. She picked up the flashlight again, its beam flashing across her silver cocktail dress. "Come on, Brade. Maybe I can help."

He glared at her.

"I've been up in Olive's empty house," she said. "I left the gallery just after you did. I've been up there at Olive's dining table reading her research." She squeezed his hand tighter. "Before that, when I left the gallery, I followed you."

He felt himself shiver.

"I saw Melissa, I saw her on the street. I saw the flash of her eyes in the headlights. I saw a crowd of people around her—around you both.

"And after you got in the car I saw people change into cats and run away into the darkness."

She led him out of the tool room and up the dark garden. The only sound was their footsteps and the faint brushing of his pant legs against the tangled flowers. She said, "After you and Melissa drove away, and the cats ran away, I came home and let myself into Olive's. I dug into her notebook." She led him up the steps to Olive's front door. Lights were on in the living room, the draperies closed. Inside, the room was cold and damp from being unoccupied. Morian sat him down at the dining table as if she were herding a small child, and she opened the notebook.

He didn't want to read it; he pushed the book away. "I don't need this, Mor. I know all this. She told me."

She sat down at the table across from him.

"She went down there, Mor. Hell, it doesn't help to know where she went. She shut me out. She shut me out of her life. I saw her go through a damn solid stone wall into another world, another life."

He stared at Morian. "I have known Terrel Black for years. We have taught each other's classes. Got drunk together, won awards in the same shows. Tonight I saw Terrel Black change into a black cat with one white foot.

"And I saw Melissa go through a solid stone wall into a world that can't exist. And you knew about this. All the time, you knew." He slammed the notebook shut.

"Not all the time, Brade. It took me a while to work it out. It took me a very long while to believe it."

"She promised to wait for me in the tool room, but she didn't wait. Christ, Mor, she's going down there into the middle of a war. She told me that. She can't—she can't go back there alone."

"Are you sure?"

"She went into the Cat Museum. She insisted I stay in the car. She came out wearing an emerald pendant. She said it had powers, I could—I could feel the powers."

"She loves you, Brade."

He stared past her toward the drapery-shrouded windows, realizing that for some time lights had been flashing and shifting against the pale cloth.

Morian turned to look, then rose and opened the draperies. "Sam's is crowded, the lane is jammed with cars."

He got up woodenly and went into the kitchen and began opening cupboards looking for a bottle. "Doesn't Olive have a damned thing to drink in here?"

"The tool shed door is open, Brade. I know I closed it behind us. It—Brade . . . come here."

He couldn't find a bottle. Where Olive usually kept a fifth of brandy there was only a half pint of seltzer. He went back into the living room and stood beside Morian, who was looking out at the arcing lights swinging across the window as more cars pulled into the lane. He saw that the tool room door stood open. Beyond the door in the lane where cars were parked double, triple, the people getting out were not heading for Sam's; they were heading for the portal. That was what it was called: the Catswold Portal. The damned door that had lured Alice.

There were cats in the lane, too; cats leaping out of open car doors and cats suddenly appearing in the lane as people vanished. Soon there were more cats than people; in the flash of headlights dozens of pairs of eyes flashed. Cats and humans moved together toward the Catswold Portal. Braden saw Terrel Black in human form. He watched Terrel push in through the portal and watched the dark, quick shapes of cats slip in past his ankles, cats only half-seen in the fragmented light.

"How the hell did Terrel know? Melissa didn't tell him. How did he know to come here?"

"Terrel came back to the gallery. He wanted to know where Melissa lived; he wanted to know if she lived here with you. He remembered the door from the times he's been to the studio. He talked about the cats carved on the door."

More car lights were going dark like huge pairs of eyes winking closed. Soon most of the parked cars were dark. A few last figures hurried after the others up the garden and through the portal, pushing into the tool room which was, like the airlock in a submarine, the anteroom to another world.

Morian said, "Can they open the wall?"

"I don't know. Back there on Farrel Street, she didn't tell them how. Christ, I don't know if they can open it."

"What did she tell them, Brade? Exactly what?"

"She told them—how to change into cats. It was a rhyme. A spell. Christ, this isn't happening—it can't be happening."

She moved away from him and picked up her keys from the dining table. She took his hand and led him out and down the steps and across the dim garden toward Anne's darkened house. He watched the lane, the portal, trying to figure out what to do. He felt numb, incapable of thought.

Morian unlocked Anne's front door and pulled him inside and across the dark living room toward Tom's room. The room smelled closed and musty. She leaned over the bed and shook the boy awake. He came up fighting and crying out, and she clapped her hand over his mouth. "Shut up. You don't want to wake Anne." She pulled him out of the bed, holding his hands so he couldn't fight her. "Get dressed. Hurry up."

"Go to hell. Why should I get dressed? Leave me alone."

She twisted his arm behind him. "If you don't get dressed at once I'll wake Anne. I'll tell her the truth—all of it."

The boy subsided and stooped to rummage on the floor for the pants and shirt he had dropped when he went to bed. He pulled them in angry jerks, glaring at them. When he was dressed and had tied his shoes, Morian propelled him out of the dark bedroom and out through the unlit house, down the steps and down through the garden. They entered the tool room and pushed through the crowd toward the stone wall, through the flickering light of an oil lamp. The boy stared at the crowd of people and cats as if he walked among snakes. Morian faced him toward the wall. "Open it."

He stared at her white-faced. "What are you talking about?"

She twisted his arm until the boy dropped to his knees. "Open the wall." When he didn't move or speak she pulled him upright, shoved him against the wall, and slapped him. The crowd of Catswold folk watched her silently, intent and predatory. After seven slaps the boy began to whimper, soon he choked back a cry. Braden was growing alarmed for him when finally he whined, "I'll open it. Stop hitting me and I'll open it."

Morian smiled. She seemed to have no pity for the child, as if the fact of his youth did nothing to deceive her perception of his true nature. "Hurry up and open the wall. What is your name?"

Braden said, "He is Wylles, prince of Affandar. Melissa told me that."

Wylles' eyes raked Braden. But he whispered the words, his voice furtive and nearly inaudible. The wall swung away, revealing the black tunnel beneath the hill.

Cats leaped past them. A man pushed through, then two women. The smell of damp earth breathed out cold from the hollow blackness. Terrel hurried through swinging a lantern, glancing shyly at Braden. Someone behind Braden in the tool room said, "There are more lamps," and soon five lanterns had been lit. Braden found he was gripping Wylles' arm hard. He grabbed the canvas bag he had dropped earlier, when Melissa had slammed the wall in his face, and dragged the boy into the tunnel behind Terrel and the cats. Already the crowd of Catswold had disappeared into the dropping blackness. Digging his fingers into Wylles' shoulder, Braden paused to look back into the tool room, at Morian.

She stood beside the table, her dark eyes reflecting wonder and fear. She looked at him deeply for a long moment, then she turned away.

"Close the wall," Braden said hoarsely.

Wylles' spell swung the door closed with a hush of compressed air. They were in darkness. The faint light of the lanterns was fast disappearing ahead.

Chapter 64

The swinging light of the lanterns jabbed and shifted along the tunnel walls. The shadows of humans and cats tangled together hurrying down into earth. Voices interlaced in whispers, as if to speak too loudly might call forth from the earth things one would not want to summon. As the tunnel dropped, the glancing light picked out falling chasms, picked out stone slabs tilting over them. Spaces yawned, then suddenly the tunnel closed in, the walls soon pressed against Braden's shoulders. Fear traveled with them, fear of being trapped beneath the earth. But his companions seemed unafraid. A powerful longing drew the Catswold on, a need Braden could only guess at as the Catswold hurried deeper down into the core of the earth. He felt above him the weight of tons of stone, and he began to sweat. He had never suffered from claustrophobia, but now a nearly uncontrollable fear gripped him; he fought the panic, fought a screaming need for space and air. If not for Melissa somewhere down there in that cavernous world he would have gone racing back to pound uselessly on the stone wall that separated him from the world of light and air, would have dug with his hands at the tunnel walls, trying to break through.

He still held Wylles' shoulder, alternately pushing the boy along and then, when Wylles tried to bolt, jerking him back. Wylles was their only source of information, the only source of the spells which the Catswold folk must learn if they were to survive in the world they approached. And when after several hours they stopped to rest, Braden forced Wylles to say for the gathered Catswold the spell for changing, then the spell for light, then spells for turning away weapons. The Catswold tested each. In the hoary half-dark among lantern shadows the Catswold folk changed from human to cat, and from cat to human, a metamorphosis that made Braden's skin crawl. Sharply now, he realized that without magic he would be severely crippled in the Netherworld.

Melissa had told him that.

Well, hell, he had fought in other wars. If this war was different he would compensate for his weakness. War couldn't all be fought by magic, not all swords and spears would be deflected. To calm his fears he concentrated on the exotic glimpses of the inner earth given him by the lanterns, images like sudden scenes from a slide projector: waterfalls snaking down fissures, slabs of stone swinging out over black emptiness, echoing spaces dropping as if into hell itself. He imagined he could hear the whispers of dark gods, of Hecate, of Cerberus; he imagined the voices of the Hell Beasts Melissa had described too graphically. And now, no human figure shared the tunnel with him, except Prince Wylles. They all had turned to cats. He picked up the abandoned lanterns one by one, strewn down the tunnels. Alternately dragging Wylles then restraining him, burdened with lanterns he was unwilling to leave behind, Braden felt like some modern day, clumsy Diogenes.

He had no idea how long they had been in the tunnel moving ever downward. All ability to measure time had left him—the journey seemed outside of time. Several days might have passed; endless nights might have gone by stacked one on another as if someone had shuffled all the dark cards together.

The end of the world would be like this. Unrelieved blackness hiding whatever waited, so that neither size nor scale nor space could be clearly understood; mankind would be flung into dimensions of which they had no comprehension.

Suddenly ahead a figure appeared in his light: one of the cats had changed back to human. Then another. Another. Voices rose. Soon a crowd again filled the tunnel. But he did not see Terrel change, he saw the black cat with a white foot running on ahead, swift as wind. And far ahead a faint green light stained the blackness.

Around a bend they entered a green glow, then around another bend they saw the ragged hole, green lit, that marked the cave's mouth. He pushed Wylles ahead faster.

The boy was too docile now, almost sleepy. Braden tightened his grip before the prince could jerk away and run. Together, captive and captor, they hurried toward the hole filled with green mist.

The stream they had followed flowed out into the light, and the few remaining cats leaped through the water and away into the Netherworld. On the far shore they shook their paws then sat licking them dry, looking around them at the green world, at the home they had never seen.

Melissa's world. He imagined her in the ambient greenness reaching out for him, her green eyes loving him, and he was riven with longing for her. And with fear for her—and, perhaps, with fear *of* her.

The gathered Catswold were silent; the only sound was the bleating cry of a dove from the forest, a homey, familiar sound as he might hear on the brown grass hills of Marin. And in the silence the few remaining cats began to regain human form as if this world might be too unsafe to remain small.

But suddenly something exploded toward them out of the sky above the woods. A huge white shape flew straight at them, a creature far bigger than any bird, winging clumsily. It gave a human cry and its white-feathered breasts swung as it flapped down to an ungainly landing on its long bird legs.

The Harpy landed in a storm of beating wings and immediately embraced Braden, smothering him in dusty feathers. The feel of her feathered body against him was shocking. Like holding a bird—warm and too soft. He thought of Melissa's description of the Harpy, but in real life the beast was quite beyond description.

Her voice was rasping and querulous. "Why did you bring Wylles? I didn't see that in the mirror. We don't need that burden."

"I needed him to open the wall. And to teach the Catswold the spells." He glanced at her mirror, dangling between her breasts. "If you could see us coming, you could see that we needed Wylles."

The Harpy laughed. "I suppose we can deal with the boy. Tired," she said, leaning against Braden. "I thought you'd never get here. Can your Catswold folk ride?" Then she saw their blank looks. "Have to teach them that, as well. Can anyone use a sword?"

"We can learn," Terrel said.

"I suppose," said the Harpy without enthusiasm. "There is precious little time." She tucked Braden's hand beneath her arm and led the little band toward the forest. Braden moved swiftly, but the Harpy kept hopping and flapping as if impatient with earthbound creatures. The woods were low, twisted, filled with black hollows beneath low growth and with tortured, oddly rounded shadows. Low branches like deformed arms reached out at them; everything in the forest seemed to be watching them.

Braden thought they had traveled for about an hour when he saw they were approaching a village. The thatched huts were made of mud and straw and were surrounded by an outer circle of animal pens and of lopsided storage sheds. Between the huts, inside the central compound a dozen old men and women and four small children were saddling a herd of tired-looking ponies. Beside the fence lay a stack of weapons, a sorry arsenal of axes and rusty swords. "Give Wylles to me," said the Harpy.

Gladly Braden handed the boy over. He watched the Harpy lead him away and shut him into a hut, pulling a bolt across the door. When the ponies were saddled she made the Catswold mount up, and began to teach them to ride. She gave Braden the only decent horse—the gray gelding Melissa had left. "I suppose you can ride. I heard you tell Melissa you could."

He looked the Harpy over. "What else did you hear me tell Melissa?"

The Harpy smiled in a way that made his face heat; he

recalled Melissa's description of how vividly the mirror re-
produced its visions. The Harpy smiled and handed him a
battered sword. "Go practice on the hay mow. That old
man in the blue jerkin will show you what you need to
know. Be quick, Braden West. I have a more important job
for you to do."

Chapter 65

Melissa descended the cellar stairs among the roars of the
Hell Beasts. She cast a spell-light as she moved downward
past bins of onions and hanging hams, then soon was dodging the reaching claws of the caged Hell Beasts. She had removed the blue-and-green dress and put on the hunting
leathers that Terlis had fetched for her from Efil's closet. She
felt warm for the first time since she had left the tool room
and garden. Thoughts of the garden stirred pain, but she
must not think of Braden now.

The borrowed sword she had taken from the queen's soldiers' barracks hung at her side heavy and comforting as she
approached the Griffon's cage. She found the lioneagle
sound asleep, his golden body forced against the bars, his
golden wings jammed between the bars, a few bright feathers sticking out into the passage. He was very thin, his ribs
curving beneath his yellow pelt. But still he seemed filled
with power. She paused, remembering tales of the Griffon's
unpredictable nature. She removed her sword and laid it on
the stone floor of the passage, to show her good faith. Then
she said the spell that swung open his cage door, and she
stepped inside.

Within the cage she knelt before the Griffon. He slept

deeply. She touched his smooth, thick beak that could crush her arm with one bite. His eagle head rested heavily upon his lion's paws, his feathered neck emerged powerfully from his golden lion's mane. As she stroked him, the tuft of his tail began to flick. For a moment she longed to run, to slam the cell door behind her and lock it. She thought of the Toad's homily, *Kiss of emerald blessed by Bast can please the steed of Nemesis,* and, leaning over the Griffon, she touched his feathered cheek with the Amulet.

When he moved, her heart skipped. When he opened his eyes, she forgot to breathe. He stared at her muzzily then he woke fully and lunged at her, knocking her flat.

He stood over her roaring, his yellow eyes blazing, his broad beak open above her throat.

She shoved the Amulet into his face.

He drew back blinking.

She got up and stood facing him. He watched her intently, his golden eyes searching her face at first hungily and then with curiosity. When she didn't back away, his look softened. Gently he lifted a broad lion's paw and touched her face, a paw soft as velvet, and warm. He slid his paw down from her cheek over her chest to rest upon the Amulet. She daren't move. He opened his beak in the grin of the hunting eagle as if he would rip her suddenly, and when he spoke in a coughing roar she was faint.

"What do you want, child of Bast? How come you to have the Amulet?"

She swallowed, trying to make her voice work. "I—I have a right to the Amulet, it was my mother's. I—have no mount powerful enough to carry me into battle."

He looked hard at her. "What battle?"

"The Netherworld is at war." She looked into his broad, avian face. "Siddonie of Affandar has gone to war to conquer all the Netherworld."

He looked hard at her. "You come here alone."

"Yes."

"You would go alone to fight her? And how would you stop her?"

"I would stop her with truth. She wins with lies, with deception, but the Amulet can destroy lies."

"You have only the Amulet with which to defeat her?"

"And a sword. And—and your power, if you would carry me."

"And what would I gain by doing that?"

"Siddonie caged you. She took you from your forests. If you help me defeat her, you will fly free again."

The Griffon shifted his weight. When he tried to lift his cramped wings, she could see they were stiff. His gaze didn't leave her. She stared back at him boldly. He stroked his beak across his paws, then turned his head and with his thick beak he groomed the golden fur over his thin ribs. He seemed to be listening to something far away, or to something within himself. She waited.

At last he looked full at her again. "There is more at stake in this battle, young woman, than you yet know."

He said, "Old, dark powers are rising. The queen has waked the primal dark which is the sire of all evil." He looked at her intently. "Do you not sense this? Does not the rising power of that deep and primary evil touch you, daughter of Bast?"

The Griffon nodded sagely. "The serpent rises, Catswold queen. The dark enemy of Bast again rises." He poked his thick beak at her. "Show me the Amulet. Hold it up so I can look at it."

She held the emerald before him and brought a spell-light to shine on it. Deep within, the emblem of Ra burned. The Griffon's gaze grew intense. When he had looked a long time he snapped his gaze on her suddenly. "We are kin, daughter of Bast. You bear the blood of Sekhmet. You bear the lion's blood."

She shivered.

The Griffon placed a heavy paw on her shoulder. "Dark stirs now across the Netherworld. The Serpent Apep stirs and wakes; the primal dark wakes." The Griffon's broad golden beak opened wide enough to swallow her face. His breath smelled like spoiled meat. "I must eat a proper meal before we start out. I am weak; they know nothing about feeding griffons."

She led him up the stone stairs to the next level, and watched him cut down hams with a sharp snap of his beak and tear them apart and devour them. Up the next flight, in the scullery, he drank dry the water barrel. She could see through the scullery windows that Terlis and Briccha still worked in the garden, picking beans. As she led the Griffon out toward the courtyard he said, "What made you think you could wake me and not be eaten?"

She laughed. "I had to try." She gave him a wink, as she had seen Morian wink, and a slow smile. "The Harpy warned me you were fierce." They moved into the empty courtyard, and Melissa slid onto his warm back.

He looked around at her and spread his golden wings and he leaped skyward in a rush of wind, rising straight up above the palace. She stared down at Terlis, saw the white oval of the child's face looking up, then they had left the palace behind, tilting so close to the granite sky she had to duck. He shouted, "Are you afraid?"

"Yes, I am afraid." She stroked his neck as her heels dug comfortably into his sides. The Griffon twisted around again and gave her an appraising look. Under his old, wise gaze Melissa felt very young.

He said, "Remember, daughter of Bast—daughter of Sekhmet—one must ride into battle meaning to kill. Any other thought courts defeat." He banked low over a forest. "If you die, you die. One cannot think of that; it saps the strength." He sped above a deep valley, then above rising white cliffs. "The battle has centered at Cressteane. I sense it like a stench blowing. I sense her there: the dark queen."

Chapter 66

On a narrow ridge east of Shenndeth, Siddonie sat on her horse watching a band of mountain elven driven screaming and fighting over the cliff. The pale little people grabbed at the soldiers' horses and jabbed with their lances as her horse soldiers clubbed them. For three days her armies had been routing these small, hidden bands, working north from Lettlehem toward the main area of battle. Her troops had swept Lettlehem clean, as well as Pearilleth and now Shenndeth, leaving the villages stripped of life and food.

Below her a dozen winged lizards banked and dove at the bodies strewn along the cliff, lapping their blood. When a new lizard, a big male, heaved down out of the sky she held out her arm to it.

It wore a collar. It landed so heavily it nearly unseated her. Its eyes seemed still filled with the Hell fires from which it had just returned. Its long, slick body shone like ebony, its leathery wings glinted with black scales. It grunted a greeting, then spoke in a guttural hiss forced up through its long, narrow throat.

"Three rebel bands west of Cressteane," it said, "hiding in the mountains." It smiled a toothy grimace. "Fear touches them, the spirit of the dark beast has found them. It plays with their fear like dragons play with a lamb." The lizard's black tongue flicked with satisfaction.

Siddonie nodded. "And what else? What of the main rebel army? And what of the Catswold? What has the dark beast done to the Catswold?"

The lizard turned its face away, as if she would strike it.

"The Catswold do not heed the dark beast. I flew all the way through that endless tunnel to Zzadarray. I saw the spirit of the beast lying like fog over Zzadarray darkening the streets and chambers, but the Catswold moved through it never seeing it, never aware of it."

"That is not possible. *I* can see it, and so can they! I see it every night in dream."

She did not speak of her fear at night as the dark beast came exploding into her dreams. She would not speak of that to a lizard. The dream filled her with rage. *She* had called the beast, it must obey *her.* No creature, no being, dare have power over her. She said, "The beast should be driving terror into the Catswold. Why is it not?"

The lizard gazed at her intently.

"Go back. Go back there and find out!"

"But I can tell you why."

"Why, then? Speak up!"

"The primal dark has risen at your call, but that does not mean it is your servant, Queen Siddonie. You have summoned the dark that lived before the earth was formed. You have challenged it, but it goes where it pleases and it destroys only as it pleases. That beast will never be ruled by you."

Her hand circled its throat. "I am its heir! *I* am daughter of Lillith. It *must* obey me."

The lizard opened its wet mouth in a mirthless smile, and wriggled as her hand tightened. "You have found the power to summon it. It is drawn to you as surely as I am drawn to blood, but that does not mean it will obey you.

"The primal dark is not your slave, Siddonie. You are its slave." It choked suddenly, strangled by her throttling grip; she cast it away from her. It dropped, then righted itself and flew above her clumsily.

"Go back," she shouted. "Go back and learn more about the Catswold. I want to know why they resist."

From the stone sky, the beast glared at her, then plunged away flapping.

Chapter 67

Zzadarray's towers were airy, open to the Netherworld breezes. The city was built of pale stone, the pillars and stone facades carved into leaf and flower designs. The upper chambers let onto balconies, and the lower chambers onto small private gardens scaled to a cat. In the main city, preparations for war were under way, conducted as smoothly and seemingly without effort as the stalking of small game through Zzadarray's grassy meadows. The Catswold from Marchell and Cathenn and Ebenth had joined those of Zzadarray, and they were heavily armed.

All the Catswold women had taken human form. They wore their finest silks and their sacred jewelry, golden anklets, amber necklaces, ruby and emerald girdles. Lapis and emerald combs were fastened into piebald locks, religious treasures all, brought down to the Netherworld in ancient times from the Celtic lands and from Egypt. In the white stone temple as the women knelt, their jewelry was blessed by the five Catswold priests, and their weapons and the weapons of the Catswold men were blessed. As midnight approached the Catswold nation prepared with feasting and then with spells and with prayer. Tomorrow they would ride against the dark queen.

Their rituals spoke to the sun god Ra, though none of them had ever seen the sun. They prayed to Bast and to Sekhmet, speaking in the lost cadences of Cyprus and Crete, or in the tongue of Mycenae and Knossos. But in spite of the ritual spells a tenseness held the Catswold, a fear none could name, a sense of threat far greater than Siddonie. As dawn began to green Zzadarray's towers, the rituals ended. The Catswold went silent; a wariness held them. And then they sensed a nearer threat. Something approached the city. Someone moved through the forest toward Zzadarray and it was not one of their own.

Weapons were sheathed, spells were repeated. And a dozen Catswold took feline form and moved into shadow among the trees, listening, watching.

Soon every Catswold heard the hushed footfall of a lone horse, and smelled the crushed leaves and grass. At the edge of the forest a branch moved and a rider emerged on a tall, fiery horse: not a horse of this world.

The rider was a woman, young and thin, hard muscled. Her black hair was streaked with orange, her face sharp-planed, and the shadow image of a darkly mottled cat clung about her. She was dressed in the golden robes of the Catswold queen, yet the Catswold did not lay down their weapons for her. They did not kneel. Why would a queen appear now, when no queen had appeared in Zzadarray in a generation?

When they saw that she was followed by a consort, an ermine-robed king who rode in the shadows behind her, whispers flared across the crowd and arrows were fitted to bow.

Her consort was Efil of Affandar. And from out of the forest behind him emerged an army of horse soldiers. The Catswold warriors mounted their steeds, and faced the advancing party quietly.

The approaching warriors were hard-looking men and women. They were Catswold but they were strange. And far more alarming than their looks was the fact that they rode upperworld horses and wielded oddly shaped swords and knives of unfamiliar design. Their clothes, though seeming at first to be Netherworld garments, were not of the Netherworld.

The approaching army paused in the forest shadow. Their eyes gleamed like jewels in the dimness, and then as they moved out of the forest the darkness of their tanned faces struck another foreign note.

The Catswold queen—if such she be—sat her mount haughtily, studying the gathered Catswold, studying each priest intently. The Catswold nation watched her.

Then she shook her dark, mottled hair, and fingered her golden robe open, revealing a thin, sheer gown which draped over her breasts. And between her breasts against the gold filament hung an emerald. It was huge and tear-shaped. It was held by two gold cats, their paws joined. It was the Amulet of Bast, or it pretended to be.

"I am Helsa. I am your queen. The wisdom of the Amulet has brought me to seek you."

"For what purpose?" said a priest.

"Because you are my subjects," she said, smiling gently. "And also I come to free you—to lead you against Siddonie of Affandar. I mean to free you from her subjugation. I mean to free all Catswold and to strengthen the four eastern nations. I come," said Helsa smoothly, "to free the Netherworld." She smiled again, speaking softly. "Won't you kneel to your queen?"

No one moved. No one knelt. Helsa's eyes narrowed in thinly concealed anger. But she was Catswold; she knew better than to demand that they kneel. She said, "Within the hour I mean to ride to defeat Siddonie. I hope you will join me in setting our nations free. I pray, as Catswold queen, that you will see fit to arm and provision yourselves to ride against Siddonie."

When still no one spoke or moved, Helsa's color rose and her eyes blazed. But still her words were soft. "Would you see Siddonie of Affandar destroy us all and defeat Zzadarray?"

A priest said, "We are only shocked, my lady. The Netherworld Catswold have seen no queen in my lifetime. Indeed," he said smoothly, "we will follow you to destroy Siddonie."

Helsa nodded. "I mean to ride out in an hour, once my troops are rested. I pray you to sharpen your heaviest weapons. If Siddonie should win this war, all the Netherworld will be enslaved. And for nothing," she continued. "Siddonie has no longer any right to the throne of Affandar."

A puzzled hush held the gathered Catswold. The five priests glanced at one another.

Helsa said, "By Netherworld law, Siddonie has no valid claim, now, to the throne." She gave Efil a bold look. "I am now queen of promise. I carry within me the future prince of Affandar. I carry King Efil's child. The soothsayers have so confirmed."

After a long silence, someone among the Catswold said, "The child of Efil and Siddonie is well again. All the Netherworld knows that."

Efil sat his horse calmly. He looked very pale beside the sun-darkened Catswold woman. He said, "The boy who travels with Siddonie is not her son nor mine. The boy is a changeling. He was brought by Siddonie from the upperworld." The Catswold folk shifted and glanced at one another but no one spoke. Efil said, "Soon I will produce Wylles. I will show you the two boys side by side. Meantime, hear your queen. She is not only Catswold queen but queen of promise of Affandar. Hear the plan we have structured."

Helsa waited for their full attention. Her creamy voice carried as insidiously as a breeding cat's rich mewl. "I have promised Queen Siddonie that I will lead you with my own band of upperworld Catswold to fight beside her. I have told her that together we will defeat the rebel bands."

Her voice softened to a haunting murmur. "We join with Siddonie's armies on the battlefield. And then," Helsa said, her hands curving as if she made claws, "we will turn on them. We will destroy Siddonie's troops and destroy Siddonie. We will kill her and free the Netherworld."

There were nods among the Catswold. But again the priests glanced at one another. Helsa watched them and smiled, and raised her fist. "One hour."

And as she turned away, one among the crowd said, "My name is Oeden the Black." And another said, "I am Galvino Grayleg." Helsa turned back and nodded, smiling at them because they had given her, by such greeting, admission of their belief and fealty.

When Helsa had gone to rest, the Catswold moved about their hasty chores, their eyes meeting slyly at the lies their men had been able to speak to this false queen. If, while wearing the Amulet, she could not detect lies, then she was not of queen's blood and likely the amulet was as false as she.

Yet quickly they made their final preparations for war, readying supplies, inspecting horses and equipment. King Efil moved among them, greeting one then another. He spoke for a long while with the Catswold priests. He did not notice an occasional cat slip away between the robes of its companions; he had no notion that three dozen cats left the ranks of the preparing warriors.

Helsa was escorted to the most luxurious apartments to rest. She was led through the honeycomb of pale stone bowers and grottoes to a high tower, to a chamber walled in white marble and carpeted with embroidered cushions. She took off the outer, ceremonial robe of gold lamé, and in her transparent gold shift she stretched out on the damask covers of an ornate bed. She did not change to cat. Glancing above her at the high, small alcove lined with silk, she studied the true bed of the apartment's occupant. The alcove looked deliciously comfortable, but she did not intend to abandon her human form. She lay relaxed, stretching, thinking with satisfaction of the web she and Siddonie had woven.

She had told the Catswold she would pretend to join Siddonie, then destroy her. Efil, too, believed this. The fool thought he would remain king. He thought he had charmed her, won her. Only Siddonie knew that Helsa would, in truth, lead the Catswold to be slaughtered. Plan and counterplan, lie and counter lie wove an intriguing tangle.

She smiled, warm with Siddonie's promise. Her tough street loyalty had been securely won during Siddonie's three visits to the upperworld ranch. She respected Siddonie; the queen was strong. Soon she would ride by Siddonie's side as her disciple, and when Siddonie died she would be heir to the throne of Affandar and to all the thrones of the Netherworld, for surely in this war they would win every nation. When Siddonie died, she would be queen of the Netherworld.

She slept briefly and lightly, hearing every sound near the chamber. She woke and lay supine for a moment, then flipped up, drew on the gold robe, adjusted the hood, belted on her sword, and was prepared to ride.

Chapter 68

The army moved out of Zzadarray with Netherworld Catswold and upperworld Catswold riding side by side. The upperworld horses were several hands taller than those of Zzadarray, and the upperworld Catswold were edgy, predatory, and impatient. The mixed band moved quickly down the steep ridges heading for the valley and the mountains beyond, making directly for the valley of Cressteane.

But not all Helsa's troops were with them. A cadre of mounted San Francisco street rabble waited unseen in the forest, and when only the old folk and children remained in Zzadarray these riders stormed the city with the violence born of Siddonie's training. They ransacked the chambers for jewels, tore at the walls of the buildings, cudgeling and breaking the soft stone. They were primed to kill and torture, but they found no Catswold—the city was deserted. The old and the frail had turned to cats and vanished into the forest. Then suddenly out from the forest rode three dozen Zzadarray Catswold armed with bows and with heavy, spell-cast swords.

Soon on the streets of Zzadarray, Siddonie's soldiers lay dead.

*   *   *

Helsa's army moved slowly down the steep, corrugated ridges formed of sandstone and clumps of twisted trees growing stunted from the stone. Far below lay the plain hidden by mists of steam rising from hot underground springs. They must cross the plain then cross beneath the mountains on the other side to reach the plains of Cressteane. The sky above them was low, and broken by streaks of white crystal. They rode silently. Helsa and King Efil, at the head of the army, were flanked by two Zzadarray priests. Helsa had dispersed the three other priests to ride at the head of three battalions, perhaps as leaders or perhaps to separate them. A Catswold priest was a military captain as well, a freely elected leader. The refinements of corruption which elect most officials had not touched Zzadarray. The Catswold folk were too stubbornly independent to tolerate corruption. Thus Helsa felt it best that these priests be separated.

The upperworld Catswold troops sat their horses eagerly looking across the plain toward the far mountains, primed and honed for battle. And the warriors of Zzadarray who rode beside them watched them closely, wondering at the fervor of upperworld folk to save a foreign land.

They did not reach the plain that night but camped on the escarpments, and finished their descent the next morning. By the evening of the second day they had crossed the plain and were at the foot of the mountains, nearing the deep passage that, two days hence, would bring them up into the heart of battle. They were dismounting to make camp at the foot of the mountains when a captain shouted, and men began to point up toward the peaks. Something was flying toward them above the mountain, its thin shadow shifting and gliding across the granite sky. In the falling green light its wings shone golden. It flew with great power, its broad wings describing long, slow sweeps. "A griffon," whispered one of the priests, and the Zzadarray warriors smiled and sheathed their swords. But Helsa rode tense in the saddle and the swords of her troops were drawn.

The Griffon dropped toward them. At the last moment its

golden wings snapped out to break its fall; it thundered earthward, driving the horses back so they reared and shied. Its rider's sword was drawn, and as the Griffon came to rest and his rider faced the Catswold troops, a sigh escaped the Zzadarray warriors. She was Catswold and there was about her a presence that held them staring.

She was beautiful and slim. Her piebald hair was tangled from the wind of the Griffon's wings, hair of red and gold and platinum and black, the hair of a true Catswold queen. She was dressed in fighting leathers, and she held her sword comfortably. Her eyes were as green as the emerald which hung between her breasts, drawing the gaze of every warrior—an emerald circled by two golden cats, twin of the pendant Helsa wore. The young Catswold woman ignored Helsa; she seemed to see only the faces of the warriors. Helsa stared at her, white and still, then lunged suddenly, spurring her horse to a leaping charge, her sword leveled at the woman's throat.

Melissa felt the Griffon tense, and a dozen emotions swept her as the girl's sword flashed and she parried with her own. The Griffon twisted, knocking the girl's horse to its knees, and Melissa slashed her sword aside. She grabbed the horse's bridle, snubbing him, and pressed her sword to the girl's chest, knowing she could kill her with one thrust. She was shocked at how young the girl was, maybe fifteen. Though her green stare was far older, brazen with street cunning.

"Who are you? What is your name?"

"Helsa!" the girl spat. "I am Helsa." She lunged and tried to snatch away the reins. Melissa slashed her arm, drawing blood, and Helsa's face filled with hatred.

"Why do you wear the golden robes of a Catswold queen? And what is that stone you wear? Do you claim *that* to be the Amulet of Bast?" She felt pity for the girl, and she feared her. "Answer me! What is that stone you wear?"

"The Am . . . It is the Am . . ."

The lie would not come; the girl could not lie within the

true amulet's presence. She stared at the true stone, trying to speak, her face white.

"Name that stone for me. Name the stone you wear."

Silence.

"Name it! What is it?" Her sword pressed harder. "Where did you get it?"

Still Helsa was silent.

Melissa pulled the reins tighter, jerking Helsa's horse close. "Name it."

"It . . ." She choked, stared at Melissa with rage, and spoke at last as if she could not help but speak, as if she had been forced to do so. "It is—it is a common emerald."

"Has it power?" Melissa glanced past the girl to the listening troops.

No answer.

"Has it power?"

"It has . . . It has no power." The girl sat up straighter in the saddle, her face sharp with hatred.

"Where do you come from?"

"From—from the upperworld."

"Tell me why you wear a false amulet."

Helsa stared into the brilliance of the true amulet, clenching her lips, refusing to speak. Melissa prodded her hard with the tip of her sword. "Do you wear it to deceive the Catswold warriors?"

Reluctantly she nodded.

"Why do you deceive them?"

The choice of silence seemed no longer to remain to her. "I—I deceive them to defeat them. I—mean to defeat the Zzadarray armies."

"Throw away the false stone, into the dirt."

Helsa didn't move. Melissa prodded her again, drawing a deep wound. The girl glared but did not cry out; now her eyes showed fear. Melissa prodded again, cutting down her arm, sickened at doing this and knowing she must. At last Helsa removed the false emerald and dropped it in the dust.

"Take off the robe."

She removed the golden robe and lay it over her saddle,

her eyes filled with ruined dreams. Melissa took up the robe with the tip of her sword, and pulled it on over her leathers as two Zzadarray soldiers took the reins of Helsa's mount. The girl, nearly naked in her thin shift, seemed frail and vulnerable. Melissa touched the Amulet at her throat. "Tell the Catswold warriors your true mission. Tell them what they would have found if they had followed you."

"Their death," Helsa said tightly. "My mission was to lead them into Siddonie's trap."

"This was your real promise to Siddonie," Melissa said, "that you would bring the Catswold to her to die."

"Yes."

One of the five Zzadarray priests rode up close to Helsa, spurring his shaggy horse, his white robes open to reveal his fighting leathers. He faced Helsa angrily, showing no pity for her frailty and youth. "You are a Catswold woman. By what perversion would you destroy your own people?"

"By this perversion, priest," Helsa said boldly. "I am to rule Zzadarray! I am to be Siddonie's only heir. She has promised I will rule all the Netherworld after her death." And suddenly Helsa turned, knocking Melissa's sword aside, snatching up her reins and spurring her startled mount. Melissa caught the girl's arm as the priest swung his blade. He struck Helsa from the saddle, cutting her throat in one blow.

Melissa stared down, shocked at the girl sprawled in the dust, and Helsa, as life bled from her, slowly changed to cat. Soon a thin, darkly mottled cat lay bleeding in the dust at the feet of the circling horses. Melissa turned away, shaken.

The priests of Zzadarray buried Helsa deep in the earth of a world she had never known. And Melissa saw, in the eyes of the upperworld Catswold who had come here with Helsa, the beginning of uncertainty.

She mounted Helsa's horse and pulled the golden hood up to hide her hair. The horse was a tall, distinctly marked pinto that she suspected Siddonie had chosen so Helsa would be easy to see during battle. She turned to look at the Catswold troops gathered behind her, then led them out toward the tunnel that would bring them into Cressteane.

Earlier she had seen from the sky the lines of battle, the plains of Cressteane crowded with the armies of eight nations, their tents filling the dry plain some distance from the Hell Pit. And in the Hell Pit she had seen the leaping flames stirring wildly, licking up at the sky as if they would leap from the pit to run unchecked across the desert, consuming warriors and horses. She had seen deep down within the fires a darkness writhing, growing denser. She had watched a huge black beast take form among the flames, and watched it fight to leave the Hell Pit rearing, falling back to rear again. The Griffon had dived down close above the beast, looking, and she had felt its evil engulf her, more malevolent than any Hell Beast. She had never seen the beast before, but a deep race knowledge filled her, a memory that washed her with panic. This was the primal dark—this was the seed of evil. Nothing anywhere, in any world, could match its evil. This beast *was* the core, the primal corruption. The black beast had lunged up reaching for the Griffon as if they were toys flung in the air.

Now she looked at her troops for a long moment, then looked up at the sky where the Griffon glided. And, filled with fear of war, and with terror of what waited in the pit, she pressed on quickly, leading her armies toward Cressteane.

Chapter 69

It was midnight, the battle was stilled by darkness. Siddonie made her way alone from her tent across the sleeping battlefield toward the red glow of the pit. Around her, exhausted soldiers slept. She could hear the occasional snort of a horse and the moans of the wounded. She approached the pit, lusting to touch the dark beast.

"Apep," she said softly. "Eblis. Apollyon." Powerfully she willed the dark beast to her. Willed it to invade the minds of her enemies. She stepped nearer the edge where flames licked and exploded, and suddenly she wanted to climb down the sheer sides and leap into the fires. She longed to embrace the black dragon.

But suddenly that desire struck terror through her; she drew away shaking and sweating. *She* was daughter of Lillith. The dark beast had no right to control her. *She* had the right to use it. *She—Siddonie—*she alone was heir to the primal dark.

Chapter 70

The ponies jogged along steadily behind Braden's gray gelding. The Catswold folk from the upperworld, dressed in borrowed Netherworld leathers, were hardly distinguishable from Netherworld peasants. Except, on closer inspection, they had better styled haircuts, and the women had pierced ears and painted nails. They handled their horses passably; they had learned more quickly than Braden had thought possible. Likely it was their feline balance. The sturdy ponies had made good time across Affandar.

By now, the women had wiped off their lipstick and tied their hair back or slicked it under caps, and their manicured hands were dirty and blistered, and they carried sharpened shovels and axes and crudely made bows. Above them the Harpy circled impatiently.

For Braden, the upperworld had faded, the Netherworld was all that was real. The earth beneath him was solid. The hard stones under the gelding's hooves struck sparks. The smell of pine and juniper filled his nostrils. The cold rush of the river where they had stopped to water the horses had left his boots wet. The stone sky above him seemed totally normal, so that if he were again to face the emptiness of the upperworld sky he would feel too exposed.

He rode with one thought in mind, one goal. Melissa.

He turned once to urge on the pack pony he led. Each rider led a pack animal, heavily burdened with a long, cumbersome bundle.

And when suddenly the Harpy did a wingover and dove at

the horses, he responded at once, moving his mount on fast. "Kick those ponies," he shouted, "get them moving!"

"The pit is beyond that mountain," shouted the Harpy. "We will camp at the crest. On the other side, the valley is thick with Affandar warriors."

Chapter 71

Melissa, riding the upperworld stallion meant for Helsa, wearing the golden robe Helsa had worn, led the Catswold warriors into the dark tunnel. The green of the Netherworld night disappeared behind them. As they pushed into total blackness they brought spell-lights. The Griffon walked among them, his wings folded in the tight space; he was cross and nervous confined thus, and the Catswold warriors kept their distance from him. Melissa was surprised he had stayed with them.

The journey took all night. They stopped once, at the tunnel's deep springs, to water and rest the horses and feed them from the bags of grain they carried. It was well past midnight when they came up out of the black tunnel and turned south. The Griffon had burst out ahead of them, lifted away, and was gone.

Soon the stone sky grew red, reflecting the fires of the Hell Pit. Beyond the flaming pit burned hundreds of small fires in the camps of the two armies as the enemies waited, facing each other across an expanse of empty plain in the enforced truce of darkness. The air was filled with smoke.

Fear made Melissa's hands sweat on the reins, and with her uncertainty the stallion began to fuss and shiver. She could hear, ahead, occasional low voices and the muffled

cries of the wounded. They pushed on to the lip of the Hell
Pit then drew back startled. The pit was broad here, and it
seethed with liquid fire in rolling waves. But deep within the
fire a blackness writhed—a dragon, its thick coils stretching
away in both directions—humping, sliding, disappearing as
the fires shifted. Melissa backed her trembling horse away.

Watching the dragon, they dismounted and led their balking mounts fast up the steep cliffs beside the pit. They entered a narrow overhead pass tunneling through the granite
sky above the Hell Pit. The terrified horses went slowly,
sweating and shivering. Melissa alternately fought her stallion and talked to him, drawing him on.

They came out of the tunnel and onto the battlefield in the
first green light of approaching dawn, greeted by the crash
of metal and by soldiers boiling out of the two camps.
Hooves thundered as rebel troops swept in waves toward
Siddonie's armies. Melissa's horse lunged and pawed, wanting to join battle. Already the fighting stretched for more
than a mile, and the clashing and screams filled the valley.
But suddenly an enchantment of terror hit the battlefield.
The spell weakened Melissa as if water ran in her veins.
Rebel horses bolted, their riders frozen with fear in the saddle to fall under the blades of Siddonie's army. All across the
plain the rebel lines fell back. Fleeing horses stumbled over
their fallen riders. Could this be Siddonie's magic? Did the
dark queen, alone, have such power?

Fighting her fear she led the Catswold warriors straight
into battle, though many upperworld Catswold drew back.
Ahead, Siddonie loomed suddenly among her fighting men,
the black stallion rearing and charging. Melissa gave the
sign and leaned low in the saddle, and they charged the
queen at a dead run. She saw Siddonie's warriors separate to
surround the Catswold. This was Siddonie's plan. She would
expect Helsa to draw back and be captured. She signaled
again and her troops separated, swerving away in two arms
circling the Affandar troops. She saw Siddonie's movement
of surprise, saw her jerk her horse, saw her shout orders but
couldn't hear the words.

Siddonie's soldiers wheeled to form a wider pincer. The Catswold warriors wheeled and cut them off. They had lost more of the upperworld Catswold; Melissa could see them, galloping away to safety. She could see also, behind Siddonie's troops, the rebel bands closing in. And suddenly a roar came from above and the Griffon dropped over her, sweeping low, knocking Affandar soldiers from the saddle. At the same moment Melissa charged, her soldiers with her. Beneath the Griffon's diving attacks they began to drive Siddonie's troops back. They cut the Affandar soldiers down and forced them into the swords of the pursuing rebels. Again and again the Griffon dove and they attacked, and with each sweep a wave of the queen's troops fell. Men lay dying. Loose horses pounded away. Melissa thought Siddonie was shouting a spell. But the queen, surrounded by enemies, shouted suddenly, "Truce! I want truce!"

The Catswold warriors paused, looking to Melissa.

"Truce," Melissa breathed warily. Her hood was tight around her face, and in the confusion of battle surely Siddonie still thought she was Helsa. Was this the moment the two had planned, when Helsa would turn on her own troops and help kill them?

Siddonie rode forward alone to face the gold-hooded Catswold queen. But then she half-turned, aware of something behind her. And Melissa saw within the flames of the pit the black dragon rising up. Its thick body looked like a gigantic, endless tree rising. Its head touched the granite sky snaking, seeking. And now suddenly Siddonie recognized her, her face was transfixed with rage. Suddenly she dropped low over the saddle, her sword drawn, and charged Melissa. Melissa could see her lips moving in a spell, could feel the cold power weaken her, enervating and lulling her . . .

No!

She roused herself, grasping the Amulet shouting a spell against Siddonie, as their swords met.

Melissa felt Siddonie's blow like fire in her arm. She saw the Griffon dive to distract Siddonie, and she struck the queen, nearly unseating her. "Now, Griffon! Again!" He

dove and she struck again. The queen twisted. Her mount
stumbled under the Griffon's driving weight, and the Griffon
grabbed the queen's arm in his powerful beak, as Melissa
struck the sword from her hand.

Facing Siddonie, Melissa shook back her hood, and
opened her cloak to reveal the Amulet.

Siddonie went white, but then she laughed at her. "That is
not the true Amulet! A useless toy. A common emerald."

"Is it?" Melissa said softly. Then, "Speak to your armies,
Siddonie. Tell your soldiers that you fight to free the Netherworld."

Siddonie smiled and turned to face her armies. Her cap-
tains pressed their horses nearer. But when the queen tried to
speak, she could not. She opened her mouth but her voice
would not come.

Melissa said, "You cannot lie before the Amulet." She
watched Siddonie's rising uncertainty and anger. "Tell your
soldiers, Siddonie, that you fight to free the Netherworld."

The kings who had ridden with Siddonie were close
around her now, her brother King Ithilel, King Moriethsten
of Wexten, King Craysche and others. But as the gathered
armies waited for the queen to speak, and as they realized
the queen could not speak, Melissa saw one king then another draw back.

King Bedini of Ferrathil left Siddonie's side, then
Hevveth of Chillings. Soon other kings turned away, and
only four monarchs remained beside the queen of Affandar.

Melissa said, "Can't you speak to your armies, Siddonie?
Can't you tell them they fight for freedom against the slave-
making rebels?"

When Siddonie remained mute and the silence had
stretched taut, some of Siddonie's own officers turned their
horses away.

But other soldiers drew closer to her, watching their
queen. And suddenly with no warning a dozen Affandar soldiers attacked Siddonie, grabbing her horse, trying to pull
her from the saddle. Her stallion plunged. Siddonie
screamed a spell that sent the men reeling, and sitting her

fighting horse, she laughed. But Melissa rode at her hard, grabbing the stallion's bridle. *"Tell them!"* she shouted, jerking the horse to her, her sword poised at Siddonie's throat. "Tell them what they fight for."

When Siddonie tried to shout her lies her voice strictured and broke as if hands circled her throat.

"Tell them!" Melissa thrust her blade, blooding the queen's cheek.

"I'll tell them," the queen shouted suddenly. She stood up in the saddle looking out at her armies. Her face was flushed, her eyes blazed, and she was laughing, a cold, brittle cry of sound. "You fought to become my slaves!

"You fought to enslave the Netherworld. To enslave yourselves." Again she laughed, harsh and challenging. Standing tall in the stirrups, laughing in the faces of the kings who had followed her and in the faces of her soldiers, she shouted, "That is my power over you! Total power! You fought to become slaves to me. You have killed your brothers for me and have thanked me for the privilege of killing them!"

Her laughter broke as she shouted a spell toward the pit. At the same moment Melissa saw the Griffon dive directly for the pit, and as Siddonie's spell spilled across the battlefield, Melissa's blade was knocked from her hand and the queen lunged at her, her knife flashing as she pulled Melissa into the blade.

Chapter 72

Pain shot through Melissa's shoulder. She unsheathed her knife as the two horses lunged and spun. The queen struck her a glancing blow that nearly jolted her out of the saddle. But suddenly Siddonie hesitated, and Melissa was aware of silence around them. No soldier moved, all were staring beyond Siddonie.

Behind Siddonie the black dragon had risen up out of the pit, its coils humping above the flames. As the black beast towered against the stone sky it became a dozen serpents reaching and striking, then became one again. It lunged at them, its head scraping the sky, its eyes blazing with the Hell fires. Deep within its gaping mouth Melissa saw the Hell fires burning. Its roar rang with the tortured screams of the damned souls that were a part of it.

Melissa's horse was shivering, his eyes were white-rimmed, his nostrils distended. Siddonie sat her horse smiling, waiting, licking her lips as the serpent slid swiftly toward them across the battlefield.

It lunged at them like a mountain unleashed. Horses wheeled away, foot soldiers fled. But a dozen mounted soldiers attacked the beast, their spears striking at it like pins hitting a mountain. It snatched them up and drooled their blood. Melissa spun her horse, charging beside her troops. She saw the Griffon appear out of the smoke of the Hell Pit.

He dove at the dragon but the beast flung him aside. The Catswold troops charged the beast, and only absently did Melissa realize she was wounded, or pay attention to the faintness that gripped her. She thought her dizziness was fear. But as she rode straight for the beast she heard Siddonie cry a changing spell.

The change hit her: she was suddenly cat, clinging to the saddle of the running horse, her knife gone, the black dragon coiled over her.

Her scream was a yowl. As she was lifted in the dragon's flaming mouth, she saw that all the Catswold warriors had changed. Around her hundreds of cats were sucked up from the saddle, fighting, twisting, into the black maw of the dragon. His body was like dense smoke. Choking, she tried to change to human and could not. She tried to bring a spell against the dragon and was powerless. The beast's shifting form revealed glints of stone sky that vanished again as around her cats screamed, falling against her. She thought she heard Braden shout her name and felt rage at the deception.

A louder shout made the beast pause. Now suddenly the suspended cats dropped twisting down as if scattered from a cloudburst. Cats dropped to the battlefield and fled, changing to human. She saw Siddonie near to her. The queen had gone dead white. She sat frozen in the saddle, staring off to the south.

The calico leaped to the back of a riderless horse and saw across the battlefield a group of riders approaching, running their scruffy ponies straight at the massed armies. She dug her claws into the saddle, unbelieving.

Fifty immense white banners, slung from poles, flapped above the running horses. Melissa heard from the massed armies a sigh of shock. Siddonie seemed unable to look away from the banners. Her hands trembled, and the reins dropped loose under her fingers as she faced their powerful magic.

Each banner was blazoned with Siddonie's face. A huge, lifelike portrait. The queen's face was repeated fifty times, and in the wind of the galloping horses the banners stirred and flapped and the faces seemed alive, twisting and grimacing.

The Affandar queen cringed in the saddle, diminished.

The serpent she had called from the pit grew thin in breadth and thinner in substance so the mountains showed plainly through its coils, and it began to blow like smoke back toward the pit.

The banners snapped. Siddonie's fifty faces writhed. Siddonie herself seemed powerless. The four kings who had remained beside her wheeled their horses and fled as if the power that held them had snapped. Siddonie kicked her horse, trying to flee too, but now her reins were held by her own warriors. She screamed and hit at them, her face a parody of the banner images. Her curses raked the air. And it was then that Melissa saw the image maker.

Braden rode standing in the saddle. She wanted to ride galloping to him. She brought the spell, but could not change from cat. She was wounded, her shoulder drenched with blood. She kneaded her claws uselessly as Siddonie's sword swept at her.

Braden saw the queen raise her sword. He spurred his horse, felt the unwieldy banner jerk in his hand. He hung on to it, riding hard for Siddonie as she lunged at the calico cat.

He swung the banner so hard Siddonie was knocked from the saddle. The calico's horse bolted, the little cat clinging to the saddle. "For Christ sake, Melissa! Change!"

Silently crying the spell, she was suddenly sent reeling up tall. She was awkwardly astride a racing horse; she snatched up the reins and pulled him up. Her right hand was clutching the Amulet.

She saw the smoky coils of the serpent twisting across the sky above the Pit, growing thinner as it descended down into the flames. Then light struck the battlefield, glancing through the serpent's coils. Light bathed both armies, and within the light shone a woman tall as the mountain. Her body was robed in gold. Her face was the face of cat—leonine, bold.

Sekhmet stood over the battlefield, her eyes burning with light. The serpent was gone, blown apart.

At Melissa's breast, the Amulet burned with light. And then Braden was holding her, his lips against her forehead. Together they watched the golden lion-woman, her glow embracing the warriors, watched her until the goddess vanished. And when at last Melissa looked up into Braden's eyes she saw that he was different. As if something lost long ago had been given back to him; as if the chasm between his own two worlds had been bridged.

Chapter 73

Siddonie stood captive, held by her own warriors. Melissa remembered a younger Siddonie bringing dolls to the house in San Francisco, remembered the frightening games Siddonie had tried to make her play. She watched the kings gather, King Bendini of Ferrathil, gray and grizzled; young, dark King Allmond of Shenndeth; King Terragren of Cressteane, sitting his horse straight as a rod; King Plaguell of Pearilleth, a great rock of a man. She watched each of the twelve kings accept a banner from a Catswold upperworlder—the bed sheet banners that Braden had painted to liberate the Netherworld rulers. The kings raised the images solemnly. Melissa listened to their prayers of thanks for Siddonie's defeat, their voices carrying across the battlefield. Every head was bowed.

When the prayers were finished, King Plaguell said, "We will not execute the queen of Affandar here on the battlefield. There will be a formal court at the palace of Affandar. Our own transgressions will be recounted, as will hers, to become a part of Netherworld history. The events of this year will be documented, never in future to be forgotten."

The twelve kings circled Siddonie, holding high their

banners, her portraits turned toward the center of the circle where she must face them.

As the kings completed their circle around the cold-faced queen, Melissa saw Wylles sitting astride a shaggy pony among the upperworld Catswold. The prince's arm was held securely by Terrel Black as the boy watched his mother's defeat. Seeing this, Melissa turned away, pressing her face against Braden's shoulder.

Chapter 74

It was midnight. Few lights burned in Affandar Palace, though smoke from many chimneys drifted toward the granite sky. In a large second-floor chamber Melissa undressed before the hearth's bright flames. Firelight flickered and shifted against the pale walls. As she slipped into bed, the creamy silk sheets felt delicious against her bare skin. She slid against Braden's nakedness, letting his warmth engulf her. They did not make love. They were silent, thinking about the dead queen.

Siddonie's trial had ended at noon. She had been hanged two hours later in the palace courtyard, in a ceremony Melissa hadn't watched.

It was stupid to feel sad for Siddonie. She had brought only misery and fear.

"What was she?" Braden said. "What kind of creature? A totally evil woman . . ."

"Daughter of Lillith. Slavemaker. A destroyer of the spirit, Mag said."

"I like Mag," Braden said. He laughed. "Mag and Olive hit it off, all right."

"And the Harpy," she said, smiling.

He kissed her forehead lightly, stroked her hair. "Three grand old girls. Best thing that ever happened to Olive."

They had watched the two old women and the Harpy wander off together as the gathering in the main hall finished and folk, yawning, headed for the chambers that Briccha and Terlis had prepared. They had watched Tom and Wylles, too, as the two boys made the first tentative advances in a wary, uncomfortable relationship.

Wylles and Tom had ridden together side by side as the Affandar troops returned to their homeland. The two boys, prince and changeling, were visual proof of Siddonie's deception. To the peasants they passed in the villages, the living signs of the queen's betrayal had been as impressive as word of her defeat.

Melissa didn't know where Efil had gone, or care. Anyway, Affandar had no more royalty. King and queen had been replaced by a council. Soon all the Netherworld would be ruled by elected councils.

Only Tom had spoken well of Efil. King Efil had shown him how to resist Siddonie, and had caused him to be awake when Pippin came to the window of the palace. "When I saw my yellow tomcat looking in from the balcony," Tom had said, "that was pretty great. I didn't believe it at first, but then suddenly Pippin wasn't a cat anymore." He had grinned broadly. "A warrior was there. But," Tom said, "the warrior had Pippin's eyes."

Melissa turned, watching Braden. "I'll miss Pippin."

"And so will Tom. I think Pippin has become a true Netherworlder."

"Maybe he'll come back sometime," she said wistfully. "Maybe he'll come up with Olive when she's ready to leave."

"If she's ever ready. She's as at home as if she belongs here."

"Olive longed for years to know about this world." Melissa slid closer against him. "So many things to sort out, so much for the new councils to do. And at home—all the legal things about Siddonie's enterprises. So complicated."

"Did you say, at home?"

"I guess I did," she said, grinning.

"You would leave the magic?"

"There's magic there," she said.

"And what about the legal complications? Do you want to stay here, forget them?" He stroked her cheek.

"I want to be where you are."

"No one said we can't live in both worlds."

"No one said that . . ." She sighed. "We can live where we want to live, as long as we're together."

He kissed her and drew her to him, kissing her throat, her breasts. She returned his kisses at first lazily then with a hot, magical passion more powerful than any spell. He put his hands under her, lifted her to him. The fire's shadows played across them, cloaking their slow, sensuous lovemaking. He saw the room for an instant as a painting, then he was lost to her; saw the chamber cloaked in breast-shaped shadows forming a rich, dark world, with two pale lovers at its center; and the shadows trembled in the firelight.

Near to dawn she woke with the sudden need to become cat. She whispered the spell and, as the calico, she snuggled on Braden's chest; he was deliciously warm, hard muscled, safe. She kept her claws in, but let her pleasure rumble deep in her throat. And of course her purring woke him; he raised his head, surprised, then lay stroking her, laughing at her.

She rolled over on her back and lashed her tail, biting at his hand. She felt giddy, wild. As cat she was small and vulnerable, but she was safe with him. He stroked her until she bit his hand too hard, then he swore at her. She leaped off the bed, raced to the dressing room, changed to girl, and pulled on her leathers and boots.

Within half an hour they rode out through the palace gates, heading northeast. When Melissa looked back at the palace windows, their departing reflections were sharply defined: two lovers riding out with a picnic basket tied behind his saddle.

By mid-morning they were skirting the Affandar River.

They had passed through half a dozen villages teeming with returned warriors already plowing and planting crops. They had passed children who had yesterday gone to war as grooms and pages, now gathering wild roots and mushrooms and small wild fruits, and hunting the game birds that yesterday had been forbidden to them. Melissa had shown Braden the dry underground river with its water-carved caves, and they had crossed the high ridges above the sheep meadows. Where the Affandar River ran deepest, foaming over boulders, they tied the horses and spread out their blanket. And on the banks of the deep Affandar River they made slow, easy love, then dozed.

They woke ravenous, and attacked the picnic. She had packed cold roast dove and fresh bread, peaches and berries and grapes. They had not finished eating when the river began to change.

Within the foaming rush, the center of the river grew still. A glassy pool formed, reflecting the low stone sky. At its center, deep down, something dark stirred. Braden sat up, watching.

The dark shadow moved again. Then the pool's glassy surface broke into ripples, circling outward. And suddenly, a hump broke the water. Another. Another, until seven humps made a line across the river like the back of a huge water beast. Braden had eased his knife from its sheath, but Melissa stayed his hand. And then the farthest hump pushed up out of the pool, and they saw it was a horselike head, its nostrils distended, its mane streaming water. Then another surfaced. Another. She laughed out loud at his surprise when he realized he was looking at seven horses swimming.

The horses heaved up out of the water onto the opposite bank. They were wild-looking, stocky beasts with wide nostrils, wide eyes, and tangled, sodden manes. The water ran from their manes and tails. They stared at Braden. Their eyes were dark, mysterious. And suddenly the horses were gone and in their places stood seven stocky men with wide, dark eyes, their beards streaming water. They spoke as one.

"Welcome, image maker."

Braden looked amazed, then grinned. He lifted his hand in greeting to the selkies. The seven old selkie men looked at Melissa. "Welcome, sister—shape shifter. Welcome, Catswold queen. Your work has been well done. The whelp of Lillith is dead." They turned, expecting no answer, and moved away upriver walking single file. Only far upriver did they turn into stocky ponies again. They switched their tails, cocked their ears, and leaped straight down into the fast water.

She said, "Few have seen the selkies. It is a sign of peace that they have returned."

"I would say wonder was more descriptive. How long do you suppose they were there?"

"Not long," she said, coloring.

He laughed. "Gram would have loved seeing them."

"I think your Gram would have been at home in the Netherworld."

He nodded. "She would have."

"Maybe she was, once," Melissa said.

"Maybe," he said, laughing. "Anything's possible." He reached for her and held her by the shoulders, looking at her seriously. "I want to paint this world." He searched her face. "But I never can. It would reveal too much."

She touched his face. "It would reveal too much only if the paintings were seen in the upperworld."

"But no one—there are no—"

"There is no one here to feel the power of your paintings? Are you so sure?"

"I didn't mean that."

"No galleries. No critics," she said. "No one learned enough to praise you."

His eyes blazed. Then he laughed.

"They know power when they see it," she said. "They know magic when they see it. And they know love. They don't need a degree for that.

"You could," she said softly, "be the first image maker this world has known. You could bring to the Netherworld a new kind of magic."

Chapter 75

Sun flooded through the windows of Mathew Rhain's reception room. Melissa stood within the warm light looking down at the city. Five stories below her lay neat squares of clipped grass and beds of flowers. The streets bordering Union Square were solid cars, moving in a tangle of noon traffic.

They had arrived early; Rhain was still with a client. Braden sat on the leather couch facing the window, reading a newspaper clipping that the blond secretary had given him when they arrived. It was Mettleson's review of the show. He looked up at Melissa and grinned. " '. . . Symphonic mystery . . . West's best work to date.' " He handed her the clipping. "You'll like the 'beautiful and elusive young woman' part."

"Is he always so right?"

"Not always," he said, laughing.

Rhain came out with an elderly woman dressed in a stiff navy suit. He ushered her out, then led them into his office. They sat at the conference table, and he pushed a thick file across to them.

"These are the financial particulars of Lillith Corporation. This is a preliminary report only, a collection of letters, cables, bank statements, summonses, court documents, legal research. You can take it, go over it at your leisure." Rhain paused, looking them over. "What you have in mind will not be easy."

"But it can be done?" Melissa asked, watching him.

"I think we might do it. We won't be sure until we get

deeper into it, but I think we can do it." He smiled. "I know the Kitchens will be pleased. Of course you know you could start from scratch more easily."

She said, "We want to do it this way."

Rhain nodded. "The Alice Kitchen West Foundation. Yes, the Kitchens will be pleased."

Braden said, "Thanks for the review of the show."

Rhain smiled. "I liked the show. There was a second news release, too. But not about the show."

As he leaned back, his red hair caught the light. "I have a friend at the Museum of History. He showed me a release he prepared last week, a bit of publicity meant for a feature article. I—persuaded—him this wasn't worthwhile publicity, that perhaps the whole project was not worthwhile. I told him that perhaps the museum would fare better by accepting, say, some donated antiques?"

"He let me keep the article. There is no other copy." Rhain picked up a plain file and withdrew a single sheet.

September 28, 1957:
A medieval carving valued at possibly half a million dollars drew the attention of museum experts this week. The oak door, carved with the faces of cats, stands in a Marin County garden. It came to the attention of Field West Museum Director Suel Jenkins while he was searching the museum archives. Jenkins found nine photostats of drawings of the door done by Bay Area artist Alice Kitchen shortly before she died in 1955. She was the wife of painter Braden West. Mrs. West had asked the previous director to investigate the authenticity of the door, but after her death the project was shelved.

Dr. Jenkins said the door is a fine example of tenth century Celtic art. It has long stood in the weather, enclosing a hillside cave where garden tools are stored. He had no idea why such a valuable door would be left outdoors, in the elements. He said the wood and the carvings are in remarkably good condition. Nota-

*tions by the previous director, Dr. Lewis Langleno, in-
dicate that the owner of the door and of the property
on which it stands is retired Marin librarian and local
author Olive Cleaver.*

*The museum is now in the process of making an
offer on the door. They have photographed it, and with
Miss Cleaver's permission they will exhibit the photographs along with copies of Mrs. West's drawings in a
small exhibition early next year.*

Braden handed the release back to Rhain. He did not comment. There was no way the museum could do anything
without Olive, and Olive, when she returned, would not sell
the door. Nor would she agree to such an exhibit.

Melissa said, "There are some lovely antiques I know
of—small desks, early medieval chairs—that the museum
might like. It might take a little while to get them—here."

Rhain looked at her a long time. "I think the museum
would be very pleased to have them." He nodded, grinned at
them, and tore the article into small pieces.

Then he leaned back, studying them. "I have some other
interesting connections besides the young man at the museum, folk from whom I get occasional bits of news. May I
say that I am, ah, very impressed with your recent adven-
ture?" He smiled and leaned back, closing the file.

They rose, a satisfied smile linking the three of them. And
as they parted, Melissa hugged Rhain. He hugged her back
warmly. She felt a hot rush of gratitude and kinship; as if she
had not left those she loved so very far away after all.

Crossing the street, Braden gave her his arm. "We'll walk
to lunch, it isn't far. I like Rhain—he's a nice mix of cul-
tures."

"Yes, I like him, too. And he makes me feel—closer to
McCabe. Where are we having lunch?"

"It's a French restaurant where Alice and I used to go.
They collect local paintings and prints—there's a drawing I
want you to see."

"Alice's drawing?"

He nodded. "An early one."

She stopped on the sidewalk, holding his hand. "Done when she was a child?"

"Yes, it was."

"A drawing of a cat?"

"Yes," he said.

"I think I remember it. I think I remember the restaurant. Alice—Alice had a birthday party there. It's a small place—small rooms all connected, with skylights?"

He nodded. They moved on again along the sunwashed street, but she was shivering. He said, "Would you rather not go there?"

"I want to go. I want to see it." But she moved close to him. Remembering the drawing too sharply. He glanced at her, holding her hand tightly.

She knew she could not avoid this kind of encounter. She knew she must learn to make such things a part of herself. But fear filled her.

The cat in Alice's drawing in the restaurant, the same cat as in Alice's diary, the same cat that had been buried years ago in the front yard of the Russian Hill house—the cat that died before she, Melissa, was born.

She knew that that cat, when she faced its picture in the restaurant, would look exactly like her own cat self. Its colors and markings would mirror exactly her calico patterns. Its face would be her face, the exact same white markings, the same green eyes. She glanced up at Braden, upset that he would take her there. But yet she knew that he must take her, that the last piece of the puzzle must be touched, and perhaps understood. She knew she could not have gone there without him, that she would not have had the strength without him. She smiled at him, striding beside him along the sun-warmed street, hardly aware of the cars that sped past them, cars that, a few weeks earlier, would have made her cringe with terror. And above them the unending sky rolled away, wind tossed. And everything was all right. With Braden beside her, it was all right.

Epilogue

San Francisco Chronicle, September 14, 1957.

The female figure is a time-honored theme in painting. The female figure reflected in shop windows, and those reflections woven through with abstract city scapes, produces a richness of subject unerringly right for Braden West. This is West's best work to date, a difficult feat for one who has long been admired for the richness of his palette.

West's show, which opened last night at the Chapman to a jostling crowd, was a smashing success. By the close of the evening, nearly all the work had been sold. The richness of this work is overwhelming. West's entire Reflection series is of the same elusive young woman, yet not one painting is repetitive, except in the mysterious, symphonic mystery that graces them all. This fascinating show will remain at the Chapman through October 31. It will open in New York at Swarthmann's in December in a group show with the work of Garcheff, Lake, and Debenheldt. The foursome will move on to the Metropolitan early next year.

San Francisco Chronicle, September 20, 1957.

A strange disappearance of San Francisco's cats has led to complaints over the last week to police and to the Humane Society. Most of the disappearances seem to have occurred last Sunday night. Cat owners reported their pets acting unusually nervous, pacing and yowling. The cats that were let out were not seen again.

The same night, Marin County residents reported seeing groups of cats running into a garden near Sam's Bar, a well-known jazz cafe. Cats were seen by the dozens in the head-lights of heavy traffic, and there were more than the usual number of complaints about barking dogs. About three A.M. the barking stopped. No more sightings were reported.

San Francisco Chronicle, August 8, 1959.

Business News:

Meyer and Finley appointed their first woman broker today. Anne Hollingsworth, brokers' assistant with the firm for twelve years, was appointed head of the San Francisco office. And in another surprise move, nine previously termi-nated brokers and key personnel were re-hired, after their mass firing two years ago.

The firm has been completely restructured, though it will remain in its Union Square offices. It had been virtually bought out by the Lillith Corporation in early 1957, but that corporation has since filed for bankruptcy. Lillith's exten-sive charitable branch has been sold to the new philan-thropic *Alice West Cat Rescue Foundation,* named for the late and well-known animal artist, Alice Kitchen West.

If you enjoyed *The Catswold Portal*, you'll love Shirley Rousseau Murphy's award-winning Joe Grey Mystery series. Joe Grey is not your average sleuth—he's a tomcat who, with the help of his feline friends Dulcie and Kit, uncovers the nefarious doings in his sleepy hometown of Molena Point, California. Besides their exceptional sleuthing skills, Joe, Dulcie, and Kit have one more advantage over your average cats—they can communicate with humans. But these fine felines don't talk to just any Tom, Dick, or Harry; they choose their human friends carefully, and only when the case is at stake. From fighting an evil, green-eyed "cat" burglar, to solving murders of a more human nature, they take the case and use a healthy dose of feline intuition to collar the killer.

Turn the page for a glimpse into the mysterious and intriguing world of Shirley Rousseau Murphy's Joe Grey series.

Joe Grey was content just being a regular old tomcat. But after a mysterious accident, everything started to change. First he found he could understand human speech, then he found he could talk (quite useful for scaring dogs), and then even read! But he really wanted to worry when he found himself feeling human emotions like guilt and sympathy. And now he's in a real predicament—when a man is murdered in a dark alley behind the local deli, Joe is the only witness. He must put his newly acquired skills to the test to make sure the killer ends up behind bars. Now Joe has to deal with the responsibility that comes with being a *Cat on the Edge*—not a human, but no longer just a regular old tomcat!

Perusal of the human mind was not a feline concern. Cats didn't *think* about human perversion. Cats *felt* human depravity. They knew that human lust and dark human hatred existed, and they accepted those aberrations. Cats did not analyze those warped human conditions. Cats left the philosophizing to men.

Yet all the time he had been fleeing from the killer, a part of him had been trying to analyze the man. Trying to guess at the man's motives. Trying to figure out his intentions not only at chasing him, but his purpose in killing Beckwhite. Trying to unravel the mystery that had transformed that thin human face into a killer's mask.

What did he care what drove the man to kill? He wasn't connected to this man's problem, and he didn't want to be. And inside him, alarms were going off. These thoughts were new and terrifying. A gut level signal was warning him that he was in the throes of mental and emotional change. A new facet of himself had awakened, new concerns were surfacing.

The transformation had been coming on him for some weeks, but it had not been stirred violently alive, not until tonight. Now, some foreign presence within him had come alert. And it was clawing to get out, to break free.

He ran the last two blocks caught in a distressing tangle of fears and wanting nothing more complicated than his warm, safe bed, wanted to curl up safe on the blanket next to Clyde, protected by his human housemate.

Joe Grey never regretted the mysterious accident that gave him the ability to talk and understand human speech. And now he has company—this mysterious gift has been given to his girlfriend Dulcie, too. The problem is, Dulcie isn't only listening to humans, she's believing them! She is convinced that the man in jail for killing a famous artist and burning her studio is innocent. And, leave it to Dulcie, she is determined to find the evidence that would convict the real murderer—even if she has to get Joe Grey—a real *Cat Under Fire*—killed in the process!

At least if Dulcie had to solve puzzles, the murder of Janet Jeannot was better than agonizing over the mystery of their own pasts. They'd done enough of that this summer. Their sudden onslaught of uncatlike thoughts, and their ability to speak human words had been a shocker. When Joe had first experienced his new and alarming talent, he had tried to remain cool and laid-back. Scared as he was, he'd attempted to handle the matter with some restraint. But not Dulcie. She had exploded into her new life with wild eagerness, embracing her sudden new talents with hot feline passion. Wanting to learn everything about the world all at once, trying to make sense of the entire universe, she'd just about driven him crazy. Even watching TV had become a challenge as she soaked up information.

Ever since she had been a kitten, Dulcie had watched TV with her elderly housemate. Curled cozily on Wilma Getz's lap, she had basked in the music and motion of the programs, and in the incomprehensible but fascinating voices. Then suddenly this summer, when she had begun to understand human words, she'd fixed her attention on the programs, eagerly lapping up the smallest detail. Sitting rigid on Wilma's lap, like a little furry scholar, she had soaked up the daunting new experiences and ideas as if, her entire life, she had been waiting for this moment to learn and discover.

Joe Grey is, well, peeved. His human housemate Clyde has been trying to volunteer him as a once-a-week Animal Therapy cuddle-kitty. And just when Joe is about to nab the cat burglar who's been terrifying his usually quiet coast town, he has to add this to his plate as well! But when Joe finds out that this "pet-a-pet" scheme is really his girlfriend Dulcie's idea, he can't say no. Dulcie needs Joe's help to prove that the old folks' home is hiding more than just lonely seniors—she's already uncovered a severed finger and a very, very busy open grave. In *Cat Raise the Dead,* Joe can't resist Dulcie's feline feminine charms, even if he sees nothing but trouble from butting into yet another human mess!

Leaping up, she wandered among the bottles and crowded jars, stepping carefully, sniffing at the lids, trying to identify the contents. Makeup, certainly, but some smells were very strange. Stepping over an array of lipsticks and little boxes of eye makeup, over eyebrow pencils, cotton swabs, and a pair of tweezers, she paused to look into the three-way mirror, enchanted by her multiple reflections. To see herself from all angles at once, see herself from the back as if looking at another cat, was like an out-of-body experience.

Forgetting Joe, preening shamefully, she heard, from the drive below, from somewhere beyond the kitchen, a car start up and pull away, heard it move around the front of the house and head off up the long drive.

A miniature chest of drawers stood beside the hat-boxes, a little, perfect piece of furniture no taller than her shoulder. She nosed at it, and with a careful claw she pulled out one of the drawers—and she raised her paw to strike, her eyes blazing.

But these were not mice. In the small drawer, the furry bodies looked, in fact, more like dead caterpillars lying fuzzy and still.

Some were gray, some brown, some nearly white. They did not smell like anything that had ever lived. Puzzled by the lifeless fuzzy creatures, she shoved the drawer closed and opened the next.

She froze, staring.

Eyeballs. The drawer contained human eyes.

There's a bad new cat in sleepy little Molena Point: a rene-
gade tom with a penchant for robbery, a scorn for his fellow
felines, and a disdain for human laws. And this *Cat in the
Dark* is masterminding a crime spree that's quickly
headed toward murder most foul. Dulcie and Joe Grey both
know the score— they've seen Azrael in action. But how
can they expose the criminal without letting ordinary, un-
trustworthy humans in on the secret that certain select
cats think—and talk? Cats like them . . .

It was not until the next morning that Joe, brushing past
Clyde's bare feet, leaping to the kitchen table and pawing
open the morning *Gazette,* learned more about the burglary
at Medder's Antiques.

"What are you reading?" Clyde picked Joe up as if he
were a bag of flour, so he could see the paper.

Joe dangled impatiently, twitching his tail, as Clyde read.

Clyde sat down at the table and dumped pepper on his
eggs. "So this is why you've been scowling and snarling all
morning, this burglary."

"I haven't been scowling and snarling. Why would I
bother with a simple break-and-enter? The police can handle the simple stuff."

Clyde raised an eyebrow.

"So there's a new cat in the village. So are you satisfied?
It's nothing to worry you, nothing to fret over."

Clyde was silent a moment, watching him. "I take it this
is a tomcat. What did he do, come onto Dulcie?"

Joe glared at him. Stupid humans could be all too perceptive at the wrong times.

Ever since the earthquake, things have been going from bad to worse in Molena Point, usually the most tranquil little town on the Northern California coast. It started with that suspicious "accident" on Hellhag Hill. In *Cat to the Dogs*, the police might write off the deadly accident to the night fog, but Joe Grey knows a cut brake line when he sees it—he may be a cat, but he's solved more murders than your average police detective!

Frowning, the white strip down his gray face pinched into puzzled worry lines, the big tomcat padded along a fallen sapling between the upturned wheels.

What had he heard?

Dropping down on the far side of the wrecked car, his mind played back the crash in a quick rerun: the squeal of brakes, then the skid just about where Deadman's Curve began. Hellhag Hill was famous for that double twist. If a driver lost control on the first bend, he was hard put, when he hit the second one, to regain command. The too-sharp turn was on him, the canyon dropping straight down away from his front wheels. The locals took that road slowly. The warning signs were numerous and insistent—but in the fog a driver wouldn't see them. Even a local might not realize just where he was on the hairpin road.

Had he heard another sound before the squeal of brakes? Had he heard a horn farther away, muffled in the fog? The faint, quick stutter of a warning horn?

He squinched closed his eyes, trying to remember.

Yes. First a faint triple beep, then the skid and the crash and the car careening down at him—but had that earlier honking come from a second car, or had this driver honked at something looming out of the fog? Had there been one car or two, moving blindly along that narrow road?

He thought he remembered the hush of two sets of tires;

but had they been coming from opposite directions? Then
the faint stutter of the horn, then the scream of brakes and
the heart-jolting thunder as the car came careening over.

The other car must have gone on. Why hadn't it stopped?
Hadn't the other driver heard the wreck?

While Joe Grey has played tricks on Max Harper, Molena Point's head lawman, he's never had anything but respect for the dedicated sheriff. Now Harper's in trouble, suspected of murdering two friends, and the only witness, a young girl named Dillon, has disappeared. Both Dulcie and Joe know Harper is innocent, and Joe is a *Cat Spitting Mad,* determined to prove his pal's innocence—and find Dillon.

They looked and looked at the two women, at their poor, torn throats, at their pooled blood drying on their clothes and seeping into the earth.

The cats knew them.

"Ruthie Marner," Dulcie whispered. The younger woman was so white, and her long blond hair caked with blood. Dulcie crouched, touching her nose to Ruthie's icy arm, and drew back shivering. Blood covered the woman's torn white blouse and blue sweater. She had a deep chest wound, as well as the wide slash across her throat. So much clotted blood that it was hard to be sure how the wounds might have been made.

Helen Marner's wounds were much the same. Her blond hair, styled in a short bob, was matted with dirt where she had fallen. She was well dressed, much like her daughter, in tan tights, paddock boots, a tweed jacket over a white turtleneck shirt, her clothes stained dark with blood. A hard hat lay upside down against a pine tree like a sacrificial bowl.

No horse was in sight. The horses would have left the fallen riders, would have bolted in panic, the moment they could break free.

Dulcie backed away, her tail and ears down. She'd seen murders before, but the deaths of these two handsome women made her tremble as if her nerves were cross-wired.

It's bad enough that Molena Point has been invaded by a famous writer and his suspiciously rude wife. Now the local yard sales have set off a host of puzzling thefts. In *Cat Laughing Last*, Joe and Dulcie take the case and soon discover that those sales hold a secret treasure someone will kill to possess. But before the fur can fly, these talented cats will unmask a murderer—and unearth a few other surprises along the way.

Since their arrival, Elliott Traynor had kept largely to himself as he finished the last chapters of *Twilight Silver*, the third novel in his historical trilogy. But Vivi had made herself known around the village, and not pleasantly—as if she enjoyed being rude to shopkeepers, as if she took pleasure in being abrupt and demanding.

The Traynors had not wanted a staff for the cottage they were renting, but had hired the cleaning service provided by Wilma Getz's redheaded niece, Charlie. Charlie tended the Traynor house herself, early each morning, then left the couple to their privacy.

Molena Point's residents, numbering so many writers and artists, were not put off by Elliott's reclusive ways. They talked among themselves about his books and about the play, waved when occasionally they saw him on the streets or in the black Lincoln, as they headed to the theater; otherwise they left him to his own devices. The presence, alone, of the prestigious writer, seemed adequate enrichment to their well-appointed lives.

But no one had warmed to Vivi.

Traynor's previous wife had died three years before. Six months later, he married Vivi, a woman forty years his junior. Besides her loud, rude ways, something else about her made the cats want to back away, hissing, a chill that perhaps only a cat would sense. Whatever reason she had for appearing this morning in the McLeary garden could only, in Joe Grey's opinion, mean trouble.

Romance is in the air in the charming seaside village of
Molena Point, California. Everyone is excited about the
upcoming wedding of chief of police Charlie Getz, even
cool feline detective Joe Grey. But the festivities are interrupted when two uninvited guests try to blow up the
church. Then one of the bride's good friends, building contractor Ryan Flannery, lands in a heap of trouble when her
philandering husband is found dead. In *Cat Seeing Double,* Joe and his feline sidekicks sign on to the case, finding
themselves in the biggest cat fight of their lives—a bare-
clawed battle with a prey who is as cunning as he is
deadly . . .

"Those stained-glass windows," Dulcie said softly. "How
could the killer have wedged the body in like that? To lift a
deadweight, pardon the pun, at that angle and ease the body
down between the windows . . . That would be like standing
on your hind legs lifting a dead rabbit as heavy as you, hoist-
ing it way out at an angle and slowly down without dropping
it. The killer had to be strong. But why bother? What was the
point of leaving the body there?"

"You don't think he was shot there?" Joe said.

"Nor do you," she said, cutting her eyes at him. "Those
windows are old and frail. You heard Ryan last night telling
Clyde. That glass has to be brittle, and those strips of lead
fragile. Those old stained-glass windows in the English Pub,
the way if you rub against them, the glass will push loose
from the leading? If Rupert had fallen there he'd have
smashed those windows to confetti."

Dallas said, "We'll have to take your gun." The cats heard
chair legs scrape, then the front door open, heard the officers
and Ryan going down the stairs.

Leaping from the bathroom window and down the hill,
they were just at the edge of the drive when the officers and

Ryan came down; and the medics set down their stretcher, prepared to take Rupert away. Slipping into the bushes, they watched Dallas unlock Ryan's truck door then unlock her glove compartment. Flipping the glove compartment open, he turned to look at her.

"You said your gun was here?"

When antiques and valuables begin disappearing from residents' homes, Joe Grey knows that something is very wrong in sleepy Melona Point. Could the thief be a local, or, even worse, is it the old crook who may be connected to Azrael, the sinister, yellow-eyed cat who terrorized Joe and Dulcie years ago? And when a young, healthy waiter drops dead at a local art opening, the town is on full alert. *Cat Fear No Evil* brings Joe and Dulcie the most dramatic investigation of their lives, as they follow diverse leads, scratch out the truth, and try to restore a distraught village to its usual cozy tranquility.

Clyde shrugged, engendering a moment of miscalculation in which the black tom raked his hind claws down Clyde's shoulder, bringing new blood spurting, one claw dug deep. Joe stopped smiling and leaped from the tower like a swooping eagle, knocking the tomcat from Clyde's grip. The two cats hit the floor locked in screaming battle, then Joe flipped the tom twice, forcing him into the cold fireplace.

Crouched over Azrael among the ashes, Joe blocked his retreat with a degree of viciousness Clyde had never before seen in his feline pal. Azrael, driven by Joe's frenzied attack, backed against the fire wall pressing hard into the bricks—as if wishing the wall would give way and let him through into the dark chimney.

Watching the two tomcats, Clyde stood clutching his arm and applying pressure to the wound. The cats communicated now only in silence, their body language primal. Clyde could read Joe's superiority of the moment as Joe goaded and stalked his quarry. The black tom showed only uncertainty in the twitch of his ears and the drop of his whiskers.

Joe moved from the fireplace just enough so Azrael could step out. His meaningful glance toward the glass doors at the south end of the study was more than clear. As Joe herded the flinching black tom toward the roof deck, Clyde stepped to open the door.

Silently Azrael padded past them onto the deck, as docile as any pet kitty. Silently Joe Grey stood in the doorway beside Clyde watching as Azrael crossed the wide deck over the roof of the carport, leaped into the oak tree, and fled down it to the sidewalk. As Azrael disappeared up the street, Joe Grey turned back inside, never looking to see which route the cat would take. Azrael had left the premises cowed and obedient, and that was all he cared about—for the moment. If, before the black tom was driven from the village, he presented more serious problems, Joe would deal with trouble as trouble arose.